THE
CHALK MAN

An absolutely gripping crime mystery with a massive twist

ADAM LYNDON

Detective Rutherford Barnes Mysteries Book 4

JOFFE
BOOKS

Joffe Books, London
www.joffebooks.com

First published in Great Britain in 2024

Cover art by Nick Castle

ISBN: 978-1-83526-524-6

AUTHOR'S NOTE

Modern policing is awash with acronyms and abbreviations, particularly those — such as "PACE" — that can be pronounced phonetically. In the interests of authenticity and procedural accuracy, this story employs both in dialogue. The reader will find a glossary of these terms at the end of the book.

PROLOGUE

September 2013

Barnes's knees buckled and he sank to the cold concrete floor, like a marionette whose strings had been cut. Fear began to course through him, and he thought, *This is it. I'm dead.*

Stratton Pearce stood over him, the harsh strip lights of the empty warehouse bouncing off his zero-grade skinhead, his pale eyes registering nothing but cold hate. Eyes that cared nothing for the consequences, eyes that saw *consequences* as an occupational hazard. No one was going to talk him out of *anything*.

This was what really terrified Barnes, what made his whole body shudder. Made him acutely aware of how insubstantial was the layer of flesh that stood between his vital organs and twenty inches of cold steel.

Pearce took another step forward and lifted the gleaming cutlass above his head, the tendons in his arm taut, the tip of the heavy blade pointing at the ceiling. Paralysed by fear, Barnes was unable to tear his eyes from the tip of the weapon.

A cruel smile appeared on Pearce's thin fish-lips, and he opened his mouth to speak.

Great, thought Barnes. *A pre-mortem soliloquy.*

Pearce leaned down, so close that Barnes could smell the Old Spice, seasoned with the blood of Pearce's previous victims.

"Ladies and gentlemen, boys and girls, this is your captain speaking."

Barnes blinked. What?

"We've had a good tail wind, and I'm pleased to say we'll be arriving a little ahead of schedule."

Barnes woke with a sharp intake of breath, the rumble of the cabin suddenly deafening in his ears. Cool air chilled the sweat on his top lip. His heart was still racing.

Beside him, Tamsin stirred. "You okay?"

He nodded, and reached for some water.

"Just a dream."

"We aim to touch down at around 10 a.m. local time, so if I could just ask you to fasten your seat belts, we will be starting our descent. The weather in London is fine, with a light north-easterly. Local temperature, nineteen degrees Celsius. I hope you have enjoyed your flight, and thank you once again for flying with BA. We hope to see you again soon."

Around Barnes, the passengers stirred. After the turbulence earlier in the flight, the captain's authoritative voice was reassuring.

Barnes's disorientation slowly began to dissipate, and he got his breathing under control. He attempted to fasten his seat belt while Ellie scrambled across his lap to get to her mother.

"Ellie, come on, sweetheart. Time to buckle up," he said, wincing as one of her flailing pink sandals found purchase in his groin.

Ellie completed her mission and regarded him from her mother's lap.

"You're not my daddy," she said, tilting her head to the side.

"Ellie!" Tamsin said.

"It's okay," Barnes said, touching her lightly on the arm. They both knew Ellie intended no malice. In the two years or so that he had been her *de facto* stepdad, the four-year-old had come to realise that this particular statement of fact could be a handy lever whenever she didn't fancy obeying Barnes. Nevertheless, this didn't make her words any less cutting.

While Tamsin attempted to persuade Ellie to get back in her own seat, Barnes tried to erase Stratton Pearce's cruel face from his mind.

They were on their way back to Eastbourne from a gloriously warm week on the edge of Loch Fyne. The holiday had been marked by the news that Stratton Pearce, the man that, as far as Barnes was concerned, had murdered his wife, had finally been captured after more than three years on the run.

Barnes felt a nervous surge in his stomach. Spending a week with the girls in a nineteenth-century inn on the water's edge had been lovely, but Barnes hadn't been able to shake the feeling that they were hiding out. Moreover, the remote location meant that if Pearce had decided to come looking for him — and, God forbid, actually found him — the four of them were sitting ducks.

None of Barnes's superiors had deigned to confirm in bald terms that Pearce was on the warpath, merely suggesting that a leave of absence for a week or two might be good for his constitution. When Barnes had asked outright if he was in danger, those same superiors had suddenly needed to dash off for important meetings.

Not that Barnes needed confirmation. He knew Pearce would carry out a lifelong vendetta against him. Some chin-stroking third party might even have suggested that the two of them were square — Barnes near as dammit knew Pearce killed his wife; in turn, Pearce held Barnes responsible for the death of his girlfriend and son. Barnes didn't buy into that kind of rationalising, so there was no way a garden-variety headcase like Pearce was going to.

He shook his head clear of the last remnants of the dream, and felt a small hand wriggle into his. He looked down at Maggie next to him. Barnes and his ready-made family were occupying a row of four seats in the centre of the cabin, and his seven-year-old stepdaughter was craning her neck, trying to catch a glimpse out of a window of the approaching London cityscape.

The aircraft began its descent, leaving Barnes's stomach somewhere up near his heart.

"You okay, honey?" Barnes asked Maggie. "Tummy feel funny?"

She nodded, wide-eyed. She bit her lip as everyone's stomach went for another lurch, and he squeezed her hand.

Of his two stepdaughters, seven-year-old Maggie was a considerably easier proposition than Ellie. Maggie had been four when Barnes and Tamsin met, Ellie just over a year old. Maggie had unconditionally latched onto Barnes like a limpet and refused to budge, whereas the more guarded Ellie had manipulated the situation at every turn. Barnes had always thought it would be the other way around, given that — unlike Ellie — Maggie at least had some vague memories of her father being around.

Tamsin found his other hand, and she leaned her head on his shoulder as the aircraft made its final approach.

After the rough flight, a murmur of quiet applause rippled through the cabin as the undercarriage thumped and squealed on the tarmac, and British Airways Flight 1472 began to taxi towards the terminal.

Through one of the windows, partially obscured by an enormous American, the terminal building swam into view, and Barnes felt another surge of inexplicable apprehension in his gut. He felt Tamsin watching him, as if she could sense his anxiety. He turned to look at her. How was it possible for a woman to load a single look with such meaning?

How, in fact, had he ended up here? After Eve, he'd not consciously decided to retreat into a state of widower limbo; by the same token, it was a pit he'd found increasingly difficult to climb out of.

And then Tamsin.

She'd known what she was signing up for in terms of emotional baggage, but had jumped in with both feet anyway, with a typically Tamsin-brand approach: "Let's sit down and sort your shit out." Somehow, she understood without saying so and he was able to lean on her in a way that he couldn't have done with Eve.

He tried hard not to make comparisons, but sometimes it was tough. Tamsin had a sweep of perfectly straight ash-blonde hair cut to just below the earlobe and green, almond-shaped eyes, while the arch of her brow gave her a serious, no-nonsense look. Barnes wondered if that was the para-medic in her, but when she laughed — generally at jokes that only emergency services personnel would find funny — he felt the buzz of having won her over. He would never have described Eve as a shrinking violet, but Tamsin could beat you in a road race and then drink you under the table with-out breaking sweat. Some men might have felt threatened by this, but not Barnes.

Ready-made family. Would-be stepchildren. Maybe, now Pearce was finally locked up, the time was right to make things more official. Consign those awkward moments at passport control explaining why they all had different surnames to history. There was emotional baggage, but then there was sociopath-ic-criminal-with-a-grudge baggage. Nevertheless, Tamsin had stayed the course. Maybe now they could break out of this limbo and get on with their lives.

He wanted to say: *We did it, we're back, we're finally free*, but it was not necessary. She knew what he was thinking, and she was thinking the same.

We're finally free.

THREE MONTHS LATER

CHAPTER ONE

7 December 2013
Terminus Road, Eastbourne

The courier with the surgical mask on his face parked at the kerb and locked the car. It was an old Toyota hatchback that he had picked up for peanuts from an agoraphobic in Hangleton with a limp and four Saint Bernards. The glass was practically opaque with a generation's worth of dog slobber, but mechanically it ran well, with surprisingly low mileage. No one was going to give it a second look.

He looked around quickly, then headed off towards the seafront, momentarily disappearing into a café sandwiched between two department stores.

He went unnoticed by the flurry of Christmas shoppers.

* * *

DC Will Howlett gazed at his reflection and wondered whether, despite the incredible cut, the pink-and-white candy stripe shirt was a bit much.

What the hell, he thought. Brighten the place up a bit. He looked at the name badge clipped to his tie: *T/DC Will*

Howlett. T for *Trainee*. Three months, he reckoned, and that *T* would be gone. Sooner, if he had his way.

He took a deep breath.

"Game face," he said to his reflection, then pulled out his phone and keyed a quick text message: *Gonna make you proud x*

He grabbed his cardboard box of belongings and headed over to the new office — "new" being relative. Since the closure of the Grove Road police station, Eastbourne's main base was one long single-storey open-plan office with uniform at one end, CID at the other, and a clutch of supervisors gatekeeping the middle.

He spotted a desk with his name on — *T/DC* again — and dumped his box next to a stack of files in green folders also bearing his name. His first day in the CID happened to be a late shift, and the office was in full swing. Apart from one DC on the phone, whose disinterested gaze flicked momentarily over to Howlett — the shirt probably catching his eye — no one else acknowledged him.

"DC Howlett?" called a voice, mercifully interrupting his swelling feelings of awkwardness.

He turned. The DI was eyeballing him from the doorway of his corner office. Howlett hurried over and took a seat opposite the boss.

Howlett knew the DI by name — guy called Barnes — but had never met him. He was tall, with a slight stoop and built like a distance runner. Howlett liked that. Physical self-discipline was important in a leader, he thought. That was part of the reason he himself spent practically every spare moment in the gym.

"Welcome," Barnes said, his eyes going straight to the shirt. Howlett tried not to grimace. "Find your caseload?"

"I did, sir."

"You've inherited Sean Maxwell's files. He's off to the Met in a couple of weeks. You've lucked out — he's pretty diligent, so there shouldn't be any shockers in there."

"Yes, sir."

"You're going to have a busy time — you've got the exam, the course and then the workbook to do before you can be confirmed as a detective. That's with the day job as well."

"I can do it, sir. I don't plan on being a trainee for long. Then I want to take the sergeant's exam as soon as I can."

Barnes gave him a small smile.

"Good for you," he said, quietly. "So, there's a couple of things I just want to—"

His desktop phone rang, interrupting the briefing. He picked it up — it was a ten-second conversation, and all the DI said was, "Okay."

DI Barnes stood up and grabbed his jacket off the back of the chair.

"You fit?"

Howlett stood up, a lightning bolt of excitement firing through him.

"What is it?"

"Dead body."

* * *

They drove to the town centre, the seafront its usual slow crawl of traffic, thronged with walkers in brightly coloured winter gear. The Channel was behaving itself today as the sun warmed its surface. On the horizon, beyond the Royal Sovereign Lighthouse, a container ship moved slowly west.

DI Barnes continued his pep talk in the car. It was nothing that Howlett hadn't been expecting — all except the bit about making sure he married outside the police in the interests of self-preservation.

According to Barnes, the call was a good one to get started on. A cleaner on their lunchtime rounds had found a body in the public toilets in North Street, a quiet, narrow lane one block back from the seafront. No obvious sign of death but there was an assortment of drug paraphernalia on the floor around the deceased and, as the body appeared to be no older than twenty-five, CID had been called.

"There will come a point, probably quite soon," Barnes said, as they pulled up outside a line of scene tape closing off the junction of North Street and Seaside Road, "when the call to a crime scene comes in and your heart sinks, because it's another day you aren't getting to the files on your desk. It will be tough, but try not to lose sight of that, okay?"

"Always happy to get out of the office, sir," Howlett said.

They approached the cordon. A uniformed officer held up a hand as they approached.

"Duty DI," Barnes said, showing his warrant card, and the officer held the scene tape up for them to pass.

Howlett looked up and down the street. Despite being Sussex born and bred, he hadn't even known North Street was here, much less that it featured public toilets. It connected Seaside Road and Pevensey Road; both were well known to the police, playing host as they did to lively and rambunctious activity of one form or another — pretty much twenty-four-seven.

The street was about two hundred metres long and barely wide enough for a car. There was a tiny café and a studio of sorts, but, in the main, the quiet road featured little else besides the loading bays, bin stores and delivery doors that serviced the rear of the shops and department stores that lined Terminus Road, Eastbourne's main thoroughfare.

The toilet was little more than a damp concrete bunker. The cold and the stink of urine hit Howlett as he followed Barnes in. You wouldn't use it if you were beyond desperate, Howlett thought — even without a dead body present.

Barnes patted his pockets; Howlett passed him a pair of latex gloves. Barnes nodded.

The body was in one of two cubicles, partially folded forwards, the wall of the narrow cubicle propping it up, so it was still more or less sitting on the toilet. It was male, mid-twenties, dressed from head to toe in black leather, with inch-long ginger roots visible underneath the jet-black hair dye. Needles and caps were littered at its feet — which of them belonged to the body was anybody's guess.

The face was blue-white, the mouth stretched open in a silent yawn; the eyes were only partially closed, and the sclera underneath looked like silver coins.

"So, in the main, four reasons we're here," Barnes said, gently moving the body's chin from side to side with a gloved hand. "One is to underwrite a decision that this isn't a homicide. Second is to open an investigation into the supply of controlled drugs — if in fact this is an overdose. Third, feed the intelligence machine in case there's a bad batch circulating. Fourth, put together a file for the coroner. So, what do you think?"

Howlett glanced at the DI, his mind suddenly blank.

"Well," he began, "it's a public place, so forced entry is a moot point. No obvious signs of injury. No defensive wounds. I imagine it's pretty tough to inject someone who doesn't want to be injected.

"That said," he continued, his brain loosening up, "just because you can't show a deliberate act, there's still someone out there who has provided the deceased with the hotshot. In terms of causation, I mean."

"All good observations," Barnes said with a smile. "But you're looking at me, not at the body."

Howlett flushed, and moved in a little closer to the pinched white face.

He frowned, and tilted his head.

"You okay?" Barnes said. "You're not going to faint on me, are you?"

"I . . . I know this guy," Howlett said. "I was at . . . primary school with him. God, that must have been twenty years ago."

Barnes crouched down and carefully extracted a wallet from the jacket pocket.

"'Charlie Rees,'" he said, peering down at an ID card.

"That's him," Howlett murmured. "Wow."

They emerged from the toilet and stood for a moment in the cold air, a sliver of winter sun providing a narrow beam of warmth in the urban canyon.

They walked back up the road to the cordon. Howlett remembered Charlie Rees well. A loner, very quiet, somebody who sought out attention by either pestering his peers to the point of irritation or trying to amuse them with lame magic tricks, or both. Somebody that even the more reserved, well-behaved kids felt entitled to thump.

Even the teachers hated him. Howlett remembered one lunch break — he'd been sitting at a table with his friends in the packed hall. Charlie had been at a table on his own — as usual — a few tables over. Howlett never saw exactly what had pushed the headmaster's buttons, but remembered his red, bearded face as he strode over, clouted Charlie on the back of the head and screamed at him, his nose inches from Charlie's ear, to get his elbows off the table.

Charlie had acted like he wasn't even there, and continued munching on his sandwiches while staring into space.

At the time, Howlett had thought this act of supreme defiance was simply because he was used to such behaviour; in retrospect, Howlett realised the kid was probably scared witless and unable to react any other way when the headmaster lost his shit.

Howlett looked up at the seagulls as a finger of guilt jabbed at him. At the time, it had never even occurred to him to invite Charlie to sit at their table. He wasn't sure he'd have done so even if it *had* occurred to him.

He let out a long sigh and shook his head. Reviled by all for having bright red hair and fish paste sandwiches; a brief, inauspicious life cut short by, it seemed, an ignominious death.

Howlett stared up at the seagulls screeching against the pale-blue winter sky, and made a silent promise to himself to make sure somebody saw justice for the death of Charlie Rees — he had never been a friend to him, but he would try to make up for that now.

"How long you want to keep the cordon on?" Barnes asked.

"Huh?"

"You with us?" Barnes said. "The cordon. It's not a main route, but it *is* right in the middle of the town centre."

"Oh, I see," Howlett said. "Get undertakers rolling, then close the scene, I guess."

"Works for me," Barnes said. "You'll need to track down next of kin."

Howlett looked back at the small building. Somehow, he didn't think there would be any.

They walked back up to Seaside Road and ducked under the scene tape. A skinny man in a tracksuit — head down, baseball cap pulled low — approached. His eyes widened as he took in the scene tape, uniformed guard and detectives, and he stopped short.

Howlett was on him before he had a chance to run. He flashed his warrant card and gently steered the man into a doorway so as to minimise the amount of gawking, politely explaining as he did so that he was investigating a drugs overdose nearby — and that the man had all the hallmarks of someone in the wrong place at the wrong time.

CHAPTER TWO

Barnes took up position as Howlett's cover officer, and eyed his protégé while he continued talking to the man in the tracksuit, realising, to his surprise, that he was impressed. Howlett spoke to the man politely but firmly; in minute detail, he also explained what he was doing and why he was doing it. A poorly executed stop-and-search lay at the root of many a complaint or obstruction charge, but the man in the tracksuit was practically high-fiving Howlett by the end of it.

Barnes didn't know much about Howlett, beyond the fact that his father had retired from the Met at the rank of chief inspector a few years previously, while his older brother had just been promoted to sergeant. He was tall, physically fit with clean-cut features — whether you liked it or not, that was a big tick in the public's book, and would likely pave the way for a promising career. The years had passed like lightning, but if you rewound to when Barnes had been in Howlett's bright young shoes, even he hadn't been as good as this — and back then, many had thought Barnes was extremely hot shit, himself included.

Howlett appeared sincere, and didn't seem to have any of that casual arrogance so common in new recruits — that much was obvious from this encounter alone. Watching Howlett work brought C. S. Lewis to mind — that quote about doing the right thing, even when no one is looking. His parentage aside, Barnes felt sure that if he asked Howlett why he had joined the police, he would answer — without a hint of irony — that he wanted to help his community.

Howlett finished the search, gave the man a receipt and turned back to Barnes while the man practically skipped off into the sunset.

"Very thorough," Barnes said. "Now let's . . . what is it?"

Howlett's face had creased into a frown of concern, his gaze fixed on something happening over Barnes's shoulder.

Barnes turned and looked away down Seaside Road at the huge inflatable Santa that dangled precariously between the respective corners of T. J. Hughes and the Qualisea fish and chip restaurant, flanked by giant snowflakes lining Terminus Road all the way down to the seafront.

Terminus Road was just a regular town centre in the pre-Christmas shopping rush, packed with determined people walking the canyon of buildings from one destination to the next, their cargo increasing in size as they went.

A Stagecoach bus roared off from outside the distinctive multi-coloured hoarding that was wrapped around the four-storey former Co-op department store on the corner of Terminus Road and Trinity Trees that had been boarded up for as long as Barnes could remember. Barnes's eye was caught by movement, sudden movement incongruent to this tableau. He dropped his gaze down from the giant Santa to street level, and saw what Howlett was seeing.

A woman had fallen over on the other side of the crossroads intersecting Terminus Road and Seaside Road, on the pavement just outside one of the steakhouses. Most people continued straight past, not wishing to interrupt the urgency of their rigid Christmas itineraries, but two or three stopped to help.

"Looks like someone's feeling crook," Howlett said. "Come on, boss."

The pair of them jogged towards Terminus Road, Howlett calling on his radio for an ambulance as they ran.

They were nearly at the intersection when Barnes saw a second person collapse, close to where the first woman had fallen. A young man, fit. He hadn't tripped. His body started to convulse on the ground.

Barnes stopped dead in his tracks, grabbing at Howlett's sleeve.

"Will . . . wait."

Howlett slowed, and turned to Barnes. He looked confused.

"What is it?"

"Stop. *Stop*. Don't get any closer," Barnes called.

"What?"

"There's a second casualty. Something's wrong."

Howlett looked at Barnes as if to say: *well, obviously*. He pulled his sleeve away from Barnes. Barnes held on tightly.

"Will, it's dangerous. We need to be away from here."

Howlett looked Barnes dead in the eye.

"I have to help them. I have to try."

He wrenched his arm free and continued running across the road.

"Will, *no!*"

Barnes made a flailing grab for Howlett, but he was already out of reach, and besides, it would doubtless have been like trying to stop a Scots pine rolling down a hill.

Howlett sprinted the last thirty metres, and arrived at the kerb just as two more people dropped to the ground.

He turned to look back at Barnes, confusion spreading wider across his face. He opened his mouth to call something — just as his eyes rolled back into his head and his knees buckled.

He dropped heavily onto the road, in that unnatural, doll-like way people fall when they are already unconscious; limbs lifeless, no attempt to break the fall with their hands. Howlett's head took most of the impact with the kerb, and Barnes knew the young DC was dead.

CHAPTER THREE

Barnes looked around frantically, and grabbed for his radio as he backed away across the road. He reached the car, and flung open the driver's door. It was a standard CID pool car — no lights, no sirens, no PA, nothing.

Barnes knew what his job was — to stay safe, observe, assess and report, using CHALET as his guide — what is it, where is it, what do you need and what is the best way in without inadvertently stumbling into the threat? This was not easy, and ran contrary to his instinct to run and help. This was why he was standing still, taking deep breaths, trying to muster the self-control he needed to resist the accusing stares of people wondering why the hell the bloke in the suit holding a warrant card wasn't helping anyone.

He stood still long enough to gauge the wind direction. A gentle south-easterly, blowing in off the Channel. He checked around for something to confirm it — a flag, a plume of smoke or steam somewhere — but saw nothing. He shut his eyes and concentrated, just to be sure.

When he opened them again, the crowd had taken on a very distinct shape, one familiar to Barnes from years of protests, football matches and industrial incidents. There was clear space where the casualties had fallen, and the onlookers surrounding them had pressed this vacuum into a tight circle.

Barnes ran around to the boot. In the box was a large plastic crate crammed with scene suits, latex gloves, scene logs and — to Barnes's astonishment — a megaphone. He grabbed it, pulled his radio handset from his bag and slammed the boot lid shut.

"Ladies and gentlemen, this is the police. Please listen carefully." His amplified voice rattled out across the street. "Please do not panic. Move quickly and carefully across the road towards the sea. Look after each other, please, and try not to push. I repeat, look after each other."

Anxious faces turned to him, wide-eyed. Had they heard him? Or had they just heard a tinny robotic voice squawking at them in a way that suggested bad news?

"People, please cross the road. You need to move *upwind*."

The majority of them were now looking at him, and while he had their attention, he began to repeat his instructions. Crowds such as these took on their own dynamics, and individual nuances and characteristics tended to be lost in the collective.

For a moment, Barnes thought he had them under control.

Then the screaming began.

The crowd began to stampede across the road, bent on self-preservation. The smallest and weakest of their number fell and were trampled on the tarmac.

The panic spread like a bush fire, and Barnes's instructions were lost in the yelling. His voice became a high-pitched yell as he watched those failing to heed his instructions collapsing as they started to run, their bodies crumpling heavily onto the road.

Barnes fumbled for his radio and began yelling orders into it.

CHAPTER FOUR

Tina Guestling's heart sank a little when she saw the cluster of men gathered around the free weights. Big, muscular guys, glistening with sweat, talking loudly and laughing in deep, braying voices while swigging from gallon tankards of water and peering at their mobile phones.

She thought momentarily about performing a swift U-turn, but Nicky was patiently pushing a trolley around the supermarket while she waited to collect her mum, and Tina didn't want to waste her daughter's time.

The subjects of their conversations were indiscernible from thirty feet away, but, given the way the chat dried up and all eyes turned to her as she approached, she took an educated guess. There was a brief impasse while two of them stood between her and the barbells.

"Come on, boys," she said with a broad grin, fists on hips in a Wonder Woman pose, "time is money. Mind if I crack on?"

"'Course, love," one said, dabbing at his brow with the towel hanging around his neck. "Shove over, you lot. Don't crowd the lady."

They dispersed. She beamed at the alpha, stuck her headphones on and began sliding plates onto the bar.

As she launched into deadlifts, she wondered — and not for the first time — about transferring to another gym, but figured she would only run into the same boilerplate fraternity hogging the squat rack.

The rest of the session was uneventful. Until her phone rang. She tutted and ignored it, but it rang, and then rang again. And then again. Same number — one she didn't recognise. A mobile.

The number persisted. Just in case some hideous disaster had befallen Nicky in Asda's produce aisle, she answered.

"Yes?"

"Tina? Sorry to bother you. I'm calling from FIB . . ."

Work. Her irritation bloomed. She wasn't on call.

"I'm not at work," she said, and, in her impatience, missed the caller's name. Some DI she didn't know, but whom she assumed featured somewhere in the complicated spiderweb that made up the management structure of Intelligence.

"Yes, I know. I'm really sorry to bother you. I'm trying to get as many people in as possible."

"What's happened?" she said, curiosity getting the better of her.

"There's been some kind of CBRN incident in Eastbourne town centre. Looking like several casualties with at least two deceased. Maybe more. Major incident's been declared."

"Oh shit. Terrorism?"

A couple of the meatheads looked over at her. She turned away.

"Not sure yet. For all we know it's some kind of accidental spill, but maybe not. Hence the call. Whatever it is, the world and his wife are going to want a piece of it, as you can imagine. Gold wants to line up all the ducks before COBRA start calling."

"Do we know what the stuff is?"

"Again, no." Now it was the DI's turn to sound irritated. "It's only just happened. Can you come in?"

"Of course. Where do you want me? HQ?"

"RVP is the Major Incident Suite at Hammonds Drive."

"OK. I'm in the gym. I need thirty — no, twenty minutes."

"Fantastic. See you shortly."

He hung up. Tina looked at herself in the mirror for a moment, then called Nicky.

Nicky, Tina's seventeen-year-old daughter, arrived early without complaint. Tina felt the familiar stab of guilt and shame as she got in the passenger seat. Nicky was resourceful and reliable, and never complained at having to ferry her mother around. Tina often wondered if these were inherent traits, or whether her mother losing her licence as a consequence of a drink-drive conviction in the throes of divorce simply meant Nicky had needed to grow up a bit quicker than expected.

The run to the Major Incident Suite took ten minutes in the traffic, but it was still handy that Tina's home station had been selected as the RVP for the incident.

Or maybe not — Tina remembered that a CBRN incident had happened not four miles up the road. Maybe she'd have been better off going to HQ after all.

Nicky stopped outside Wickes.

"What time you want collecting?" she said as Tina got out.

"Oh, hun, don't worry. I'll get a cab."

"Mum, don't be silly. I've got no plans."

"Nic, listen, I don't know when I'm going to finish. It sounds like it's going to be a long one."

"What about food?"

Tina smiled. "I'm sure the boss will sort out a bulk order of Domino's."

"That's not on the diet plan."

"Call today a cheat day. Nicky, listen — go home and stay there, okay? Keep the windows and doors shut. Don't go into town, whatever you do."

Her daughter's eyes widened.

"I'm probably just being paranoid, but until I know exactly what has happened, I want you to be safe."

"Okay, Mum."

"Try not to worry, okay?"

Nicky grinned. "Have a good shift."

Tina watched Nicky reverse and pull away, idly noting that the Corsa needed a new brake light, then turned and walked into work.

She sensed the buzz in the office when she was still in the corridor. The duty team had their heads down, clacking keyboards furiously, while the surplus staff recalled to duty — Tina among them — were shrugging off bags and jackets and trying to find somewhere to sit. A couple of the sergeants — neither of whom Tina recognised — were trying to meet, greet and organise desk space while their phones ran hot.

Eventually Tina found a workstation and turned to listen to the snatched briefing from the supervisor — four analysts were needed for the RVP, to staff a mobile command unit. As the supervisor spoke, she reflected that most incidents and crimes did not encroach into the personal fears and anxieties of the police working the cases, who usually found it relatively easy to maintain an objective distance.

This was not one of those. This was most certainly one to be worried about, and she was glad she had insisted that Nicky stay home.

A police officer was dead, one of the first casualties. He had been practically on scene, dealing with something else, when he ran to assist one of the collapsed victims. Moments later he was dead also. All signs pointed to some kind of CBRN release, and while it was too early to identify the substance or suggest a deliberate act, it was being treated as such. If it was deliberate, there were no suspects.

Intelligence had a significant job to do.

CHAPTER FIVE

With the precision of a Jonny Wilkinson place kick, Maggie finished writing her name on the front of her exercise book, just as the bell sounded. It made her smile. The bell at her old school had been so loud it made her teeth chatter; here, the hall monitors came out with a hand bell and rang it. It reminded her that it was only eighteen sleeps until Christmas. She couldn't wait till it was her turn to ring it. She would ring it louder than anyone else.

She gathered up her collection of exercise books and counted them before she dropped them into her bag. There were nine in all, and the covers were all different colours. Blue for maths, green for English and so on. She loved brand new exercise books, loved the smooth feeling of them in her hands and the smell of the unspoiled pages.

Nine times she had written her name. It was good practice. *BARNES* was a bit harder to write than *WALL* and she could never remember whether it had an "E" in it or not, but she much preferred it. *MAGGIE BARNES*. She liked the way it sounded. She wondered if Mummy would like it too.

She finished packing her bag and skipped out onto the playground. She didn't have long before practice started, and she had to get changed.

The winter sun smelled good on the funny rubber floor of the playground. She couldn't believe it was nearly Christmas. There was a hint of salt in the air as well. She loved that she could smell the sea at her new school. She thought of all her old friends back in London, all wrapped up warm for winter, and just for a moment she felt a sad feeling in her stomach.

Then the field came into view, and the sad feeling went away. She enjoyed rugby. The ball was egg-shaped, and she found it easier than football because you were allowed to carry it and run as fast as you could. Her teacher, Mr Shan, said she was really good. A natural, he'd said. She liked Mr Shan. He smiled a lot, and didn't shout. He was even nice when things weren't going well, like when she tripped over and dropped the ball. She wished more of her teachers were like Mr Shan.

She couldn't see anyone on the field yet. Maybe they were still getting changed, although the cones and big sacks full of rugby balls were normally out on the field by now. She didn't let it worry her, though, as she skipped towards the field, the sun through the trees making patterns on the ground.

The school was huge, and looked like a castle. (She tried not to think of the word *haunted*.) The sun disappeared behind one of the enormous towers and her footsteps began to echo as she headed inside and made her way down the corridor towards the changing rooms.

She turned the corner, and stopped.

A man was standing there, right outside the changing rooms. He was smiling at her. He was wearing a Summerdown House tracksuit, and a whistle hung around his neck. He was very thin, with long black hair combed back over his head.

"Hello, Maggie," the man said.

She didn't answer.

"Mr Shan's not very well. I'm taking practice today. I'm Mr Davidson."

"You look like a boy," Maggie said.

Mr Davidson kept smiling. He stood very still. Maggie looked around. There was nobody else in the corridor.

"It's all right," the man said, holding out a hand. "You can trust me."

Maggie suddenly felt unhappy. Not sad, but . . . maybe a bit scared. She felt it around people she didn't know. She'd felt it a lot since changing schools and moving house, and once before that, when a stranger had spoken to her and Ellie while Mummy was talking to someone in a shop.

"Mr . . ."

"Mr Davidson." He moved closer to Maggie, and dropped down onto one knee.

"Mr Shan's told me how good you are at rugby," he said, still smiling. "I thought we'd start you as captain today. How do you feel about that? Sound good?"

A little of the unhappy feeling vanished, and she managed a smile. *Captain?*

"Come on," he said, standing up. "The others are waiting."

She made to go into the changing room, but he placed a hand on her shoulder to stop her.

"Let's get straight onto the field, okay? You need to pick the teams. You can come back and change while the others are warming up."

The unhappy feeling came back, but Mr Davidson's hand was already holding hers. It was cold and slimy. He led her towards the doors at the end of the corridor and out onto Carlisle Road.

"Where are we going?" she said.

"Just up here," he said. "We're using the big field today."

A small voice inside her shouted *Get away! Run!* but she wasn't sure why, and she allowed Mr Davidson to lead her up the road. She looked back at the castle as they walked.

Where was everybody?

They walked along Carlisle Road towards the sea, and, after a few minutes, arrived at New Field. The afternoon sun was right in her face and, after the gloom of the inside of the school, it took a few moments for her eyesight to adjust in the sunlight. Maggie saw the big H-shaped posts at either end of the field, but she also saw that there was no one on the field. No balls, cones or tackle-bags.

There was, however, something else on the field.

An ambulance.

She knew it straight away. They were always racing past them on the motorway. The sirens made her jump, and she was always fascinated by the fact that the word AMBULANCE was the wrong way round on the front, like in a mirror.

But why was there one on the school field?

"Is somebody hurt?" she asked, looking up at Mr Davidson.

"Not sure," he answered. "Let's go take a look."

They walked over to the ambulance. It looked like there was nobody in it. Mr Davidson led her to the back. The doors were shut. Mr Davidson knocked.

"Maybe the paramedics will show you how all their equipment works," he said, turning the handle that opened the door.

Maggie peered inside, her curiosity suddenly strong. She'd never seen inside an ambulance before. There was a bed and computer screens and other things she'd seen at the doctor's surgery.

But there was no one in there. The back of the ambulance was empty.

She turned around to tell Mr Davidson, but before she could, she felt two hands pick her up and shove her roughly inside the ambulance. Her leg bent sideways on the floor and she fell over forwards.

Then the door slammed shut behind her.

CHAPTER SIX

An eerie silence had descended over the intersection of Terminus Road and Seaside Road. Even the gulls were quiet. The portion of street in Barnes's line of sight had virtually cleared itself of traffic and people — exactly how, Barnes wasn't sure — but the traffic lights governing the empty road continued blinking silently from green to amber to red and back again.

Barnes strained to look and listen — for drifting vapour clouds, dead seagulls, rapidly departing vehicles, anything out of place. There was nothing obvious, but then he could hear little beyond his heart ramming against his ribcage and his own rapid-fire breathing as he fought to stay calm and keep his mind from freezing completely.

The patrol base was less than three miles east; ordinarily, the sound of multiple sirens drawing closer as the cavalry came over the hill — or, in this case, along the seafront — tended to bring a sense of relief, but Barnes was still struggling to work out exactly what he was going to tell them when they arrived.

After a moment or two, he cobbled together enough presence of mind to call up on the radio and direct the first three units to set up road closures — one at the seafront end of Terminus Road, one at Memorial Roundabout and one at Cavendish Place. "When you get out of your cars," Barnes said over the air, "shout for as many people as you can to come towards you. Do not come any closer."

* * *

As more units started to arrive along the seafront — Barnes didn't think he'd ever seen so many marked cars at once — he ordered further road closures to complete the circle and create as much of a sterile area as was possible at four in the afternoon on Eastbourne's main drag three weeks before Christmas. The rest of the units he summoned to where he stood. It wasn't pretty, but it had more or less done the job.

Barnes's own car was still half on, half off the pavement outside the Royal Sovereign pub, at the junction with North Street. He had intended to dress back some distance from where he was standing when Will Howlett fell, but as the patrol cars pulled alongside him, it became increasingly difficult to do so. As FCPs went, it was a bit closer for comfort than Barnes was entirely comfortable with, but, given the circumstances, it would have to do. Such things were usually best endeavours anyway.

Next to the former Co-op was a convenience store and this, judging by the small cluster of bodies on the pavement, seemed to be the nucleus of whatever the hell had happened.

The principles of a major incident response were, Barnes mused, like the cross-section of a felled oak. Ground zero right in the centre, with inner, central and outer cordons radiating outwards in expanding circles. In those early stages, with precise information in short supply and the extent of the potential damage as yet unknown, the scene control needed to assume the worst — and, accordingly, be as wide as possible.

Clearing the area around the immediate scene had been pretty easy — the public had more or less done it for them, to the extent that trying to identify and speak to potential casualties and witnesses before they left (or, rather, *escaped*) the area had been virtually impossible. But when Fire & Rescue had insisted on a 400-metre evacuated cordon, well, that required some phone calls up top. This radius took in most of the town centre, including the Arndale shopping centre and the train station.

Barnes managed to marshal his backup into some kind of inner cordon before the press arrived. A suitably vague "stay away" message went out on the Force's social media channel, but that didn't stop Sky News from hovering overhead far sooner than Barnes would have thought possible.

HART paramedics in protective hazmat suits, who had made extraordinarily good time from their Gatwick base, moved swiftly among the casualties in the hot zone, while Fire & Rescue attempted to set up a decontamination area and protect the stunned faces of the dead from the press.

The triage was brutal in its efficiency — casualties were labelled with brightly coloured snap-on bracelets. Green: walking wounded. Amber: serious, but not life-threatening. Red: immediate care needed to save life.

Black: beyond help.

So far, there were six wearing black bracelets, including the body of T/DC Will Howlett. Barnes made an estimate that at least two of the casualties had sustained crush injuries having fallen and been trampled in the exodus. Whether any of those succumbed to their injuries remained to be seen.

Six was a lot of bodies. Any more than three in one incident and the national media came sniffing. More than three, connected only by the — as yet unknown — cause of death, was a lot of front pages.

Once Barnes had organised all the manpower he was going to get — at least in this first wave — to drop a net over everything, it became Fire & Rescue's roadshow, closely followed by the paramedics. A flotilla of TV news trucks had assembled at the seafront end of Terminus Road some two hundred metres away, and long-range lenses started to appear on the cordon.

Barnes frowned. He was with Fire on this one. In this scenario — multiple casualties, no obvious cause — the outer cordon needed to be another two hundred metres further out, minimum. He wasn't quite sure why he himself was still so close to the action.

He angled himself away from the cameras as he pulled out his phone. Tamsin guessed immediately that something was up.

"Hey, honey," she said, in that throaty voice of hers that sounded like she had just woken up. Despite the situation, Barnes got that feeling of butterflies in his stomach whenever he heard her voice. Husky, but matter-of-fact. "Everything okay?"

"Tamsin . . . where are you? Out?"

"No. Home."

"And the kids?"

"Ellie's with me. Maggie's at school. I'm about to go and get her from rugby practice."

Barnes breathed a sigh of relief.

"Tam, do me a favour, okay? Grab Maggie and then stay home. Don't come to town. Stay well away."

She didn't panic, or question him, or fall apart. Those butterflies again.

"Does this have something to do with my phone going batshit?"

"Work?"

"Probably. I haven't answered it."

Tamsin's full-time paramedic career had tapered off once the girls arrived, but she still kept her hand in, part-time. And like most emergency services personnel, she knew how to keep calm when it was all going off.

"Okay."

"Barnes — are you okay?"

He thought about it. Was he? He was a good fifty or sixty metres from where Howlett had fallen, and, as far as he could work out, he seemed to be all right. No burning sensation in the throat, no coughing, no red eyes, no inexplicable spasms or loss of feeling anywhere.

"Barnes? You there?"

"I . . . I am. Yes, I'm fine. I'll see you soon, okay?"

"Be careful. I'll kiss the girls for you."

Barnes put his phone away and, for a moment, thought about quitting the police altogether. This kind of shit might have been fun when he was a widower living alone, but now . . .

He looked behind him. Seaside Road was empty, the cafés, convenience stores and charity shops silent. It looked like a scene from some post-apocalyptic film — a couple of cars had been abandoned on the kerb by their occupants with the doors still open. The shops, too, had their doors open and the lights on, but the staff were gone, hustled away to the Sovereign Centre, which had very quickly opened its doors as a temporary shelter.

It was a one-way road, the pavements having been widened and sprinkled with bollards some years previously, both as a traffic-calming initiative and to create a more al fresco appeal to the coffee shops — chuck a few metal chairs and tables outside, that kind of thing.

That did mean that the single-file road very quickly became snarled up with a train of liveried mobile command units, incident support vehicles and a decontamination unit — an enormous red container that somehow brought Dr Seuss to mind.

A muffled voice spoke sharply behind him; Barnes found himself and a few of the other uniformed response officers who had pushed forward to assist him hustled down towards the decon unit by large figures in what looked like spacesuits, or deep-sea diving apparatus.

As the gaggle of officers was steered past the scene tape guarding the entrance to North Street, Barnes remembered that he still had a dead body sitting on a public toilet awaiting collection by an undertaker.

To all intents and purposes, a Class A overdose.

But maybe not.

Barnes tried to point this out to the astronaut who was guiding him gently but firmly towards the giant red container, but the muffled voice told him it would have to wait.

It was rather like herding cats — police officers, in such situations, prefer to be the shepherds, rather than the sheep — but eventually they went through on a conveyor belt of being disrobed, lathered with what seemed to be jet-powered foam, hosed down and shoehorned into some kind of rubbery orange jumpsuit with gloves and a face mask.

"I'm going to want those," Barnes said as his clothes were shoved into a biohazard bag. "That's a crime scene back there. I'll need to get into it."

The astronaut just looked at him through the vapour that had formed on its mask and nodded towards a folded stack of generic tracksuits.

After decon, Barnes was triaged by a paramedic who, after establishing that he was symptom-free, cautiously allowed Barnes to move about within the cordon.

Barnes found himself pulled back towards ground zero, back towards the scene of whatever it was that had happened.

Back towards Will Howlett's body.

He stopped himself, realised his car was boxed in by five or six enormous red vehicles and was going nowhere quickly, and instead started to walk east towards where, on the intersection of Cavendish Place and Seaside Road, a police operational support HGV was dutifully bringing up the rear of the long red line. It rolled to a halt outside the cordon with a hiss of air brakes.

It was a strangely reassuring sight, the staff from the emergency planning team busying themselves setting up a refuel station.

Reassuring, that is, until he saw the white shirt and scrambled egg adorning the diminutive-if-solid frame of its wearer, whose eager eyes darted around like a meerkat's in search of television cameras.

Barnes's least favourite command officer.

Gabby.

Or, to give him his full title, Assistant Chief Constable Gabriel Glover. On Gabby's scale of pet dislikes, Barnes had long theorised that he was placed maybe on a par with fish tank slime and hives.

Barnes knew, however, that he did rank slightly above his only trusted police colleague, Superintendent Samson Kane. Gabby's loathing of Kane was so nakedly unabashed that Barnes looked like the Milkybar Kid in comparison.

If it had been anyone else, Barnes would have been surprised to see the Gold Commander for an incident like this so close to the action, but, where Gabby was concerned, it was entirely on brand. Something about not wanting to be lumped in with the General Melchett school of commanders, sending troops forward as cannon fodder while he played tiddlywinks thirty miles behind enemy lines.

Barnes pulled down his face mask. Gabby did a double-take.

"Barnes. It's you," he said. "Why is it always you?"

"It's good to see you too, sir."

Dispensing with further pleasantries, Gabby shouldered his way past Barnes in order to manoeuvre himself under the scene tape and through the cordon. To say he looked disgruntled when Barnes stopped him was a significant understatement.

"Sir, you can't go in."

"You what?"

"Cold zone ends here. We can't begin the investigation until the scene has been declared safe."

Barnes looked over his shoulder to where plastic sheeting now covered the fallen casualties, which were themselves being treated as extremely hazardous crime scenes.

Gabby edged closer. Barnes had a good six inches on him, but Gabby tilted his nose up towards Barnes's chin without any hint of disquiet.

"We have a dead DC. First officer to fall in the line of duty on our patch for over ten years." He came closer still. "They're not exactly going to be queuing up to work with you, are they?"

Barnes's insides bloomed with anger. "I did everything I could to save him."

Gabby said nothing. Barnes wasn't finished.

"It's basic training for a CBRN incident. One casualty — approach as normal. Two casualties — approach with caution, stay upwind and report back. Three or more casualties — *stay the fuck away*. I tried to stop him."

Gabby shook his head in disbelief. "You know we're broke, right? Recruitment freeze. Forced retirements. It's bad enough without the officers we do have dropping like flies. If the exodus continues, we'll have no one left."

Barnes's fist balled. Gabby made another attempt to go under the tape. Barnes grabbed him by the upper arm — it was either that or bash him in the jaw.

"I'll tell his family. It has to be me," Barnes said.

Gabby looked Barnes up and down, and jerked a thumb toward his garishly decorated epaulettes. "I think not."

For a third time, Gabby pushed his way into the scene. This time, Barnes let him go.

With a distant public inquiry half in mind, he resolved to start collating his thoughts into some form of cogent written log, when his mobile rang again.

Preparing for tacit interrogation by some other senior officer, Barnes didn't look at the screen.

It was Tamsin.

"Barnes . . ." His normally unflappable partner sounded frantic.

"What is it? Are you okay?"

"It's . . . it's Maggie."

Barnes went cold. "What about her?"

"She was supposed to be at rugby practice, but the coach said she never showed up. No one has seen her."

"Oh God."

"Barnes, she's . . . she's missing."

CHAPTER SEVEN

His breath coming in serrated gasps, Barnes crammed himself into a hazmat suit and scanned the casualties from a distance. He checked the suit's integrity for a fourth time and pushed towards the hot zone.

It wasn't coincidence. It couldn't be. Maggie *missing*? At the very time an apparent chemical attack had crippled the middle of Eastbourne? Barnes couldn't work out how or why, but he'd never believed in coincidences.

When he got to the FCP — his car — an enormous firefighter clad, like a red Darth Vader in CBRN PPE, blocked his way.

"You can't go any further." His voice was muffled by the mask.

"You don't understand—"

"I know, it's a crime scene. You said. But no one is getting near it until we have a better idea of what it is."

"No, listen. My daughter is missing. She . . . she might be . . ."

Barnes pointed to the mound of bodies. The firefighter tilted his head. He didn't understand.

"She's vanished from school. I just want to make sure she isn't over there."

"Look, there's going to be any number of people calling in worried that their loved ones are caught up in this. Police will be setting up a casualty bureau. Why should you get special treatment?"

Because all this might be because of me, Barnes thought.

"Look, you're right," he said, fighting to keep calm. "I don't want special treatment. But you — we — are going to have to start cross-checking missing person reports with casualties at some point. Why not cross one off the list while we can?"

The firefighter, breathing heavily behind his mask, thought about it.

"Okay," he said, eventually. "Got a photo?"

Barnes pulled out his phone and flicked through it until he found one of Maggie in her powder-blue Summerdown House uniform. He showed it to him.

The firefighter turned on his heel. Barnes remained at the FCP and stared at the bodies, the town's usual hubbub absent from the hot zone.

The firefighter took his time. Barnes's body began to tense with the anxiety of the wait. He'd thought a quick visual sweep, no more than thirty seconds, and Darth Vader would have been able to quickly confirm Maggie's absence.

Or presence.

The bodies had been left where they had fallen, sprawled and twisted in a mesh of limbs whose owners were not immediately obvious. Even from this distance, Barnes could see the expressions of some — frozen in horror, streams of blood and the thick white foam of wrecked internal organs caked on their faces.

He'd originally estimated twenty casualties, with maybe a third of that number deceased. It was clear that the number had risen. Most of those wearing black bracelets were adults, but there were some smaller limbs visible among the wreckage. Underneath a large corpse he saw the bright pink of Howlett's shirt.

The firefighter was careful. He didn't go piling in, pulling bodies this way and that. He was strictly hands off, using visuals only. Despite the situation, Barnes was impressed. It was still a crime scene, after all.

He suddenly worried that the firefighter would miss her. He'd only glanced at her picture for a second. And people looked different in death. They went an unfamiliar colour. Their muscles stopped working and their faces took on expressions never used before. Would the guy even recognise her?

Then he saw it. A flash of distinctive powder blue among the carnage. The bright blue shirt of Summerdown House's regulation uniform. The firefighter peered down at her.

Please God, not Maggie. No, not . . .

It was a girl, maybe about ten. Her sightless eyes were wide and glassy.

Not Maggie.

But it was still a fellow pupil. One who wouldn't ever be going back to school. It could so easily have been Maggie.

The firefighter walked over.

"She's not there."

"Are you sure?"

"I'm sure."

"Thank you."

He loped off. Barnes pulled off the headgear with relief, the fresh air and sounds of the seagulls a welcome change from the muffled silence inside the mask and the putrid air inside the hot zone.

He leaned on suddenly rubbery knees and tried to marshal his thoughts. Maybe it was coincidence after all. Some kind of chemical incident, multiple casualties, the likes of which Eastbourne had not seen before. At the same time, his seven-year-old stepdaughter was missing.

Maybe she wasn't missing. Tamsin might be trying to call him right now, to tell him Maggie had turned up and all was well.

He reached in his pocket for his mobile and dialled her number.

"Tam? Any news?"

"No. No news." Her voice was hoarse and strained. "Barnes, I'm . . . I'm just giving the report to the policeman. Can I . . ."

"Of course. Call me when you're done. I've checked the casualties here. She isn't here."

"Oh, thank Christ. Your lot had better find whoever's done this before I do. I'll rip his bollocks off. What the sodding hell is going on, Barnes?"

"I . . . I'm not sure. Call me when you're done, okay? I'll have a better idea then."

Barnes's jaw tightened as he approached the mobile incident command vehicle. He was already at the foot of the steps when the side door opened.

As if on cue, Gabby Glover appeared in the doorway. He stood for a moment, surveying the street, hands on hips. He caught Barnes's eye, briefly held his stare, and then disappeared inside the vehicle.

Barnes stared at the vacant doorway for a moment, and then clomped up the steps after his boss into the cool gloom of the command centre.

Despite himself, Barnes was impressed. A bank of monitors lined one side of the centre, with two analysts and two controllers furiously working the keyboards while relaying information to ground units. A CCTV feed was supplying views of Eastbourne to six different screens, and radio chatter clipped the air. None of the operators noticed Barnes.

In the corner of the vehicle an animated conversation was taking place between Gabby, his counterparts from the ambulance and fire services, and a fourth man who looked like a caricature of a university professor, with a cheap houndstooth jacket and red wiry hair like dancing flames.

Barnes hesitated, and then marched over. The conversation petered out as the four men realised Barnes was standing there, but he still caught words like "suffocation", "toxic", and "nerve agent".

"My daughter's missing," Barnes said, addressing Gabby.

"Barnes? What the hell are you doing in here?" Gabby's voice was trembling.

"My daughter's missing," Barnes said again.

"What do you mean, your daughter's missing?" Gabby said. "In case you hadn't noticed, we're a little busy here."

"I think it's connected," Barnes said. "I don't believe it's a coincidence."

"Well, what do you expect us to do about it?"

Barnes had to count to five to stop himself planting his fist in Gabby's ear. The fire and ambulance guys looked uncomfortable.

"Apologies, we've not met," Barnes said, offering a hand to each of them. "Detective Inspector Rutherford Barnes, CID. First on scene. One of my team didn't make it."

They each returned the shake, muttering condolences. Barnes turned to the man with the red hair with his eyebrows raised, who introduced himself as some professor of toxicology and pharmacology or other from UCL.

"You made good time," Barnes said.

"I'm part of STAC. I'm sort of on call."

"Any update on substance identification?" Barnes asked.

The man cleared his throat. "Still too early to tell, but it might be sarin."

"Jesus," Barnes muttered under his breath. "That would mean it *was* a deliberate act."

"Difficult to be sure because it evaporates so quickly, but the symptoms of the casualties are — so far — consistent."

Barnes eyed him. "You've been up and had a look?"

The professor cleared his throat again. "Just an early hypothesis from what I've been told by our fire colleagues. There's still plenty of work to do."

Barnes left it. He'd have to assume there was no such thing as a STAC hack. For now, anyway.

He turned back to Gabby.

"My daughter. She had rugby practice after school, but the coach called my wife and said she never showed up."

Gabby said nothing, but held Barnes's stare.

"She called me minutes after this happened. Seconds, even."

Still nobody spoke. All eyes were on Barnes now.

"You're not telling me you think it's coincidence?" Barnes said to the silence. "It's connected. It has to be. I want . . . I need some resources to look for her."

Gabby took a deep breath, as if not being a twat required significant effort.

"Look, Barnes. This is your daughter, so I get it. But there is no intelligence to link these two . . . episodes. Am I right?"

Barnes said nothing, and his shoulders slumped a little. He knew exactly where this was going.

"My partner — Maggie's mother — has already reported it," he said. "I checked the casualties. She's not there. She's only seven . . ."

Gabby's restraint evaporated.

"You did *what*?" He stepped forward. "That's a fucking controlled area. It's a *crime scene*."

"I didn't *personally*. Fire did. They had the necessary protection. What are you fretting about? Is it *your* daughter that's missing?"

"Oh, they had the necessary protection? Well, I'm relieved. What about you? Did you bag your suit? Did you update the scene log? Did you go through the decon process?" He threw his hands in the air, and then grabbed Barnes's upper arm and pointed at the door.

"Get yourself outside and into the decontamination chamber. You can't miss it. Big queue of fucking people. Then maybe we'll talk."

"Take your hands off me!"

Barnes pulled his arm free. The ambient noise in the vehicle stopped. The four operators working the console behind the men stopped typing, and for a moment there was only background radio chatter and the sounds of the street outside.

Barnes turned on his heel and walked towards the door, feeling every pair of eyes in the vehicle on him.

At the doorway he paused, and looked back at the vehicle full of people. Gabby was staring at him, angry breaths jetting out of his nostrils. The fire and ambulance commanders, along with the STAC professor, were staring at their feet. The operators turned back to their workstations and refocused on their screens as the sound of clicking keyboards slowly resumed.

All, that is, except one. She was dark-haired, not more than forty. Her name badge said *TINA*. She was staring at Barnes with a mixture of sympathy and bewilderment, and the moment Barnes caught her eye, he knew she was a parent too.

Raindrops began drumming onto the roof of the command vehicle, and Barnes stepped outside into the sudden downpour. Vapour began to rise off the street as the rain battered the tarmac.

He stood in the rain and watched the hazmat responders diligently work around the edges of the contaminated area. Despite his feelings towards the man, he knew Gabby was right. There *was* no intelligence to suggest Maggie's disappearance was linked to this chaos, and he had been correct in his refusal to provide resources on the back of an emotive plea. In fact, how many times in his service had young children been reported missing by frantic parents, only to turn up safe and well minutes later? Who was to say Maggie and Tamsin hadn't already been reunited?

He snorted at the thought. Experience had told him to trust his gut, and right now his gut was ringing all kinds of alarm bells. If there was no intelligence to suggest Maggie's disappearance had anything to do with a chemical incident, then he was just going to have to go find it.

CHAPTER EIGHT

The courier pulled off at Pease Pottage and tucked the ambulance into a far corner of the services car park. It was relatively quiet. Trucks and vans crawled in and out, the odd family people-carrier loaded to the gills with bicycles and roof racks. People wandered in and out of the main concourse clutching lattes and mega-size meal deals, no urgency to their movements. News from the seaside had not yet filtered up the A23 corridor.

The courier stared at the phone as he waited, his gaze impassive. He cared for nothing but collecting his money in time to make his evening flight. With any luck, he would be in the air while the cops were still scrabbling around on the ground like ants.

The mobile phone buzzed.

The courier flipped it open.

"Well?" The voice on the other end was clear and loud.

"It is done."

"There's nothing on the news yet." The voice was impatient. The courier understood that. This kind of risk was too great to brook failure.

"It won't be long. One hour, maybe two."

"How did it go?"

The courier hissed laughter through his teeth.

"It was a success. Many casualties."

"And the girl?"

The caller's tone was beginning to irritate the courier.

"Everything went as planned. There is nothing unexpected to report."

"Did you hurt her?"

The courier smiled to himself.

"Only a little. Do you have my money?"

"The transfer is going ahead as we speak. One hour, maybe two."

The caller's paraphrasing was not lost on the courier, but he did not wish to argue. This man would not dare cross him.

"Good. My flight leaves in two hours."

"Call me when you land."

"No. There is no need for us to speak again. As soon as my payment is transferred, our business is complete. Unless, of course, there is something else you wish to hire me for?"

There was a pause on the other end of the line.

"Maybe you think about it, and call me when you've made up your mind."

The caller inhaled, ready to speak, but the courier ended the call. He pulled out the phone's innards, pocketing the battery and snapping the SIM card in two. He leaned out of the ambulance window and dropped the handset in a bin on his way out of the car park, then pulled back onto the motorway and north towards Gatwick International Airport.

The courier smiled to himself as he drove. He had been baiting the caller, and he knew it. He knew full well there was more work coming his way.

There was much more to the caller's plan.

CHAPTER NINE

Barnes staggered back up Terminus Road in a daze. The usual sights, sounds and smells of the town were now completely absent. There were people pressed against the cordons at the outer boundaries of the warm zone at Memorial Roundabout to the west, the Crown & Anchor to the east and the railway station to the north, but, for the most part, the areas outside the cordons were deathly silent. News of a chemical incident was beginning to filter through, and people were leaving the town centre in droves.

Barnes found the picture of Maggie on his phone, and approached the few people he did see wandering about — mainly store owners closing up shop before starting their retreat — asking if they had seen her.

Those that didn't ignore him completely simply gave him strange or hostile looks, and Barnes realised his warrant card was still hooked over his waistband. In situations like this people expected cops to be in charge, directing people away from the danger, rescuing casualties, answering questions. Barnes had effectively taken himself out of context by approaching people like a wild-eyed beggar, and all he was doing was alienating himself from the public.

This realisation served to put his thought processes back on a more linear trajectory. How did he expect to find Maggie by wandering around the town alone?

Gabby didn't believe that Maggie's disappearance was in any way linked to the chemical incident. And, much as it galled him, Barnes realised he would probably have taken the same view had he been in Gabby's shoes.

So, if Barnes couldn't prove a link by searching for Maggie in the midst of the town centre carnage, he might be able to prove it by focusing on her disappearance. Less chaotic, more of an isolated incident. Easier to identify lines of enquiry.

Part of him, he realised, wanted Gabby to be *right*. Because if Maggie's disappearance *was* linked to what was looking increasingly like some kind of deliberate chemical act, what the hell did that mean?

He looked down at the picture of Maggie on his phone. Her smile was happy and radiant, and her eyes sparkled. He remembered the picture being taken. He remembered Tamsin styling Maggie's hair in a French plait, and the school dress he had ironed for her.

Maggie's image disappeared as the phone began to ring. He closed his eyes. Tamsin.

"Hi, Tam," he managed, wishing he had news for her, hoping that *she* had good news for *him*. "Any news?"

Tamsin's voice was calm, if hoarse, and her steady tone made Barnes feel frantic.

"Barnes . . . I'm at the school with the police. We're speaking to the principal. They . . . think Maggie's been taken."

Taken?

The small fragment of hope disappeared.

"What do you mean, taken?" he said.

"It seems that . . ." Her voice hitched. There was a shuffling sound as the phone was handed over.

"Hello? Barnes? It's Samson. I'm with Tamsin."

"Samson? You're at the school?"

"I got a call from Gabby Glover."

"I can imagine how that went."

Samson chuckled. "At least he called, right?"

"You did well to get here from HQ."

"Getting in doesn't seem to be a problem. It's getting out that's causing some headaches."

"I meant with your car intact."

Samson Kane. If ever there was an outsider in the police service, Kane was it. He'd arrived on day one as a fresh-out-the-box lateral entry superintendent, skin raw from a hundred tattoos having been freshly lasered off, dotted with holes where piercings once sat, yellow-blond hair spiked into some kind of Ziggy Stardust arrangement with The Clash blaring from his claptrap Lancer.

Someone — and Barnes knew who — had thought Kane's appointment might edge the modern service towards greater representation of society's fringe elements. Barnes himself had never been able to shake the feeling it was some sort of cruel joke. The comment about his car being intact was only half a joke — checking the tarmac around his tyres for scattered drawing pins was now part of Kane's daily ritual, and that was *inside* the police station.

But here he was, almost four years' service now, and showing every indication of going the distance. He was still a superintendent — it would be a cold day in hell before any of the senior administration saw fit to promote him — but he hadn't thrown in the towel either. That he was Barnes's only real confidante in the service spoke all kinds of alt-rock volumes.

Reports of missing children numbered in the thousands each year. For a comforting moment Barnes told himself that Kane would have responded personally even if Maggie had simply wandered off in the supermarket, but, once their strange bromance was taken out of it, the fact remained that there was a superintendent promptly on scene at a missing child report. Barnes knew about resources, knew about proportionate responses and he knew that the moderately reassuring feeling that Kane's arrival invoked was offset by the enormity of what it potentially meant.

"What have you got, Samson, please?" Barnes asked.

"There isn't really an easy way to say this, but I'm afraid it does look like your daughter may have been abducted."

"Go on." Barnes fought to stay calm, but the shrieking in his head was amplified by Kane's use of the words *your daughter*.

"Well, as you know, she never showed up for rugby practice after school. We've canvassed her classmates and teachers, including her rugby coach. There isn't a great deal of information, but what the jigsaw looks like at the moment is that she left on foot with a man, possibly posing as a teacher, and that they may have left the school grounds in a bus or similar vehicle. That's a theory, mind. Not concrete yet."

"CCTV?" Barnes asked, the fear boiling up in his chest.

"Disabled."

"Oh, Christ."

"It's a fairly decent system here, by all accounts. The maintenance guy has confirmed that it was manually switched off at some point this afternoon."

"Samson . . . sir . . . you don't think . . ."

"Barnes, I don't think anything at the moment. But Stratton Pearce is in a cell. We don't know it's anything to do with him."

"What about CRA?"

There was a pause on the line. The Child Rescue Alert was a big deal. It meant angry warning alerts sent to every mobile device in the region and beyond. It meant priority messaging on digital motorway signs. It meant normal service interrupted. It meant Kane nailing his theory to the mast very early, and very publicly.

"It qualifies," Kane said slowly. "There's two problems. One: it might, potentially, scare the offender into a course of action they might not otherwise take. And I take it you've heard about the incident in Eastbourne town centre?"

"I'm standing in the middle of it. People are leaving like rats from a ship."

"That's the other problem. I don't think a CRA would necessarily make it to the front of the queue."

48

Barnes, deliberately, said nothing. He knew all this.

"A coincidence?" he said, finally.

"I know what you're saying," Kane said. "And if there's a link to Pearce, I'll find it. My bigger problem is resources. Ordinarily, we — I — would have everything at my disposal, but the chemical incident makes that a bit difficult. Everyone's being pulled off their deployments."

"What are you saying, Samson?"

"Look, Barnes, I'll do my absolute best, I promise you, but it's going to be with half the staff I would want for a kidnap operation, at least for now."

Barnes imagined Tamsin saying, *My daughter is not a kidnap operation.*

"Okay, I understand," he said, with a calm he did not feel. He understood the pressures of competing demands. Tamsin would not, however. Let her give Kane the hard time. "Keep me posted."

"Barnes . . ."

Barnes ended the call. He turned and started jogging back down Terminus Road towards the cordons.

It had been like a switch being pulled inside him. Kane had given him a clear message — with all the attention on the chemical incident, Barnes was, Kane aside, more or less on his own. Kane's own presence at the scene was no doubt intended to take a little of the sting out of this realisation.

So be it.

CHAPTER TEN

Barnes worked the scene. He banished the desultory feelings welling up in him, and instead turned his attention to the outer edges of the cold zone. He moved from point to point, taking in the sightlines, looking at the escape routes. As he circled the cold zone, he began to feel a little better. He was still working for Maggie, but his mind had shifted from parent back to detective.

He looked at the empty streets outside the cordons, and the space-suited scientists hurrying around inside them.

He worked outwards in a spiral, taking in every detail, every innocuous item of street scenery, looking for anomalies, checking for kinks in the fabric of everyday life.

He shut his eyes on the corner of Seaside and Elms Road. *I want to release a deadly chemical with the primary objective being to exact the maximum number of casualties. What do I do?*

Assume for now that the stuff was already here, Barnes thought. He didn't know a huge amount about nerve agents, but he knew that, once you had hold of them, they weren't necessarily difficult to carry about undetected.

This didn't feel like a suicide attack. The team sifting through the casualties would confirm that soon enough, but a suicide attack would be more likely to involve explosives, wouldn't it? Explosives meant maximum impact, maximum media exposure, and the consequent advancing of whatever ideology you had signed up to.

So, assume also that the perpetrator is a professional. A mercenary. A gun for sale. Not a believer.

And a professional would need an out. An escape route.

It occurred to Barnes that a professional might have any number of reasons for executing such an attack. He tried not to dwell on the fact that one of them might be to cause a distraction. If that *were* the case, then it was working.

Barnes pressed his fingertips to his temples and turned around on the spot.

Two options. You get out of the country pronto, using the chaos as cover, or you go to ground somewhere remote until the dust settles.

And you didn't have to go far to achieve that. You could hide out in a shed in Wester Ross and the cabin fever would get you before the feds did.

But a professional had to keep moving. Had to keep earning. Had to keep themselves available and attractive to other bidders. Hide out too long and you take yourself out of the market.

Another sudden burst of rain swept across the buildings in a sheet of freezing spray, soaking Barnes in seconds. It hissed onto the tarmac and then it was gone again, passing over Barnes on its way to the water's edge like a flock of migrating birds. Almost immediately the clouds broke again and Barnes's skin started to itch as the winter sun hit his damp clothing.

An idea came to him. Beyond the outer cordons of the cold zone, the streets were more or less completely devoid of vehicles. Once news had filtered through, people had grabbed their cars and fled.

Inside the cordons, however, their cars were off limits. You need to get away, but you can't use your car to do it. It made for some ugly scenes, and more than one disgruntled citizen had breached the scene perimeter to get to their car, and to blazes with the risks.

Barnes moved down to the seafront, along Grand Parade and back up Trinity Place to the multi-storey, circumnavigating the hot zone in a U-shape. Both sides of the street were packed with cars, as was the multi-storey. Nothing unusual about that.

He rounded the corner and kept heading north-west towards Memorial Roundabout along Hartington Place — and then he saw it.

A space in the parked cars. A bare patch of light-grey tarmac on the otherwise wet ground between a Ford Mondeo and a Toyota Carina. Barnes walked over and knelt down. The patch was bone dry. Whatever had been parked here had left recently.

He got up and stepped back. Difficult to gauge the width, but it was too long for a normal car. Maybe an estate or a pickup. Kane had said a vehicle similar to a bus. The dry patch was not big enough to fit a bus into, but maybe something bigger than an estate. Maybe a van.

It might not mean anything at all. But it might mean everything.

He looked up and down the empty street. There was nothing moving at all. Language schools, dental surgeries, Trinity Church — all silent and closed up in a hurry. An empty bus sat in a stop, the doors wide open, hazards blinking slowly. It was as if someone had switched off the town.

He headed back down the way he came, and found himself outside the hot zone, the centrepiece of which was still the mobile command vehicle he had been thrown out of less than twenty minutes ago.

Investigative policy, contingency plans and major incident manuals differed the world over, but in essence, they boiled down to the same thing. Whoever ended up leading the enquiry would doubtless set an action to log all the vehicles in the area surrounding ground zero, but Barnes had no idea *when*. Besides, that was an investigative action. A secondary action. At present they were still in the phase of trying to contain the unidentified threat and maintain public safety.

And *he* had to know. *He* had to be the one to find out.

But how? No way Gabby was going to allow him to do anything other than stand in the rain with his hands in his pockets. He certainly wasn't going to let Barnes back into the command vehicle.

At that moment, the answer descended the steps of the mobile command vehicle. Tina, the analyst he'd almost met, looked around at the activity going on around her, gave a visible shudder, and then lit a cigarette.

She drew in a big puff, then closed her eyes and pressed the palm of the hand holding the cigarette to her forehead. A number of cops on the cordon turned appreciatively in Tina's direction, and Barnes could understand why. She was tall — about five-nine, Barnes reckoned — and built like a swimmer. Her hair was dark brown and shiny, like the glaze of a devil's cake tumbling from her head, and her olive skin was smooth.

They hadn't met, hadn't spoken. All the eyes in the vehicle had followed him when Gabby had manhandled him outside earlier, but he'd caught a trace of sympathy in hers, and it was this alone that he was basing his play on.

Her large green eyes swept back and forth over the flurry of cops, and then settled on the one striding purposefully towards her with an intense stare.

She didn't flinch. Didn't look away. She fixed his gaze and held it as he approached.

"Hey," she said. "Come back for round two?"

"I need your help. My stepdaughter's been taken."

"Taken?"

"My boss is at her school. Superintendent Samson Kane. You know him?" Barnes asked.

Tina Guestling took another draw on the cigarette and shook her head.

"Should I?"

"It's linked to all this. I just know it . . ." He pointed towards the command vehicle with his chin.

"What makes you—" she began.

"Listen, you're a parent, yes?"

"Yes, but I—"

"Then you've got to help me. I don't need much. I just need you to do a CCTV sweep of all the streets inside the warm zone. I'm looking for a van or something of a similar size leaving the area from, say, 2.20 to 3 p.m."

"I don't think they're going to give you a big welcome in there," she said.

"That's why you're going to help me. I'll keep my distance until I can prove a link between Maggie's disappearance and this mess." He gestured at the empty street. "Then I'll be all over Gabby like a rash."

"I'm not too sure about this. I could . . . I could lose my job."

"That won't happen, I promise. If you get in trouble I'll take the rap for it. Besides, you're not doing anything illegal. You're just bumping a task up the queue."

Indecision and uncertainty crept across Tina's face.

"Please, Tina? She . . . she's only seven."

Barnes was not a manipulator, and he couldn't have controlled it, but he felt his eyes sting. Tina Guestling rolled her eyes and appeared to capitulate.

"Okay, okay. I'll do what I can. But there's camera crews everywhere," she said. "This shit's all over the news. I can't do anything without the ACC noticing."

"Then let him. Nothing makes you look suspicious like behaving suspiciously. Be bold and brassy — I'm sure you can manage that. Act like you're meant to be doing what you're doing, and no one will give you a second look. Any questions?"

"How about you tell me your name?"

Despite himself, he smiled.

"I'm Barnes. Rutherford Barnes. Sorry. It's been kind of a crap day."

She nodded, connecting his face, he knew, with emails and minutes of meetings and phone calls from her professional past. In an organisation the size of theirs, you could go years before you met someone you'd been corresponding with, if ever.

She turned to go, and placed one hand on the handrail of the command vehicle.

"Hey," he called. She turned to face him. "Have you had a chance to, you know, call your family? Are they all . . . accounted for?"

She smiled. "Yes, they are, thank you. Mum doesn't come to town unless she has to, and after today I don't suppose she ever will again."

"What about kids?"

"I have a daughter. Teenager. She's . . . she's at home."

"I'm glad."

Tina smiled and disappeared into the cool gloom of the command vehicle.

Barnes returned to the cordon. His churning insides had settled into a steady simmering anxiety — his parent's heart wanted answers, but his detective's head knew that a kidnap enquiry, like most police work, was to a large extent a waiting game.

He recognised one of the uniformed constables standing on a point outside the cordon as Adrian Willow. He and Willow had joined together back in 1999 — Willow, a former car mechanic who nevertheless had the drop on Barnes at training school when it came to bulling shoes and pleating tunics, and was happy to share his skills, had remained as a response officer for the entirety of his service to date, while Barnes's career had ebbed and flowed from sudden ascent to crashing depths on a cyclical basis. Willow was cynical and weathered, but, in fourteen years, his heart and conscience had remained resolutely on the rails. For all his chuntering, you would never hear, for instance, PC Adrian Willow comment that a victim of domestic abuse brought it on themselves.

Barnes showed Willow Maggie's picture, and asked him to show it to his colleagues; Willow, his usual humour absent, placed his hand on Barnes's shoulder and asked him if he was okay.

Before he could reply, Barnes's attention was drawn by a small gaggle leaving the command vehicle. Front and centre was Gabby, flanked by the Fire and Ambulance commanders and three women in business dress.

The group were fixed on a point in the distance. Barnes turned his head to where they were looking, and saw a group of waiting journalists with microphones and cameras about a hundred metres further east along Seaside Road — well outside the cordons. They too were flanked by officers.

Gabby looked tense as the group approached the edge of the cordon. His pace slowed a fraction. Willow lifted the scene tape to let them through. Barnes stepped forward and took hold of Gabby's arm as he passed.

The group stopped. Gabby looked down at the hand on his arm, then over at the waiting journalists before meeting Barnes's eye.

"What is it?" he hissed. Barnes could feel the tension in his arm.

"Will Howlett," Barnes said. "I want to tell his family he's dead."

"I don't think you're the right person for that job, do you? Seeing as how you got him killed."

Barnes squeezed. Gabby grimaced, and looked over again at the journalists. He clearly wanted to react, but the pressure of the cameras had paralysed him. Barnes had control of this situation.

"I can answer questions no one else can answer. I can tell her how he died. I was there. She deserves that."

"Barnes, that needs to be a commanding—"

Barnes squeezed again.

"I have to do it. Understand?"

Barnes sensed Willow shifting uncomfortably in the background, and he released Gabby's arm.

There was a brief stand-off, before one of the media advisers ushered the group onwards. They passed through the cordon to the waiting ensemble, and Barnes slipped under the tape.

Barnes waited until Gabby had the full attention of the assembled journalists, and then he broke off from the cordon and headed straight for the command vehicle.

He stepped into the gloom and found Tina Guestling engrossed in a bank of video screens. He stood behind her for a moment, and took in the images. Nine screens displayed the video feed from different town CCTV cameras, playing simultaneously from 2.20 p.m.

She jumped and spun round in her seat.

"Fuck!" she said, her eyes sweeping the room before landing on Barnes. "I thought you were Glover. What are you *doing* in here?"

"The boss and his entourage are busy entertaining the press," Barnes said, staring at the screens in wonder. All the answers were before him, and he felt like he was trying to find buried treasure. "What have you got?"

"Well, it's good you're here," she said. "I think I may have found something, and I was wondering how to find you to tell you."

"Go on." Barnes moved closer to the screens.

Tina looked over at her fellow analysts. One had noticed Barnes entering, clearly having remembered him from the earlier altercation, but had since turned her attention elsewhere.

She turned back to the screen, and her voice dropped to a whisper.

"This is the Memorial Roundabout feed," she said.

"Speak normally," Barnes said. "You'll just draw attention to yourself."

Tina cleared her throat and tried again. "This is the Memorial Roundabout feed, covering the south-west corner of Trinity Trees, 3.05 p.m."

"That's better."

"People were just starting to fall ill, yes?"

Barnes shut his eyes. An image of Howlett collapsing and striking the tarmac appeared in the black.

"Yes, that's right." He opened his eyes.

"Look at this." She pointed at the centre screen. A jerky image appeared. The tarmac was dark with the recent coating of rain. "Between Trinity Trees, Hartington and Devonshire Place. Traffic is slow. The camera's on random rotation, but you can just see here . . ."

She paused the video. Barnes bent down and squinted at the screen. Tina shifted in her seat, but Barnes was oblivious to how close he was to her.

"This is the Memorial Roundabout feed, covering the south-west corner of Trinity Trees. 3:05 p.m.," she said.

Barnes felt the butterflies surge in his stomach. The parking space untouched by rain he'd found in Hartington Place, just south of the Esperance Hospital. This was practically the same location.

"Play it again," he said. "Slow it down."

Tina fiddled with some controls. The images sped backwards, and then she hit the play button. The video began again at half-speed.

The camera only just caught it as it spun, but a flash of green and yellow moved through the south-east corner of the picture.

Barnes's phone rang. He answered it without straightening up or taking his eyes from the screen.

"Yes?"

"Barnes? It's Samson. Think we might have ID'd the vehicle. We found another witness. Works at a retirement home in Salisbury Road. Backs onto the playing field. It's looking like Maggie wasn't placed in a bus at all, but an ambulance."

"Yes," Barnes said, looking down at Tina. "I think you're right."

CHAPTER ELEVEN

Kane rubbed his hands slowly down his face and held them there for a moment. When he looked up, he wanted to have answers for the anxious woman sitting opposite him in the principal's office. Tamsin had been as polite and patient as could be expected in the circumstances, and he desperately wanted to be able to help her — while keeping her from becoming a headline.

He rubbed his face again. Reports of missing children tended to go only one of two ways: the majority eventually turned up safe and well, while the tiny remainder . . .

This investigation was already leaning towards the latter. Independent, credible witnesses had corroborated the now very strong likelihood that a man posing as a substitute rugby coach had come onto the school grounds for the express purpose of abducting Maggie.

The *why* was eluding him, but that would have to wait. The use of the ambulance and the rugby coach disguise suggested more than a simply opportunistic snatch. Neither Barnes nor Tamsin were particularly wealthy, which meant the favoured hypothesis was the worst possible one — some kind of predatory paedophile. He had not yet used these words in front of Tamsin, however.

The other issue confounding him was the chemical incident in the town centre. He hadn't yet heard too much about it — focused as he was on Maggie's disappearance — but no doubt it was going to be a headline grabber. Statistically, bona fide child abductions were rare, and major incidents at the seaside rarer still. So what were the odds of the two happening at once?

Kane didn't believe in coincidences, and now he and Barnes had potentially connected the two incidents.

He tried to see the whole investigation in his head. Ordinarily, he would have scooped up and directed officers from across the county to trace and question all known RSOs in the tri-district area. He would have instigated the CRA. He would have search officers doing fingertip line searches of the school grounds and beyond.

The chaos in town had prevented all that. All he had was this potential lead on the ambulance, which he wanted to verify before he went running anything further up the chain of command.

SECAMB were in the process of accounting for all their vehicles, and had promised a call back within the hour. This was what Kane was waiting for. He had started to explain to Tamsin that a significant amount of a kidnap investigation involved waiting, but had given it up on the basis that it sounded like he was making excuses.

The witness from the retirement home was a groundsman. He was reasonably sensible, sober, and a quick check of his record did not throw up any credibility issues. Kane had scared up a couple of detectives to do Jedi mind tricks on him to see if he could recall a better description of the driver than the one they had.

Kane's Motorola buzzed in his pocket. He'd had the presence of mind to change the ringtone from "I Fought the Law" to a simple vibrate setting before sitting down with Tamsin.

"Superintendent Kane," he said.

"Hi, this is SECAMB area control room," said a chirpy female voice. "You called us about our fleet? Well, all of our vehicles are accounted for, except one."

All the hairs on Kane's neck stood up.

"Go on."

"Fleet 1007. Reg mark GY60 DYW. Off the road for service in Lewes workshops from about nine yesterday morning. Fleet manager's done an inventory of all those vehicles not on a callsign, and this one couldn't be found."

Kane stood up. The girl continued.

"It was off the road, so we'd have found out sooner or later — if you hadn't called it might have taken longer to discover it was missing. Fortunately our fleet is fitted with GPS, so it wasn't too hard to get a fix on its location . . ."

"Where is it?" Kane tried to shrug on his jacket with his free hand.

"According to this, it's static in a residential street in Crawley. Hold on . . . according to this, it's in Cherry Lane, Langley Green . . ."

"Langley . . ."

"Off the London Road. Right near the airport."

Right near the airport.

Kane was already on his way out the door.

* * *

He ran for the car and stopped with his hand on the door. How the hell was he going to get there? He only had his Lancer — no blue lights, no sirens, strictly no-frills — and all through routes were going to be snarled up with traffic trying to escape the town centre. His best hope was NPAS, but that was out of the question. No doubt all air support would be assigned to the chemical incident, and wouldn't be released for anyone.

Unless he could prove the link between the abduction and the chemical incident. The ambulance itself wasn't enough. He needed more.

He pulled out his phone and dialled Barnes. The DI picked up immediately.

"Barnes? It's Samson. Listen, are you able to get to Gatwick?"

"I don't see how. What for?"

"SECAMB reckon one of their fleet was stolen from Lewes at some point between yesterday and this morning, and they've got a fix on its location in Crawley. I can't go. My car doesn't have any bells or whistles."

"Is it the same one?"

"Got to be. The VRM is . . ."

"No plate visible on my screen," Barnes interrupted. "Picture's not good enough. All routes out of here are going to be gridlocked with people leaving — A22, A27, A23. Can you get NPAS up there?"

"I thought of that. There's no way I'll be able to get it released from the town, unless I can prove the ambulance is connected to the CBRN thing."

"You don't think the fact a stolen ambulance fled the hot zone five minutes after the stuff was released is a lead?"

"Of course I do. But it's not me you need to convince."

CHAPTER TWELVE

Barnes clapped the phone shut and looked around, his breath coming in ragged gasps. Even as he had been rationalising, he knew that the final arbiter here was going to be Gabby, which meant Kane was absolutely right.

Gabby was still entertaining the press. Activity around the cordons had levelled off. It was as close to static as it was going to get until all the families had been informed and they started removing bodies. One thing was for sure — he couldn't stand around here knowing the ambulance Maggie had been bundled into had been found and was sitting unattended.

Barnes marched up to Willow and commandeered the keys to his patrol vehicle. Before he left, he rescued his handcuffs, baton and pepper spray from the boot of his own car — leaving the items in the boot was generally frowned upon, but if he hadn't, they would have been sequestered by Fire & Rescue along with the rest of his clothing.

The two main routes north out of Eastbourne were like the prongs of a tuning fork branching out of town. Crawley was about an hour away, just off the M23.

An hour in normal conditions.

Silver Ford Focus patrol cars littered the areas outside the cordons and had been staggered as makeshift roadblocks at the intersections up and down Seaside. Barnes walked from one to another, pressing the key fob until one of the cars responded with an accommodating *thunk* and the blink of hazard lights.

Barnes slid into the driver's seat and fired up the car. He hit the lights and sirens and pulled away onto Royal Parade, gritting his teeth as he prepared to churn through the static metal line of outbound traffic.

Eastbourne was a dome on the coast, encased on all sides by the rural spread of Wealden District and the green embrace of the South Downs. He had three choices — west into Meads then over Beachy Head towards Seaford, picking up the A27 in a straight line to the motorway; east along the seafront towards Pevensey Bay and then cut north; or plough straight through the middle of the town and hope for the best.

He opted pretty quickly for the first option — he could go via Summerdown House and scoop up Kane without too much of a detour, plus, he figured, of the three routes, away and over the South Downs would be the least likely to be snarled up by the exodus of departing traffic.

As it turned out, he was half right.

He spun in the road and pulled out onto Royal Parade, the serpentine Channel now moving listlessly on his left in the winter haze. He instinctively eased off the acceleration at one of numerous zebra crossings dotted along the parade, before realising that the streets were silent and empty. The road seemed unusually wide, until Barnes realised that the angled parking bays nosing up to the sea, full all year round in daylight hours and usually resembling a Formula 1 starting grid, were completely empty. Long aprons of set-down bays outside the hotels lining the seafront were bereft of coaches, while the joggers and casual strollers that typically peopled the three-tier promenade in all weathers, at all hours, had vanished.

Barnes slowed the car and turned the sirens off, and, winding down his window, took in the raging emptiness of the silent streets. For a moment it alarmed him, like waking after an apocalyptic event to find you are the only one left.

He stepped on the accelerator and raced out of the silence. The sense of exhilaration he felt at the emptiness of the parade's westbound lane was short-lived; as the road inclined up towards Meads he almost collided with the rear-most car of an eight-mile tailback at Upper Dukes Drive. Vapour and engine shimmer rose into a fine smog above the traffic. It was going nowhere fast, a solid snake of metal and rubber filling every inch of the parade. People's patience — and lane discipline — had already worn thin, and cars had spilled out over the pavement, onto the grass verge and across the opposing lane.

Barnes reactivated the lights and sirens. The light bar on the roof threw out a disco-ball of blue, while the howl of the siren cut through the air.

He stamped on the throttle, then, suddenly realising the tailback was moving for no one, had no choice but to stand on the brakes. Barnes winced — the speedo needle dropped from around seventy to less than twenty, and the car juddered as the ABS kicked in and came to a stop. A cloud of grit and dust kicked up from the verge as he cut too close to the kerb.

"Bloody cars!" he yelled as he jabbed the steering wheel, intermittently interrupting the sirens with the horn.

It was not the right move, however. Drivers were already clambering out of their cars to remonstrate with each other over the increasingly impassable snaking road, and when they saw the police car they each rushed over to state their case. Barnes grudgingly switched the sirens off.

"Officer, this idiot's blocked the lane . . ."

"I can't move my car . . ."

"She's on the shoulder . . ."

"What are you going to *do* about it?"

This last comment was uttered by a large, angry-looking gentleman in overalls with salt-and-pepper stubble and a thick vein in his forehead.

The man banged on Barnes's window, and the patrol car was slowly surrounded by a horde of scared motorists, each bent on the preservation of self, and to hell with the others.

The car began to rock slowly, and Barnes started to feel like he was in a zombie B-movie as the faces pressed against his windows started to grow in number and obliterate the sight of the road ahead of him.

In any other circumstances, he might have felt fear. But all he could think about was Maggie, the one slim lead he might have, and he thought, *I don't have time for this.*

Yanking the handbrake on, he managed to form the presence of mind to activate the vehicle's failsafe switch — a mechanism that allowed the engine to keep running with the keys out of the ignition. It was intended to prevent the lights, sirens and radio equipment from draining the battery during prolonged static deployments. To prevent theft, however, releasing the handbrake caused the engine to cut out.

Barnes took a deep breath, pocketed the keys and rolled down his window. Two huge arms forced their way through the gap and Barnes felt the material of his shirt tighten around him as the man took hold.

Barnes forced himself to relax, and reached for the small canister of mercifully rescued pepper spray.

"What the *fuaaarrrgh* . . ." the man yelled, his demands descending into a paroxysm of coughing as Barnes unloaded the contents of the canister into his face.

The man released Barnes, as his hands flew to his burning skin. He backed away from the car, and Barnes saw his chance. He flung open the driver's door and scrambled to get out.

In his haste, his foot got caught in the seat belt, and he felt the grit of the road on his face as he landed heavily on the tarmac.

Landing prone was the worst mistake to make, and in a panic he tried to pull himself into a sitting position to fend off whatever attack was forthcoming.

As he sat up, however, he noticed that the angry crowd was not interested in him at all, but his patrol car. Apart from the man with the burning eyes, they all crowded around it, trying to bundle into the driver's seat.

Barnes shuffled backwards on his backside until he thumped against the concrete of the kerb. He pulled himself to his feet, threw the keys over a garden hedge and barrelled off down Cliff Road on foot. He heard a shout of dismay as the engine of the patrol vehicle died, and realised that one of the mob must have released the handbrake fully. No doubt they would shortly discover that there were no keys in the ignition either, and he scrambled over a wall and garden-hopped into Meads in case they decided to channel their disappointment into retribution.

Meads was a ghost town. The usually teeming Pilot Inn, the huge red-brick townhouses, the sprawling Gothic prep schools, All Saints Park, the genteel lattice-pane frontage of Ridgways restaurant and the small parade of chocolate-box shops — it could have been five in the morning on New Year's Day.

Summerdown House was on the outskirts of Meads, the last stop before Paradise Drive and the rolling green of the Royal golf course. Barnes had to pass through Meads and out the other side, and, despite a lifetime of running, he arrived at the school a breathless, sweaty mess ten minutes later. He leaned on his knees while he got his breath back; when he straightened up, he was reassured to see more activity than he'd expected — there were a couple of uniformed constables and a square of the playing field was sealed off with crime scene tape.

Kane and Tamsin came over. He pulled her to him in a fierce hug.

"You okay?" he said.

She shook her head.

"When I find this bastard, Barnes . . ."

"You didn't run all the way here, surely?" Kane said.

"Long story," Barnes said, shaking his head.

"We'd better take my car, then," Kane said, pointing to the Lancer.

They walked off towards it. Barnes hesitated and turned back to Tamsin. She didn't look like she was going to go to pieces. That wasn't her style. She had a steel about her that tended to present itself when she needed it most. He figured a lifetime of trying to jump-start murder victims and picking up body parts from railway lines would do that to a person.

"Are you . . . do you want to . . . ?"

He nodded towards the car. Kane was already in the driver's seat.

"No. I need to stay here in case she comes back."

She pressed her lips against his. He held the back of her neck.

"Bring our girl back, Barnes. Get her home safely."

CHAPTER THIRTEEN

"You okay?" Kane kept his eyes on the road.

"Fine."

"It could be a coincidence, you know."

"I don't believe in them. And what difference would it make?"

Despite a notable reluctance on the part of the stream of motorists to yield them access — with Kane driving equally robustly, having collected a few scrapes and dings along the way as he forced his way through the traffic — the Lancer was making reasonable progress. From Summerdown House, they had continued up towards Beachy Head, where the exodus of traffic had started to clear a little, and then cut back onto the A27 past Seaford.

"Gabby is going to shit," Barnes said.

"Now you've stopped pestering him, I honestly don't think he's going to give you a second thought."

Barnes held up his phone.

"Six missed calls."

Kane expelled air.

"Maybe answer next time. If you can convince him of a connection, we might get some shit done."

Barnes switched on the radio. News of the episode in Eastbourne town centre was starting to filter through. There was a whole heap of padding in the broadcast, lots of dramatic *"we can bring you updates from the scene . . ."* and *"this just in . . ."* but it was a triumph of style over substance. *Over deadly substance*, Barnes thought grimly.

The media were skirting around confirmation of a deliberate act, but they were speculating on it rather gleefully, and giving precious little airtime to other possible theories.

Barnes switched it off.

"Tell me again what happened," Kane said, off-siding a keep-left bollard to the annoyance of a flatbed truck.

"Straightforward G5 call. Young man, early twenties, overdosed in a public toilet in the town centre. Me and a DC. We were just about to stand down when someone collapsed in the street. The DC ran over to help, then he went too. After that it was like a domino rally," Barnes murmured.

"Then what?"

"I was in decon when Tam called to tell me about Maggie."

"More or less the same time, two miles up the road."

"Indeed."

"A DI would only normally go to an OD if it was suspicious, no?"

Barnes eyed him. Not because he was being interrogated — Kane was sounding out the coincidence theory — but because only a couple of years or so previously he wouldn't have thought to ask the question.

"Usually, yes. But he was new, and I wanted to show him the ropes. Plus I've got the usual shortage of DSs."

"What was his name?" Kane said, quietly.

"Will. Will Howlett. Keen as mustard, reminded me of me at that age. Shit. I need to tell his family."

"Someone else will take care of that," Kane said.

"I told Gabby it had to be me."

"You've got a full plate, Barnes."

The road inclined over the Glynde Reach and the railway line, the South Downs looming on the horizon at the end of a carpet of green. As the carriageway passed over the River Ouse, the traffic resumed something like normal levels, and it was as if nothing had happened.

But it had.

An image of Maggie appeared in Barnes's mind, and his stomach twisted with a slice of fear and pain. Where was she? Was she okay? Why was he not with her? Why had he not protected her?

As if sensing his disquiet, Kane pushed the Lancer harder, the needle tipping a hundred as they raced along the inside lane.

"If it isn't coincidence, then what is it?" Kane said.

"I don't know," Barnes said. "Any other time, everything stops for a genuine child abduction. But not when you've got a major incident unfolding at the same time. What better cover can you think of?"

"By killing indiscriminately?"

"If it *was* indiscriminate."

Kane looked over at him.

"Kill ten when you only want to kill one, and you keep the investigators weighing up motives for ever and a day."

"That's pretty extreme."

"There's some extreme people out there."

Barnes tapped the LCD clock display on the dash.

"We're still an hour away yet."

"We'll switch up. Get a marked car from HQ."

Kane pulled off the A27 into Lewes and, after an interminably slow crawl through the Cuilfail Tunnel, drove into Police HQ. They swapped the Lancer out for a marked Focus — it was a bit sorry looking, but it was liveried up and had all the bells and whistles needed for a blue-light run up the motorway. Mercifully, and by some freak miracle, it also had a full tank of diesel.

Kane pulled the keys out of the wall safe in the multi-storey car park and tossed them to Barnes.

"No permit yet?" Barnes said.

"I need to make some calls en route," he said.

Barnes didn't need telling twice. He screamed out of HQ, the tyres groaning in protest as he wrenched the car around this corner and that, blasting past lines of traffic as they shot towards the motorway.

Beside him, Kane was barking orders into his phone. Despite himself, Barnes was impressed.

"I need a unit to the East Surrey Hospital, stat. They're looking for an ambulance . . . yes, I know that, that's why suspect has dumped it there. Fleet one thousand and seven, index Golf-Yankee-six-zero, Delta-Yankee-Whisky . . . I've got a live time fix from SECAMB — it's there somewhere. When they find it, don't approach. Get out of sight, keep eyeball on and report . . ."

Barnes heard a tinny voice protesting at the other end of the line. Something about strict instructions to hold all units on standby in case of further chemical incidents.

"Listen, this is a hot lead on that." Barnes looked at Kane. He was making a link that wasn't strictly confirmed yet. He was sticking his neck out. For Barnes.

Again.

"I don't have time to explain it to you, but I have good reason to believe that the suspect for the abduction is con-nected to the chemical incident in Eastbourne . . . yes, you can. It's Superintendent Kane. Superintendent. Capital 'S'. Yes, okay. Fine. Let me know when they pitch up on scene. We're en route. Thirty minutes, best speed."

He ended the call and held up the phone.

"Control room inspector. He's nervous. I don't blame him. But he's sending a unit to find the ambulance."

CHAPTER FOURTEEN

Maggie pulled her knees to her chest and made a tight ball. The sirens were loud. She felt sick, but wasn't sure if it was because the ambulance was lurching around corners like a rollercoaster or because she was so, so scared.

She couldn't understand what was happening, or why, or what the man wanted with her. What had she done? Had she been bad? Was this punishment? She'd had some mean teachers before, but nothing like this. She knew it was wrong, that her mum would not be happy at all with the school after this.

The ambulance slowed down a few times but didn't stop, and Maggie thought that maybe it was slowing down for red traffic lights but then carrying on anyway. She knew that other cars were meant to get out of the way for an ambulance with its blue lights on. But that was when they needed to help a poorly person. She had no idea where this ambulance was going, but she didn't think it was off to help anyone. Besides, the man driving wasn't an ambulance man.

The next time it slowed, she managed to pull herself up off the floor into the grey bucket seat fixed to the wall of the ambulance. She clipped the seat belt into place and held on tight.

She had tried to work out where she was, but they had been driving so long now that she no longer had any idea. Barnes had taken her, Ellie and her mum to Cornwall last year. She liked Cornwall. It had pretty beaches with jellyfish and caves. She didn't think they'd been driving long enough to get to Cornwall. She liked shopping at Bluewater with her mum, and she reckoned they'd been driving for at least as long as it took to get there. But traffic to Bluewater was always bad. If they had an ambulance they could get there much quicker. That wouldn't be allowed, though.

She needed a wee really badly and she had a hot, tight, sick feeling in her chest. The longer they drove, the further she got from her mum, the worse it became. She could feel tears and screaming inside her, but she tried really hard to keep calm.

This was a Bad Thing. Bad things could happen to anyone. You might fall off your bike and hurt your knee, or you might be in a car crash, or you might lose your favourite toy, or break your mum's best vase. You couldn't *undo* any of those things, but you had to try to fix them. And to fix them, you had to think. Had to stay calm. Had to be sensible.

Had to be brave.

* * *

Eventually, after what felt like a million hours, the sirens stopped. The ambulance turned lots of corners and began to slow down.

And then it stopped. The engine stopped. A clicky noise as the handbrake went on.

Maggie heard the driver's door open and slam closed. Footsteps.

The back door opened. Maggie squinted as the sunshine burst in.

A shadow. The man. The teacher-not-teacher.

A voice.

"Come."

* * *

74

Barnes had stopped hearing the sirens. Certainly, the other motorists on the road seemed to have done. Barnes vaguely remembered something from his driver training about how, if you were travelling above fifty miles per hour, other drivers couldn't hear them anyway.

He'd had his foot pressed to the floor from the Brighton on-slip all the way up to Crawley. He'd eased off here and there, but hadn't used the brake pedal once. Kane had been shouting into his radio and phone for most of the journey, fighting to generate some interest in Barnes's stolen child.

They weren't far off now. Fifteen minutes, maybe.

Kane ended another phone call and looked over at Barnes.

"The unit on scene has found it. VRM checks out. It's not in the emergency bays. North-east corner of the footprint, right out by the helicopter landing site. They're keeping obs."

"Any movement? Anyone with it?"

"Not that they can see. It's just a big spread of empty land, so they're at a distance to avoid being spotted."

Barnes set his jaw and focused on the road.

"I know you know this, but this is just one lead," Kane said. "The link isn't concrete. We've got what we think is an ambulance at the school and an ambulance near the hot zone that left in a hurry — in the opposite direction to a site of mass casualties. All we know is that neither was on a call, and that it's a bit odd. It's very suspicious. But it's not concrete."

"It has to be her," Barnes mumbled.

"Look," Kane said, "I know you're fearing the worst. But, even if you discount the CBRN incident in Eastbourne, there's a degree of subterfuge at play here. An ambulance? A supply teacher ruse? It feels organised. It feels *professional*. You might get a ransom demand. She could well be unhurt."

"I appreciate that, Samson, but I'm not driving any slower."

But he hoped Kane was right.

He prayed she was all right.

He prayed it wasn't too late.

He extracted a little more from the car.

* * *

The man was rough. He pulled her arm up as he walked — she couldn't keep up and her shoulder began to ache. He didn't speak or look at her, just kept walking.

"I really need to go wee," she said. "I'm going to have an accident. I need the toilet."

"Later. Keep walking."

They were headed away from the ambulance across a large field next to a virtually empty car park. Behind the ambulance, in the distance, was a large building that looked like a hospital, or maybe a big school.

She looked back at the ambulance with a strange kind of longing. Although the journey had been bad, it was better than not knowing what was coming next. There was nothing ahead of them except fields and trees and the end of an empty road that seemed to go all around the car parks.

This was bad. This was wrong. She didn't know what was going to happen, but suddenly she was angry.

She pulled her arm away.

"Leave me alone!" she shouted. "You're a bad man."

He turned, momentarily surprised — and then back-handed her across the face.

"Bad girl. You come with me. Do as you are told, or things will be much worse."

She was stunned. The noise was loud, much louder than she would have expected. Like a big handclap. Barnes had big hands, and when he clapped, it was really loud. He clapped at her last school Christmas concert. He was proud. He told her so.

Her face stung, and she felt the tears fill her up behind her face like an overflowing tap. She couldn't stop, and then she felt warm wetness between her legs as her tummy lost control.

She kept crying, her chest hitching in huge, wailing sobs.

"Shut up," the man hissed. "Stop that noise."

"I want my mummy," Maggie cried, as the brave feeling slipped away.

He grabbed her arm again, and pulled her across the field.

The anger flashed again, unexpectedly, like a ray of sunshine in her head.

She kicked out with her foot, toes pointed like she was practising for penalties, and caught the man on the back of his heel.

He swore and turned, looming up over her with an angry snarl.

She turned and ran.

CHAPTER FIFTEEN

Barnes finally killed the siren as they pulled into the East Surrey Hospital.

"Where are they? Are they in a marked car?"

"Keep driving," Kane said, pointing at the perimeter road.

Barnes brought the speed down. If this was a full-on assault with a parade of marked cars behind him, then he'd have kept it loud.

But there wasn't. It was just him, his weird boss, and a bemused local patrol car that had been co-opted into helping against all their other orders.

He couldn't see the other unit. He cruised past A&E as casually as he could muster, pushing past the spread of car parking towards the helipad.

"Are they still here?" Barnes said.

Kane started dialling a number.

"This thing's going to need charging soon," he muttered.

"Come on. Let's get out on foot."

He pulled the patrol car up onto the kerb. Heads turned as the two of them exited. A couple of people pulled out their phones, and Barnes realised that he was still in his post-de-contamination tracksuit, while his oppo, despite a year of trying to get in step with his peers, still looked like a garage band punk rocker. They were hardly Butch and Sundance.

"Warrant card out," Kane hissed, pulling out his own. "They'll think we've stolen it."

Barnes obliged, and they moved cautiously east. Barnes stayed on the pavement, while Kane fanned out into the car park to provide a flank of sorts.

As they moved further along the perimeter road, Barnes clocked the patrol car up ahead. It was tucked out of sight, between a large industrial skip and the side of a single-storey brick outbuilding.

Good boys, Barnes thought. Their choice of location alone told him all he needed to know. *Sensible lads.*

The doors of the patrol car opened, and two female officers got out. Barnes chided himself internally. He imagined Tamsin, arms folded. *You sexist twat*, she'd be saying, with that potty mouth of hers.

The officers pulled their hats on as they moved towards Barnes. He stepped out into the road to meet them. As he did so, a van moved slowly across his line of vision, and he saw it.

A flash of fluorescent lime green, about a hundred yards in the distance. It was on the other side of the large grassy spread of land that acted as the hospital's helicopter landing site.

The need for stealth deserted him.

"There!" he shouted, and broke into a run.

"Barnes, wait!" Kane shouted.

But Barnes couldn't hear him, or didn't want to. He ran around a couple of slow-moving cars exiting the car park and began to sprint towards the ambulance. He was dimly aware of the other three following — Kane moving out wide while the two patrol officers moved around to his right as they ran, so they were coming at it in some sort of formation.

He hopped over a low barrier at the car park edge — and then there was nothing between them besides an expanse of grass.

Unless HEMS were landing imminently, it was all kinds of wrong. On its own in the corner of a field, well away from the main hospital building. Nothing around the ambulance. No signs of movement.

Barnes pumped his knees. The ambulance grew in size before him as he got closer, a square of yellow and green shining bright against the backdrop of fields and trees.

"Maggie!"

Kane was right. Barnes should have waited.

Wisps of smoke appeared at the rear of the vehicle, curling up and out from the doors, like grey snakes escaping a pressure cooker. A hungry flicker of orange appeared in the cab, spreading along the fascia and turning the glass black.

"No . . ." Barnes whispered, the heat and stench lighting up his own dimly lit memories — his unconscious wife, his frantic dog, his own house melting beneath his feet.

The cab caught just as Barnes arrived. It went with a lazy growl, and fingers of flame stretched up over the windscreen.

He grabbed the driver's door handle and pulled. A wall of red like a skillet raced out and hit him in the face, driving him backwards onto the grass. He was aware of shouting from behind him, but it was muffled by the rumble of the flames.

"Stay back," he coughed in Kane's general direction, and then hauled himself forward on his belly to check the cab. He had a matter of seconds before the thing exploded properly or before the fire grew to such a magnitude that it drove him out of there.

Or both.

Staying as low as he could, he peered through the black sheet of smoke, straining his streaming eyes.

The footwells were both empty. Nothing on the front seats.

He ran around to the back of the ambulance. The fire was dancing over the roof now, orange waving hands enveloping it in a halo of heat.

He wrenched the back door open and scanned the treatment area. Heat pushed its way into his face.

Patient trolley — empty. Bucket seat — empty.

His eyes burning, he staggered backwards and fell to his knees.

She wasn't here.

Strong arms underneath him.

"Come on, we need to get back," Kane said.

Barnes scrambled backwards, Kane pulling him. The two uniformed officers joined them and helped him get to his feet.

They'd managed to get about twenty feet back when something exploded, maybe an oxygen cylinder, and the ambulance was encased in a raging fireball.

"She . . . she's not in there," Barnes said.

"That's good, right?" one of the officers said.

"But then where is she?" he wanted to scream. "Where?"

CHAPTER SIXTEEN

Maggie didn't know where she was. A large branch was digging into her neck, and she flattened herself further into the frozen, muddy ground to try to make herself less visible.

The minute she'd started running she knew she'd made a mistake. She should have headed back to where there were people, cars, buildings. But she hadn't been thinking — she just ran, in a straight line.

The straight line had led her along a service road stacked high with junk — massive metal bins, old cars, wooden crates — onto a field where there were bushes, muddy tracks, hedges — and nothing else. No people. Hardly anywhere to hide.

But she was going to try.

She ran as fast as she could, bringing her knees up high and trying to watch the ground so she didn't trip. The teacher-not-teacher wouldn't be far behind her. But she was fast.

There was a cluster of trees ahead of her. Like a small wood. What was it called? A copse. She'd read a joke in one of her books about it. Copse and robbers. She hadn't got the joke, so she'd looked it up.

She ran around the outside of it and then doubled back, plunging herself into the trees, in the hope that she would be already out of sight when the man came around the corner.

She was surprised at how dark it was in there under the winter sun. The branches and leaves made a huge ceiling. But that was good.

Her body very quickly started to become cold, and she wondered how long she could stay there. Her legs felt damp and sore from where she had wet herself. She pulled her school cardigan tightly around her.

She scrunched her eyes shut and tried to listen. Wherever she was, there were an awful lot of aeroplanes overhead. Far more than she was used to. And they were flying low. The sky was a constant scream of engines — as soon as one faded away another one took its place.

In one way, this was good, but in another, it didn't help her with trying to work out where the man was.

And then, in a lull between the sound of the aeroplanes, she heard him.

"Maggie? Where are you, Maggie?" He was making his voice sound gentle. It was almost playful. "Come out, now."

The anger flashed inside her again. Why was he doing this to her? Why couldn't he just give up and go away? How did he even know her name?

"You're very good at hide and seek, Maggie," the voice called. "But I . . ."

His voice was drowned out by another engine in the sky. Maggie wanted to jump up and wave at it, in the hope that the pilot would see her and send help. All those people on board — reading, eating, looking out of the window. So close to her, right above her head, but they had no idea she was here.

"But I'm very good at it, Maggie," the man continued. "I will find you."

What should she do? Stay put and hope for the best? Or make another run for it? She carefully looked behind her. Through the trees, she could just about see the glint of metal from the edge of the service road. Back there — buildings, cars, people. *Help.* Up ahead — a lot of green, and not much else.

"Maggie."

The voice was much closer now. And then, through the leaves and branches, she saw his ankles. White socks, trainers and what looked like the hem of blue pyjamas.

She couldn't run now. He'd spot her. And catch her. She kept her eyes tightly closed and pressed herself flatter into the mud.

Another engine. Another aeroplane. Another chance to escape come and gone.

A flash of daylight in her little bunker as the branches were parted.

"Hello, Maggie."

* * *

Barnes sat on a trolley with a space blanket around his shoulders, holding a plastic cup of some kind of hot mud.

Kane was engaged in an intense conversation with the Fire & Rescue incident commander. It looked like it was winding up. Kane clapped the man on the shoulder and walked over.

"It's empty. The ambulance," Kane said. "There's no one in it. Fire have confirmed."

Barnes wanted to feel relief, but he didn't. If anything, he felt worse.

"But it's the same ambo," Kane continued.

"Same?"

"Same one stolen from the Lewes workshops," Kane said. "Number plate's cooked. But the fleet number's on the side panel. Still just about visible."

"Same one as at ground zero?"

"Maybe. But not confirmed." Kane looked down at Barnes. "We need to get you some new clothes."

Barnes stared down at the cup.

"Later," he said.

"Fire started in the cab," Kane said. "The investigator is trying to scrape out some traces of accelerant and there's some glass fragments in the footwell. Early indications are that this was pretty amateur. This was not a sophisticated rig."

Barnes looked at him and hopped off the trolley. He dropped the cup in a bin.

"That means it was done in a hurry. Something's put a kink in his plans. We're still close, Samson."

He shrugged the space blanket off, gave it back to one of the paramedics, and headed off towards the main hospital building.

One of the uniformed officers ran over to him as he walked. She wasn't more than about twenty-three, but her eyes sparkled with intelligence, and her jaw was set with determination, having already, Barnes mused, seen more sights than many people would see in a lifetime.

"Sir," she said, her notebook out. "Are you okay?"

"You did well, Officer. I'm grateful."

"Sir, thank you. Listen, we've been canvassing witnesses. People queuing for the pay-and-display machine, mainly."

Barnes stopped and turned to her.

"And?"

"Couple of people think they saw someone near the ambulance. Male, tall, thin build. Black hair. Possibly in a tracksuit. Not a brilliant description, but it is at least consistent among the witnesses."

"Alone? Was he alone?"

"Yes, sir." Her voice was small. "No one has reported seeing anybody with the suspect."

Barnes thought about this for a moment.

"Okay. Thanks, Officer. Good job."

He turned to go.

"Sir?"

He looked down. There was a gentle hand on his arm.

"I hope you find her, sir."

Barnes nodded, then turned and headed into the main hospital building.

* * *

Maggie felt the fight go out of her, like when you blow up a balloon and then let it go and it whizzes around the room. She wished she could do that. He'd never catch her then.

She remembered once how her mum had taken her swimming. She couldn't swim yet, and she was nervous. She couldn't understand how you kept yourself above the surface of the water. During the lesson, she'd gone under and there was a moment where she'd thrashed with her legs, hoping to touch the bottom, but there was nothing there. No matter how much she thrashed her legs, she kept sinking. She remembered the feeling in her chest — the tightness of not being able to breathe, but also the feeling of panic, clutched around her heart like a fist.

And then there were arms around her, pulling her up and out and into the air. Her mother pulled Maggie to her in a tight hug, telling her not to worry and how she would be okay. She'd only been under for a second, but she remembered that fist gripping her heart and how it was like a curtain coming down over her mind. She'd felt it again in the ambulance, and if she let it grip her heart again now she would not be able to get herself out of this.

When she played hide-and-seek with her sister, she would get cross if Ellie found her easily. Cross with herself, cross with her sister, cross with her mum for not having a bigger house with better places to hide.

But she'd felt it slip away when the man found her. Like she was giving up.

Maggie prided herself on her good behaviour. It impressed her teachers, her mum's friends, Barnes's work colleagues, people she met in the street. She sort of knew that bad behaviour could be okay in certain situations.

Like this one.

But that didn't mean it came easily.

What would her mum want her to do? If her mum was here, what would she be saying?

She wouldn't say: *Don't kick that man, Maggie. That's not polite.*

She'd say: *Fight, Maggie. You must help yourself. You must be brave, and think. Don't freeze. Fight.*

She rolled over onto her back as the man parted the branches and stepped into her little hiding spot, and then, as he leaned in, she kicked out as hard as she could with her foot.

Her shoe caught him square in the face, and his hands flew to his nose. She scrambled backwards, stones and briar thorns cutting her hands, and out into the daylight.

She could see the big metal bins and old cars on the service road, and for a moment she thought she could make it.

But then there were rough hands on her, and she felt herself lifted up into the air.

She fought. She screamed and thrashed her legs and arms, and as the man's hand clamped itself around her mouth to stifle her screaming, she bit down hard. And kept biting.

She heard him grunt. She tasted blood. He dropped her. She ran. He caught her again, and she repeated her efforts. She might not succeed the first time, but she was going to keep trying until he got fed up and went away.

But he didn't.

This time, instead of picking her up again, she felt a dull *thud* on the side of her head, and suddenly the world became dark grey, and there was a loud ringing in her ears.

She was still awake, but her legs had turned to jelly.

That's not fair, she thought, as the man scooped her up again.

* * *

"Police," Barnes said, his warrant card held aloft. The door clanged against the breeze block wall of the tiny security lodge, making the man at the desk jump. "We need to see your CCTV."

"Please," Kane added, appearing beside Barnes in the doorway.

The man looked befuddled. Barnes was wide-eyed and soot-stained, with a large dressing on the side of his neck, and his post-decon, prison-issue tracksuit was only just about hanging together.

"CCTV," Barnes said again.

The man looked as if he was going to bite, and Kane stepped forward, holding out his own warrant card.

"Superintendent Samson Kane. This is urgent. Life or . . . death."

He looked sideways at Barnes, then pulled out his phone and found a news page showing coverage of the chemical incident in Eastbourne.

"We have reason to believe the main suspect for this incident dumped a stolen ambulance in your car park as part of an escape plan."

Now it was Barnes's turn to look sideways at Kane.

"We have a description," Kane continued. "We need to track his movements on your CCTV — and then find him."

They stepped into the office. It smelled of cigarettes and old takeaways. The man set down his mug and brushed crumbs off the front of his polyester uniform shirt — nevertheless looking more presentable than Barnes — and then wheeled his chair over to a computer.

Police CCTV enquiries were usually something of a lottery, and tended to go any one of a number of ways. Often, the system wasn't actually real, or someone had forgotten to load a tape, or there was only one tape continually being overwritten and reused on an endless loop every twenty-eight days. Staff quite often had no access to, knowledge of or interest in the system, and usually deferred any such activity to "Head Office", which was often, in Barnes's experience, an entirely apocryphal line of enquiry. On more than one occasion Barnes had threatened to excavate entire CCTV systems from the site in order to focus the minds of the unwilling staff — in a few cases actually making good on his promise. The frustration of these types of enquiries was compounded by public expectation and perceptions of CCTV as the zenith of crime-fighting tools. Failure to check CCTV was at the root of many a police complaint.

Today — and God knew Barnes felt he was due some luck — they were fortunate. The man's name was Gordon, and he proved, once he'd got over the shock, to be a competent and helpful security industry ally.

They stood by Gordon's shoulder while he muttered to himself and cycled through a number of feeds on a screen split nine ways.

"This is the main access road, coming by the front of A&E. Busy, as you can see. Lot of traffic. Lot of ambulances. Not really surprising."

He was speaking mainly for his own benefit. Barnes and Kane stood behind Gordon's chair — Kane patient, Barnes shot through with nervous energy. In the brief lull he took a moment to look at his phone. A ton of missed calls. Three more from Gabby. Two more from Tamsin. Several voicemail alerts. He didn't listen to them. He knew what they were going to say.

He should call Tamsin back. But he couldn't. Not just yet. They were on his tail. He could feel it. For the sake of twenty more minutes — admittedly interminable, to Tamsin — he might be able to call her with good news.

He leaned forwards and peered at the on-screen display.

"That's too early," Barnes said, fighting to keep the irritation from his voice. "That's before school finished. She'd have been in class."

"Huh?" Gordon said.

"What he means is, the chemical thing in Eastbourne didn't happen until just after three," Kane said. "We're working on the basis that the suspect skipped out more or less immediately and came straight here. Try skipping forward by forty-five minutes or so."

Gordon obliged, and sped through the footage until just before four in the afternoon.

That was the other thing, Barnes thought. Time and date displays were so often out of sync. It gave defence lawyers lots of fun opportunities to dangle SIOs like puppets. He had to hope Gordon's meticulous nature was just well hidden. They didn't have time to watch hours of footage.

"Maybe play it at double-speed," Kane suggested. "Just so we can get to the right bit, eh?"

Gordon pressed a button. They peered at the footage. Entirely ordinary. Patients coming and going. Service vehicles idling. Transport buses. Deliveries. Taxis.

And ambulances. Plenty of them. They came, they went, they parked in A&E.

"Wait," Barnes said. "There."

"What have you seen?" Kane said.

"Maybe nothing. Back up a bit. Couple of minutes."

Gordon thumbed some sort of wheel on a bank of controls and all the activity ran backwards.

It was an ambulance. Not stopping at A&E, but continuing past on the service road.

"Just another ambo," Gordon offered.

"No, look," Kane said. "It goes out of shot, then . . . look. There."

Gordon hit pause.

There it was, in the top corner of the screen. A flash of lime green on the perimeter road, heading past the outer car parks and towards the helipad.

"You have coverage of the landing site?" Barnes said.

"No," Gordon said. "Blind spot."

Kane leaned in towards Barnes.

"We're close," he said, his voice almost a whisper. "We're going to get him."

Barnes's gaze remained fixed on the screen, his arms folded, his fist pushed against his mouth.

"I don't think so," Barnes said. "It's too easy. You plan something like this, in an ambulance, you're hiding in plain sight. You know they can track the things, so you're banking on doing what you need to do and getting out before it's noticed. You say he's organised, but that's a long shot. Something like this, you need to plan for anything and everything that could go wrong. Like, the eventuality that someone might notice it's missing before you're done with it."

"Maybe it's just a coincidence," Kane said. "If it is, you should be thanking your lucky stars that the thing in the town centre happened when it did. No better cover for an escape than a distraction. Maybe he let his guard down."

"And if it isn't a coincidence?"

Kane thought about this, then shook his head.

"That's a whole lot of ifs, buts and maybes."

"If he didn't plan for someone to notice the ambulance was missing as soon as we did, then his planning is weak. Which means he isn't as organised as he'd like to think. Which means he might panic. Which means . . ."

He didn't say it. He didn't want to think about it. Kane got it. So did Gordon, probably.

"Something else might have come in from left field and dinked his plans. Life's full of the unexpected," Kane said.

Maybe. Maybe even Maggie. Barnes knew she had her mother's grit and stubbornness.

"This is the best I can do," Gordon said. "The ambulance goes out of shot somewhere near the edge of the car park. There's too much footfall to pick anyone out — unless you have a description of your man?"

Barnes relayed the description the officer had given him in the car park, and Gordon went to work.

"Where's he going?" Kane said, more to himself than anything. "What's next?"

"The ambulance was on the edge of the footprint, beyond the helipad," Barnes said to Gordon. "Could he get out that way?"

"Sure, he could," Gordon said. "Nothing north of here except fields. He could go east and be at the aerodrome in five minutes. Or keep going north and then cut back onto the main road. Lots of residential areas. Train station is twenty minutes away on foot. Or Gatwick is five miles south."

"So no reason at all to come back the way he came? Back past A&E and out the main entrance?"

"None at all," Gordon said.

Barnes's heart sank a little.

Kane moved away and began making calls on his phone. His voice was quiet, but insistent — directing the deployment of dogs, air support and lowland searchers. He dropped his rank into it wherever he could, but Barnes mused that seniority was worthless if there was someone more senior directing the opposite of everything you were trying to get done.

He'd have to get back to Gabby. But he just needed a little more. Barnes knew Gabby still wouldn't entertain a confirmed connection between Maggie's disappearance and the chemical incident in Eastbourne. He wasn't even sure Gabby believed Maggie had been abducted at all. And Barnes's failure to answer a catalogue of phone calls from the man in the last hour meant he would have gone from merely purple with rage to utterly apoplectic.

"Keep scanning," Barnes said. "He's been hiding in plain sight this far, so my instinct is he'll keep doing so. On foot across a field exposes you. Public transport exposes you. Aerodrome is a possibility, but someone would remember you. Release a nerve agent in a busy town, you can make your getaway while everyone is running around like headless chickens. Same applies if you blow up an ambulance. And besides—"

"Wait," Gordon said. "Look here."

He froze the shot and zeroed in on the image. Barnes peered at it.

There he was. Bottom corner of the screen, walking past the entrance to A&E.

A man. Thirties, maybe. Tall, slender, upright, in control of his movements. Not rushing, but moving purposefully, even on the jerky footage. He reminded Barnes of a ballet dancer, or a marathon runner. Shiny black hair combed back over his head. The description given was that he was wearing a tracksuit, but the witnesses were either mistaken or, more likely, he'd changed his clothes. He was wearing theatre blues, and he was heading straight into the main entrance of the hospital's A&E department.

And he was completely alone.

"How long ago was this?" Barnes said.

Gordon squinted at the screen.

"Forty-five minutes ago."

Kane clapped Gordon on the shoulder.

"That's good work, Gordon. Thanks. Now bring up your live feed and see if you can find him in the hospital. Start searching."

Kane made for the door. Barnes was already there.

"Hey, wait," Gordon called.

Kane turned.

"Here," Gordon said, tossing Kane a radio handset from a cardboard box.

"Channel 17. If I find him on the footage, I'll radio you."

"Good job. Can you print that screenshot of him? Circulate copies out to the wards?"

"Well, actually, I—"

"Top man," Kane said, and the two men ran out into the hospital proper.

"Want to split?" Kane said.

"We should," Barnes said. "You go west, I'll go east."

"How thorough are we being?"

"Cursory," Barnes said. "Do it at a jog and start scanning. Room to room. My gut is telling me he isn't hanging around. He'd have to go to ground — hide in a cupboard and wait for all this to blow over, and that's a boatload of risk. More likely he's passed straight through and out into the ether before someone asks him to deliver a baby or something. The blues could have been just for moving about freely. He may even have had another change of clothes stashed somewhere in the hospital."

"Roger," Kane said, and jogged off towards the corridors.

Barnes watched him go. He took a moment to gather his thoughts, standing there in the main concourse with his hands on his hips.

Kane was right. The trail was warm. Hot, even. But it was going to rapidly cool unless they could drop a net over it.

And that meant resources. Kane was trying, but with limited success so far.

But why was it hot in the first place? Someone organised enough to plan to steal an ambulance to cover their tracks was organised enough to get out.

Unless something had interfered with Plan A to the extent that Plan B had been activated and was very much now in play.

Blowing up ambulances.

Cutting losses.

Something?

Or someone?

CHAPTER SEVENTEEN

The man was angry. She'd drawn blood on the back of his heel, and it had leaked out onto his white sock. Her head was throbbing, and he had hurt her arm, pulling her this way and that, but when she told him to let go and that she would walk beside him and do as she was told, he'd agreed.

She had no idea where they were going. The ambulance was on fire in the distance, and there was nothing around them but fields. She wanted water, and a bath. Her legs were starting to ache, her head was pounding and she felt dizzy.

But still he walked, and walked, and walked. She could see huge planes with orange tails flying low overhead, as well as little planes with propellers flying the other way — they were landing, she realised, at a small airport across the fields.

Eventually, a row of houses came into view. They headed into the estate between two new-looking houses, and emerged on a dead-end road with lots of cars parked along it. Across the road was a small playground with a yellow slide and a roundabout with a smiling turtle painted on the side. Three children were playing there, and she suddenly felt her stomach plunge, like she was watching them through inch-thick glass.

As the children turned to look at her, a bright red-and-yellow van entered the close and slowed down. Maggie didn't pay it much attention — it was obviously a delivery van, and she'd seen thousands before.

She only looked at it properly when it stopped in front of them; the side door grumbled as it slid open, and she came face-to-face with a yellow-haired skinny man who looked like he was going to be sick, he was so pale. He held out a hand; Maggie recoiled, then the other man — the one with the bleeding heel — gave her a shove and she tumbled onto the dusty plywood floor of the van.

The door slid shut, she heard the driver and passenger doors slam shut, and then they took off again.

She jumped up, thinking she might be able to open the sliding side door herself and jump out before the van started going too fast.

She gripped the handle and pulled.

And pulled, and pulled, and pulled.

It wouldn't budge.

She sank to the dusty floor and tried really hard not to cry.

* * *

This is ridiculous, Barnes thought. They couldn't do this alone, and every unsuccessful visit to a ward room was wasting precious time. Gordon was getting his printouts circulated, but they needed air support, dogs, tannoy announcements, media appeals, officers standing at the entrance passing out images to patients and families leaving and arriving.

Forty-five minutes had elapsed between the suspect entering the hospital and Gordon finding him on CCTV. That had been fifteen minutes ago. You could go anywhere in an hour. You could be fifty miles north of London. You could be out of the country. You could even drive back down to Eastbourne to chant *nyeh-nyeh-nyeh* at Tamsin.

And then, chatter on the radio Gordon had given him.

"Officer, are you there? Officer? Come in. This is Gordon. Over."

"Go ahead," Barnes said.

"Looks like your first thought was right. He's gone straight through the hospital building and out the other side."

"What's there?"

"Accommodation block, X-ray centre, creche, deliveries, staff car park, that kind of thing."

"Taxi rank? Airport shuttles?"

"Nah, that'd be out the front. Right by where he came in."

"Okay. Bus stops and things out that way?"

"All out front. There's a big estate to the south where you could pick up a bus, but not a lot else. But listen, I think he's changed."

"He's what?"

"Yeah, he's ditched the blues. He's in some kind of delivery uniform now. Like a courier. Sure it's the same guy, though."

"How sure?"

"Pretty sure."

"That's a good spot, Gordon. How long ago was this?"

"Getting on for an hour."

Barnes kept himself from exclaiming in frustration.

"OK, listen. How many in your team? Just you?"

"There's three of us. But I can use the porters too."

"Okay, I need you to go and cross-check all your scheduled deliveries for today with anything unexpected. Any delivery vans parked up anywhere, go put in a challenge. Where do theatre blues go when you're done with them?"

"They all go into the biohazard laundry. There'll be tons of the things."

"Fine. Keep an eye out for any that have been dumped in a regular bin. I'm coming back to look at the image. And do me a favour — get someone to go to the creche and make sure all the kids are accounted for. Discreetly."

"Okay."

"Thanks, Gordon. Good work."

It was new information. As long as new information was still coming through, the trail was still warm. And if it came in twos and threes, you knew you were doing okay.

His mobile phone rang. He didn't recognise the number.

"DI Barnes."

"Hello, Barnes . . . sir. This is Tina." Her voice was hushed, and Barnes imagined her crouched down in the corner of the command vehicle, a hand over her mouth, trying to look inconspicuous.

"Tina? Are you okay?"

"Yes, I'm fine. Listen, I may have something."

Barnes inhaled. Adrenaline crackled through him.

"I'm listening," he said, trying to stay calm.

"I've done some convoy analysis using ANPR, and it looks like there's a second vehicle."

"Don't tell me. A delivery van."

"Yes, it looks like it. An Iveco Daily. Registered to DHL. How did you know that?"

"Intuition."

"Well, it looks like this van followed the ambulance out of Eastbourne and then up the A23 into Crawley. It's stopped pinging cameras north of Gatwick."

"Found the ambulance. Burnt out."

Barnes heard Tina inhale.

"And . . . and . . . your . . ."

"Maggie wasn't in it. She's still missing. What's the reg of the Iveco?"

"Papa-November-zero-five, Foxtrot-Kilo-Tango."

"Keep working on that plate. Call me back."

"There's something else."

"Yes?"

"I've played around with the CCTV image of the ambulance from Hartington Place. Enhancement isn't my strongest suit, it needs to get sent away for that—"

"What have you got, Tina?"

"Well, I can — I think — make out the fleet number. I wouldn't bet my house on it, but it looks like one-double-zero-seven."

"One thousand and seven."

"Yes."

"How sure are you, Tina?"

"Sure enough to call you."

"Okay." Barnes's voice was trembling. "That's the fleet number of the one that just blew up in front of me. The stolen one."

"Yes. It's the same one."

CHAPTER EIGHTEEN

Barnes tried to contain himself. It didn't conclusively connect it to the chemical attack, but it had to be a viable hypothesis now. Stolen ambulance parked three hundred metres away from ground zero leaves the scene just before the bodies start dropping? That was enough for him to front up Gabby. Face the music. And maybe get some resources rolling, especially if it meant the main suspect could be cornered like a rat.

"Fantastic work, Tina. Call me back."

He picked up his police radio and relayed the information to Kane, and the two of them regrouped at the main entrance before heading off to find Gordon.

It was indeed a good spot. The suspect was now in a distinctive red-and-yellow uniform with a cap pulled low over his head. It was almost certainly the same man, but easy to miss.

"Turns out a DHL van has been double-parked out by the accommodation block for most of the day with its hazards on," Gordon told them. "One of the porters thought it was odd, but hadn't got around to doing anything about it."

"It's gone now, presumably," Barnes said.

Gordon nodded.

They obtained a bunch more printouts of the best shot — Barnes taking a snap of the screen using his phone camera for good measure — and headed back to the car.

"What now?" Kane said.

"We just need to wait."

"Wait?"

"Just a few minutes. Tina's going to call me back. That courier van isn't stolen, or it would have been lighting up cameras all the way up the motorway. Either that or it hasn't been noticed yet."

"Well, that line of thinking worked for the ambo. I'll get on to DHL."

Barnes passed him the details of the Iveco's number plate.

"Soon as she calls me back, I'll front Glover," Barnes said. "That connection still isn't watertight, but any investigator worth his salt would have to give it serious consideration. Which means he can't refuse my resource requests any longer. It might stick in his craw, but if he can claim credit for catching the chemical suspect mere hours after the fact, then his next promotion is all but safe."

As it happened, it was another seventeen interminable minutes before Tina called back.

Barnes snatched at the phone. Kane was engrossed in a phone call with a DHL operations manager. Barnes dug him in the ribs with an elbow.

"Tina?"

"Sorry about the wait. Couple of other bits came up."

"It's okay. I'm only going out of my mind."

Silence.

"Tina. Sorry. I was trying to make a joke. Poor attempt."

"Okay, well, this courier van . . ."

"Yeah. We think it was parked to the south of the footprint. Rear entrance. Our suspect came in one door wearing theatre blues, walked straight through the hospital and came out the other side in a courier get-up. Like Mr-sodding-Benn.

Looks like the van bugged out of here about an hour ago. Direction of travel unknown."

"Well, that would compute."

"Oh yes?" Barnes started the engine, and put the phone on loudspeaker.

"Like I say, it stopped pinging cameras around Crawley about ninety minutes after the CBRN job. Nothing since, and then it tripped the southbound camera heading onto the Gatwick South Terminal perimeter road."

Barnes took a deep breath.

"When was this?"

"Five minutes ago."

"Tina, I will thank you later. We're heading there now. If you happen to see Gabby, tell him there's a confirmed link between the CBRN incident and my daughter's abduction. Principal suspect is headed into the airport. He might want to ring me."

He ended the call, hit the blues and swung the knackered marked Focus out of the hospital and southbound towards the airport.

Kane called the control room inspector again and made some kind of sticky-tape-and-glue arrangement to get the CCTV still of the suspect in the courier uniform into the control room and thence to police patrols on the concourse and beyond.

"Tell them he's likely to have changed clothes again. If you assume he isn't about to go out like a martyr, then he's trying to get a commercial flight out of the country. That being the case, he won't be going in a courier costume."

"He's going into the lion's den, isn't he?" Kane asked. "Airport's the one place you don't have to scrounge around for a policeman."

"Get them looking for the van too," Barnes said. "He'll have dumped it in a drop zone with the hazards on, most likely. Buy some time. Dog might be able to start a track. Footfall's likely too high, but worth a go. And get GRC to ask the SDM to start scanning the monitors. CCTV-wise, there's no blind spots here. This prick should be like a lab rat under a soldering iron."

They screamed south down the Horley Road towards the airport, Barnes wrenching every last drop of power out of the war-torn Focus.

"This thing's earned its retirement," Kane remarked.

They pulled onto the Gatwick Airport perimeter road five minutes later, by which time all available AFOs were deployed around the concourse — watching, waiting and primed for action. Brightly lit hotels rose up all around them, the elevated intertwined monorail shuttles that connected the north and south terminals creating a kind of space-age city. They raced along the perimeter road, chain-link fences with razor wire crowns stretching alongside them, preserving the sanctity of airside operations that chugged and bleeped and growled on the other side.

"No pushback from Ops1? About deploying the Gatwick crews?" Barnes said.

"None," Kane answered. "Tina must have briefed Gabby."

Barnes felt a moment's guilt. He shouldn't have asked her to do that. He should have put his own stresses aside long enough to do that himself.

Kane had his ear to his Airwave handset, frowning as he concentrated on the clipped, tinny transmissions. Barnes couldn't make out the words, but the urgency was obvious.

"Turn it up," Barnes said. "Get it on the car set."

"... I repeat, subject vehicle located. VRM confirms. It's parked off the Eastway, outside the Gatwick Hilton. Unattended, hazards on. Vehicle has been cleared — no trace of any persons ..."

"Good site to use," Kane said. "He can go straight through the hotel and out the tier side. There's an airbridge right into the terminal."

Barnes pulled up behind the van two minutes later. A couple of unarmed Gatwick officers — yet to embark on their firearms training — were guarding it. As at the hospital, they did a double-take at the sight of the odd characters emerging from the marked patrol car. Warrant cards were produced again — suspicions neutralised, a cure for many a social ill.

The double doors at the rear of the van were open. Barnes stood for a moment, taking in the empty cabin. Had Maggie been in here? Were traces of her meshed into the plywood floor?

"This is a crime scene, okay?" Barnes said to the officers. "Stay with it."

He ran into the hotel, Kane behind him. He tugged at Barnes's shoulder.

"I know we look like we're out of *Stir Crazy* or something, but try to walk normally. We're not in uniform. We have an advantage. We can spot him before he spots us. Talk the crews in."

Barnes looked at him and slowed. It took considerable self-control, but the boss was right.

"Keep 'em peeled," Kane said.

They headed off along the walkway, passing over Westway and the dizzying circular spirals of the multi-storey car park exit ramps.

Barnes suddenly felt extraordinarily self-conscious. He looked down at himself, then caught a look at his reflection in the windows of the walkway.

"Escaped convict" didn't really do it justice. Nor did "dragged through a hedge backwards". His usually ordinary hair was unkempt and sticking up, his expression wild-eyed and strained, while his blood- and grime-smeared tracksuit was just about hanging on in there.

"You'd better circulate my description too," he muttered. "Firearms are liable to faceplant me into the terminal floor."

They emerged onto the concourse, Kane passing updates quietly onto the radio. This gave the operation a long-over-due sense of officialdom, as well as giving Barnes a degree of self-assurance that their activity was now, more or less, above board. Not that he cared about that, particularly — his only priority was finding Maggie — but it was nevertheless good to know the list of enemies had reduced slightly.

Armed officers were stationed in pairs around the concourse, baseball caps pulled low, carbines held at low port. They looked alert, tense, but they were also behaving no differently to their usual patrol activity. They didn't — thankfully — draw the eye, particularly. But they were waiting.

And watching.

"This could be a short search," Barnes muttered to Kane. "This isn't the hospital. There isn't a single CCTV blind spot in the place."

Which was true. But there were also several thousand people, and more than a few uniformed couriers — the purple, white and orange of FedEx, the gold and brown of UPS, and the red and yellow of DHL.

He should be easy to spot.

But he could also be easy to miss.

Kane and Barnes fanned out across the terminal's arrivals hall, trying to look as casual as possible. They hugged the edges of the concourse, passing WHSmith, M&S and Tie Rack. They scanned the crowds — elated couples reunited, irritable lines of passengers at the check-in desks, tired global commuters passing through one more gateway, their natural body rhythms left somewhere on the other side of the world.

Barnes strained to pick out abnormalities above the ambient sounds — a hum of conversation, tinny announcements on the public address, transport buggies beeping and chirping as their electric motors whined across the polished floors.

There was nothing out of the ordinary.

Barnes caught the eye of one of the firearms officers. The officer's gaze rested on him for a moment. Barnes thought he was about to be approached, but the officer gave an almost imperceptible nod and continued scanning.

"We're adding nothing here," Barnes said to Kane. "The eyeballs on the place are like a fishing net."

"The more the merrier," Kane said.

"Balls. He's not buying a prawn sandwich. He's either changed clothes again and is going straight through the other side, or he's getting out of the country."

They watched.

They waited.

Nothing happened.

Barnes suddenly felt a powerful urge to start checking the cabins of all the aircraft lined up at each of the piers. He suddenly felt as though every second spent static, standing in the arrivals hall like a tit, was a second their quarry was making good use of to put time, space and distance between himself and his pursuers.

Barnes tapped his foot. He gripped his mobile phone in his pocket. It had barely stopped vibrating. He didn't answer it. Couldn't. The distraction would prove costly, and besides, he didn't think the battery would survive even a five-minute phone call.

There was a last call for a flight to Oslo.

There was a page for an absent passenger.

The digital billboards flicked from one brightly coloured ad to another — vitamins, good organic eating on the upper concourse, island paradise package deals.

Travellers stood rigid and surveyed the information boards, arms folded, waiting for a change.

Barnes blinked.

Kane stepped towards him, his ear pressed to his Airwave handset.

"Got a sighting."

CHAPTER NINETEEN

Barnes felt as if he'd been electrocuted.

"Where?"

"Airside. He's cleared customs. Not confirmed. He's ditched the courier outfit."

Barnes's fists bunched by his sides.

"Which gate?"

"Seventeen. There's a crew making an approach."

There was a burst of chatter on the radio. The other armed officers dotted around the concourse heard it too. One pressed his earpiece deeper into his ear canal.

"What?" Barnes said.

The armed officers began to move towards the customs and security area, walking briskly, and then "*Runner! I have a runner! Gate 10, Pier 2. West, towards the runway . . .*" burst out of the radio and the armed crews began to sprint.

"Stay with them," Barnes yelled. "We'll never get airside without them, even with a warrant card."

They barrelled across the concourse, heads turning as they tried to catch up with the AFOs. The pre-security briefing was on point; as they approached, one of the Gatwick security team opened a secure side door embedded in a glass wall next to the customs queue, and the six officers — Barnes, Kane and two pairs of AFOs — were able to get airside and into the duty-free channel without troubling Her Majesty's Customs.

They ran through the duty-free hall, Barnes straining to listen for updates coming through on Kane's radio.

"*Gate 27 . . .*" came the update over air. "*He's going to run out of road. Six-foot, black hair, grey suit. Can't see any weapons.*"

It was a painfully long journey; from the duty-free hall to Gate 27, at the very end of Pier 2, was the best part of half a kilometre, and the travelators were only of limited use, thronged as they were with shuffling passengers.

They thundered along the wide walkway of Pier 2, thudding footsteps echoing up into the whitewashed ceilings, the last scraps of the day's winter sun blinking through the windows, aircraft moving this way and that on the pale-brown concrete outside, backlit advertising screens and rows of yellow plastic seats stretching away down the pier on either side of them.

They caught up with the AFO crew that had done the spotting in the corner of a large area at the end of one of the piers that appeared to be some kind of atrium under construction. Stepladders and dust sheets were scattered around the area, and the AFOs formed a dome to contain their subject who, having run into a dead end, was cornered.

Barnes and Kane caught up with the AFOs. Barnes moved up, but was ushered backwards by one of them, who shooed Barnes back with a wave of the hand, without turning round or taking his eyes from his target.

Barnes flattened himself against the wall — and then he saw him.

It was him. No doubt whatsoever. Tall, slender, shiny, wet-looking black hair combed back over his head. And empty, staring eyes.

He'd ditched the courier get-up for the nondescript grey suit of the professional traveller, but there were no doubts at all. It was a good spot.

It took every ounce of Barnes's self-control to stop himself running forward and grabbing the man and demanding to know where Maggie was.

What he'd done with her.

To her.

But he couldn't. He was experienced enough to know that this was an armed operation, and a civilian getting caught in the crossfire — which is what it amounted to, warrant card or no — risked making things worse, not better.

So, he waited and listened, hovering behind the line of AFOs as they attempted to negotiate with the man.

"Take it easy, fella," the lead AFO said. "Keep your hands in front of you, and don't make sudden movements, okay?"

The man was not focused on the officer. His eyes were wide, almost unseeing, and Barnes knew he was formulating some kind of plan, buying time, his mind working furiously. He didn't look under the influence, but then even professional criminals don't necessarily react well to staring down the collective barrel of a semi-circle of MP5s.

The lead AFO caught this. He was standing just off to the side of the man's twelve o'clock.

"Focus on me, mate. Look at me. Just keep chill and think about how you want today to finish up. Now, slowly, lie face down on the floor."

The man tensed. He'd been given an instruction, and Barnes knew he'd realised that anything other than compliance could mean a number of things, which in turn could be interpreted a number of ways.

His eyes drifted off again. He was thinking. Unless he had some spectacular trump card that involved a Boeing piloted by a suggestible colleague crashing through the concrete wall, those options were limited to run, fight, or passive refusal that involved hours and hours of negotiation. Theoretically, as long as he didn't present a threat, they could be there all day.

"What's your name, fella?" the lead officer said, his barrel still holding steady, pointing directly at the centre of the man's torso. "Tell me your name."

"You want to be my friend."

It was a statement, not a question, but one with a faint sneer about it. Barnes shut his eyes and replayed the phrase in his head. There was a hint of an accent. He couldn't place it.

Barnes inched forward, closer to the lead officer.

"If he cleared customs," Barnes said quietly, "he's unlikely to be armed."

"I know that," the officer said, a touch of irritation in his voice, his eyes remaining on his subject. "Keep back . . . sir."

"I want him alive," Barnes said.

The officer turned his head over his shoulder, just a fraction.

"Tell me your name," the officer said again.

He inched closer. The man caught this, and spread his hands in front of him as if he were offering bread.

Barnes chanced a look behind him. They were alone in this corner of the airport. No travellers, maintenance people, press, nothing. The first sign of life was a cleaning cart almost two hundred yards up the corridor.

"Mate," the officer said. "We can stand here all day. But there's a little girl out there. Tell me where she is, tell me she's okay, and we can all go and get a brew."

Barnes thought he saw the faintest hint of a smirk on the man's face, and he shut his eyes before the urge to rush forward and strangle him became too much.

"Where is she?" the officer asked again. "Where?"

The grin got wider.

"Hands!" the officer on the right flank yelled.

The man was slowly putting his hands down, and then he began gradually moving them backwards.

"Come on, mate," the lead AFO said. "Don't do this."

Barnes frowned. It didn't make sense. It certainly wasn't, to his mind, fitting any conventional criminological models. A mercenary, a professional, wants paid and out. You plan to avoid the unexpected, but getting caught is just one of those possibilities. An occupational hazard, almost. Do as you're told, keep your mouth shut, listen to the lawyer and you had a fifty-fifty of beating it anyway. A jilted lover, by contrast, was all heart and no head. Raging at the world, they'd take as many down with them as possible, maybe enjoying the stand-off before the blaze of glory. A paedophile — God help him, it was the first time he'd permitted himself to think the word, let alone say it — works to the urges. In many cases, they might cut their losses in the hope that they might live to fight another day. Prison didn't suit . . . that.

This guy seemed to be a hybrid of all of the above.

"There's no way out of this, mate," the officer continued, and then, out of the corner of his mouth, back over his shoulder to Barnes. "One of you put a call in to the duty hostage and crisis negotiator? We could be here a while."

The man hadn't noticed — and nor had Barnes, come to that — that the semi-circle was very gradually moving in on the man.

"What's happening on the coast?" the officer asked. "That got something to do with this? Nerve agents at the seaside? Do you know about that?"

The man frowned. He looked genuinely puzzled, and then seemed to comply. He raised his hands above his head, elbows bent, fingers splayed and dropped first to one knee, then the other.

There was no crescendo, no natural progression, no anticipated change in positioning. Just his right hand suddenly dropping and . . .

"Gun!" one of the officers screamed.

Barnes didn't see it, didn't react, didn't really know what was going on. On a very primal level, he was able to later piece together that he saw muzzle flash, then heard the one shot, then saw the gun, in that order.

"No!" he screamed.

The man didn't go down immediately. The pistol was still in his hand. He sank to his knees.

"Drop the gun!" somebody yelled.

He couldn't or wouldn't respond. He certainly didn't comply. Another shot, and he fell face first onto the concourse, his already lifeless head taking the brunt of the impact like an egg smashing on a tiled kitchen floor.

The AFOs rushed towards their subject. The lead officer began barking orders at them — stop the bleeding, intubate, start CPR — and the crews rushed into a different kind of action.

Barnes inched forward as they worked, pulling all manner of equipment from enormous first-aid kits, discarded dressing packaging and defibrillator pads scattered on the floor around them.

Kane spoke calmly into his radio. "Threat presented, two shots fired, subject neutralised by primary weapon, now receiving first aid. Post incident measures required."

Barnes barely heard it.

He moved forward around to the man's head as they worked on him, positioning himself so he could see the face.

The eyes were milky and sightless. His skin was already fading. Whatever wounds had been caused by the rounds, they were clearly unsurvivable.

"Where is she?" Barnes muttered. Nobody heard. "Where is she?" he said again.

Nothing.

"*Where is she?!*" he screamed, in a voice he had never heard emanate from his own body before.

The AFOs turned. Two stood.

"He's gone. I'm sorry, sir." This was the lead AFO. He put his hand on Barnes's shoulder.

Barnes shrugged it off and collapsed to his knees next to the dead body of the only person in the world that knew where his stepdaughter was.

He grabbed the lapels of the grey suit.

"*Where is she? Where is she? Where is she?*"

He continued his mantra, shaking the lifeless body as if to restart it somehow, even if only long enough to impart the small piece of knowledge that was already fading into a meaningless organic sludge behind the dead eyes.

Barnes felt hands on him, lifting him gently up. Samson Kane spun him around and pulled Barnes to him in a fierce hug.

CHAPTER TWENTY

"So, who is he?" Kane asked.

They were standing in an incident room of sorts, a four-by-four office hastily purged of desks to create a briefing area, wall screen and whiteboard with a few workstations pushed to the edges. Night had fallen in a freezing sheet, and the golf course outside the windows of the Major Incident Suite was dark and silent.

After the Gatwick officers had summoned the paramedics — who had wasted little time declaring life extinct — and the armed operation became an investigative one, Barnes had insisted on primacy and directed that the body, the route taken, the DHL van and more besides were preserved as crime scenes, with a view to squeezing every last drop of forensic material from each one.

Barnes shut the door. In the incident room proper — next door, as it happened — Gabby Glover was holding court with a roomful of investigators, analysts and scientific experts attempting to unpick the chemical incident in Eastbourne town centre, now badged as Operation Element. Besides half a theory involving a stolen ambulance, the only thing connecting the two episodes was a gossamer thread named Tina Guestling, who, during intervals from her principal tasking, periodically visited Kane and Barnes with food and updates.

That was it. That was the extent of their team. Barnes let it ride, for now. Once he got some concrete leads he was going to go ten rounds with Gabby to get something resembling a half-decent unit. The less persuading Gabby needed, however, the better. If the link between the two incidents was so incontrovertible that even Gabby with his bright-pink pig-headedness couldn't refute it, then it might be more economical all round.

If, indeed, they were linked. Even Barnes couldn't quite bring himself to believe it.

Yet.

"The name on his passport and boarding pass is Andrew Lau," Barnes said.

Kane immediately screwed his face up.

"What?"

"That's an alias. Andrew Lau is a cult film director."

"Well, that figures. Passport is genuine, though. The papers were found in his inside jacket pocket. He didn't have anything else on him. No bag, wallet, nothing."

"Phone?"

"Not on him. Probably ditched it. I've got a skeleton search team retracing his steps, upending the bins, et cetera."

"What about checked baggage?"

"It's being pulled off the carousel as we speak. It's being treated with a degree of caution, as you might imagine. Besides that, he had nothing else."

"Just a nine-mil."

"Viable one, too. Full clip."

"How the hell did he get that airside?"

Barnes shook his head.

"Well, it's not a standard weapon. Early indications are some kind of polymer construction. Very lightweight and technically undetectable. NABIS are running some checks to see if it's been used in any other shootings, but it doesn't look like it's a pool weapon."

"Not an easy gun to get hold of," Kane said.

"No, exactly. You have to have the contacts and the funding, as a minimum. There's also a possibility it was made to order."

"It still doesn't answer the question of how he got it airside."

"The Gatwick inspector is investigating that right now with the SDM. It's proving a bit political. You've got Gatwick security, police, Border Force, NCA. No one agency is going to readily admit to being the weak link. Not when the line of suspects is long enough to give you half a chance of blaming someone else. In any case, he either slipped it past border checks or had it pre-stashed airside."

"What the hell was he thinking? Those odds were never going to be good. Suicide by cop, maybe?"

"Impossible to discount it. Strange choice for a professional, but even professionals can have an aversion to going back to prison."

"You still holding to that?"

"At the moment, everything else points to it," Barnes said. "Either that, or he saw my face and wanted to twist the knife at the death . . ."

He took a moment, covering his eyes with his hands. Was this his fault? Was the AFO team leader right? Should he have backed right off? How would the guy have even known who he was?

"You okay?" Kane said.

"Passport and boarding pass have gone off for examination," Barnes continued, as if he hadn't heard. "Dental imprints too. Interpol have been told to order some pizza and not expect an early bath."

"Anything in the van?" Kane said.

"Nothing so far. Nothing obvious, anyway. The senior SOCO is a friend of mine. He's making sure of a thorough job. Luck, not judgement," he added, seeing Kane's look.

"You talk to Tamsin?" Kane asked.

"I will," Barnes said, a little too quickly.

"You need to."

"I said I will. I . . . I want to be able to give her news."

Kane straightened up.

"I know you want to make this right for her. I know you want to be the one to fix it. But she needs you. She can't just sit and wait at home alone."

"I need to do this."

"Have you asked her what she needs?"

Barnes glared at him. Kane didn't back down.

"You should be well away from here. Don't be a cop on this one. Be a partner. Be a father."

Barnes felt rage swell and then subside. His shoulders slumped a little.

"I'll make you a deal. If Gabby starts taking me seriously, then I'll back off. Okay?"

"Fair enough. But it's not me you need to be making a deal with."

* * *

Barnes sat under the dim light of a desk lamp, poring over a morass of papers, seeing nothing, his mind a whirlwind.

He was alone in his makeshift incident room. Kane had gone somewhere. Home, probably. Barnes knew he himself should sleep. Should eat. Take a bath. But it didn't seem right when he didn't know if Maggie was able to do any of those things.

Darkness had fallen, and the thought of Maggie gripped his mind with a new ferocity now there was a lull in activity. People were retiring for the night. The temperature was dropping. Traffic was thinning. All the things that went in your favour when trying to find your victim alive dulled under nightfall.

Next door, by contrast, the pace of Operation Element had not waned. That was going to be a twenty-four-seven operation for some days yet.

Barnes called the control room and asked for an operational name to be assigned to Maggie's disappearance, but, as it turned out, as a suspect had been shot dead by police, one already existed.

Operation Console.

He finally deigned to pull his mobile phone out of his pocket and saw it was dead. He plugged it in, and after a few minutes it had been sufficiently resuscitated to come alive and start vibrating and buzzing with missed calls and messages.

There were several from Tamsin. The last one just said: *Hope you're okay. Call me x*

He keyed one back: *Sorry, I can't come home yet. I have to be here. I think I found him. Now I'm going to find her.*

He awoke an hour or so later, his face pressed into his sleeve on the keyboard. He sat up suddenly and rubbed his face, wondering what it was that had woken him.

He turned and saw Tina Guestling in the doorway. She was holding a bottle of Coke and a pizza box.

"Few slices left. Barbecue chicken and sweetcorn."

"Neither of which should be anywhere near a pizza."

"That's probably why there's some left."

She brought the box over and set it down next to him. He backed off slightly, worried about morning breath, and discreetly wiped his face with the back of his hand in case he'd been drooling into the keyboard.

She perched on the edge of the desk. He took the Coke.

"Thanks," he said. "Winding down in there?" He nodded towards the Op Element incident room.

"Skeleton crew now. Couple of night detectives and a supervisor. Most have gone to grab some sleep. They'll be back on early. You should do the same."

He took some pizza. It was cold and dry, but his stomach growled as he slowly chewed.

"Any more on what happened?"

"Still working on that. Scene is still open, albeit work's paused overnight. Working theory is that it's some kind of nerve agent, but they're not sure what. The STAC cell has been stroking its collective chin all day."

"Deliberate, then."

"Took a while for them — the ACC — to want to go public with that, but yes. Looking like it. Not confirmed though."

"Method?"

"Not sure of that either. Depends on what it is. Liquid preparation could be released by smashing a vial on the ground. Something like fentanyl, you wouldn't need much to wreak a fair amount of havoc."

"They're going with fentanyl?"

"I'm just saying."

"What's the body count?"

"Six confirmed dead. Fourteen ill — five seriously, two life-threatening. The rest with respiratory symptoms but otherwise walking wounded. That's just ground zero."

"There's more casualties?"

"Funnily enough, yes. But they were down by the seafront. South of Trinity Place."

Jesus. Barnes had walked straight through there.

"No fatalities there, though. Sore throats, vomiting, streaming eyes, that kind of thing. The main concentration was . . . well, where you were."

"Blown downwind, maybe?"

"Yes, maybe."

"Who was the intended victim?"

"They're going with random victim selection at the moment. Indiscriminate."

Barnes screwed up his face.

"You don't buy that?" she said.

"It's possible, but, to me, it doesn't fit. You want to pick off a load of Christmas shoppers for no reason, you use a gun, or a knife, or a truck. Scattering toxic agents around the place doesn't have the same cachet. That's the mark of someone who doesn't want to leave a trace, or at least wants people to think that the Russians have popped over with their poisoned umbrellas to keep the memory of the Cold War alive in between cream teas."

"Well, not all the victims have been identified yet. Some are still in situ, even. I gather there's been a few conversations about the spooks or CTC wading in and taking the investigation off the local constabulary, but those are a bit above my pay grade."

She toed the floor.

"How are you doing? Why aren't you at home with your wife? She must be going out of her mind."

"I'm more help here."

"That the only reason? Or are you blaming yourself?"

"I can't go home knowing she's out there. I just can't. Sitting around wringing my hands knowing Gabby doesn't give two fucks about it. About her.

"And we're not married. Not yet, anyway. Can't say we're likely to be, after this. It depends on how this all . . . ends.

"And . . . listen. I wanted to say: thank you. For sticking your neck out and helping me when no one else would."

"I didn't really have much of a choice. But you're welcome."

"We got the bastard in the airport. Bled out before I could ask him where she was."

Tina's face blanched. "Oh, shit."

"In a way, that's good. Means he's not with her. Can't hurt her. And there's opportunities now — ID, travel itinerary, the van he was in. Matching his MO to other cases."

"The . . . the convoy analysis," she said, in a small voice. "There's likely more than one."

Barnes shrugged.

"I know."

"Jesus, how can you be so matter-of-fact about it all?" she said. "I would be going mad."

"It's my head that's going to find her. Not my heart."

She looked at him sideways.

"I'm not going to go to pieces," he said. "Besides—"

"Oh, shit!" she cried again. "I forgot."

She barrelled out of the room and returned a few minutes later clutching a sheaf of A4 prints of what looked like photographs.

"Look at this," she said. "Stills from footfall in a fifty-metre radius around ground zero. Ten minutes before and after the attack."

She rifled through them and then brought one to the top of the pile.

"Here."

She pointed at the grainy image. It had been taken from some distance, but still showed the intersection with Terminus Road and Seaside Road. The pavement was thronged with shoppers, and, in the top left corner, Barnes could make out his car at the junction with North Street.

He peered at the image and checked the time stamp. This was less than five minutes after the bodies started dropping.

"Bottom right. Trinity Trees, south pavement. Heading west."

Barnes looked — he couldn't see him.

And then he did.

Tall, slender, black shiny hair combed back. He was wearing a paramedic's uniform, but was otherwise, despite the low-res image, clearly the man Barnes had pursued into the airport.

Andrew Lau.

"Christ," he said. "That's him."

CHAPTER TWENTY-ONE

8 December

Barnes hedged his bets and, on balance, worked out it would be marginally quicker to walk over to Tesco to buy a toothbrush and a change of clothes than it would to go home and get them.

To offset what this ostensibly said about him, he sent another message to Tamsin:

I'm going to find her. I'm close. And she will be okay.

He couldn't promise all those things, but reasoned that Tamsin needed to hear it. If he turned out to be wrong, her world would be smashed to pieces anyway. What difference would a false promise make then, if she felt better in the moment?

Once he was slightly more presentable, he went into the office Gabby had commandeered from the Divisional Commander and waited for him.

Tina had made him a strong coffee and had then gone home, but he didn't need the pep now. He wasn't going to fall asleep.

Gabby walked in about quarter past six, in a deerstalker and some kind of ski jacket. He slowly pulled off his outerwear, his eyes fixed on Barnes, the corners of his mouth slowly curling downwards.

"They're connected," Barnes said. "It's incontrovertible. The chemical attack and my stepdaughter's abduction."

Barnes read the look: *Then this is all your fault.*

"And how did you arrive at that conclusion?" Gabby said, hanging up his hat. His freshly shaved head was pink all over.

"The same man took her from her school in an ambulance. He drove to the town centre, probably with her in it, did whatever he did with whatever chemical it was, and then tried to leave the country. He dumped the ambulance in plain sight — outside A&E five miles north of Gatwick, switched to a courier van, and was shot dead by TFU after he cleared customs."

He stood, and held out the printout of the CCTV still that Tina had given him.

"That's fact, sir."

Gabby didn't move, didn't make to sit or otherwise go about his day. He stood by the coat stand, his fists by his side. His shoulders seemed to relax a little.

"So, what does that mean, Barnes?"

"It means he's dead, and my stepdaughter is still missing. Convoy analysis suggests he was working with at least one other person. His body, his phone, the van, the ambulance — they all have some forensic potential. There are opportunities, but she's still out there."

"You do realise, Barnes, that the Home Office, the spooks, COBRA, CTC . . . they all want a piece of this. For all we know, this is a trigger event for another Cold War. State actors on UK soil. I'm lucky we've managed to keep our grubby little mitts on it. If that changes, and we get evicted from our own police station, then no one is going to call your stepdaughter anything other than collateral damage. An unfortunate citizen caught in an East–West crossfire."

"That's why I'm here."

"You're suggesting that the chemical attack is some sort of cover for kidnapping your child?"

"Her name is Maggie. But, yes, I am."

"That's a hell of a leap. It must mean there's someone out there that hates your guts even more than I do."

Barnes let that one go, acted like he hadn't heard it. To give Gabby credit, at least you knew where you stood with him.

"But it plays to the argument to keep it local," Barnes said. "If it's not espionage — just that someone wants it to look that way — then you can shift the focus over. The government are not going to be unhappy if you can say conclusively that it wasn't a foreign power at play."

"We can't say that for sure. Not yet. Not until we establish the identity of all the victims. And I mean their true identities. If one of those poor fuckers was in some kind of protection programme, then that changes everything back again. Agreed?"

"Agreed."

"Has the media linked the shooting at the airport with what happened in Eastbourne?"

"Not as far as I'm aware. It won't be long, though. I think you should front it up, too."

"Do you, now?" Gabby screwed up his face, like he was swilling a cup of cold, stale coffee around his mouth and trying to decide whether or not to swallow it.

"Please know, sir, that I am summoning considerable effort to remain calm and polite."

Gabby eyed him.

"So, does your incident room want to meet mine?"

Barnes chewed this over.

"No. If you assume every one of our staff is suggestible — which you should — then it's better to keep the two separate, for the sake of appearances. I just need some extra pairs of hands. Tina Guestling, for one."

"You should not be anywhere near it, much less running it."

"I'm not running it. Samson Kane is."

Gabby twitched, but he let it go.

"These forensic . . . opportunities. How soon can you get them back?"

"With your name on the submissions — and the cheque — twenty-four hours. Hopefully less."

Gabby thought about it.

"Maggie may not have twenty-four hours, sir."

"Okay, Barnes. Go do it."

* * *

Barnes called Kane's mobile, then, when he heard the tinny ringtone of "Bulls on Parade" he walked down the corridor to find him.

He was in the main Op Element incident room talking earnestly to a couple of the night detectives, who were about to head off.

"Op Element. Funny," Barnes said.

Kane looked up.

"You're still here."

"I'm going home. See Tamsin and Ellie."

"Does that mean—"

"I fronted Gabby. He's not happy, but Tina — God love her — has proved the link. He's accepted the connection. I've told him you're running it. He doesn't want me anywhere near it."

"I already said that."

"Priorities?"

"ID the second suspect. ID Andrew Lau's movements, including, ideally, where he was laying his head. Find his phone. Forensic harvest to maximise likelihood of finding Maggie. Priority submissions. Rapid turnaround. Origins of his paperwork — passport and the like. PolSA-led searches of the airport and site of the ambulance fire. Media appeal. Intel, intel, intel. That about it?"

"More or less. Gabby won't sign off on the media, though."

Kane inched forward.

"I don't give a shit. If it costs me my job, I don't care. Unless you tell me no."

"You decide," Barnes said. "Pros and cons."

"You put fingertip line searches in a field next to a burnt-out ambo, the hacks will be ringing off the hook anyway. May as well get on the front foot."

"You get something, you call me."

"I will. Get some sleep. Hug your family. I'll call you."

CHAPTER TWENTY-TWO

Maggie was tired. She didn't know where she was. Some kind of cupboard maybe. It was dark, but there was a crack of light under the door. She was cold, and her legs and feet were sore, but at least she'd been given some food. She didn't know who had given it to her, or when, and it wasn't very nice, but she figured that it was . . . something.

She didn't know how long she'd been here, or how long she was going to be here. How this was going to end, or when.

When she ran from the man, she felt strong. Her mind felt strong. She didn't know that then, but now her brain felt like porridge, and she kept wanting to fall asleep. She felt like she should be sad or scared, but she wasn't. She should be trying to work out a way out of this place. She did it before, and she could do it again. She should be listening for clues, testing the door, screaming for help. But she couldn't summon the energy. She just felt . . . dull.

* * *

Barnes pulled onto the driveway. The tyres crunched on the gravel. The street was otherwise unremarkable. Quiet. Elderly neighbours hidden away behind net curtains. Bins left out for collection. Decaying autumn leaves backed up into the corner wind pockets of driveways that needed weeding.

Ellie, in a crumpled school uniform, looked tired and confused. Disrupted. Tamsin, in a grey hoody and pyjama bottoms, looked blank, empty, but that edge was still apparent. The steel. There was still fight there. She still believed.

In a parallel universe — another home, another set of circumstances, another woman — he might have expected the full force of despair and wrath at his absence during a time when she needed him most.

But he had given his party line — that if he wasn't the one actively trying to find Maggie, then she would slide to the bottom of a pile whose order was controlled by someone like Gabby. And Tamsin knew all about someones like Gabby.

That was his line, and she accepted it.

She didn't blame him.

But he did.

If someone had used a chemical spill as a cover to abduct a child, then it was because of him.

If he had not got together with Tamsin, this would not have happened.

It was his fault.

That's what this meant, right?

She reached out a hand to him as he walked up the driveway, and led him into the house.

Barnes went into the lounge. They'd put the Christmas tree up pretty early this year. There were stacks of presents in shiny wrapping underneath it, but the lights were off. Barnes could barely bring himself to look at it.

Tamsin boiled the kettle and made tea for them all, and then, when he stood as she brought the mugs in, she saw him looking at the tree and sort of collapsed into his arms. Ellie watched, worried; the tea spilled down Barnes's trouser legs as he caught her.

He absorbed the pain of the scald. Didn't cry out or flinch. Just quietly held Tamsin and gently lowered her onto the sofa next to him. Maggie was suffering. Why shouldn't he?

After five minutes or so, she got herself together, and pulled both Barnes and Ellie towards her until they were all wedged together on the sofa like some sort of nursery rhyme where the person on the end falls off.

As is often the case in such scenarios, Barnes mused, the conversation was utilitarian. Emotion, blame, raw despair would come later.

Inevitable.

"You guys had something to eat?" he said.

"Domino's for dinner. There's some left." Her voice was almost a whisper, like she'd used it for screaming and not much else in the last twenty-four hours.

"Thanks. I'm all pizza'd out. Want me to order ice cream?"

He smiled. It was nearly eight in the morning. Ellie and Tamsin both shook their heads. He stroked Ellie's hair.

"You going to school, poppet? Still got time."

"I don't want to," she said, in a tiny voice. "Mummy will be lonely."

"Fair enough."

"How come you're home?" Tamsin said.

"Gabby finally listened to me. Kane's running it. He's stood up a full operation."

"How did that come about?" she asked, in a flat tone, like she already knew the answer.

He looked her straight in the eye.

"The incident in the town centre. It's linked to Maggie's disappearance."

"You mean kidnap, Barnes. She hasn't disappeared." Her tone was brittle.

"Yes, you're right. Kidnap."

"The police are calling it a kidnap, yes? Not just you? They're not going to suggest she's just playing a particularly long game of hide-and-seek?"

"Samson's leading it. I trust him. They — we — are doing everything. We'll find her."

She didn't reply. He continued.

"There's a link. The person that took her is the same one that released the chemical in town."

"I read about that. Six dead? Why would somebody do something like that?"

"I wish I knew."

"Was he just on some kind of fucking bender? Was she exposed to that shit? Sorry, Ellie. Cover your ears."

"I don't know the answer to that. Yet," he added.

"Was she chosen specifically? Or wrong place, wrong time?"

"I don't know that, either."

"You don't know much, do you?" It was out of her mouth, he knew, before she could stop it, and it was the first time he fully considered that, as a burgeoning family unit, they might not survive this ordeal. Especially if it turned out that he — his job, his seemingly endless stream of emotional baggage — was the common denominator. He stared again at the dull, lifeless Christmas tree.

"I'm sorry," she said, her eyes closed. "What happened to the suspect?"

He looked briefly at Ellie, then back at Tamsin.

"He's dead."

Tamsin's hands flew to her mouth, and an involuntary noise escaped her, somewhere between a sob and a gasp.

"He's dead," she said. "Dead how? Did you . . ."

"Shot by armed police."

"Was he the only one that knows where she is?"

"Maybe, but unlikely. We have his papers, his van, and it's just a matter of time before we find his phone. These all give us leads that we didn't have before. He had help too."

"Help?"

"To steal the ambulance and the courier van. There's a second suspect."

"Oh, God."

"We'll find her. And she will be fine. I promise."

She looked him dead in the eye, but didn't say anything.

"She will. The signs point to a reasonably organised operation. Not opportunistic. Not necessarily sexually motivated . . ."

"Oh, Jesus Christ."

". . . Not revenge or a precursor to self-righteous familicide. It's not inconceivable that we could receive a ransom demand."

She covered her face with her hands.

"You might . . . could you turn your detective switch off, just for ten minutes? It's bad enough when I think these things, but hearing them is worse."

Barnes stood.

"I have to go back. I can't just sit here."

"Stay," she said, squeezing his hand. "Just for a while."

"I'll be back."

"I . . . I've had to tell their father."

Barnes turned in the doorway. This, too, was something else that had been inevitable.

"How did that go?"

"As well as expected."

"Okay. I'll be back later. I'll call you. Try to get some sleep. Can your mum come over?"

"She's been over most of the night. She's coming back later."

"She tell you that you should have married a chartered surveyor?"

"She actually told me I should lay off men altogether, but that women are no less hassle."

He hissed a chuckle, then kissed them both. Tamsin whispered in his ear, "*Find my girl. Don't pay attention to me. I'm railing at the world,*" and then Ellie jumped up and threw her arms around him. He could feel her tears on his neck, and her little shoulders shook as he held her.

CHAPTER TWENTY-THREE

Tina appeared at the man's shoulder, placed a paper coaster onto the baize and gently set down the cocktail glass.

"Thank you, love," the man mumbled, looking back over his shoulder at her cleavage and knocking over his small pile of chips in so doing. He had a head like a boulder and the stink of liquor and Old Spice rose off him in waves. "Why don't you come join me? I need a little luck."

You need more than that, Tina thought. She smiled sweetly at him.

"Duty calls, I'm afraid," she said, gliding away to the bar, where the next order awaited her.

Whether they were on a winning streak, or the house was about to eat them whole, it didn't seem to matter. They wanted a kiss for luck, they wanted to give her a sob story, or they wanted her to sit on their laps and talk about whatever popped up.

She wanted to tell them that after nine more months of study she would have her PhD and wouldn't need this job anymore. Not that it would make much difference in this place. "That's nice, love," is what she would get. Except it wouldn't be "Love", any longer, it would be "Dr Love".

She couldn't complain. If it was that bad, she could have left. She could have gone and got a part-time night job in Tesco, rather than a casino. Nicky had said as much. Put up with it or ship out. The pay was good, it would get rid of the student loan in no time and it fitted — despite her DI's initial reservations — around her day job. Intelligence analyst by day, glamorous cocktail waitress by night.

And doctor in waiting, she thought, as she loaded martini glasses onto her tray.

The place was never quiet, but for a weeknight it was unusually busy, and, by the end of her shift, she was exhausted. Just for a moment she wondered if she was possibly overdoing the whole burning-the-candle-at-both-ends thing.

Who are you kidding? she thought as she pulled on her coat. *My candle has been a melted puddle of mess for months now.* The place was largely empty now except for the most desperate diehards, and she wrote her lonely hearts ad in her head as she marched across the gaming floor: *Knackered, academically minded single mum holding down two jobs while waiting for drink-driving ban to lapse. Seeks like-minded loser with own teeth.*

The tiredness hit her properly as she stepped out into the fresh air. Unlike the casino, Tesco didn't, as far as she knew, pump oxygen in through the vents twenty-four-seven to keep the punters from fading — so maybe she should stop fretting about her lot.

Her heart sank at the prospect of the night bus. A taxi would cost a bomb, but it would be worth it to get home in relative comfort. For a brief, ridiculous moment she thought about walking, and as her tired brain refused to settle on a sensible decision, she saw the familiar faulty brake light of the Corsa and her heart leaped.

"What are you doing here?" Tina said as she opened the passenger door. "It's three in the morning!"

"Hello to you too, Mum," Nicky said. "I figured you could use a lift."

"You're very naughty. You should be in bed. You've got exams coming up."

"So have you," Nicky smiled. "And besides . . ."

Tina leaned over and hugged her daughter.

"I'm so pleased to see you. God, thank you so much," she said, reclining the seat. "I think I would have cried if I'd had to get on that bloody night bus. You're still naughty, though."

Nicky released the handbrake and they headed out of the marina.

"I worked out that you should get your licence back about the same time as your graduation ceremony," Nicky said. "You're nearly there, Mum."

All she got in response was her mother gently snoring in the passenger seat.

* * *

Tina dreamed. She was in a speeding car on the motorway. She was in the driving seat, but the steering wheel didn't work, nor did the brakes. Nicky was in the back, laughing as she slid from side to side with the momentum of the car, having too much fun to put on her seat belt, despite Tina's pleas. The car veered from lane to lane, narrowly missing car after car, before going into a skid and heading straight for the solid metal of the central reservation. Tina screamed, but nothing came out.

She woke up suddenly, her heart pounding, sweat matting her hair, and realised her buzzsaw alarm was blaring.

She sat on the bed for a moment, trying to calm her breathing, even as the faint snatches of the dream faded away.

This wouldn't do, she thought as she showered under a steaming blast of water. Nobody could function properly on three hours' sleep. It was such a blessed relief that Nicky was so independent, or Tina would have performed a good impression of a combustion engine having a meltdown.

Work was part of the problem. Generally, her work was methodical, quiet and ordered. She conducted research, extrapolated patterns and submitted reports.

Generally.

Like anyone working the police, however, when the shit hit the fan, everyone felt it. In her career to date, she'd endured only a handful of major incidents, but this was something completely different to anything she was used to.

Her mind turned to the DI with the big eyes. Barnes. Half mad with worry, blamed for a dead DC and unable to get anything resembling traction from anyone on the inside for the enquiry into his missing stepdaughter.

Policing was made up of a network of tightly woven rules. There wasn't a lot of room to move outside those rules; in the aftermath of a couple of bad *Daily Mail* headlines, they wound together even tighter.

But DI Barnes seemed to need help, and no one was willing to give it. He was a parent, like Tina. She could imagine how she would be feeling in the same position. If someone had taken Nicky. Jesus, she'd be screaming from the rooftops. She wasn't quite sure how DI Barnes had managed to keep his composure.

Tina stepped out of the shower. She knew she shouldn't make decisions when tired. For Tina, being exhausted was a little like being drunk. She tended to be less inhibited. Less inclined to check herself before giving her honest opinion. More inclined to swear.

More inclined to think, *To hell with it.*

CHAPTER TWENTY-FOUR

The steady chirp and flashing amber lights of the bin lorry woke him. Barnes took a moment to come to, having woken from a dream about being pursued by a particularly savage police dog. The three of them were still crammed together on the sofa, half under a throw.

He looked at his watch. Nearly lunchtime. He carefully snuck out from where Ellie's legs were resting on his lap. Neither she nor her mother stirred, and Barnes was glad he'd been persuaded to stay a little longer. Tamsin's eyes were tightly shut, her breathing deep, her brow knotted in a frown.

He cleaned his teeth and changed his shirt, and then headed out, peering in the living room as he went. Nothing. Fast asleep.

He made for the door, and then, for reasons he couldn't immediately articulate, he entered the living room and switched on the Christmas tree lights.

Their relationship might not survive, he mused. But they hadn't fallen asleep until he got home.

* * *

He drove to the station. There were thin curls of snow pushed to the verges, sitting atop cold muddy grass like clumps of hair mousse. The December sky was like a sheet of iron.

The few hours he'd been asleep seemed to have passed in a heartbeat. He checked his phone — three missed calls, all Kane.

"Shit," he said, calling back.

"Finally," Kane said when he answered.

"What have you got?"

"Partial lift from the front cover of Andrew Lau's passport."

Adrenaline, like he'd been shot in the heart. The edges of desperation now.

"Good enough for an ident?"

"Maybe. We're fast-tracking the submission through NAFIS."

"How long?"

"Hours, not days. We've run DNA samples from the body up to the lab for work too. Dental will take longer."

"Okay."

"You know a PC called Adrian Willow?"

"Yes, why?"

"He personally insisted on taking the samples to the lab himself, on a blue-light run. That's not a short journey."

"Did he, now?" Barnes said, quietly.

"That means either it's an inside job and he wanted to make sure all the samples went in the sea, or he cares very much about finding your daughter."

"Let's both hope it's the latter."

"Don't overthink it. See you when you get here."

Barnes switched on the radio. There was talk of the chemical incident in Eastbourne, but it hadn't caught in the way Barnes had been expecting. It wasn't even the lead story — there was as much coverage being given to some cyclone inbound from the Netherlands, the death of Nelson Mandela and Australia creaming the English in the winter Ashes.

There was no mention of Maggie.

On balance, Barnes preferred it this way. Otherwise, whoever had her might panic and do something rash. The more eyes the better, but, in Barnes's view, relying too much on a public appeal made it look like there was nothing else in their toolbox. He wasn't sure Tamsin would see it that way.

There was a second suspect. That was a given. If there wasn't, then, yes, go hell for leather on the newspapers. But they had a lead.

Kane met him in the incident room.

"Anything?"

"Nothing yet. Soon on the fingerprint."

"What about the media? CRA?"

"I don't think we know enough yet. We'll get a boatload of calls, most of which will be duff. If we didn't have a second suspect, I'd say yes — in and around the hospital where we found the ambulance. But we do, and, as of right now, she could be anywhere. Likely somewhere between Eastbourne and Gatwick, but anywhere."

Barnes turned. Two display boards on wheels had been joined together, and now formed the centrepiece of their unofficial incident room. A long sheet of A1 paper stretched across the boards, with a tube stop line running from one end to the other, CCTV stills and other images posted at key points along the line.

The last eighteen inches or so were empty. *A story they didn't yet know the end to*, Barnes thought.

Tina bustled into the room, engrossed in a bunch of printouts. She looked up and stopped suddenly when she saw Barnes.

"Oh . . . hi," she said. "I see you found the timeline."

Barnes touched the paper.

"You got her on CCTV," he murmured.

The image was grainy, taken from some low-end private installation from one of the apartment buildings close to the school.

The quality was poor, but, taken from behind them, it showed a man and a small girl, walking hand in hand along the pavement. The man had dark hair and seemed to be in some kind of tracksuit, while the child was clearly in a school uniform.

He considered. Why would she hold his hand? She was smart, switched on, knew about stranger danger and all that stuff.

He shook his head. Children with no deep-seated reason to do otherwise just trusted, he figured. Just did as they were told, especially if the one doing the telling was an authority figure.

He felt the anger bubbling up again. Tina looked awkward, like she hadn't meant him to see the graphic.

Kane's phone rang, puncturing the loaded silence.

"Superintendent Kane. Yes, hi, Brian. Uh-huh, yes . . ."

He eyeballed Barnes, wedged the phone under his jaw and grabbed a piece of paper and a pen.

"Yes, go on. Okay. No, I just need the name. We can do the rest, unless . . . do you have the last address in front of you? Okay, yes, go on . . ."

He scribbled on the paper, then carried it over to his laptop and copied whatever was on the paper into the machine.

"No, that's great. Thanks, Brian," Kane said. "Call me later about the other bits."

He ended the call and then lifted up the laptop to show Barnes.

"Get your jacket," he said. "That was the CSM. Ident on the partial. Callum King, twenty-three years old, 12 Azalea Drive, Maidenbower. Not good enough for court, but enough to shake the tree."

Barnes looked at the map of the address on the screen, every hair on his body standing up.

"You know what this means?" he said.

"Yeah," Kane said. "It means we're going back to sodding Crawley."

* * *

Crawley meant another hour-plus in the car with the sirens and lights on, every single conceivable emotion racing through Barnes as they drove — fear, hope, anticipation,

138

dread, anxiety. Most of all was the sense that, one way or another, this was *it* — and trying to hedge his bets against disappointment, being back to square one, or worse. The desperation was borne as much from his brittle sense of foreboding as the fact it was already getting on for mid-afternoon in December, and he didn't think he — much less Tamsin — could go another night of knowing Maggie was still *out there*.

Tina ran intelligence checks back at the factory, and kept Kane updated by phone.

"From what Tina describes on the system checks, it's some kind of flophouse. Bail hostel or something. King is a resident."

"What's his profile?"

"Nothing that leaps out. Petty theft, drugs possession, FTA, handling, burglary, some minor aggravation on arrest."

"Employment?"

"She's working on that. Nothing on the system. He's not long out of prison, so she's trying to get hold of his probation officer."

"Sounds like a typical bottom-feeder," Barnes said. There was a blast of winter sun through the windscreen as they dipped into and then ascended Handcross Hill and passed the weighbridge, flanked on both sides by Mid Sussex firs and acres of National Trust gardens.

"Couple of ARVs have put a discreet containment on. Uniform patrols have closed the road at either end," Kane said, looking up from his radio.

"What is this place?" Barnes said.

"Not completely sure," Kane said. "From how they're describing it, it sounds like a largeish bungalow in a cul-de-sac full of retired couples with prize-winning rose bushes. Seems a bit odd to me."

Barnes was minded to agree. They headed straight through a neat, largely deserted, new-build industrial park south-west of the airport, which, in turn — and to Barnes's surprise — led onto a new residential development which was so neat, new and tidy that it looked like a model village, with green plastic Lego squares for front gardens. A row of pines rose up behind them, the motorway on the other side, and Barnes realised they had doubled back on themselves.

They showed ID to get through the roadblock, parked at the end of the driveway and got out of the car. Barnes noticed one ARV, but not the other.

He had thought the "flophouse" description was erroneous, but no — there it was. A sprawling bungalow at the end of a short cul-de-sac was flanked by two smaller ones — the ones with the rose bushes — and Barnes wondered what horrible turn of events had led to it being placed here.

There was a low thumping bassline being played at high volume from somewhere inside. There were two abandoned washing machines, a mattress and a motorcycle with no wheels on the front driveway. The bike was leaking oil onto the tarmac, and the grass hadn't been cut in months. Two of the windows had been smashed, and an invisible cloud of pungent cannabis stink enveloped the whole place.

Barnes turned back to the houses with the rose bushes and wondered what they had done to deserve it. Nothing like a bail hostel falling out of the sky to shave a couple of years off your retirement.

"Containment is on," Kane said, in a low voice. "How you want to play this? We don't have a warrant."

"I'm going to knock on the bloody door," Barnes said, and marched up the driveway.

There was no answer at the front door, which, apart from a crudely sprayed tag across the timber, was in reasonably good order. Barnes looked left and right, and realised that it was a kind of chalet, with two wings and at least eight bedrooms.

"Get Tina back on the phone," he hissed at Kane. "See if this King has got a room number."

He gave the door a bump with his shoulder, and it popped open. They went into a dark hallway where the smell of damp and cannabis was stronger. The music was louder now, but there were no signs of any people.

Opposite the hallway was a small kitchen area; the hall then split into a "T" and led away into the two wings, each with rooms leading off them. To their right was a small room that was once, Barnes presumed, the entrance cloakroom. Now, the presence of an old inkjet printer, glass screen and desk phone suggested it was being used as some kind of administrative office. There was no one in it.

"Room six," Kane whispered.

Barnes inched forward, then stalked down the left-hand corridor and started hammering on all the doors.

"Callum King!" he roared. "Police. Get your arse out here before I set fire to the place."

A couple of sleepy, curious heads emerged to see what all the ruckus was, and then went back to bed.

Barnes walked down to the end of the corridor. There was a communal lounge in pea green at the opposite end with a broken TV and an overflowing ashtray. The carpet was surprisingly soft underfoot; he hoped that wasn't because it was soaked through.

He bashed at the door of room six.

"You've got ten seconds, Callum King, and then I'm kicking the door in."

After five seconds, Barnes shouldered it open. He found himself in a single room with a dirty-looking bed, a small wardrobe — and a pair of denim-clad legs dangling out of the sash window.

Barnes made a flailing grab and came back with a handful of cloth, but no Callum.

He grabbed his radio.

"Runner! He's gone out the back window, round to the . . . east. White male, jeans, white T-shirt. Someone grab him."

"Got him, boss," a cheerful voice said. "Helps that there's only one floor."

Barnes heard shouts and protests coming over the air. They met the ARV crew out the front, who — with one hand only, each — were controlling and restraining a struggling Callum King.

"Hold him there a minute," Barnes said. He held up an exhibit bag with Andrew Lau's passport in it.

"Lawyer," Callum said. "Not speaking."

Barnes squatted down to his level.

"This passport has your fingerprint on it," he said.

"Bullshit. Says you. Fucking let go of me!" Callum said, wriggling. "Prove it."

Barnes frowned.

"Callum, please think about this. If you don't cooperate, you are in a whole heap of shit."

"What do you mean?"

Barnes brought up a printout of the passport's photo page, copied before the exhibit bag was sealed.

"The passport belongs to this man. He's implicated in an attack down in Eastbourne that killed six people, and the abduction of a seven-year-old girl who is still missing."

"Well, why don't you fucking ask him instead of me?"

"He's dead." Barnes leaned in. "We killed him."

That got Callum's attention. And the ARV crew's, come to that.

Barnes straightened up.

"What do you know about boosting — sorry, I mean *driving* — courier vans, Callum?"

Callum stopped struggling and he went from loud protests to looking extraordinarily shifty. Barnes could practically see his brain racing as he tried to work out exactly what he'd done, what the detectives knew and how much he could impart without implicating himself. He wondered if the man realised just how much he was giving away.

"I'll ask you again . . ."

"Okay, look. There was a new guy. In the, you know . . ." He jerked his head towards the bungalow.

"He's not your usual type. Looked pretty well-dressed. So, I might have had a peek around his place one day while he was out. Might have picked up his passport. I put it down again. Then I left. I didn't take anything."

Callum folded his arms: *that's all you're getting from me.*

142

Barnes looked at him and shook his head, inwardly fascinated by the logic. The man thought that half an admission to burglary gave his story a sheen of unyielding credibility.

Maybe he was right to do so.

"What room was he in?"

"Three."

Kane was already on his radio, asking for more units to help search.

"What shall we do with him, boss?" one of the armed officers said, pointing at Callum. "Is he under arrest?"

Callum's eyes widened, apparently gearing himself up for more righteous indignation.

Kane's phone answered the question for him. The conversation was hushed and rapid.

He hung up, and leaned in towards Barnes.

"Tina. She said chummy here got a part-time cleaning job with an agency as part of his licence conditions. Tina's spoken to the agency. They're based here in Crawley. One of the clients is DHL. Their Gatwick hub."

Barnes looked at the ARV crew.

"Cuff him."

They did as bidden. At the sound of the metal bracelets being ratcheted, Callum flew into a rage, which was quickly extinguished by the ARV crew as they laid him prone.

"I haven't done anything!" he screamed. "I helped you! What am I under arrest for?"

Kane squatted down on one knee.

"Theft of a motor vehicle and conspiracy to abduct a child," he said quietly.

A double-crewed unit turned up a few minutes later and bussed Callum off to custody, leaving Barnes, Kane and the ARV crew to go and boot the door to room three open.

They paused outside the door. Barnes and Kane stood shoulder to shoulder.

"No warrant," Kane said. His eyes were fixed on the door.

"The occupier's dead. It's not like the case against him can be thrown out," Barnes said.

He planted a boot against the door and it sprang open, crashing against the wall behind it.

They stood for a moment on the threshold, Barnes scanning for any obvious booby traps.

Nothing jumped out as being out of the ordinary. It was much like Callum's — single bed, wardrobe, fitted shelving unit — only neater, tidier and with fewer belongings.

Kane stepped in and scanned the surroundings. He checked the wardrobe, then looked behind the door.

"Ensuite," he remarked. "These people really fell on their feet, didn't they? Room service too, no doubt."

Kane poked his head in the bathroom and checked the shower cubicle. He held Barnes's eye when he emerged.

No Maggie.

"We need LSOs here," Barnes said. "It needs ripping up by a proper search team."

They didn't have to wait long. The effort required to convince Gabby that the case was deserving of official treatment had been time well spent.

Barnes left Kane to brief the LSOs and stepped outside.

He stood on the driveway and let the low winter sun momentarily warm his face. Two, three hours, it would be dark, and the monsters would come out again.

He was close. He could feel it. He had the second suspect. He would let Callum stew in his cell for half an hour or so, then get an interview into him. It was likely he knew nothing — Barnes theorised that Lau had offered the first roommate he found with car-thievery skills a chunk of money to help him steal a van and then an ambulance, but beyond that, nothing. If that was the case, then Callum would likely tell the truth. He was a stooge, a skivvy, the help. A nobody. Barnes would even let him walk out scot-free in exchange for information about Maggie — Kane might not like that, and nor would Gabby, but they could be persuaded.

He saw a wrinkled face with gloves and a watering can looking at him from one of the neighbouring gardens. He walked over, warrant card aloft.

"DI Barnes, CID."

"Are you finally shutting the place down?"

Barnes looked back at the hostel.

"You get much hassle?"

The man puckered his lips.

"They've made our life hell. It'll put my Mary in the ground before her time, you mark my words. Drinking, drugs, fighting, smashing things up. All hours of the day and night. We're scared. I haven't slept in months."

Barnes frowned.

"How long has it been here?"

"Five or so months. Five too many, if you ask me. It used to be a rest home, but the firm went under. It was up for sale for a while, then the government bought it."

"Government?"

"Yes. The people who look after prisons and the like."

"Ministry of Justice?"

"That's them. They held some kind of community meeting. We all went, and we told them what would happen. They pretended to listen, and then said, 'Well, they've got to go somewhere.' And that was that. Now everything that we said would happen has happened. I've written to them, told the local police, told my MP. Nothing's changed. I'm going to the papers next."

Even Barnes was perplexed. Why on earth would they put it here, of all places?

"The owner was pleased as punch, of course. He couldn't sell the place — too big for a family, but too small to do anything else with. No one wants a B&B on a retirement estate next to a motorway. It's on a dead end, no links to anywhere. Nothing to do. The government have buying power, so of course the sale went straight through. For a businessman, it's good — rooms, onsite management, solar, even a little garden. That's been decimated, of course. Lots of storage. Parking. Garage. Close to the airport, if such a thing would be useful to such people. Why can't they lock them up and throw away the key? It's not like . . ."

Barnes had more than a handful of sympathy for the man, but he turned away as the monologue continued.

Then he stopped.

Turned back.

"Storage? Did you say storage?"

The man frowned.

"Yes, storage. Quite a few around here have basements, which is pretty unusual. It's a bungalow, but the loft has been fitted and boarded throughout, so you could fit a small army up there . . ."

Barnes was off and running.

CHAPTER TWENTY-FIVE

He burst into the main corridor — attracting curious stares from Kane and the others — and found a large loft hatch in a small vestibule at the rear of the house. He reached up, pushed at it, and it clicked and slowly opened. A stair-case-cum-ladder slowly uncurled towards the floor; it was newly installed, and the wood smelled fresh.

He ascended the steps two at a time and found himself in darkness. He fumbled around in the gloom until his fingers settled on a small piece of hard plastic. He flicked the switch and ceiling-mounted LED strip lights came on with a low *click*. They were powerful, and reached all corners of the loft space.

Barnes pulled himself up. It had indeed been boarded end to end with new plywood, and was largely empty, apart from some rolls of unused loft insulation and a couple of cardboard boxes that, Barnes quickly discovered, were empty. The loft space was not partitioned, and ran the entire length of the building.

It was not quite high enough to stand up in, and Barnes shuffled along in a kind of running squat. He scanned the space and moved slowly through it, checking the corners and testing cross-beams and plasterboard walls for concealed spaces.

Halfway along he stopped and listened. Strained his ears for something.

Anything.

He got the muffled, low voices of the officers in Andrew Lau's room and, very faintly, the distant hiss of motorway traffic.

Nothing.

Nothing to hear, nothing to smell besides chipboard and the synthetic stink of the thick insulation's rough wool.

He climbed back down and started going room to room. The ones that were occupied were the subject of rapid searching, whether the occupants liked it or not, while the unoccupied rooms — only two, as it turned out, excluding Andrew Lau's — were unceremoniously entered and subjected to similarly perfunctory searches.

He did another circuit of the building, looking for exterior hatches and doors. He returned inside and checked the kitchenette, the staff office cubicle, a large cupboard that acted as a sort of cloakroom and the communal lounge.

He was just about to leave the lounge when he noticed a latched door in the corner, off to the left of the television. It was normal height, but narrow, and Barnes chalked it up to being a cleaning cupboard of sorts — ironing board, Henry hoover, that sort of thing.

He popped the latch and inhaled sharply. There was a staircase.

He'd found the basement.

There was no light switch that he could find, and he stepped carefully down, the boards creaking underfoot, the square of light above him gradually reducing in size.

At the bottom was another door, and he reached for the Maglite on his belt. It was flimsy, cheap plywood, and although it had a Yale lock, it was easily overcome.

It opened inwards to a rectangle of absolute black. A draught of cold air came out to greet him — musty, dank, laundry powder sludge.

And something else. He couldn't put a name to it, but it smelled like, like . . .

Like someone else was here.

Take hair, skin, bodily fluid, reduce it to a memory and lock it away, and it would smell like this.

He shone the Maglite around until he found the light switch. Unlike the loft, there was a single naked sixty-watt bulb suspended from the ceiling, barely making any dent in the darkness at all.

He stepped forward onto a cold, unfinished concrete floor. The room was about the size of a single garage plus a bit. There was a washing machine, dryer and chest freezer to his left, and, in the far corner on the right, a row of padlocked cupboards about four feet tall. The coloured labels on the front of each one suggested to him that this was the bin store. There was a further set of double doors over to his immediate right; again, they were about the same height, and from the tiny strip of daylight underneath, Barnes realised these led outside. God knew exactly where though — he'd checked the perimeter twice.

He made himself check the freezer first. There was nothing in it but frost and a family-size box of some very old fish fingers. Then the dryer, then the washing machine.

He shut his eyes, and strained to listen.

Maggie?

He wanted to call out, but if she thought he was the enemy . . .

"Maggie? It's me. It's Barnes."

Please be here.

Something. A scratching, shuffling sound. Mewing, or squeaking. Distress.

The padlocks were cheap, and Barnes's hefty Maglite was more than equal to the task.

The first one went with a pop. Inside was a large metal bin, filled with plastic and cardboard.

The second one — the same. Glass bottles and jars in this one.

The third — metal cans.

The fourth . . .

Darkness.

And the smell — unwashed skin, matted hair, ketones on the breath of someone poorly fed and dehydrated. Urine on the cold concrete ground.

Barnes saw the plate with crumbs on, and the plastic buckets side by side.

And eyes, gleaming in the darkness at the back of the cupboard.

"Maggie? It's me, Barnes." He made his voice as soft and soothing as he'd ever made it, fighting to keep it steady. "It's okay, baby. I found you. You're safe now. Come out. I'll take you to your mummy."

Slow breathing in the darkness.

"No one can hurt you, honey. The bad men are gone. Come on, sweetheart."

Barnes could feel his chest about to burst with unending, unimaginable relief, joy, sheer exhaustion. He reached out, and then, slowly, ever so slowly, a small, pink, grubby hand reached out of the gloom to meet his.

CHAPTER TWENTY-SIX

Barnes watched Maggie through the glass as she slept. Tamsin and Ellie were next to her, on a cot that the nursing staff had wheeled in to be next to Maggie's bed. The soft, rhythmic chirps of the various machines were reassuring in their steadiness.

Mercifully, the physical damage was minimal, but every so often Maggie would twitch, or a frown would cross her face, and Barnes wondered what demons would yet lurk for her. Now she was able to touch her daughter's hand as they slept, Tamsin's face was relaxed, untroubled, in stark contrast to the fitful rest she had endured less than twenty-four hours ago.

"She looks peaceful."

Barnes turned. He pegged the man as a cop straightaway. It wasn't obvious — in terms of physical stereotypes, Barnes would have gone with accountant or something — but it was something in the eyes, the way they seemed to regard the world.

The man extended a hand.

"Graham Wall. I can't tell you how grateful I am to you for rescuing my daughter."

Barnes slowly returned the shake, recognising the man from photos on the girls' bookshelves. Encountering the ex was an anticipated — if not especially welcome — by-product of recent events. It tended to happen; you'd be bimbling along quite happily in your own little world, then you want to go on holiday, or Auntie Beryl dies, or your kid falls off the swing, and then the doors to that world open by default.

Barnes forced himself to take the man at face value. They'd not met before, and his opinions to date were based on what Tamsin had told him and the snippets of the odd telephone conversation he had overheard. The girls spoke reasonably fondly of him, however; they toddled off to weekend visits without complaint, and tended to return in similarly upbeat frames of mind.

"You're welcome," Barnes said, eventually.

"Seems she isn't badly hurt. We can be thankful for that."

Barnes nodded. He tried to place the accent — an edge of Manchester, maybe.

"She's dehydrated, and hasn't eaten. She's got cuts and grazes, as well as some skin damage from . . . from where she had to go to the toilet. But besides that . . ."

"Why would anyone want to do this?" Graham Wall said, shaking his head. He looked at Barnes, rather than Maggie, as he asked this.

"People do bad things," Barnes offered. "You — we — know that better than most."

"But why her particularly?" Graham turned to look at Maggie again. "It could have been any one of a number of children. Why her?"

He screwed his eyes shut, pinched the bridge of his nose and bowed his head. Barnes thought momentarily about placing a reassuring hand on the man's shoulder, then opted not to. It was, he found, not a hard decision to make.

Graham composed himself after a moment or two.

"Well, I imagine you must be busy. With the investigation, I mean."

"Strictly speaking, I'm not part of the investigation. Standard practice when there's a crime involving one of your family. You know how it is."

He held Graham's gaze on the word *family*.

"Nevertheless," Graham said. "How is it looking? The investigation, I mean. Now she's been found."

"As I say, not really my place. The SIO will update Tamsin soon, I'm sure."

"Well, hopefully they can speak to us both at the same time. Save delivering it twice."

Barnes tried to dial it back down to small talk.

"Where did you serve?" he asked. "Metpol, am I right?"

Graham gave a thin smile.

"Some and some. But yes, indeed. Happily retired now, thank goodness. The commute was an absolute killer. Hardly ever home. Likely contributed to . . ." He pointed at Tamsin through the glass, then back at himself, and then repeated the motion.

"Were you CID?"

"I dipped my toe in a few pools. I did work CID for a time. Did my stint on uniform. Carried a weapon briefly. But I seemed to find my niche with digital forensics. It's a growth industry, you know."

"And a neat segue into a career in civvy street, I imagine."

Graham shrugged and smiled. Given that, to his own ears, Barnes's subtle attempts at small talk had sounded anything but, the man seemed to remain remarkably gracious.

"Well, look, we must let her rest. I'm going to head off and hopefully catch up with Tamsin and the SIO later," Graham said. "Do let me know if you want to sit in on that meeting."

Barnes bristled, but he kept it hidden. Fair play to Wall. He got the last word, and the smile hadn't slipped.

"I'm really sorry to be finally meeting you under such circumstances," Graham continued, extending a hand again. "Thank you again for rescuing my daughter alive and well. You can imagine it's some relief to know that your beloved children are in —" Graham paused, as if searching for the right words — "*safe* hands."

Barnes returned the shake but didn't say anything. He watched Graham glide away down the corridor and out of the ward, the sound of chirping and beeping machines suddenly loud in his head.

* * *

He caught up with Tamsin a couple of hours later. She was in the ward lounge, arguing with a vending machine over a Kit-Kat and a plastic beaker of coffee.

"Tam."

She turned and gave him a smile he didn't think he'd ever see again. His insides felt like he'd just reached the surface of the sea and broken through into glorious salty air after hours underwater in the darkness.

"Any other time, I'd be putting this machine in a headlock," she said, sliding her arms around his shoulders. "But it's just a joy to have only that to worry about."

"Where's Ellie?" he asked.

"Mum's just arrived. She's reading them both a story. Maggie's still asleep. I tell you, Barnes, I'll never let either of them out of my sight ever again."

He nodded.

"How are you doing?" he asked. "Genuine question."

She sat down on a puffy, pea-green sofa and thought about it.

"You know, I feel guilty," she said. "I came so close to losing her in the worst way imaginable. And there are parents out there who have had to endure the same, only their stories ended the wrong way, and they live with that for ever. We came close to it, but we might actually be able to get back to some kind of normal life at some point. And it's all thanks to you. You're my sodding hero, Barnes."

She kissed him on the cheek.

Before he could stop it, he thought, *And if you hadn't met me, it wouldn't have happened at all.*

"I met Graham," he said.

She gave him a sour look.

"I shouldn't complain," she said. "If he hadn't visited, I'd have been chuntering about how he doesn't give a shit. Now he's here, I'd rather he wasn't. No pleasing some people."

She smiled.

"You're only human," Barnes said. "Exes are exes for a reason. He was pleasant to me. Pleasant enough, anyway."

"So what now?" she said. "One of the fuckers is dead, the other is in the cells, right?"

"Pretty much. He's been interviewed. Reckons our main guy — the dead one — paid him to steal the courier van, help him steal an ambulance, and that's all he knew. He didn't know why, and he didn't ask. Reckons if he had known why, he'd have said no and then called us. Gave us some high-horse stuff about having a child of his own."

"And you believe that?"

"Honestly? It's probably not a million miles from the truth. It makes sense that he would be given plausible denia-bility, if for no other reason than he would have put his prices up if he'd known all of it.

"But there's a bit of work to do, yet. Need to cross-check his version of events with his phone, computer, stuff found at the scene, that kind of thing."

"And the dead one? What was he, some kind of paedophile?"

Barnes swallowed.

"We don't know yet. Lots to do. And now she's been found, I'm kind of out of it. I'll see Samson later, get an update."

She leaned her head on his shoulder.

"Let's get away," she said. "Paris or something. Take the girls out of school. Put my mum in an adjoining room so we can go out for dinner. Get her to take the girls on a day trip so I can thank you properly."

"Sounds nice," he said.

"I don't care," she said. "Even if you take a fortnight off and we spend the whole time on the sofa with boxsets. It doesn't matter. She's safe now. *We're* safe."

CHAPTER TWENTY-SEVEN

"He's a ghost."

Barnes and Kane were sitting in a low-ceilinged smugglers' pub dating back to the sixteenth century. It had solid oak beams and a thatched roof, and was tucked well away in the depths of the Arlington countryside. There was a fire going and the smell of burning wood helped Barnes unwind a bit — that is, until Kane opened his mouth.

"Ghost?"

"PNC, PND, local systems — no trace. No trace NAFIS, no trace NDNAD. Dental's coming back via Interpol, but nothing yet. It's a slim hope. Same for the passport — it's likely he's used fraudulently obtained documents to get hold of a genuine passport, as opposed to being a black market fake. Callum King did most of his local recon work."

Barnes exhaled heavily.

"Things that point away from it being opportunistic, or driven by some kind of sexual motivation: one, the total absence of footprint. Two, the polymer gun. Three, we found a phone — unregistered pay-as-you-go, naturally — and cash in his room. Multiple currencies. No other devices. The ambulance fire was low-sophistication, but that could have been because it wasn't planned."

"He'd have vanished completely," Barnes murmured. "She could have died in that cupboard."

"But she didn't. And we don't think that was Plan A. He only bolted for the airport because we were on his heels. He cut his losses. If he'd thought he was home and dry, he'd have—"

"He'd have what?"

"Well, that's the point. We don't know. We don't know what the endgame was. Ransom, maybe? To all intents and purposes, he's a gun for hire, which means there was another phase that never got to play out."

"So what *do* you have?"

"We're trying to trace the sale of the burner. There might be CCTV. Still waiting on dental, as I say. The NCA have been asked to play around with facial recognition, but that's very much an embryonic technology. All very much a long shot.

"The more encouraging lines of enquiry are his room in the bail hostel — how did he come to be there? He'd have had some kind of legend, which could present some opportunities — that is, if the MoJ play ball before the turn of the century.

"The other is Callum King. He's been charged with various offences and remanded in custody. He was on licence, so he's going to be recalled to serve the rest of his sentence. He's none too happy about that, so I'm going to offer him a pass on the charges in exchange for everything he knows."

Barnes shook his head.

"If he knows anything."

Kane shrugged: *We've got to try.*

Barnes sat forward.

"If he was a gun for hire — and I'm not seeing any other theories that get anywhere close to that one — then who hired him? And why? And what does it have to do with the attack in Eastbourne?"

"Those are the three sixty-four-thousand-dollar questions at the moment. Unfortunately, and as you can imagine, Gabby isn't too keen to entertain them."

Barnes fought to keep calm.

"Tamsin wants to go to Paris."

"That's a good idea."

"She thinks she's dodged a bullet, God's smiled on her, and everything's rosy again."

"She's not far wrong."

"My point is — what if there are more bullets?"

"I'm working on it, Barnes. I'll get you some protection. Discreetly, of course. We don't really want her to think there's an ongoing threat."

"You think?"

Barnes shut his eyes and took a deep breath.

"I'm sorry, Samson."

"Want another beer?"

Barnes nodded, and Kane got up.

"I had no idea this place was even here," Barnes said, taking the pint when Kane returned. "I don't normally drink Harvey's; rude not to in here."

"It's one of Uncle Jimmy's favourites. All my old haunts are out of bounds, for one reason or another — in most cases, a prevalence of coke dealers. And this is good and discreet."

Barnes looked over at the only other punter in the place — a seventy-year-old man in a gilet and wellies perched on a bar stool with a collie at his feet. He was as still as a waxwork, and Barnes wondered if he was about to doze off in his pint glass.

"Uncle Jimmy?"

"Lives in a caravan down on the Cuckoo Line. The only family I've got that wouldn't string me up by my ankles for joining the job."

"Bit risky, you coming here, then, no?"

"Jimmy's another pariah. That's why he likes it here."

Barnes wanted to ask more, but got a sense Kane would only disclose at his own pace, like a seabound rescuer letting out a line a foot at a time.

"Samson . . . sir. Do me a favour. Find out what Stratton Pearce is up to."

He saw Kane fight to not roll his eyes.

"Barnes, there's nothing to suggest he's involved. Nothing at all. He's still in custody."

"Is he back here yet? Has he been extradited?"

Kane was silent.

"I don't know that. I'll find out. I can add it to the intelligence requirement. But that's all I can do. There isn't even a sniff of his involvement."

"I get that. Of course I do. But, sir—"

"Stop calling me 'sir'."

"Okay, Samson. We could front up Duquesne Kenley. Visit him in prison. Witness interview. We don't need evidence for that."

Kane thought about it.

"We could. What are you going to ask him? 'Has Stratton Pearce been in touch?' Don't forget: Pearce has three names on his shitlist — you, me and Kenley. I'm amazed Kenley is even still alive."

Duquesne "Duke" Kenley had been vice-captain of the Keber crime group, a regional subsidiary of a crime network whose tentacles stretched across the UK and Europe. Kenley had been keeping the seat warm for Pearce, himself a fugitive for numerous historic activities on UK soil, and who had been arrested as an unexpected bonus during an armed operation. Pearce had been out for Kenley's blood ever since.

Barnes thought about it. There was a hook. Kenley had got close to his next-door neighbour — Natalie Morgan, herself a police officer — and there was a theory that she had melted his cold heart. *Bloody heart-warming*, Barnes had thought at the time; the man was suspected of at least two murders.

"You're thinking about it, aren't you?" Kane said.

"I'll think about nothing else until I know the girls are safe." He stood, and dropped a couple of notes on the table.

"Don't go without me. You'll compromise everything. You shouldn't be anywhere near this. If there's a link, I'll find it. If there's a shred of intel, we'll go to work on it. I promise."

Barnes nodded, and shrugged on his coat. "I appreciate that. You know my take on this — Andrew Lau didn't snatch Maggie for himself. Which means he snatched her for someone else."

* * *

Gabby, however, didn't want to hear it.

Barnes went in to work the following day feeling slightly unsure of what he should be doing. Tamsin and Ellie were still at Maggie's bedside — it didn't seem likely she'd be discharged today. Maybe tomorrow. He would be there for that.

He couldn't relax until he could be sure Andrew Lau Mark Two wasn't going to emerge from a wheelie bin somewhere. His caseload, his day job, his manager's performance expectations, suddenly seemed like the biggest pile of banality he could conceive of. Demotivated didn't come close. There was nothing else for him besides unpicking the wider story behind Maggie's abduction.

The smell from the corner office of the incident room was oppressive — somewhere between a changing room after a rugby match and a pub at kicking-out time. Barnes happened to know that Gabby had a very large, airy, wood-panelled period office at HQ; he had, for some reason, moved lock, stock and barrel into the incident's room goldfish bowl, and it had not been a neat transition.

"What are you doing here, Barnes?" Gabby looked exhausted; his eyes were encircled with grey, while his shirt — unusually for a man so fastidious — was crumpled and looked slightly yellow.

"You been home, sir?" Barnes asked.

Gabby eyeballed him, and popped a couple of what looked like antacids.

"I asked you a question."

"I work here, sir."

"No, you don't. You work over in the main building. The CID office. This is the incident room for Op Element, the heinous chemical incident in Eastbourne town centre; next door is the scaled-back incident room for Op Console, which Superintendent Kane is running. You're involved in neither."

Barnes weighed up his response. Bite, or let it slide? He'd already voiced his concerns to a superintendent — one he trusted — so he saw no percentage in rising to it. The man was obviously exhausted.

"Sir—"

"You're to take a leave of absence."

"I'm sorry?"

"A leave of absence. Two weeks, minimum. Preferably more. When you come back, you'll have a new post in CID Training."

"You can't—"

"That's a lawful order, Barnes. It's that, or you're going to put me in an early grave."

"You know there's more to Maggie's abduction, right?"

"All the more reason."

"The main suspect—"

"The dead one."

". . . is not of interest. He has no footprint. He's most likely a mercenary. That means someone hired him."

"Is there any intelligence to back up this wild theory?"

Barnes chewed the inside of his cheek. "How many paedophiles have you heard of that can obtain a plastic gun and get it through border checks undetected?"

"Barnes, you got your kid back safe. Many don't. Take them on holiday. It's a win–win. You get to count your blessings; I get you out of my hair."

The obvious quip formed and died on Barnes's tongue. He turned to go.

"One other thing," Gabby said, apparently getting into it. "You'll likely be served with gross misconduct papers when you return."

"It wouldn't be the first time," Barnes said.

"No, indeed. You're running out of lives." There was the merest hint of a smirk on Gabby's face.

"For what, may I ask?"

"Failure to observe basic health and safety advice at the scene of a CBRN incident, resulting in the death of DC Will Howlett. Failure to observe safety protocols for unarmed officers during an armed operation, resulting in the death of suspect Andrew Lau. That's two deaths, Barnes. On your hands. That's some proper Article 2 shit. Coroner will have plenty to say to you, I'm sure."

He didn't wait for it to sink in.

"We're done, Barnes."

Barnes backed away and spun on his heel, resisting — and not for the first time — the incredible urge to bounce Gabby's head off the glass partition wall of the corner office.

He stalked out of the incident room. A worried-looking Tina Guestling was hovering in the doorway. She caught his eye.

"You okay?" she said, shaking her head. "Bastard."

"That makes two of us," Barnes said, and left.

CHAPTER TWENTY-EIGHT

"You're making the right decision, you know," Kane said.

"I just wish we'd picked another airport to fly from," Barnes said.

Ten days after Maggie's blessed reunion with her mother and sister, they were standing at the drop-off area outside Gatwick Airport's South Terminal, a hop, skip and a jump from where Andrew Lau had been dropped by armed police. After Barnes had greenlit Tamsin's idea about a city break, she had flexed her organisational muscles with gusto, and now the four of them were about to head off for a last-minute, pre-Christmas week in St Helier.

Kane had met them to see them off. It was the first time he'd met Tamsin and the girls. He'd offered a tentative handshake; she'd thrown her arms around him and stayed there for a good half a minute.

"This is pleasure, not business," Kane said. "Try to enjoy it. Anything comes up, I'll call you."

"Do so. No matter how small. And have a think about fronting Duquesne Kenley. Just don't do so without me."

"You're going to miss your plane. Go and get drunk with Tamsin. Forget all this for a week."

Barnes looked over at Tamsin. She was making a fuss of the girls and looked happier than he'd ever seen her. *Blessed*, was the word she'd used. She looked up, caught his eye and winked.

"I'll do my best. Thanks, boss."

* * *

It took a while for Barnes to unwind, but after they checked in to their holiday home and Tamsin insisted he share a bottle of champagne with her, he felt himself loosen up a little. That, coupled with the reassurance that Kane was actually considering his almost offhand suggestion that they front up Duquesne Kenley, led Barnes to tell her about Gabby's parting shot.

"What an absolute Grade-A fucking bellend," she said. "Why do you put up with that shit?"

Barnes shook his head. It was an entirely reasonable question. He somehow kept coming back for more, which he put down to his slightly self-destructive tendencies. He could get out. He could transfer. He could leave policing altogether. Go into teaching. Learn how to drive an HGV. Set up a private investigation firm. Something Tamsin worried less about.

But he knew he wouldn't do any of those things, knew that until he had a little more faith that those around him were taking him seriously, he would be looking over his shoulder until he knew Stratton Pearce was in the ground.

The cottage they had rented was near the zoo, not far from Bouley Bay. It was a converted barn with wood beams, a real fire and floor-to-ceiling glass, and they were tucked away down a lane surrounded by countryside. It was a fifteen-minute walk through the woods down to twinkling waters and a croissant of golden sand, and the girls loved it.

The girls had been asleep for about half an hour; Tamsin had already checked on them four times. He didn't discourage her — how could he? And why would he? Maggie had been beset by nightmares since leaving hospital, and the bedroom resembled a homeopath's display window, with dream-catchers, lavender pillows and oil burners dotted around the place.

It was their second night here, and despite the unfamiliar surroundings, Maggie's sleep had actually improved. He didn't know if that was because she associated their house with what had happened to her, or whether time was very gradually healing.

The sofa was large enough for the von Trapp family, and Barnes stretched out, curling his bare feet against the fabric. He took another sip of the champagne. Unwinding was proving difficult. There was something persisting at the back of his mind, like a piece of cloth snagged on barbed wire. It wouldn't budge, and the effect of the alcohol was only partially helping.

When Tamsin's phone rang on the kitchen island countertop, killing the sound of Miles Davis, Barnes set the glass down on the coffee table and swung his legs round. Maybe giving up on trying to relax would actually be more productive.

She hurried out of the bedroom and tutted quietly when she saw the display.

"Hello? Hi. Yes, I'm okay. No, we got here fine. Journey was good. Yes, they're both fine. No, they're asleep. Well, they go to bed the same time every night, Graham. We're not in a different time zone, here."

It seemed more unconscious than deliberate, but she moved further into the kitchen, away from Barnes, and then out the other side until she was in the vestibule by the front door.

Barnes flicked on the television and watched some muted snooker, trying not to listen.

". . . she's okay. Some nightmares still. Yes, of course I am. Well, maybe. It's too early to be thinking about therapy. No, I . . . what are you saying? How did you arrive at that conclusion? *You* were in the police, and she wasn't kidnapped by a nutcase then. There are thousands of other police officers whose children aren't abducted. It's not his *fault*, Graham . . ."

Barnes picked up his own phone. There was a text from Kane: *Sorry to disturb. Call me when you get a sec.*

"Well, that's as maybe, but I don't see how . . ."

Tamsin's voice was rising. Barnes looked over.

". . . she won't have to *go* to court, will she? The prick is dead, is he not? Well, I didn't see you running around trying to find her . . . no, I told you as soon as was humanly possible. I was a little preoccupied . . ."

Barnes picked up the bottle and refilled her glass.

"Fine, fine. Yes, tomorrow night. Yes. Yes, *okay*, Graham."

She ended the call and walked back into the living room.

"Prick," she said, tossing the phone on an armchair.

"He goads you," Barnes said, passing her the glass.

"I know. He did it for six years. Petulant, condescending, smug *git*. And I bite every time."

She necked the champagne in one and held out the glass for another top-up.

Barnes obliged.

"He only phoned to say goodnight to the girls, then somehow got on to the topic that you and your job were indirectly responsible for Maggie being taken. That's not true, is it?"

She looked at him over the rim of her glass.

Don't bullshit her.

"Honestly, Tamsin, I don't know. Samson's trying to find out."

She shrugged, then shook her head.

"There are some police who go in, tread water, do the bare minimum and go home. They keep their heads down for thirty years, then they cash in. There are others that *work*. They never let up, they keep up the pressure, and they get under the skin of their quarry. That's you, Barnes. You get the bad guys cornered, and they lash out. That doesn't happen to the other kind.

"What I'm saying is: good cops make enemies. Lazy ones don't. So maybe someone had an axe to grind. I wouldn't want you to stop being you."

That's only because she's alive, Barnes thought.

After the champagne bottle was empty and the fire had all but sputtered out, they retreated to the bedroom and made love under the skylight, a freezing navy sky freckled with white-gold stars visible through the glass.

Tamsin snored lightly. Barnes made tea and stepped out onto the deck to get a better look at the stars, amazed at how clear the sky was.

He tilted his head and listened. The night breeze hushed in the trees; beyond that, he could hear waves lapping on the sand. The sea was a black titan rising up on all sides. Nothing else — no traffic, no voices, no urban disruption.

It made him slightly uneasy.

He looked at his watch, weighed it up, called anyway.

"Superintendent Kane." Office chatter behind him. Still up, still at work.

"It's Barnes."

"How's the island retreat?"

"Pretty good, thanks. Quiet."

"Girls okay?"

"They . . . are, actually. I think Tamsin would like her ex-husband to lose an argument with a minotaur, but besides that—"

"I met him."

"Of course you did."

"He's harmless enough."

"Eastbourne. The chemical incident. Any update?"

"No ident on the substance yet. We've struggled to get a decent sample. Looking like it might be homemade, though."

"Method?"

"Can't be sure of that either, but Defra seem pretty sure it originated at sea. Maybe a barrel pushed off a container ship or a disturbed shipwreck. All theories at the moment."

"But deliberate?"

"Someone with enough knowledge could cast doubt on that supposition."

"What about victims?"

"Randoms. Innocents. None of them Bulgarian exiles or in witness protection. Spooks, NCA and the ROCUs all confirmed it."

"Anything else?"

"I was lucky to get that much out of Gabby, frankly. But, so you know, I'm trying to pull some strings at Belmarsh."

"Strings? Like a CHIS?"

"Listen, it's a fishing trip, and Duquesne Kenley is as sharp as they come. But it's worth a go, and if we strike out, we'll go see him."

"You've changed your tune."

"Nothing to lose, have we? Uncle Jimmy gets philosophical in my ear when his emphysema flares up: 'Square with yourself before you square with your Maker, son.' Plus . . ."

"Plus what?"

"His case has been listed for trial."

"Okay. When?"

"Next week."

"*What?* That wasn't meant to happen until the spring. At the earliest."

"I don't know what to tell you. The senior prosecutor called me directly. He's pulling his hair out. Wants you back here with me to start on the prep work. There's a case conference the day after tomorrow."

"I'm not due back until Sunday. How senior is the senior prosecutor?"

"There's not much room between the top of his head and the ceiling. I'm sorry, Barnes."

Barnes exhaled heavily.

"Okay. I'll come back for the meeting then fly back for the girls. And do me a favour, okay?"

"Yes?"

"Warn Gabby."

* * *

Tamsin protested. She didn't want to leave, but she didn't want Barnes to leave either. It took the best part of a morning, but he finally persuaded her — he would fly back for the conference then come straight back. He'd book them a couple of extra nights, and they would both chuck their phones in the fire.

She relented, eventually, and she was practical with it. She didn't throw her hands up and say the holiday was ruined. She understood. Rolled with the punches, for the most part. When Barnes said this was the most important case of his life, that Duquesne Kenley was the Premier League Keber member he wanted to put away — not least because the trial itself would be highly vulnerable; it wouldn't have surprised Barnes if a sniper took him out from the public gallery — she understood. *Go get him*, she said, and as he packed his bags, he decided he would ask her to marry him when the time was right.

Kenley convicted.

Pearce dead.

No more hitmen.

Leaving the police service.

Then the time would be right.

CHAPTER TWENTY-NINE

Barnes landed at Gatwick on a still, grey morning, the freezing air settling on him like a curtain.

He sent Tamsin a text letting her know he'd survived the flight, then decided it was a poor choice of words and apologised. She didn't reply, and he called Kane from the taxi.

"Conference is at CPS HQ, Brighton. I've booked you a seafront hotel. Freshen up, then when you've rested, we'll meet and prep some of the legwork."

"I've only flown in from the Channel Islands, Samson, not China . . . hold on. A hotel? You've checked me into a hotel? I have a house not ten minutes' drive from the nick. Why would I not use it?"

"It's a business trip, technically. Let someone else foot the bill, eh?"

"What are you not telling me?"

"Rest up. I'll speak to you later."

Barnes frowned as he put the phone away, then tried to doze in the back of the taxi.

To his amazement, Kane had put him in the Grand, Eastbourne's most expensive establishment. It was the westernmost seafront hotel, along King Edward's Parade, rather than Royal Parade and the slightly more insalubrious array of guesthouses, alehouses and flophouses. He'd have been content with a Travelodge in any case.

The taxi cruised past the junction with Terminus Road — the southernmost portion was still closed, local authority barriers providing an impenetrable blockade, and there were still crime scene tents and emergency services vehicles at the other end, but the urgency had gone. Outside the cordon, people went about their business and behaved as if ground zero wasn't there, the sea a ridged, sulphur-green constant to his left, like a crocodile's back.

The hotel, a model of nineteenth-century splendour, was an enormous white palace, two wings forming an "H" along the frontage of the main building. The Victorian architecture made Barnes think of shaped antacid tablets, and, as the door-man in the bottle-green top and tails gestured him enthusias-tically inside, he wondered what Kane would make of all this.

Barnes checked in, padded along the huge, carpeted atrium with the antique furniture to the Great Hall and thence to his room. He dropped his stuff on the bed and fought to slide the sash window up, caked as it was in thick layers of gloss.

The salt air hit him. The tide was out, and Barnes saw the bright wellies of a small child foraging in the rock pools with a net. Beachy Head loomed up in the distance. There was an adult with the child, pointing encouragingly and helping the child navigate their way over the seaweed-strewn rocks. No one would question or challenge the fact of the pair of them being together.

Maybe they should, Barnes thought. Just to be on the safe side. Feathers would be ruffled, and sensibilities bruised, but better that than the other, surely.

Why had Kane checked him in here, of all places? He was less than two miles from where Will Howlett fell, twenty minutes' walk from where Maggie had been taken, five from where the escaping hordes had jacked his patrol car like zom-bies. Never mind the fact that his own house was closer to the station than this place.

He tried Tamsin again, but it rang out. He sent her another text message, then, when Kane didn't answer either, he called a taxi.

He asked the driver to take a run past his house and hold about fifty yards away.

It looked fine. Quiet. Intact. No one around. Barnes's car still on the driveway.

He got the driver to swing by a florist's, then gave the police station as his final destination.

"Makes sense now," the driver growled, as he collected his money and drove away.

Barnes tailgated someone into the main compound and walked across the car park to the Major Incident Suite. He hefted the enormous bunch of flowers into the cradle of one arm, allowing him to dig out his warrant card.

He held it up to the reader. It gave an angry, red, rapid trill.

The door remained locked. Barnes sighed. *Don't let the door hit your arse on your way out*, he thought. Kane still wasn't answering, and so, looking at the forest of blooms he was carrying, he tried Tina.

"Tina? Special delivery."

"I'm sorry?"

"It's Barnes calling. I'm outside. Can you let me in? My hands are kind of full."

She appeared at the door a few minutes later.

"Hi," she said. "Gabby — ACC Glover — isn't here."

"He revoked my access the moment I left."

"Not a massive surprise, to be honest. Come in, but go straight to the ABE suite. Just because he's not here doesn't mean someone won't dob me in."

Barnes did as he was told, feeling completely detached from reality. He stood alone in the video interview suite, wondering momentarily how many horrific tales had been soaked up by these walls over the years.

There was a networked computer in the observation booth. He set the flowers down, sat at the desk and tried to log on. Nothing. Locked out. A complete pariah. If PSD came in and found him, he'd be carted off the premises at a minimum. Possibly arrested.

His brain started to kick in. Was his house under observation? Had Kane been sending him a message? If so, why would Kane tell him to meet here?

PSD?

Or someone else?

Tina came in.

"I should go," Barnes said. "I'm not welcome here. I've got no access to anything, which is probably a prelude to suspension."

Suspended, again. His dead wife would turn in her grave. Young and stupid, they'd both had such high hopes for his career.

"Sorry, what did you say?" he said to Tina. The unexpected, sudden memory of his late wife had dislodged him from the present. It happened from time to time, but it still caught him on the hop.

"I said: what's going on?"

He shook his head.

"I wish I knew. These are for you."

He gave her the flowers. Her face softened.

"Thank you . . . why?"

"Sometimes doing the right thing and following the rules make strange bedfellows. I can count on one hand the number of people that have been willing to stick their neck out for me over the years, but all the others go way back with me. You hardly know me. Who would do that?"

She stepped forward, and kissed him on the cheek.

"I know desperate when I see it. Thank you. They are beautiful."

He slid past her, out of the room and into the Major Incident Suite's entrance atrium, where a polished wooden roll call of WW1 war dead hung incongruously in the modern steel-and-glass building, one of very few artefacts to survive the transition from the since-closed town centre police station.

He opened the door and stepped out into the cold car park.

"Hey," she said.

He turned.

"I'm glad she's okay."

Barnes stepped across the car park. A spear of wind side-swiped him and ran down his neck, under his clothing. The sky was solid grey, and he crunched across the recently gritted tarmac to the gate.

He thought about co-opting a response car to run him back to the hotel, but then decided that wouldn't be particularly fair if the hammer was about to come down on him. He called another taxi instead — without a car, the patrol base was miles from anywhere besides McDonald's, Wickes and Tesco.

He still had his work phone. It would be sequestered in the event of suspension, but right now it was still his. He tried Kane, Gabby and the trial management unit, but the phone had been disconnected. No phone service, no internet, nothing. Those boys hadn't wasted time.

He tutted, and used the phone contacts book to input the number for the trial management unit into his personal phone. The man who answered was cheerful and helpful, but could find no record of the Kenley case being listed for trial. Barnes explained the situation to him, and the man told him not to worry — if the call had gone straight from a senior CPS lawyer to a superintendent, it probably just hadn't been input onto the system yet. Barnes asked about the case conference, and the man confirmed that, yes, the meeting room booking system showed a room booked out for the following day. *All* the following day, he added.

Barnes arrived back at the hotel and, when Kane still didn't answer, he sent him a text message.

I'm at the hotel. Can't get into work. Can't get hold of you. Call me.

He thought about an invigorating run along the cold promenade, but hadn't brought any running kit. Instead, he booted up his laptop and video-called Tamsin. It took a couple of goes, but she eventually answered.

"Hey," she said. She was smiling, but looked a little frazzled. There were the sounds of a pillow fight going on in the bedroom, the TV was on and he could hear something humming off camera, in the microwave. "You okay?"

"Yes, all fine. Uneventful journey. I'm at the hotel."

She frowned.

"Hotel? Why aren't you home?"

He kicked himself internally.

"Kane's idea. Recall from annual leave, so it's a business trip, technically. He's going to let the CPS pay to look after me. How are the girls?"

"They're good. We went to the zoo. Can you hear them?"

"I certainly can."

"Maggie! Ellie! Come say hi!"

Maggie and Ellie appeared, in Paddington and Transformers pyjamas respectively. They were red-faced and grinning, the pre-bed hair brushing having gone completely to pot. Maggie looked happy, stress-free, like she had momentarily forgotten her troubles.

"Hey, babies."

"I'm not a baby!" Ellie exclaimed.

"How was the zoo?"

"It was amazing. They've got howler monkeys, and snakes, and . . ." Maggie began.

"And I saw a bug get eaten by an ig . . . an ig . . ." Ellie looked at her mum.

"Iguana," Tamsin said.

"Igg-rana. It ate it in one go. It was gross."

"It sounds it."

"When are you coming back, Barnes?" This was Maggie.

"Tomorrow. I've got a meeting here, then as soon as it's done, I'll fly back. With any luck you'll still be up."

"Guarantee that," Tamsin said.

"Can we go to the zoo again? You can come this time," Maggie said.

175

"Of course."

"Right, you two. Stop wrecking the place and go and do your teeth. I'll come read you a story in a sec."

"Love you, girls," Barnes said.

"G'night!" they yelled, and ran off.

Tamsin reappeared on screen.

"She's missing you. Maggie."

Barnes nodded.

"You still haven't told me exactly what happened. When you found her."

"Hey. That's *my* toothpaste!" came a voice from the bedroom.

"Come on now, girls. It's meant to be quiet time," Tamsin called.

She turned back to the screen. At the same time, whatever was in the microwave stopped humming, and it trilled a triumphant *I'm done* tone: *bleep . . . bleep . . . bleep.*

"Do you really want to know?" Barnes said.

"I think I should. I need to understand it. For her sake." She rested her forearms on the countertop and leaned in towards the camera. "All I know is you were the one that brought her home. Not me, not her father, not some random rescuer. You. That's going to leave a big imprint on her. Especially as she gets older. And besides . . . Jesus. Girls! Will you stop fighting for two seconds and do your teeth!"

"Sorry, Mum," Maggie called.

"It's her!" Ellie yelled.

The microwave trilled again.

Barnes nodded.

"I'll tell you. When we're back together. Maybe when there's less going on in the background."

"I hear that. Look, let me get that bloody thing out of the microwave, get them settled and I'll be straight back."

"What is it? Sponge pudding?"

"Nah. Lavender cushion. For Maggie."

"Of course."

"You doing anything? Can you hang on?"

"I'm not doing anything," Barnes said. "Early night on the cards, I guess."

"Shame. Which hotel is it?"

"The Grand, bizarrely."

"The *Grand*? You're at the Grand? Without me? What a wasted opportunity. You're gonna have to take me, now. Dinner at the Mirabelle and a room for two."

"Deal."

"It's a date. I'll hold you to it. Be right back."

She disappeared.

He looked at the screen. Just the brickwork of the kitchen walls, stainless steel pans on butcher's hooks, Jersey-themed tea towels hanging on the oven door. And, of course, the microwave, just offstage.

It trilled again. It was jarring.

Barnes stretched back in the chair and gazed out at the lights of the promenade and the black sea beyond. He pointed a finger at the horizon and tried to work out which direction Tamsin was in.

He picked up his phone. Nothing from Kane. Or anybody. He sent another text message, the first flicker of unease creeping across the base of his skull.

On the call, the microwave trilled again.

Barnes picked up the room service menu and flicked through it, then switched to a pamphlet that offered a short history of the hotel and the surrounding area. Then it was the remote control and a bored cycling through inane television channels.

He hated wasted time. Hated the thought of being bored. Every second was precious — he'd thought that *before* Maggie's ordeal, but now? If Gabby hadn't seen fit to make him a pariah, he could have been reviewing the case file, looking for weaknesses and potential defences, preparing.

The microwave trilled, for a fifth time.

Barnes swung his feet off the table and turned back to the screen.

Nothing. Just the kitchen backdrop.

He inclined his ear to the speaker, and listened intently. Nothing. Maybe the story had finished and the girls were asleep. Maybe Tamsin was in the bathroom, or she had dozed off with the girls. Entirely possible. She'd got used to sleeping next to Maggie.

The microwave trilled.

"Tamsin? Are you there, Tam?"

Another minute went by. Then five. Then ten.

Barnes picked up his phone, sent a message.

Did you nod off?

On the call, he heard the phone vibrate on the countertop.

The microwave trilled again — *bleep . . . bleep . . . bleep.*

He got up and went to the bathroom, trying to kill time, busying himself with banalities to keep the growing sense of worry from getting any larger.

Bleep . . . bleep . . . bleep.

Another ten minutes.

Twenty-three minutes since she'd gone to put the girls down.

After half an hour, he began to call out.

"Tamsin? Tam? Can you hear me?"

Bleep . . . bleep . . . bleep.

He shut his eyes. She'd said: *I'm going to get the pillow out of the microwave.* She was going to do that, then put the girls down, then come back.

She hadn't.

The bloody thing was still beeping.

How could you settle the girls, read them a story and generally wind down, with that noise going on?

He timed it. It was incessant, but there was a good ninety-second interval between each round of chirping. Long enough for you to forget about it, and for it to jar you from your thoughts the next time it reminded you it was still here.

This was not right.

After forty minutes, he was yelling at the screen.

"Tamsin! Tam? Tamsin, answer me! Are you okay?"

Bleep . . . bleep . . . bleep.

CHAPTER THIRTY

The frantic feeling swirling around the pit of his stomach was horribly familiar. He'd felt it for the thirty hours Maggie had been missing, and it was made ten times worse by the fact that he'd neither expected nor hoped to be feeling it again so soon.

He paced the room for twenty minutes, intermittently calling out to Tamsin. The microwave kept on with its incessant trilling, and eventually he had to turn the volume down to keep from throwing the laptop out the window.

In the end, he decided that he was serving no purpose whatsoever, and that false hope couldn't keep him tied to the screen for ever. Keeping the connection live, he hurried down to the reception desk and managed to obtain a large piece of card and a marker pen. He wrote: *GONE TO GET HELP. BE RIGHT BACK. CALL ME*, and placed it on a chair in front of the screen.

He called the agency that rented them the property, but of course got their answer machine, it being gone 9 p.m. He found a mobile number for the owner of the property in a bunch of emails containing their arrival instructions. He called it and left a voicemail, and sent a few text messages. When that didn't bear fruit, he called the States of Jersey Police and explained the situation. The reaction from the call taker didn't exactly fill him with confidence, intent as she was on providing myriad alternative explanations for Tamsin disappearing into thin air. After casually — or as casually as he was able to muster, anyway — dropping his occupation and rank into the conversation, the call taker agreed to send the job to the stack for a patrol to carry out a welfare check. She warned him that they were very busy, and that she couldn't promise how quickly it would be there, but that he should call back if the situation changed or if he received further information.

"An island for the rich nine miles across," Barnes muttered, tossing his phone onto the bed. "How bloody busy can you be?"

The phone hit a pillow and bounced onto the floor, just as it began to ring. Barnes made a scrambling dive for it.

Kane.

"Finally," Barnes said. "Where have you been? I've been trying to call you all afternoon."

"I'm sorry," Kane said. "I'm Force Gold today. Had a fairly intense firearms operation running since five o'clock this morning."

"Not . . ."

"No, no. Nothing to do with . . . this. Not linked to you."

Barnes suddenly felt stupid, and small, and churlish. Samson Kane wasn't his own personal superintendent. He had ten million other things going on — Barnes was just one of them. His fists balled by his sides. He wanted to be an *ally*. Not a sodding *customer*.

"So what's up?" Kane said.

"You won't believe it," Barnes said. "Can we meet?"

Kane was up for it. They haggled for a bit over a destination, then decided that Kane may as well see the inside of the establishment he — or rather the CPS — was paying for.

While he waited, Barnes called the Jersey Police back. There was no update, and a sarcastic remark slipped out of Barnes's mouth before he could stop it. The call taker, a different one this time, adopted the tone of a Victorian headmaster and explained that adverse weather was causing unprecedented demand on the island, and maybe he would like to check the forecast.

Barnes apologised through gritted teeth and then followed the suggestion. There it was, on the BBC weather pages. Low pressure, plummeting temperatures and brutal westerlies were due to come sweeping in over the next few days, bringing heavy snow and treacherous conditions. By all accounts, the weather front was moving in from the Atlantic and had already gobbled up the north-western tip of France and the Channel Islands as it rumbled north.

Another thought occurred to him. He'd already decided that if the Jersey Police were still mired in states of apathy by midnight, he was just going to fly back himself. A quick scan of the travel webpages confirmed the suspicion that was brewing in his gut — nearly all flights were likely to be cancelled for at least twenty-four hours.

When he read that, he felt the fight go out of him like a punctured balloon. He slid into an upholstered armchair — the soft lighting, luxury décor and sea views suddenly incongruous to his situation — and covered his brow with his hands. He couldn't keep doing this, and certainly not alone. He was so exhausted. Why would no one listen to him? Why was he always fighting, fighting, fighting? Why did he have to try so damn hard to get some help?

Kane arrived fifteen minutes later. The call connection was still live, and Barnes wrote an addendum on his sign: *IN BAR. CALL ME.*

The cocktail bar was practically empty. There was a soft jazz score playing from somewhere, and — like the bedroom — the low lighting, leather furniture and winking optics of rare and vintage spirits behind the polished, crescent-shaped bar were equally incongruous, almost taunting.

Barnes sat heavily in a wingback chair in the corner of the room, the balls of his palms pressed to his eyes. Kane sat opposite him, looking equally grim. A waitress in a black-and-white suit dropped paper coasters on the circular table and left their drinks without a word.

"Try not to think the worst," Kane said. It sounded trite.

Barnes shook his head.

"I'm not one for I-told-you-so's, Samson, but you know what this feels like to me? Plan A — taking Maggie for whatever endgame — failed, so they've had a second bash. Only this time, they've taken my entire family." Even to his own ear, his voice sounded like a man who was about to deliberately walk outside his tent into an Arctic storm to perish.

"Who's 'they', Barnes?"

"Stratton Pearce."

"You don't know that."

"No, I don't. But give me a credible alternative."

"What did Jersey Police say?"

"Job's in the stack. They're flat out with weather-related calls. I'd go over there myself but there's nothing moving. All flights cancelled."

"I can help with that."

Barnes's mobile rang.

"DI Barnes?"

"Mr Barnes, this is the States of Jersey Police control room. Calling about your welfare check incident request, reference two-one-eight."

"Go on."

"A patrol attended the location in question. The premises was in darkness, with no answer at the door. No sign of a disturbance. Insufficient grounds to force entry. Assumption all occupants asleep. Call has been sent back to the stack and deferred for a further attempt in the morning."

Barnes felt the casing of his mobile phone protest as he squeezed it.

"Did . . . was the car on the driveway?"

"I do not have that information."

"Can I speak to the officer that attended? Do you have their number?"

"I'm afraid I'm not allowed to pass on that information."

Deep breaths, Barnes. *Deep breaths.*

"Well, maybe give them my number and ask them to call me?"

"I will make that request. I do not have a time frame for callback. We are very busy."

"Who is your duty Gold Commander, please? May I speak with them?"

A pause on the line.

"May I ask what about?"

"About the fact that my partner and children have vanished into thin air and nobody seems to give a flying fuck about it."

Red card. Time out. A novice error.

"You're using foul language now. I am terminating the call."

Click.

In a less opulent establishment, Barnes might have thrown his phone across the room — again.

"I can speak to their Gold," Kane said. "Leave that with me."

"That's okay," Barnes was staring at the floor.

"Look, there's nothing you can do now," Kane said. "I will try to get them to up the ante — you may as well try to get some sleep."

"When are we going to see Kenley?" Barnes said. "He was supposed to be turning Queen's, but as far as I know, he's never given us anything we didn't already have."

"He's making us work for it," Kane said. "Dangling the carrot. Nothing to lose."

"Let's go see him."

"Barnes . . ."

"What about this meeting tomorrow?" Barnes said, nodding at Kane's rucksack. "The guy at the trials unit didn't know anything about it."

Kane shrugged.

"You're not in the right frame of mind. And who could blame you?"

"Leave the case file, then. If I can't go and look for them myself, I'm hardly going to sleep."

Kane shrugged, and pulled a thick wad of papers from his rucksack, held together with an industrial-sized bulldog clip and a rubber band.

"Suit yourself. I'll call in the morning. You don't have to come to the meeting."

Barnes frowned suddenly.

"I flew back here for the meeting. My family vanished while my back was turned. I can't go anywhere or do anything about it. I may as well come to the sodding meeting."

"I'll call their Gold," Kane said, standing up. He finished his lime and soda, picked up his rucksack and walked out. Barnes had no idea if he was coming back.

Through the double doors into the garden lounge, a sudden sheet of rain spattered against the floor-to-ceiling glass.

"Tiff?" the waitress said, collecting Kane's glass.

Barnes looked up at her. She was smiling. Just trying to be nice.

"You could say that. Shouldn't really swear at the boss, though."

"That's a good life lesson. Another?" She pointed at his glass.

"No, thanks. I'm going to bed."

"No problem."

He scooped up his phone and paperwork and headed off back up the stairs, feeling about as useless as he ever had done.

He sat heavily down on the bed, unclipped the case file and spread the papers around the massive duvet.

It was a complex case. An organised crime group with slick, precise operations running — and plenty of them. A handful had been wafted under Barnes's nose for prosecution, but they were, in the main, crumbs — when compared with the wider potential, anyway. The actual charges against Kenley amounted to dangerous driving and the manslaughter of three of his criminal associates.

184

Keber's national overseer, Roxy Petrescu, deep underground. Their number one, Stratton Pearce, recently recaptured for a second time after spending a good chunk of his life as a fugitive. Their acting *capo*, Duquesne Kenley, sabotaging operations for both the detective he was in love with and the sudden attack of morals he'd developed since meeting her, and exiled for turning Queen's — or so they thought — now folding sheets in Belmarsh.

* * *

Barnes awoke suddenly — from yet another dream about being pursued by a slavering police dog — when his mobile rang, emerging from where he had fallen asleep under a pile of case papers.

"Mr Barnes? My name is Laura Balfour. I'm the duty inspector for the island of Jersey tonight."

"Hello," Barnes mumbled, squinting at his watch. Nearly three in the morning.

"I've been to your holiday home in Bouley."

"You've been? As in, personally?" Clearly Kane's phone call had made some things happen.

"Yes. I'm afraid your family are not there. I let myself in with a key from the landlady, and it appears preparations had been made to leave."

"*Preparations?*"

"Yes. A number of appliances had been turned off at the mains. There were no clothes or toiletries. I couldn't see a mobile phone or other obvious personal effects. It was clean and tidy. The car was not there."

"There were . . . we had a couple of suitcases in the wardrobe of the master bedroom. Large. Camo green. Empty, obviously."

"They were not there, Mr Barnes."

"You're quite sure?"

"Quite sure."

"When you say 'appliances' . . ."

"Oven, television, microwave, that kind of thing."

"It makes no sense," Barnes murmured.

"Look, I know it's hard," Inspector Balfour continued, "but sometimes people do just up and leave without warning."

"No, no. I had the tickets, the keys . . ."

Then he realised: she meant *leave their significant other*. Did other people think this too? Kane?

"No, I understand what you're saying, but she hasn't left me. That isn't right."

"I'm not saying it is, I'm just saying it's one explanation. I've seen it before . . . as I am sure you have."

"The car. It's a bloody island. It can't have gone far."

"We are looking around the ports, but—"

"Are they still on the island? It wouldn't be too difficult to confirm or disprove that. Check the manifests. Narrow down the search parameters."

"We can look at that, but although it's difficult to get off the island under the radar, it's not impossible . . . Mr Barnes, we have to consider the possibility that your wife does not want to be found."

"She's not . . . Look, I am reporting her missing. She is missing. She is not at a place where she is expected to be. She is in *danger*, dammit."

Silence on the line.

"Mr Barnes, we will keep looking for the car. We will make sure she is all right, if we can."

Not, *We'll tell you where she is.*

"Her phone. I've called it — it's switched off. You could ping it."

"I will formally review the risk assessment, and if it appears there is an immediate threat to life, I will explore that."

"Financials?"

"Again . . ."

Financials. *Financials.* What was he talking about? She hadn't gone off to the cashpoint. She'd been taken.

"Look, I'm sure you know, but I'm a DI on the mainland. I have an active caseload of several very unpleasant nominals who have upcoming court appearances at one time or another. At least one of them has a personal vendetta against me. Your intel people need to talk to ours."

"I can arrange—"

"Wait. The laptop."

"Laptop?"

"Yes, it was on the kitchen counter. She was on a video call with me. She walked out of shot to get something out of the microwave and didn't come back. I left the call live."

"There is no laptop here, DI Barnes."

"There must be . . ."

He scrambled over to his own machine, where a live video call showing the rustic brickwork of the holiday home's kitchen had been connected before he had gone down to the bar with Kane.

Now it was black, and silent.

Disconnected.

"Thank you, Laura. I appreciate it, I do."

"No problem. My early turn counterpart will call you with any updates."

She hung up. She was just doing her job, and doing it pretty well. Many a domestic abuser had tracked down their embattled spouse by reporting them missing and having the local constabulary unwittingly lead them straight to the horrified victim's door.

He tried Tamsin's mobile.

Dead. Dead as a dodo. In the sea, in a bin, stamped underfoot, who knew? They could ping it, but all it would likely tell them would be that it was still on the island. And, if a reasonably organised group wanted to kidnap a police officer's partner and make it look like a voluntary disappearance — which would be relatively straightforward to orchestrate, even if, as seemed likely, Tamsin had fought like a banshee — separating the phone from the owner would be the first thing they would do. You might get a location on the phone, but that wouldn't necessarily mean the owner was with it.

He had the sudden feeling of a man sinking into his own padded cell, protesting to the world that he was not insane, with a team of doctors telling him that's exactly the kind of thing a crazy person would say.

There was a seamless segue into a dream along the same lines; when he awoke, it was daylight, and the pampas and yucca decorating the Grand's gravel driveway were being blown about by spirals of violent wind. The sash windows were being battered by uneven bursts of rain, spraying across the glass intermittently as if God was bringing up His liquid lunch.

He forced himself to shower — but couldn't bring himself to look at his reflection — then, when he surveyed the mess in the bedroom, realised he had to get out of here.

He found his phone under the bed.

There was a text from Kane: *Pick you up in an hour.*

And three missed calls from Tina Guestling.

He called her back.

"It's Barnes."

"Oh, hi. Look, I don't know how helpful this is, but—"

"You've spoken to Jersey?"

"Jersey?"

"Jersey Police. I asked their intel cell to call ours."

"Oh. No. Well, not that I know of. I'm only an analyst, remember. If there's a tasking, it might not have got to me yet. Anyway . . ."

"Yes, I'm sorry. Go on."

"Well, I was trying to look at any possible links between the chemical attack and your daughter's abduction. And I remembered you said you were originally in the area for a drugs OD."

Charlie Rees. God, Barnes had forgotten all about him. He didn't even know what had happened to his body.

"Barnes? Sir? Are you there?"

"Yes, I'm here. Sorry."

"The deceased's name was Charlie Rees. His footprint is pretty limited — petty theft, bit of dealing, couple of domestic reports for having a shouting match with his mother. But I widened the search for *unlinked* associates, which meant looking for common denominators in the free-text body of the reports, rather than specific fields."

Barnes pinched the bridge of his nose.

"And I found something interesting. There's a phone number attributed to him — not one he knew we had on record, but it appears that his mother used it once to call the police during one of their arguments. She told us on the call that she was using his phone, but he may not have known about it.

"That same number was used to book a taxi on three separate occasions, each time the pickup location was Eastbourne custody centre."

Barnes sat on the edge of the bed, interested now. He felt the fight start to re-enter his body, like his heart had just been restarted and was now pumping *fight* around his system.

"I then cross-referenced the pickup times with the release time of detainees on the given days. On each occasion the taxi picked up a detainee and took them to the Crown & Anchor pub."

"You're saying Charlie Rees arranged to have these prisoners collected on their release?"

"Exactly."

"Who?"

"Chris Peake, Vernon Dodge and Len Sterling."

Barnes inhaled. "I know those names."

"They're all . . ."

"They're all linked to the same crime group. Charlie Rees was a Keber foot soldier."

189

CHAPTER THIRTY-ONE

Barnes barrelled down the stairs and checked out in a hurry, the Kenley file having been shoved, unbound, into his courier bag.

He checked his watch. Kane wasn't due for another twenty minutes. He was going to miss him.

He hurried down Grand Parade, a fierce blast of wind suddenly blowing him off course. He steadied himself against the railings outside a hotel, then carried on along the seafront towards town, when his phone rang again.

"DI Barnes? This is Gareth. From the trials management unit. We spoke yesterday."

He didn't sound cheerful today, he sounded perplexed. Barnes felt he could almost predict what the man was going to say.

"What's up?" Barnes said. "I'm just off to this case conference."

"I'm sorry? Are you outside? All I can hear is wind noise."

Barnes spun around on the spot, trying to angle himself against the wind. Waves the colour of oxidised copper, adorned with foamy white frills, crashed angrily against the shingle.

He took temporary shelter in the entrance doorway of the Lansdowne Hotel.

"How now?"

"A bit better."

"You were saying."

"This trial you've supposedly got a case conference for. *R. v. Kenley*. Numerous charges. When did you say it was?"

"Next week. Not sure of the date. Supposedly it was suddenly listed — my boss summoned me back from my holiday to attend the conference."

"So he told you it was next week?"

"Yes. Somebody senior from the CPS called him in a panic, apparently. Wanted the conference ASAP."

"You don't know the name of this prosecutor, I don't suppose?"

"No. My boss will have it. I'm just about to ring him. What are you driving at, Gareth?"

"Well, I can't find anything on the system or anywhere to confirm the trial has been brought forward. And there's a ton of stuff outstanding. Disclosure, defence statement, the enquiries on the last CPS action plan haven't been returned yet — they're with you, by the way. We are very far from being ready. Not only that, but the venue hasn't been locked down yet. Apparently there's some suggestion that the defendant may be at some risk, so it may go out of county. Possibly to the Bailey."

"Are you saying, Gareth, that this information about the sudden change in trial date is science fiction?"

"Well, unless someone knows something I don't — which is possible, but unlikely, given that we're the trials management unit. Clue's in the title. But yes, it sounds like false info."

"Thanks, Gareth."

"He's a gangster or something, isn't he? Someone getting nobbled by laying a false trail? Wouldn't be the first time I've seen it. These baddies try all sorts."

Or ensuring I'm out of the picture so my family can be got at. Again.

"You could very well be right. Thanks."

"Okay."

"Wait — one more thing. You said yesterday there was a meeting room booked for this case conference?"

"Yes, that's right."

"What name was it booked under?"

"Hold on, let me find it . . . Sandra Pearce. Hmm."

Barnes shut his eyes. "Not one of your staff, I'm guessing."

"No. Certainly not."

"OK. Thanks."

Barnes doubled his pace, not entirely sure of his destination. He tried Kane — nothing. He sent him a text: *Call me. Preferably before you leave for the case conference.* It didn't seem likely that there was anything more sinister than a wasted journey in the offing, but better not to risk it.

He kept walking, the case file in his bag getting heavier and heavier. He felt displaced — he couldn't go home, couldn't go to the station. Suddenly, he was adrift.

His instinct was to get back to Jersey as soon as possible. The train station was another fifteen-minute walk — an hour to Gatwick, then he would just have to park on a bench and wait for a flight. He could do no more here.

A sudden burst of precipitation that couldn't decide if it was rain or snow soaked him in seconds, and he took momentary refuge in the conservatory of a hotel. A gaggle of silver heads turned from their morning tea to regard the bedraggled individual that had burst in out of the rain.

As it was, neither his phone nor his laptop had enough battery power to do very much at all, and so he availed himself of a wall socket long enough to give his devices — his only lifeline, it seemed — some zap.

In the warmth of the conservatory, he accepted tea gratefully from the morning staff, and tried to compose his thoughts.

It did not take long to settle upon the theory that had begun to solidify in his brain. Someone took Maggie as a fuck-you to Barnes — hoping, maybe, that the DI would succumb to the chemical attack in the town centre at the same time. Charlie Rees's body was no coincidence — not the when, the where nor the who. He was part of Keber.

That was enough, surely? Enough to at least start harvesting intelligence to that end. Why were they not fronting him up? Or fronting up Kenley? Or getting search warrants for his cell, car and house? Who else had the motivation? Who but Stratton Pearce hated Barnes enough to go to such lengths? Pearce's girlfriend and son had perished in a deliberate fire three years ago — Pearce's logic was that, had he not been in prison, he could have protected them. And to Pearce's mind, it was Barnes's fault he was in prison in the first place. That made Barnes responsible.

The chemical incident claimed the life of Will Howlett, but Barnes had escaped unscathed, leaving him free to track down Maggie. He'd found her alive, and the main suspect — almost certainly a mercenary hired by Keber — had been killed.

Maybe Barnes had been the actual target. If he'd gone the same way as Will Howlett, then *nobody* would have looked for Maggie.

He stared at the sea while he processed this realisation.

In other words, Barnes had messed up Plan A. Plan B, therefore, must have been to fabricate a reason for Barnes to return to the mainland, leaving somebody free to have another go at kidnapping his family — all of them this time. Not only that, but engineering it in such a way as to make Barnes look like a bit of a cuckolded headcase. Having the front to do so — calling the CPS on the pretext of being the court listings office, or knowing Barnes's travel plans, or pretending to be a senior lawyer — required a bit of brass neck, but they were not difficult objectives to meet.

Panic and anxiety suddenly gripped him, and he spilled tea across the crisp white tablecloth. It oozed through the fabric as from an open wound.

Where were they? Were they all right?

Pearce had his family, of this he was convinced.

Pearce's own family died.

An eye for an eye.

Blood for blood.

CHAPTER THIRTY-TWO

The house was about as ordinary as you can get. New-build, three-bed semi, Vauxhall Insignia on the driveway. The developments were flying up everywhere, Barnes thought. The house was in Stone Cross — *God*, he thought, *we're all in each other's pockets.*

It was dark, but the porch light flicked on when Barnes knocked. He looked back down the driveway and pulled up his collar. A sage bush at the end of the path was dancing crazily in the icy wind. More snow was almost certainly on the way.

He thought maybe everybody had gone to bed, but then he heard footsteps; the hall light came on, and there was the rattling of keys in the door.

"Who's that?" He may as well have said, *Friend or foe?*

"It's me. Barnes."

"Barnes?"

Graham Wall appeared in the doorway. It was late, but he was fully dressed, wearing a grey V-neck sweater over a white shirt. He was holding a tumbler of something amber in his right hand.

"Barnes?" he repeated. "What are you doing here?"

"I came to tell you something."

"Have you been drinking?"

Barnes shook his head. "I don't drink."

"You could have fooled me." Graham was smiling. "You're swaying. Come in."

Barnes followed him in out of the cold. The house was warm, the aroma of Graham's dinner still apparent. Barnes took his shoes off and went into the lounge.

"Just you?"

"Miriam's in bed."

"Miriam?"

"My partner. Please, take a seat."

Barnes flopped into an armchair. He tried to work out the gap between Graham and Tamsin's divorce and Graham and Miriam shacking up. Probably not an unreasonable amount of time, actually.

"Nice place," Barnes said, looking around. There were tiffany lamps and a dresser with glasses and photographs on it, and a three-piece suite with frills on the arms. It looked like the set of a 1980s soap opera.

"It's okay. It's certainly a step up from where I was."

"Where you was — I mean were?"

"Divorce upsets the equilibrium in a major way, Barnes. I bounced around for a long time — hotels, friends, sleeping in my car. It's nice to have somewhere I can call my own again, even if it is suburban hell."

"Only cops understand suburban hell."

"Indeed. You're a widower, I understand."

Barnes eyed him.

"That must have been tough. So, what can I do for you, Barnes?" Graham said, passing him a tumbler.

"I came to tell you . . . because if we wait for someone official to tell you then it could be weeks."

"Tell me what?" Graham had edged forwards on his seat, and looked nervous.

"Look, I know you blame me. For Maggie's . . . ordeal. You think it was my fault."

Graham pursed his lips. "It's only the fault of the person that did it, Barnes. But I wouldn't be a parent if I didn't

195

wonder — and question — whether it was avoidable. And if, as a parent, you weren't there when it happened, wondering if it was so avoidable is all you think about."

"Maybe you're right," Barnes said, pretending to sip the drink.

"But that isn't why you're here, is it?" Graham said.

"No. It . . . it's happened again."

Graham's eyes narrowed. "What do you mean, 'It's happened again'?"

"They're gone. They've been taken."

"What?" Graham's voice was quiet, stunned.

"All of them. Tam, Mags, Ellie. We went for a holiday to Jersey. I was summoned back to work — on false pretences, as it turned out. Someone engineered it so they could snatch my family while I was out of the way. Possibly because I found Maggie and got the suspect killed. It mucked up their — someone's — plans."

"So where are they now?" Graham said.

"I don't know."

"You've—"

"Reported them missing? I certainly have. I've shouted myself hoarse trying to get someone to listen."

"But you're . . . you're . . ."

"A senior policeman? Yes, I know. And I'm being gaslit and patronised from every angle. People think I'm a suspect, or they think I'm an abuser, or they think she's left me and doesn't want to be found."

Graham's face was blank, but something flickered behind his eyes. A question: *Well, has she left you?*

"I'm here because you have a right to know. I'm also here because I've been wracking my brains trying to think of people who care about them as much as I do. I'm getting short shrift from the authorities. My boss is flexing his muscles where he can, but he's a lone voice."

Barnes stood.

"Plus, I think I need another cop to understand my theory. To everyone else I'm just a member of the public, and my theory sounds as crackpot to them as it would coming from anyone else."

"What theory?"

"I've spent a lifetime putting bad people behind bars, Graham. You make enemies that way. You must remember that.

"At least one of those holds me responsible, by virtue of his imprisonment at my behest, for the death of his own family. This is a dangerous individual who is part of a wider organisation. A coordinated revenge attempt is both plausible and probable."

Graham's eyes were glistening. His voice was small. "While my instinct is to say, 'You should have stayed away from them,' that is both unreasonable and unhelpful. Lord knows my job encroached on our marriage — and hers did too, in fairness — but not to this extent."

"She said, the more diligent the detective, the more likely you are to make enemies," Barnes added.

"Well, let's not compare collar sizes. Let's just work out what we're going to do to find them safely."

Barnes set down his glass. "I'm going to get back to Jersey."

"Nothing's flying, I imagine."

"I'll swim if I have to."

"A noble promise, but maybe not in your current condition. Do you want to stay here tonight, and then we regroup in the morning?"

"That's very kind of you, but maybe a little too weird. I'll call you with any updates."

"If I can do anything, please let me know. I care about them very much."

"Of course."

"Look after yourself," Graham said, pointing at the tumbler. "If you don't, who's going to find them?"

Barnes picked up the glass, took a final swig, nodded, and headed out.

Once he'd rounded the corner, he spat the unswallowed whisky into some rhododendrons and wiped his mouth with the back of his hand. On the whole, he thought he'd been convincing — the swaying might have been overdoing it a bit, but Graham seemed to have been fooled. Even if he wasn't, keeping *my ex's new fella turned up on my doorstep drunk* was a useful trump card for a rainy day.

Not that he'd got that vibe at all. Graham didn't give a sense of anything other than a concerned parent wanting to do what was best for his children. He'd acknowledged that he probably held Barnes responsible — who wouldn't? — but he wasn't all chest-beating and fists flying and trying to assert dominance as the alpha. He was reasonable and controlled, which was the test Barnes had wanted to put him through, thinking a faux-drunk routine would lower Graham's guard.

He'd thrown in some deliberate baiting:

My *family.*

I know you blame me.

Gaslit.

An abuser.

You must remember locking up bad guys, Graham, knowing full well that Graham had been medically retired after years of working behind a desk with a limp, ending with, as a consequence, an operational CV that barely ran to two pages.

But Graham hadn't bitten. To Barnes's surprise, he'd passed the test.

He wasn't, or didn't seem to be, a complete dick.

So maybe he was an ally.

CHAPTER THIRTY-THREE

The train to Gatwick was slow. It left Eastbourne's main terminus and chugged through the snow-carpeted countryside, fists of icy wind bashing at the windows, stopping at village stations with platforms like fingernails that couldn't accommodate more than a couple of carriages.

The check-in desks were quiet. Passengers were camped like refugees around the concourse, heaped and sprawled in a patchwork of brightly coloured coats, cases and umbrellas.

Barnes went to a couple of airline operators and tried to line himself up for the next flight to St Helier. They were non-committal about the forecast, but reckoned it wouldn't be more than twenty-four hours before flights resumed. Time is money, they said.

And more besides, Barnes thought.

He wandered aimlessly from Boots to WHSmith to M&S, the ambient sounds of the terminal echoing up into the high ceiling like flies in his head. Eventually he perched in one of the coffee lounges on the upper level and watched people milling about, the screen displays flickering and refreshing.

He stared at the screens and allowed himself to drift into a kind of trance, as a means of not thinking about the fact that less than a fortnight previously he had sprinted through here in pursuit of Andrew Lau. Suspect dead, Maggie rescued. Now he had to do it all again.

His phone rang.

Kane.

"You've got to get someone to answer your phone," Barnes said. "Don't you have a secretary?"

"The case conference was a bust."

"I tried to call you to tell you that. I would have gone to your house, but I have no idea where you live, and no one is going to give me access to your personnel file. The whole thing was engineered, Samson."

"It wasn't unproductive — the lawyer was real, the meeting room was real, the papers were real. Actually, it was pretty useful to sit down and go over it, albeit he was pretty salty that you weren't there. Then some guy called Gareth came in and said he wasn't sure why we were having an emergency case conference when the trial is months away."

"That's what I'm saying. Someone — Keber — has pulled me back here so they can get at my family. Such a diversion takes balls to pull off, but it isn't difficult. They only needed me out of the way long enough."

"Why go to the trouble? Why not just take you as well? You're one man and you're on holiday, relaxed, unarmed. Not difficult to scoop you up too."

"Because they want me to suffer. Or maybe they were banking on me coming straight back to walk into some sort of trap. The weather may actually have scuppered their plans on that front. But there's something else. Charlie Rees, the OD victim in the toilets just before the chemicals were released, was a Keber foot soldier."

"What?"

"This was not some random thing. They lined up the pieces — my rota, my duty times, the location — probably said to him, if you don't take a hotshot, you'll go out in a much worse way. Then they took Maggie and smashed a bunch of chemicals on the floor in the middle of a crowd — all so they could see the look on my face and say, *This is all your fault.*"

"Jesus. They couldn't possibly have known you would survive, though. You can't control a gas cloud."

"I don't think they were too fussed about that."

"How did you find the link?"

Barnes paused before answering. "Tina. She was digging around. Rees was organising taxi pickups for Keber troops when they were released from custody."

Kane didn't say anything.

"Samson, there's a confirmed link between Pearce and Charlie Rees now. It's not a theory anymore. It's intelligence."

"You need to go into protection. I'll call the region."

"Maybe. But not without my family."

"Okay. I'll start making some calls. I've spoken to my oppo in Jersey, and they're now taking it a bit more seriously. There's only so many places you can hide on an island that size, so they're trying to establish first of all whether they've left or not. Politically, proving that theory suits them too, because they can quickly wash their hands of it."

"Where is Pearce now? Right now."

"He's in custody, Barnes. He's on the continent in an underground cell, awaiting extradition. He's not going anywhere."

"If he's in a UK prison, he can run operations just as easily as he could on the outside."

"I'll get it ramped up. As you say, we have intelligence now. We'll get them breathing down his neck. Tossing his cell three times a day. Solitary if we can square it. And there's something else. I squared a VO for Duquesne Kenley."

"Finally."

"I failed on a production order, but a VO lets us get some face time. We'll get some private space — even looking like I do, he doesn't want the world knowing he's got two police visiting. Where are you?"

"Right now? Gatwick Airport. In the queue for a flight back to Jersey."

"How long?"

"Twenty-four hours, at least."

"Okay. I'll come get you. It's an hour to Belmarsh from there. Get your head down somewhere and I'll see you in the morning."

* * *

"I should warn you, he's been behaving pretty erratically of late." The guard extended a bunch of keys on an elastic lanyard and unlocked a solid blue metal gate with a *thunk*. "He's doing a PhD or something, in business administration. He could be going places — if he ever gets out of here. One of the inmates looked at him sideways on the wing a couple of days ago. He shoved him down the gantry stairs. Chap's in the infirmary."

It was a bleak, freezing December morning, Christmas a week away. Kane had found Barnes asleep on a sofa in Gatwick Caffè Nero, and the two of them had taken a train up to London Bridge.

Barnes wasn't quite sure how he'd done it — he may have been a superintendent, but for a governor used to daily interactions with the highest echelons of government, the security services and the Met, Kane was small fry — but he had arranged for a private room to see their charge.

Kenley had looked better. The thick brown curls were still there, but the shadows at his jaw and cheek were deeper, his Iberian complexion more grey than brown — shaded as it was in places with a spread of bruises and cuts of varying ages — and the stubble was dense and flecked with grey, covering his skin like moss on a rock. The glasses were old and smudged, and the six-two-fully-upright posture had been kinked by a slight stoop.

"You've looked better," Barnes said.

Kenley raised an eyebrow, staring directly at Barnes. Nothing broken about him, Barnes thought. Here was a man who not only still had fight, but seemed to think, despite his environment and circumstances, that he was winning.

Something still waiting for him on the outside, maybe.

Kenley spread his hands. "So, what can I do for you gentlemen?"

Kane rested his arms on the table.

"I must admit, I thought you'd be dead," Barnes said.

Kenley turned to Kane. "You must be the superintendent." Kane was silent.

Kenley laced his fingers on the tabletop. He shrugged, flicking his thumbs upwards. "So, how can I help?"

"Keber. You've still got an in. They're waging a campaign to make my life about as horrendous as it could possibly be," Barnes said.

"Yeah, they're good at that. Once they get an idea in their heads . . ." He opened his thumbs out towards the ceiling again.

"At least tell me what I know you know. You crashed a car on Eastbourne seafront to protect Natalie Morgan. You passed out in the ambulance before confirming it was Pearce that killed my wife. At least tell me that."

"You seem to be forgetting that I am even more unpopular with them than you are. Revocation of privileges, segregation, solitary — all pretty galling when they tell you it's for your own protection. As you say, I'm lucky to be alive."

He glanced at Kane.

"So, I'm afraid there's not a lot I can help you with. And even if I could help you, you would presumably have something to offer in return. I don't see why I should help for nothing. It's not—"

"We can kill your case," Barnes said.

Kenley looked at him. So did Kane. Away down the corridor, echoing voices were silenced by a metal door slamming shut.

"What?" Kenley said, in a low voice.

"We can get the whole thing binned."

"And how exactly are you going to do that, may I ask?"

"We tell them the truth. You were a high-ranking officer in the Keber group. They went in a direction you didn't like — too much risk to civilians — so you put on your holier-than-thou hat by staging a diversion on the seafront that sabotaged the operation."

"Three people died."

"Three Keber goons. No one's going to miss them particularly. And because you're so unbelievably bloody noble, we'll say it was that or twenty innocent members of the public."

"You'll recall, of course, that I took the rap for a bunch of stuff I didn't do as well. That was my penance. And as far as Keber were concerned, that was the *least* I could do."

"Again, not uncommon in your circles. We can apply for your guilty pleas to be vacated on the basis of unreliable admissions made under duress and intimidation. They'll be thrown out pretty quickly."

"You sound—"

"Desperate. I am desperate. They've got my whole family, and all they want is for me to suffer."

Kenley looked at Kane, and indicated Barnes with his thumbs.

"Should he even be here?"

"Let's not forget that Stratton Pearce didn't just hold me responsible for his pain," Barnes said. "He holds everyone in this room responsible."

"Stratton Pearce, the rascal," Kenley said. "Where is the old dog these days?"

"In a concrete box on the European mainland. Due to be extradited back to the UK any day now."

For the first time, Kenley lost some of his cocksure front.

"What's there to think about, Duquesne? We're not talking about serving time for appearance's sake — that ship has sailed. We're talking about you walking out of here. Clean slate. You have something waiting for you on the outside, we're talking about you getting there while you've got enough left in the tank to make the most of it. Something. Or someone."

Kenley held his stare. Barnes had needled him, he could tell.

"I'm a reasonable man, DI Barnes. I'm not showboating. You make a very intriguing offer. But I do think you overestimate the value I'm going to be to you. It's not like I can pick up the phone to them and pass the time of day. They want me dead almost as much as they do you."

Barnes stood. "Well, I suggest you start combing that considerable brain of yours for ideas. The alternative is that I pursue you for the rest of my life for the two murders I *know* you are responsible for, and any others I can uncover."

"That's pretty broad."

"Keep it simple," Barnes said. "To start with, anyway. Keep your ear to the ground, report some threats, get some official lines going about the risk to you. You'll pick up stuff by osmosis."

"You know I've been on remand for over three years, right? The delays in the system are a joke. I'd wager that if I threw in a bunch of guilty pleas now and turned on the waterworks, with time served I'd walk out of court. The *actual* charges are causing death by dangerous driving times three, no insurance, aggravated vehicle-taking, careless driving and criminal damage. It sounds a lot. But it isn't. The meaty stuff is conspicuously absent — no conspiracy, no murder, no robbery."

"What's your point?"

"My point is, you don't have a lot of bargaining power. If the price was right, I'd think about it. But the risk for me is real. No way could I ask any questions about Keber without some very interested ears perking up."

"I could get her in to see you," Barnes said. "Natalie."

Kane blinked slowly, stared at Barnes, and then said, "Who?"

Barnes moved around the table. His fists bunched. He bent down and got right in Kenley's face, smelling mouthwash and some kind of hair product.

"My family is in *danger*," he hissed in Kenley's ear. "Do you get that?"

"I'm really sorry to hear that," Kenley whispered back. "Have you thought about *not* abandoning them on an island in the arse-end of nowhere?"

Barnes's eyes widened. "What? What did you say?"

"I'm sorry?" Kenley said.

Barnes grabbed him by the sweater and pushed his fists into Kenley's chest.

Kane jumped up.

"What did you say? Do you know where they are? What did you just say?" he yelled, shaking Kenley back and forth.

Kenley's body went limp, like an old cotton doll, allowing himself to be shoved this way and that until Kane grabbed Barnes and pulled him off.

"Did you hear? Did you hear that?" Barnes said, pointing at Kenley. "Bastard knows something!"

"You've just broken about fourteen prison rules," Kane said. "We have to leave. Now."

He steered Barnes to the door and thumped the metal. The guard came and unlocked the door, stepping back when he saw Barnes, teeth bared, pumped like a heavyweight about to enter the ring.

In his seat, Duquesne Kenley adjusted his prison-issue clothes, the merest hint of a smirk creeping across his face.

CHAPTER THIRTY-FOUR

"Go home. Get some rest," Kane said. "I'll call you."

"You told me not to go home," Barnes mumbled.

"That's an excellent point."

They were standing by the shuttered kiosk outside Plumstead train station, a tiny brick shed surrounded by Heras fencing that rattled in the wind like chattering teeth. The wind swooped low, like a vampire, to bite them.

"Okay, so come and stay with me."

Barnes shook his head. "I'm heading back to Gatwick. If I can't get a flight, I'll get a Premier Inn or something."

"Okay. I'll give you my address," Kane said, gripping his pocketbook tight as he scribbled in it. The pages flapped in the wind.

He tore off the sheet. "Here."

"'Five, Coroner's Court?'" Barnes said. "That's cute."

"If I hear anything, I'll call you."

"What are you going to do?" Barnes said. "You barely said a word in there. Are you okay?"

"I need to start some wheels turning with this joker," Kane said, ignoring the question. "We've got enough now to start thinking about some covert options. Him running his mouth has helped, despite you losing your cool."

Barnes was silent.

"I'll check in with the duty officer in Jersey and see where they've got to, then start pulling people in to work on this properly. Major Crime should take this now. And if Jersey know we're treating it seriously, they might feel inclined to up their game."

Barnes's shoulders sagged with relief. Finally, someone was listening to him.

They shook hands and Barnes took the train back to London Bridge. He kicked his heels on the concourse, lost in the lights and footfall and tannoy announcements, feeling less and less like a detective and more like a frustrated, terrified, helpless victim with every minute that passed.

He caught his connection and booked in at the Gatwick Sofitel. He wandered over to the terminal and made a nuisance of himself at the check-in desks. One of the operators looked at him sideways, asked if he was all right, and then promised to call him at the hotel if anything came up.

In the hotel room he tried, pointlessly, to video call Tamsin on his laptop.

His phone buzzed. He looked at the display. Tina.

"Hello?"

"Barnes, it's Tina."

"Tina. You know, in this whole sorry mess, you're the only one that's ever called me with anything remotely resembling good news?"

"I am? Well . . . Barnes, are you okay? What are you doing?"

"Believe it or not, I've been making friends with my common-law wife's ex-husband. He's surprisingly difficult to dislike."

"Where are you?" she said after a pause, as if trying to work out whether or not Barnes was verging on hysterical.

"Gatwick Airport. Trying to get back to Jersey. If I'm not first in the queue when this storm finally blows over, then something has gone seriously wrong."

"Everything's cancelled, I guess."

"Indeed. I'm just lucky my phone's still working. But anyway. What magic have you performed now?"

"I wouldn't call it magic, but I've been speaking to one of my intelligence counterparts in Jersey to see if we can use ANPR to get some idea of Tamsin's car's movements. Since . . . you know."

"Yes, I know. Find anything interesting?"

"Well, for the first few hours it just moved around the island. Nothing unusual about it. Stopped at some shops, then did a wider circuit from Bouley around the west coast."

"Maybe they were making her drive it."

"Maybe. Last hit was St Helier, very close to the Elizabeth ferry terminal car park. I don't know what you want to deduce from that, but one explanation is that they did leave by commercial means."

"Or that's just what they wanted us to think. You'd need to assume there were at least three individuals, more likely four, that staged the actual taking. That being the case it would be pretty hard to board a ferry with a woman and two children who didn't want to go. For starters, it would look odd, but even with a gun pressed to her back Tamsin would raise merry hell in a public place. She's not one to just do as she's told, especially if it means kicking a plan off course that she isn't happy about."

"Good for her," Tina murmured.

"No, I think we need to assume that was for show. ANPR is not a particularly secret technology. They probably switched up into a van or something; one of them drove the car into the ferry terminal, then they regrouped and off they went — either to some predetermined hiding place on the island, or, more likely, to get off the island from some remote launch site. That would . . . that would depend on their intentions, of course."

"You still want Jersey Police to seize the car, though, right?"

Barnes thought about it. Part of him really, really didn't.

"Of course," he said.

"I'll get onto them," she said.

There was a pause on the line.

"I'm sure they're okay," Tina said. She didn't sound particularly convincing. "Either way, I'm going to try to get my oppo in Jersey to cross-check port CCTV with the timings of the ANPR hit. We might get lucky. Don't forget, the weather is horrendous. If they didn't leave the island immediately then there's a good chance they got stranded there, so there's a finite time frame to work with. And if they got stuck there when their intention was to leave — or even vice versa — then that means their plans have been knocked off course. And *that* means there'll be something for us to find."

It was a good point. Barnes was impressed.

"You don't have to keep doing this, you know," he said. "I don't want you to get in trouble."

"Bit late for that. Besides, from what you've said, no one else is doing anything."

"Kane's fighting it. He's giving it to Major Crime. There should — finally — be something resembling a commensurate response before long."

"Well, they're going to need me on the team then, aren't they? And besides—"

"Holy shit," Barnes said. His voice was strained. A bolt of adrenaline flooded his body. He swung his legs off the bed and pressed his nose up to the laptop screen.

"What? What is it?" Tina said. "Are you okay?"

"I'll call you back," he said, and ended the call.

He stared at the laptop screen. He was still logged in to his video-conferencing account. His contacts, together with tiny circular profile photographs alongside them, with even smaller coloured circles next to them denoting their status, were listed vertically on the left-hand side of the screen. Tamsin's photo was at the top, and ever since the abortive video call where she had disappeared into thin air, her status had been a grey *Offline* circle.

But to his astonishment, it had changed. The profile icon was now blinking green, with a tick inside the circle, and a caption that read:

CONTACT ONLINE.

CHAPTER THIRTY-FIVE

Barnes, with tunnel vision so sharp he felt like he was falling down a rabbit hole, clicked the *Call* button and stuck his headphones on.

The outgoing call tone emitted an inoffensive tune in his ear, and then chirped as the call was connected.

"Tamsin? Hello? Tam, are you there?"

He adjusted the headphones. There was some feedback and static on the line, and he could hear his own voice echoing back at him.

The screen was black. He squinted. Was it because the camera on the other end was off, or . . .

No, it didn't seem to be. The video feed was working fine, it seemed, it was just that whatever he was looking at had no lighting. It was complete darkness. An unlit room, or . . .

There was a click.

A light went on, a dim, low-powered overhead lamp of some kind that cast a weak yellow triangle across the screen.

Barnes could just make out a brick wall, like a garage or a warehouse or a basement or something. For an instant, he panicked that Keber weren't involved at all, and that some militant rebel faction from a crumbling overseas regime was about to deliver a live ultimatum, with Tamsin at the centre.

He tried to compose himself. How, exactly, would that scenario be any worse? It wasn't like Keber were known for their mercy. Just as his irrational mind threatened to run away with itself, another light flicked on.

What the hell was this? Parlour tricks?

"Tamsin?"

No Tamsin.

But the second light had cast its glow over an ordinary kitchen chair with white seat padding. Barnes peered at it. There appeared to be spots of red on the vinyl. Blood?

The camera's zoom function started to work. Barnes could hear it whirring. The chair grew in size on the screen.

There was a piece of A4 paper taped to it, with a message scribbled on it in thick black marker pen.

LOOK BEHIND YOU.

Footsteps. The rustling of clothing. Another presence in the room.

Barnes spun around, just as a solidly built individual in a black tracksuit launched himself across the room, arm raised above his head.

"What the hell . . . ?"

Barnes pushed himself out of the way, bracing his feet against the table, and rolled backwards away from the man.

There was something in the assailant's hand. It came down with force, shattering the two unused ceramic cups on a tray of single-serve tea and coffee.

Barnes ended up on the floor on his back, wedged between the bed and the wall, a space just wide enough for the bedside table. *Not good*, his brain screamed. He was aware of his breathing, coming in frantic gasps as he tried to connect his conscious mind with every instinct and reflex at play.

The man came again, launching himself at Barnes with some kind of metal baton in his hand. He brought it down full force with an angry scream; Barnes rolled backwards and launched his feet into the air in a double-kick. It didn't connect anywhere particularly useful, but it did catch him a deflecting blow and was enough to knock the man off balance. He crashed into the wall, and Barnes pulled himself up onto the bed before the guy could land on him. He scrambled across it and made a flailing grab for the door.

He burst into the hallway, half expecting to be clubbed on the back of the head or yanked back into the room or both. He was sprinting down the corridor when he began thinking, *Why am I running? There's only one of him. I get the better of him, that could be a straight line back to Tamsin.*

On the other hand, he thought, *if* he *gets the better of* me, *no one will* ever *find her.*

And so he kept running. He avoided the lift, and made straight for the staircase.

He took them two at a time, footsteps echoing around the dimly lit stairwell, the arc lights of Gatwick's North Terminal bouncing back off the snow-caked airfield outside, the runway empty, aircraft still and silent at the piers.

He jumped down a couple of flights and then doubled back onto the next floor and waited there, taking a moment to catch his breath, one hand on the doorframe.

He waited. He listened.

Nothing.

No pursuit, no gunshots, no angry shouting.

Barnes wasn't the only traveller stranded due to the weather, and there had been enough activity at the reception desk to suggest there were a good few passengers preferring a hotel room over a departure lounge bench, and that they would try their luck again in the morning.

So where were they all?

For just a second Barnes wondered if, in his frantic, sleep-deprived, desperate state, he'd imagined it.

But he didn't think so.

And it wasn't beyond the wit of Keber to book out an entire hotel floor. If the price was right, what would the hotel care?

Three possibilities: his attacker had knocked himself unconscious in the hotel room, he was silently stalking the halls in a slow and deliberate search for Barnes, or he'd made his point — fear and disorientation — and so had cut his losses and left.

Barnes didn't wait to find out. He quickly inventoried the contents of his room in his mind — the only essential things were his phone, his wallet and his warrant card, and they were in his pockets.

He stuck his head into the stairwell and listened intently.

He couldn't hear anything.

Then — breathing.

Slow, heavy.

He spun round.

Standing in the corridor like an apparition, the lights of the hallway stretching away behind him, was his attacker. His face was covered by a black gaiter, and a baseball cap was pulled low. His head was tilted down and he held the metal baton horizontally in front of him, a hand at each end, and his breathing was coming in a ragged hiss.

Then he approached.

He brought the baton up and then in from the side. Barnes just had time to try to block it; it crashed against the meaty part of his upper arm with a dull thud.

The pain shot through him like a heat-seeking missile, but some faraway voice from his training was saying that out of all his body parts, that bit was going to cause the least damage. *It still bloody hurts*, he thought.

The man rushed in at close quarters, throwing little rabbit punches with his fist closed around the end of the baton.

Barnes couldn't get on the front foot, couldn't gain the upper hand, couldn't get his brain switched from *defence* to *attack*; all he was able to do was to try to shield himself from this vicious onslaught of strikes that seemed to be coming from an angry octopus with metal tentacles.

The man brought a straight forearm like a plank of wood up into Barnes's jaw, forcing his head back; then, with his boot, he stamped down hard on the outside of Barnes's knee.

Barnes yelped in pain and his legs buckled. He went down on one knee, and even as he did so, he thought, *Big mistake*.

214

With Barnes's height halved, the man moved around to the rear and brought the baton around Barnes's throat.

He gripped it like a troublesome barbell, and then pulled up and in, forcing the metal against Barnes's larynx. Barnes felt his air supply shut off and a crushing feeling in his throat, and the edges of his vision began to darken as he panicked, feeling the life start to slowly leave him.

He kicked and thrashed, shoes trying to gain purchase on the soft carpeted floor, but the man was strong, and was pulling the baton towards himself like a vice closing, making little grunting noises as he did so, which signified to Barnes a certain amount of intent on the part of his attacker.

It suddenly occurred to him that this might be it. He was going to fail. He was going to die here, in a hotel corridor with thousands of stranded passengers littered about the place that had no idea what was going on. Stratton Pearce was going to win. He was going to have the last laugh.

An eye for an eye.

The thought of doing anything with his hands besides trying to prise the baton away from his throat seemed like suicide, but as it wasn't doing any good anyway, he reached up and over his head with his left hand, scrabbling for purchase.

His fingers found the man's ear, and, with as much venom as he could muster, he raked his nails down the side of his neck, hard and deep. He felt blood. The man growled in pain and anger, and squeezed harder. Barnes might die here, in the middle of an airport, but there would hopefully be enough forensic material under his nails to give the SIO of the eventual murder investigation a fighting chance.

The man was standing in the middle of the corridor, rather than braced against the wall, and Barnes managed to summon the wherewithal to drag the heel of his fairly robust shoe down the shin of his attacker, and then he drove himself backwards as hard as he could.

They crashed against the wall. It was one of the better hotels in the area, and there was little give in the solid wall. More by chance than design, the back of Barnes's head connected with the man's diaphragm; with the wall behind him giving no quarter, the impact squeezed enough wind out of him for his grip on the baton to relax just enough for Barnes to wrench it away from his throat. The man went to one knee.

Barnes staggered back, hands at his throat, sucking giant breaths into his lungs, the air scraping his damaged windpipe like the blade of a knife. He was very far from out of harm's way, and knew that if he ran, he would be caught and over-powered in no time — the man was only very temporarily sidelined. With this in mind, he swung his foot up like he was one of the Royal Ballet, and connected firmly with the man's jaw. Probably not out, but at least briefly down.

Barnes ran down the corridor. It felt like he was running along the inside of a spinning barrel. Disco-ball lights danced in front of his eyes, and he had to steady himself on the wall a couple of times.

He chanced a look back. The man was moving, but still down. Barnes reached the bank of lifts and hit the button, prepared to carry on to the opposing stairwell if they delayed too long.

He got lucky. The indicators above the door responded immediately to his summons, and the doors slid open with a soft chime moments later. Barnes threw himself inside, repeatedly jabbing the button for the ground floor like he was trying to resuscitate it.

The doors slid shut and the elevator began to move. Barnes slumped against the corner of the lift, the mirrored glass holding him up, his breath coming in ragged gasps. Parts of his body began to throb, and as he tried at least a cursory self-survey, he noticed blood — grazes on his hands and arms, and a wound winking through a rip in the leg of his trousers. He had no idea where that had come from.

He turned to look at himself in the mirror — and a wave of nausea hit him. The lights in the lift darkened, and he bent over double, hands on his knees to stop himself from passing out.

The wave passed, and he tried again. He looked like an extra from a zombie B-movie. He was pale with dark rings around his eyes like decaying fruit, and a bruise spread across his throat like a purple polo neck.

He staggered out of the lift and across the lobby. Some part of his brain was telling him, *Stop, get help, call the police, call an ambulance, there are crime scenes here and a dangerous person in the building.*

But he couldn't bring himself to stop. Whoever was doing this, they knew. They knew where he was. They knew where his family were. He was being followed, either physically or technically, or both, and *run* was the only command his body could understand.

He burst out into the night and was enveloped by the storm. There was the tang of jet fuel in the air and the ever-present backdrop of airport arc lights juddering in the wind, the usual carousel of freight and passenger aircraft performing the carefully choreographed inbound–outbound routine strangely absent, the night sky tinged purple with light pollution.

It was a five-minute walk along the perimeter road to Gatwick police station — Barnes ran up to the blue double doors and began hammering on them like a man possessed.

Nothing.

He thought about hopping the barrier and getting into the secure area via the car park, but panic gripped him — there was no one around, no signs of life, and the streetlights illuminating the path up to the station's front door were smothered by overhead foliage. He was a sitting duck.

He blindly stumbled along the perimeter road — the impenetrable razor wire fence of the airfield proper to his right, festooned as it was with red signs indicating the likely fate of anyone trying to breach it, the towering grey ripples of the acoustic concrete wall beyond, the hiss of the monorail shuttle overhead like a 1950s model of a futuristic city.

He crossed the road and ended up alone on the pedestrian underpass that led to the South Terminal railway station. He spun three-sixty on the spot — he was alone with the stink of urine and a sickly yellow light, and fully exposed if Baton Man happened to have had a car full of goons waiting outside the hotel.

He just about made it without getting collected by a passenger shuttle, and summoned the faculties to buy a ticket back down to the south coast, trying to avoid eye contact with railway staff. He thanked whichever servant of Fate had seen fit to ensure that, in the hotel room, he hadn't got around to emptying his pockets.

He waited on the platform, concealing himself behind a grimy brick pillar next to a poorly lit chain-link storage area. The rumble of the incoming train was audible after a mercifully short wait, and, once he was on board, he allowed himself to relax a little and focus on the pain that was wracking his body, particularly his throat. It felt like two metal fists were still gripping it.

He brought up Kane's number and hit *call*.

And then cancelled it.

The pain in his throat was spreading. Breathing was okay, but it hurt. He had to take his time, and he kept gently clearing his throat like a man trying to ignore the gradual onset of a vomiting fit.

He slumped lower in his seat and covered his face with his hands.

Just give them back to me. Just let them go. You can have me, I don't care. What do I have to do? Give you secrets? Sell you information? Mule drugs? I'll do it. Just let them go.

His face contorted under his hands. A family of four, laden with brightly stickered suitcases and souvenirs, pushed their way down the carriage. Barnes was surrounded by seven empty seats, but when the family chanced upon him, their holiday chatter petered out and they hurried on past.

A sliver of suspicion cut into Barnes's mind like shrapnel.

Even for a well-connected group like Keber, round-the-clock surveillance of a middle-ranking detective, even one on borrowed time, was difficult to achieve. Someone on the inside, however, feeding them information, made the proposition considerably easier.

Not you, Samson.

Kane had been elusive. Not answering calls. Not being there. Going with the flow on bogus case conferences. Did the senior CPS lawyer he namechecked and supposedly met with even exist? He'd promised lines of officialdom on every case Barnes had been personally touched by — Maggie's abduction, the chemical attack, the latest kidnap. Now Barnes had been barred from the premises, he had no means of corroborating what Kane was telling him.

Other than Tina.

She was still talking to him, wasn't she?

His thumb hovered over her number. He suddenly felt unable to make a decision.

A thought occurred to him, and he pulled the torn piece of notebook bearing Kane's address from his pocket.

He thumbed it. There was a smear of blood on one corner.

He wouldn't call him.

But he would confront him.

CHAPTER THIRTY-SIX

Coroner's Court was a block of flats converted from a Victorian courthouse in a sixteenth-century market town north of Eastbourne, squirrelled away in the endless greenery of the High Weald. Barnes's prior exposure was limited to speeding past the brown roundabout signs on the bypass indicating the way for anyone wishing to visit a "Historic Market Town".

From the outside, it looked like a complex of six retirement flats, and not the kind of place someone like Kane would go for. Then Barnes saw the frosted window with POLICE SUPERINTENDENT embossed across it, and, presuming it to be an original feature, understood a little more why it appealed to Kane.

The large spiderweb crack in the centre of the window rather spoiled the effect, Barnes thought, stopping in his tracks.

The flat, like the other five, was self-contained. Each had its own bright blue door out onto a small, neatly paved courtyard that separated the block from the narrow road that constituted the main drag.

Barnes wrapped his sleeve around his hand and gripped the doorknob.

It popped open with little resistance.

He — pointlessly, because he knew he didn't have any — patted his pockets for cuffs, baton, pepper spray, radio; utility belt staples that provided a degree of reassurance for the dogged officer stepping over a threshold into a theatre of unknown risk.

The flat was modern, well-kept, with wooden floors and the scent of residual incense. Barnes turned off a small hall-way into the front room. Half the opposite wall was taken up with floor-to-ceiling shelves half filled with books.

The remaining half littered the floor.

A large rock had been dropped through the centre of the glass coffee table, while the sofa bore tears and rips that looked like it had lost an argument with a particularly savage wolverine.

There were two framed posters over the television — the Grateful Dead and KRS-One — both smashed and defaced. A bright blue bass guitar had been removed from its stand and appeared to have been the cause of the hole in the super-intendent's window. Icy wind whistled through it.

The front room looked like a partially deliberate defile-ment of somebody's home and castle. But when Barnes stepped through into the dining area, it looked more like Samson Kane had been flung around like a puppet. A fruit bowl on the table had been smashed, the contents scattered across the floor; chairs were upended; and the clutter on the worktop looked like it had flung itself out of the way of a fast-moving, human-shaped missile.

Barnes moved into the kitchen. He crouched down. A spatter of dark brown blood and — God help him — what looked like bone fragments formed a spurting pattern down the side of the dishwasher's wooden front panel. It looked like someone had upended a cup to put in the dishwasher, forgetting it still had tea in it.

"Nice place, boss," Barnes murmured.

At the rear, a double set of uPVC patio doors swung outwards into a communal garden with a sundial and metal furniture. He stepped through the garden, following a trail of trampled foliage under a layer of slush, until he came to a wooden fence partially hidden by an overhanging willow.

He crouched down. The shrubbery had been flattened here. There were partial boot prints in the brown snow in a non-linear arrangement — tussling on the spot, maybe, turning this way and that. They didn't look like anything forensically useful, but Barnes could still see they were different sizes, different patterns.

He looked at the fence. There were clean stripes of naked wood in it where the mossy outer coating had been scraped away — by a boot scrambling to get up and over?

He peered over the fence — an enclosed concrete hardstanding surrounded by six lock-ups in varying states of repair. Nothing really overlooking it, no CCTV, any witnesses likely to be over eighty and petrified.

Van out the back with driver inside, engine running. Two to three round the front, bully or beat their way in, knock him senseless, drag him through the garden and over the fence.

Couldn't have been easier.

He stepped back inside, and his heart began to drum in his chest. He could feel options, avenues, choices, all turning to slammed doors and dead ends in front of him. He knew he should call in and report this. He should report the attack at the hotel — he still had the bloke's skin and blood under his nails, for God's sake — but he knew if he did that, the call taker would want him to stay put while they sent a patrol, particularly if he let on that he was an officer. If he didn't, then he could — would, even — quickly fall into that category of criminal who likes to report on their own handiwork from the scene before fleeing.

He could call Gabby.

Except he couldn't.

Gabby would drive there with blue lights on just to be the first one to put the cuffs on Barnes.

He tried Kane's number.

It rang in his ear; at the same time, the tinny sound of some screaming Deftones track burst out of the kitchen.

It rang off and went to voicemail.

He tried again, squatting low as he searched for it.

There it was, lying on the lino between the fridge and the cabinets.

"Goddammit, Samson."

Barnes put his hands on his hips and stared at the ceiling for a moment, trying to ignore the tempo of his heart as it drummed faster and harder, trying to quell the increasingly frantic feelings that were threatening to erupt from within.

The indecision made it worse. Leaving an obvious crime scene was anathema to him, but until he knew whom he could trust, he couldn't take the chance. Usually, if a lone detective stumbled across something, the scene was locked down and a cavalry of additional resources, bringing strength in both skill and number, descended upon the locus to freeze a moment in time and then work backward to tell the story of exactly what had happened. Barnes couldn't even get in the police station. He had been cut off from the main supply, and without the prospect of summoning reinforcements, he was, he reasoned, next to useless.

In the end, he prevailed upon the beleaguered Tina Guestling, his one lifeline into the job that continued to despise him. Even that felt like a steep line of credit.

"Barnes?"

"Tina. Do me a favour. I think Samson Kane is missing. Can you check his duties and see what he's meant to be doing?"

"I . . . okay." There was a pause and a clacking of keys. "He's due in. Hasn't booked on today. Didn't book on yesterday, either. Is he okay?"

"I don't think so. I need to raise the alarm, but under the radar. I have to keep my name out of it."

"If he hasn't turned up for work, his line manager will start asking questions, no?" she said.

"Theoretically, yes. But he's a superintendent. His supervisor won't be breathing down his neck every five minutes in the way that you and I are familiar with. I'd hazard a guess he could go a week-plus without necessarily even speaking to them."

"Well, look, I can throw in an intelligence report. Call it an anonymous source."

"That would work. It might just hasten things along enough. Soon as they knock on his door and see the blood, they'll make their own minds up."

"Blood? Oh my God. Are you there?"

"Yeah, I'm at his house. It's a crime scene. His phone's here. There's blood spatter in the kitchen."

"What are you going to do?"

"I'm running out of options here, Tina. Strange as it may sound, I think I'm going to have to lean on Graham."

"Graham?"

"Graham Wall. The ex."

"God, don't do that. You could, you know . . . hide out at mine. Shit, that sounded really wrong. Are you . . ."

"I can't stay here. And thanks for the offer. I'll be in touch."

"Barnes . . ."

He hung up, his conscience momentarily eased in the knowledge that an official check at Kane's house would not be long.

He pulled the rear doors shut, pulled the front door to, then dug his hands deep in his pockets and headed off onto the High Street. For a moment he thought about getting off the beaten track, but ultimately decided that high footfall public areas were the most expedient means for self-preservation.

A bitter wind had started to swirl, peppered with the tiny particles of another flurry of snow, and Barnes picked his way carefully as other pedestrians slipped and skidded on the increasingly icy path.

He checked his wallet. He was running low on cash and was nervous about the footprint that withdrawing more would leave. He would have jettisoned his phone too, but Tamsin, should she manage to escape from whatever personal hell she'd ended up in, would have no other means of contacting him.

He wondered if he was being paranoid, but it only took someone like Gabby — or even Kane — to record Barnes as a high-risk missing person and it would be carte blanche to trace his financial transactions, his phone activity, his vehicle movements and his presence across a sprawling network of CCTV coverage.

Both the weather and the fact that he most likely had a welcoming committee somewhere around Gatwick Airport led him to board the next southbound bus. It took a meandering route through the countryside, rumbling past fields sprinkled with frost and gnarled, dead oaks, ending up in Eastbourne nearly ninety minutes later. He couldn't go home, couldn't stay in a hotel, couldn't go to a police station, and so he went to the only other place he could think of.

CHAPTER THIRTY-SEVEN

If Graham was surprised to see Barnes, he didn't show it.

It was only lunchtime when Barnes arrived, but Graham was home. He answered the door in chinos and a white shirt, no tie.

His eyebrows shot up when he saw Barnes.

"Barnes? Are you okay? Do you have news?"

"Sort of."

"You look dreadful. Do you need an ambulance?"

Barnes's hands instinctively went to his throat.

"I don't think so."

"You'd better come in."

Barnes followed him in, feeling, oddly, like he'd reached a safe haven. But then, besides the now-absent Kane and the out-on-a-limb Tina, no one else seemed to care much about finding Tamsin and the girls.

A point Graham seemed to articulate as he fired up an espresso machine whose gleaming chrome resembled the inline six of a particularly well-preserved roadster.

"I must admit," he said, as the thing began to burble and a glorious aroma flooded the kitchen, "if this had happened to anyone else, I'd expect to see nothing else on the six o'clock news. I'd expect the press queuing up at my — your

— door. I'd expect media conferences being given by a chief officer. I'd expect detectives and family liaison officers buzzing about the place.

"I'm not seeing any of that."

Barnes opened his mouth, then closed it again.

"I presume there's a good reason. If there isn't, it just feels like nobody cares very much about finding them."

"It's complicated."

"Undoubtedly. Come through to the office," he said, passing Barnes a mug.

The room at the back of the house that had been converted into an office contained a large workstation with desktop computer, printer, phone and — of all things — a fax machine. There was a locked filing cabinet, webcam and bookshelf with various professional publications filling the shelves. In the other corner was a small conference table next to a futon, above which hung an array of carefully framed credentials, awards and qualifications.

"I wanted to ask what sort of work you'd got into. I'm a way off retirement, but it's always nice to have options."

Barnes sat on the futon, rather more heavily than he intended. The coffee just about stayed in the mug.

"You know, after thirty years . . ."

Barnes raised an eyebrow before he could stop himself.

". . . well, thirty-ish — of discipline and rank, I wanted a bit of freedom to operate. So I set myself up with a little consultancy practice."

"What sort of consultancy?"

"Well, a fair chunk of my services are universally applicable. Many enterprises operate in a similar way, it's just the end product that differs. Having said that, I do seem to have returning trade in shipping, pharmaceuticals, banking — and law enforcement, which is perhaps not a surprise."

"Busy, then. You have a team?"

"I sub a couple of contractors as my doers and Miriam does the books. But, you're right, business is good. I'll need to expand before long. It's impossible to avoid the travel and I do have an office in town — good image for passing foot trade, window shoppers and clients who insist on visiting you in person for meetings — but a fair chunk of it I do from here. Got everything I need. Video calling saves me an obscene amount of time and money, and I deliver some pretty good services with my own coffee machine right next door."

"Good for you. Genuinely."

"Thank you. It won't be for ever. Miriam wants a simple life, with clean air. Nice and simple, living off the land. Get an allotment, or a smallholding nestled in the bosom of the South Downs. Something like that."

Graham sat down at the conference table and faced Barnes.

"So, what's going on?"

Barnes told him. He told him about his exclusion from the workplace, the video call, the basement, the empty chair, the parlour games warning on the screen, the fight with the man in the tracksuit that he very nearly lost, and the missing superintendent.

As he told the story, Barnes realised that, without the overlay of the global headlines that Graham had alluded to, it sounded almost unbelievable. By the time he'd finished, however, Graham was suitably pale. Barnes thought he was going to throw him out and thank him profusely for leading the gangsters to his door.

But he didn't.

"Okay, we need to process this. You have to stay here . . . I know it's weird, but I insist. Get some food into you, rest up and then we'll regroup. In the meantime, I'll try to get hold of one of your senior officers. Jersey too. If you really are *persona non grata*, they might be more inclined to listen to me. I am a taxpaying public service user, after all. I'll threaten to go to the press. And that's not an empty threat, by the way."

Barnes didn't protest. Graham got busy in the kitchen; his new partner, Miriam, arrived home a short time later. She was polite enough when Graham introduced them, but Barnes detected a definite vibe of *why the hell is your ex-wife still proving to be a spectral presence in our lives?* Or maybe the spectral presence was in his head. He imagined Tamsin in a pit somewhere wondering why the man Barnes suspected of killing his first wife was now seeking to bring fire and brimstone down upon the heads of all of them, and whether a more conventional form of emotional baggage — maintenance payments and awkward birthday parties — were all she needed, thank you very much.

Miriam showered and then went back out. Graham plated two meals and they ate in the office in relative silence, the air heavy with the intense pace of two investigators' brains working on overdrive. Barnes washed up and then stretched out on the futon.

He was asleep in seconds.

* * *

Graham was up and dressed before Barnes had even thought about waking up. The espresso machine was going again, as was the dishwasher.

Barnes sat bolt upright and squinted at his watch. *Shit.* He'd slept for seven hours solid — no dreams, no sweats. He felt a stab of guilt; he'd slept while the girls were — where? What the hell was he *playing* at? He didn't know if they were alive or dead, and yet he'd seen fit to doze off.

After a moment or two the pain flooded through his body — his right leg was throbbing, his shoulder was raw, while every rasping breath he took made his damaged throat feel like it was on fire.

Graham came in with coffee, croissants and painkillers on a tray. Barnes grimaced. The smell was incredible, but they didn't have time for continental niceties.

"I spoke to States of Jersey Police. The duty officer," Graham said.

"You did?"

"They're scaling up the response. Full search. They may need to ask for more SAR capability from the mainland, but at the moment they're combing the island. They've locked down the holiday home and there's a search adviser on scene directing things."

"Good going." Barnes's voice was small.

"And I spoke to your ACC. Mr Glover."

"You did? How did you manage that?"

Graham shrugged. "Still have his number in my phone from when he was an inspector."

"You know him?"

"Not really. Enough to store his number back when I was a DC and needed Section 18 authorities. We also swapped a few emails last year or the year before when he was in the market for a consultancy. I didn't win that particular tender, though."

"What did he say?"

"Well, you're right, 'Barnes' is a dirty word in his lexicon, I'm afraid. But, like I said, I'm a concerned taxpaying member of the public whose entire family is missing — and that's not a front, I am all of those things. I also pointed out that the headline would be pretty grim if he continued to sit on his hands."

"Did . . . did you mention me?"

"I said you'd reached out to me because I had a right to know and because you were getting nowhere with anyone else, himself included. I didn't say you were here. I said we'd spoken on the phone. And when I mentioned that the Jersey constabulary were all over the scene and that his outfit risked some public egg on their face, he . . . well, let's just say I could hear the cogs whirring."

"Samson . . ."

"Who?"

"Superintendent Samson Kane. Did Glover mention him?"

"No. Should he have done?"

Barnes thought of Tina.

"No. Never mind."

"Anyway, I would suggest that you could now maybe focus a little more on your recovery and a little less about trying to do the work of two hundred people on your own."

Barnes sat back on the futon, feeling simultaneously relieved and useless.

"I have a client meeting at the office in half an hour. I'll be back later. Rest up. There's some clothes in my wardrobe — you're a little taller than me but they should more or less fit. Hopefully, Mr Glover will call me directly with any news, so I'll let you know if I hear anything. Are you not eating?"

"Maybe later," Barnes said. "I'll clear up."

He could hear Tamsin's voice in his head, heavy with sarcasm.

What a lovely couple you make.

Graham toddled off to work, and Barnes was left alone in the house, feeling very odd indeed. He did shovel down the croissants and coffee, grimacing at the pain in his throat as he did so, and then washed up, again, for the second time in twelve hours.

He wasn't staying another night, he knew that. He stripped the futon sheets and shoved them in the machine, then tentatively went upstairs to the bathroom, resisting any notion of having a good old poke around.

The first floor was as innocuous as the ground floor, but it was freshly decorated and had new carpets. The bathroom was particularly new, and Barnes did a double-take in the enormous mirror.

He looked marginally better for having had some sleep, but the bruise on his neck was like a tattoo spreading across the entirety of his throat. The dark circles around his eyes had reduced a little, but his clothes were bloody, grimy and tattered.

He stripped off, threw all the clothes in a bin bag and took a long shower. It was a new, powerful appliance, and the jets of water were like standing under a hot waterfall. Barnes took his time, hoping that the water would wash away not only the grime and blood from his body, but also rinse his brain of the clouds that were hampering his thinking.

The water jets were loud, and through the noise he thought he heard a knock at the door. A single, deep thud that reverberated around the house — he sensed the vibrations rather than hearing the knock.

He frowned and continued his shower. Most likely a courier — but probably better not to answer the door in only his towel, just in case it was one of Miriam's mates or something.

Then there was a second thud, and a third. Low, loud.

Barnes shut off the water and listened. Nothing. He towelled himself dry, found a first aid kit in the vanity cabinet and liberally applied antiseptic and dressings to his various punctures.

Then, despite his misgivings, he went into Miriam and Graham's bedroom to find some clothes. The dressing-up choices seemed to be *consultant* or *tennis pro*. There wasn't much in between.

He pulled on a golf shirt and some slacks — noting with juvenile competitiveness that there was a bit of give in the waistband of the trousers — and headed downstairs, intending to peer out of the living room window for doorstep interlopers.

He didn't need to bother — as he entered the living room he saw the window had been shattered. An enormous lattice of cracks spread across the pane, turning the damaged glass opaque white like the surface of a frozen lake.

Barnes backed away from the window, then spun round. He ran to the office — both glass doors at the rear had been similarly smashed.

He pulled on his shoes and headed outside, forgetting his earlier nervousness about what the neighbours must think. There were no obvious foreign objects that he could see, no notes wrapped around bricks or anything — must have been a blunt tool, a sledgehammer, maybe. In any case, he pegged it as some kind of intimidation attempt.

Shit. Had he been followed here?

He did a quick circuit of the house and the cul-de-sac it was nestled in — as a foreign visitor he didn't have a line on which vehicles should be there and which were suspicious, but he didn't see anything that jumped out at him.

He headed back in. He didn't have house keys, so once he left he couldn't get back in, and — he realised — he didn't have Graham's number either.

He looked at the time. Mid-morning. What had Graham said? Back soon?

He suddenly realised he was trapped, and he started rifling through the office for a business card, a Yellow Pages, something with a landline number for Graham's office.

Eventually, googling on his phone yielded a result. He dialled the number and, fortunately, Graham's business was robust enough for him to have hired a receptionist for the shopfront.

She was helpful, but said Graham had not long left. She wasn't sure where he was going. His diary was reasonably clear, but—

There was an enormous crash and the front door burst open.

Barnes dropped the phone and ran to the hallway. He found Graham lying on the hallway floor, bleeding.

"Jesus, Graham . . ."

Barnes looked outside. Graham's car was parked askew on the driveway, half of it on the front lawn. The windows were smashed, as were the headlights.

Barnes kicked the door shut and helped Graham up.

"I'm . . . I'm okay, I think," Graham said. "I tripped on the step."

"What happened?" Barnes said, already half knowing the answer.

"Carjacking," Graham wheezed.

"Hold on." Barnes hooked one of Graham's arms around his shoulder and supported him to the office, dropping him heavily on the futon. A smear of blood streaked across the bare white mattress.

"Carjacking? You still have your car."

"Stopped at some lights on my way back. Four guys. Surrounded the car. Smashed the windows. Hit me. I managed to drive off. Think I might have clipped one of them."

"I don't think they were interested in your car. What did they say?"

"Not sure. There was a lot of shouting. One of them might have said 'Back off.' Another definitely said they know where I live."

"When was this?"

"Came straight here."

"If it happened at traffic lights, someone must have called it in."

"These were temporary lights. Roadworks. I take the back roads to town, usually. Down through the marshes — Hankham, Rickney, that way. Pretty remote."

"Keber."

"What?"

"Nothing. Let's just say fake roadworks are a favourite MO of theirs. And they were right about knowing where you live."

Barnes nodded towards the destroyed panes in the rear doors.

"God." Graham suddenly sounded terrified.

"We've got to get out of here."

"Shouldn't we be calling the police?"

"Personally, I wouldn't recommend it at this stage, but if you're going to do so, do it from the road. Intimidation is its own end, usually, but when they've already got your family, it's a different matter. Pack some clothes."

"Miriam."

Barnes looked at him.

"She's safer if she's not with you. Does she have somewhere she can go? Her mother's or something?"

"She's got a sister in Lancing."

"Perfect. For now, anyway. She'll have to go straight there. She can't come back here first."

"She'll love that. She had a few reservations about moving in with a divorcee — I persuaded her that she needed to be realistic, that at our age there's more divorcees than not — but this is something else."

"I know. I'm sorry."

"If they're building up to something, why not just do it? Why waste time with . . ."

He pointed to the broken windows.

Barnes shook his head. "They want you softened up when they do it. They want you already scared, nervous, less likely to fight. But they are coming, Graham."

"How are we going to get out of here? Can't use my car."

"Let's try public transport for a bit of open cover. Is there a bus stop near here?"

"Yes."

"Okay. You pack while I think of somewhere for us to go."

Graham obeyed. Barnes could hear the stress in his breathing. He knew what he was thinking — he'd managed a narrow miss out on the road and had bolted to the only safe haven he knew, only to find the bad guys had already got there. It was enough to make you feel like your walls were collapsing inwards.

They bundled out of the house on foot, Graham with a holdall, leaving his smashed-up car on the driveway. Barnes wondered again what the neighbours might be thinking — a little slice of bland suburban normalcy suddenly thrown into disarray at the same time as the strange tall man with the haunted look claiming to be a detective rocked up on the doorstep.

More by luck than judgement, they managed to time their departure more or less bang on with the arrival of the bus. It was half full, and as it rumbled cautiously towards Eastbourne, sliding on the snow-covered roads, Barnes heard Graham's breathing settle a little.

Barnes reached back into his brain. Where the hell could they go? Another hotel? Risk Tamsin's house? It seemed wherever they went, they were getting found out. The night before, Barnes's exhausted mind had felt there were eyes everywhere, which he'd ascribed — partly, anyway — to paranoia; now, with the benefit of some rest, his objective analysis was more or less unchanged. It might not have been twenty-four-seven surveillance, but it couldn't have been far from it. That meant resources, equipment, skills — and numbers. That kind of undertaking needed a solid commitment, a cast-iron vision and unshakable motivation.

To do them harm.

CHAPTER THIRTY-EIGHT

Darkness, and motion.

A steady rumbling. The swish of passing traffic, and the thump of intermittently uneven tarmac.

The blindfold was tight around Tamsin's face, the corrugated metal of the vehicle floor cold against her cheek.

She was not fully with it by any stretch — her mind was like soup, and she couldn't bring herself to awaken fully nor to form coherent thoughts. All she knew was that they'd been driving for hours.

She allowed herself the temporary respite of semi-consciousness. Curled up in a ball, she could feel the warm, sleeping, steadily breathing bodies of her daughters either side of her. She would take that.

For now.

Then Maggie began to twist and squirm beside her, making little whimpering sounds, and Tamsin came awake in a flash.

"What is it, honey? I'm here, sweetheart."

"Mummy, I need the toilet."

"Okay, sweetheart, just hold on."

She snapped her head from side to side, trying to visualise where she was. She shuffled forwards on her bottom and kicked out, striking a metal wall that, she assumed, was the driver's partition.

She kicked at the metal.

"Hey! Hey! Is anybody there?" she yelled.

She swung her head from side to side again, like a pre-historic bird trying to shake its prey to death.

A low grunt of laughter sputtered beside her, making her jump.

"What the hell are you doing?" the man's voice said. "Echolocating?"

She faced the source of the voice, her breath coming in dry gasps.

"My daughter needs the toilet."

The van dropped into a pothole, causing Tamsin to lurch to the side. With her hands still bound behind her back, she only just kept her balance.

"We're nearly there. She can hold it," the man's voice said, all trace of humour gone.

"Where is 'there', exactly?" Tamsin said.

"I can't, Mummy. I've been holding it for ages. It hurts. I'm going to have an accident."

"If she says she needs to go, she needs to go," Tamsin said, trying to keep her voice even, but not backing down either.

"Listen, I don't give a shit," said the voice. "She has an accident, you clean it up."

"With what? My fucking nose?" Tamsin said, and then to Maggie, "Sorry, baby. You didn't hear the bad words. Cover your ears."

"I'm tied up, Mummy. I can't."

Tamsin spun on her bottom and began to kick the driver's partition with her bound feet. They'd taken her shoes off her some time back, but it still thudded enough to be thoroughly annoying to anyone sitting up front.

"Hey!" she yelled. "Stop this bloody van. Most kidnappers plan for toilet and food breaks. What kind of cowboy outfit are you?"

She braced herself, expecting a smack in the mouth from the man sitting next to her, but none came. In fact, to her amazement, the van slowed. She heard the *tick-tock* of the indicator, and then it veered to the left and stopped. She heard fast-moving traffic swishing past on her right.

For a second she thought she was hearing thunder, but then realised it was the metal runners of the van's side door rumbling open. And then dazzling light as her blindfold was pulled off.

She found herself face-to-face with a man. Not the man in the back with her; she could smell him behind her. This man was lean, tall, and wore sunglasses, a surgical mask and a hood over his head.

"There's a service station twenty yards ahead," the man said, in a low voice she didn't recognise. "Take your daughter and use the facilities. Your other kid stays here. If you act out of sorts in any way, shape or form, then I will personally cut all her fingers off."

Tamsin swallowed. The guy in the back was a meathead, all bravado and as thick as a stack of pancakes. This guy, though — well, she believed every word he said.

She watched as Maggie was similarly unbound, and the two of them climbed out of the van while the man with the surgical mask sat beside a still-sleeping Ellie.

"How do I know you won't drive off with my daughter?" Tamsin said.

The man in the surgical mask just stared at her.

Slowly, Maggie and Tamsin began to shuffle away from the van. Despite their situation, the fresh air smelled good, and Tamsin stretched her back, feeling guilty for doing so.

She tried to take in her surroundings. A fast, sweeping A-road slicing between a country pub and a village service station, with not much else around except a spread of fields and a ripple of green hills on the horizon. She swore she recognised it, but her bloody brain just felt like mushy peas.

She chanced a look back at their mode of transport. A dirty, weather-beaten panel van. The grime on the windscreen caught the sun, making it practically opaque. There was no front number plate. Tamsin wondered if they'd removed it before opening the side door.

They stepped onto the tiny forecourt of an independent service station, Tamsin's hand gripping Maggie's tightly. Tamsin's steps were slow, reluctant; Maggie, by contrast, was desperate to get to the bathroom.

A bell chimed as they stepped inside the shop. Tamsin scanned the interior, her heart like a timpani in her chest. Two men at the counter, paying for fuel. One other guy in the corner, inspecting the options in the chiller cabinet. Nobody else present. No sound apart from idle chit-chat at the counter, a radio playing somewhere and the *hiss-hiss-hiss* of traffic racing past on the main road outside.

Tamsin saw the sign for the toilet next to the counter, and steered Maggie towards it. The customers paid and left. Three more came in. The rotation was steady, the bell chiming each time.

Tamsin stayed focused on the sign, trying her damnedest to avoid eye contact with anyone. She would give everything away if she did, and in her mind was *Ellie, Ellie, Ellie.*

"Don't lock it, honey," Tamsin whispered. "I'll wait right here. No one will come in. Remember to wash your hands."

Maggie nodded and closed the door.

The bell chimed.

Tamsin forced herself not to turn around, but the radio was broadcasting the news, and she strained to listen. For any sound, any word, any *sniff* of anything related to her current predicament.

There was nothing. Tamsin couldn't believe it. Her world had been turned upside down, and the outside world didn't seem either to know or to care.

The bell chimed again.

Maggie appeared.

"All good?" Tamsin said.

Maggie nodded, and Tamsin took her hand. They made for the exit, hugging the wall of chiller cabinets, taking the widest route around the counter, Tamsin intending to make a ninety-degree turn halfway along the wall so as to walk the twenty feet or so straight out of the shop.

Tamsin felt Maggie's hand pull at hers. She turned; Maggie's eye had been caught by a display stand bearing treasure: tiaras, pink sunglasses, colouring books, magazines and cheap plastic toys that served no purpose other than to cause arguments between tired parents and demanding offspring on long boring journeys.

Tamsin felt heat in her chest as she watched Maggie poke about at the items. A nothing, everyday tableau, but she felt as if she were seeing it from behind bars.

"Come on, honey," Tamsin said. "Time to go."

Maggie didn't answer, and Tamsin hung back slightly, permitting her just a few seconds of normality.

She felt sweat on her brow, felt someone looking at her from behind the counter.

A woman. Middle-aged. Wearing a uniform. A supervisor of some kind. Tamsin glanced at her, held her gaze for one, two, three seconds but she felt the cries building in her chest and forced herself to break away before she completely fell apart and started screaming merry hell.

She pretended to examine the fish fingers in the chiller cabinet behind her for ten more seconds, then turned back to Maggie.

"Maggie," she said, in a voice firmer than she felt. "That's enough. It's time to go. Your sister is waiting."

Part of her wanted Maggie to scream, to protest, to throw a major tantrum in the hope that it would necessitate some kind of public intervention, one that couldn't possibly be attributed to Tamsin in any way, and which would, in turn, enable Ellie to keep all her digits.

But she didn't. That wasn't her style. Tamsin hadn't raised her that way. Maggie was a good kid; as a result, no one paid them the slightest bit of attention.

She took Tamsin's hand again, and the two of them walked out of the shop, shuffling back to the van, back to the yawning door into a chasm of black.

CHAPTER THIRTY-NINE

The sky was striped with rolls of low cloud like grey loft insulation, threatening more snow. The bus juddered into town, past the dark blue *WELCOME TO THE SUNSHINE COAST* sign with its bright yellow funfair bubble lettering, and Barnes felt like he was seeing it from the inside of a goldish bowl.

And an idea came to him.

The house.

His empty, formerly marital home.

A house with just too many memories. He'd moved out when he and Eve had split, and then he'd put it up for sale after she died. After kicking around in various states of widowed transience from one place to another, he'd then moved in with Tamsin.

It was reasonably priced, and he'd never quite worked out — and neither had the estate agent — why it wouldn't shift. In the seven years since her death, it had been intermittently on and off the market depending on varying degrees of global economic uncertainty. Offers had been made, but they fell through, or interest rates spiked, or the buyers got killed in car crashes. The universe was maybe trying to tell him something.

As such, it remained empty, completely unfurnished —
and Barnes still had a key.

The bus trundled round to the Crumbles, where Barnes
and Graham disembarked. They stopped in Asda for essentials
— Barnes pointing out to Graham that there was no power
and likely no running water — and they lugged the stuff round
to the north harbour in a fierce fist of biting wind.

The smell was as Barnes might have expected — musty
wood, lino and carpet. But there was a faint undercurrent too
— the smell not of the *house*, but the unique smell of the *home*,
something ingrained in the brickwork that was an aggregate
of every person that had spent time here, every trace of per-
fume Eve had worn, every dinner they'd shared. It was like
being pulled back into the past, into an artefact frozen in
time. Emotions so old they felt new flooded through him.

"You okay?" Graham asked, and Barnes realised he was
gripping the doorframe.

He scanned the street before closing the door. Nothing
obvious, but he headed upstairs and stood watch at the window for half an hour before retreating inside.

"Presumably the neighbours know it's been standing
empty," Graham said. "We should let the agent know."

"Let them know what?" Barnes said. "It's still technically
my house. Don't worry, I don't imagine two blokes in smart
casual will attract much attention on a day like today — most
people will be keeping their heads down and staying in. I just
hope there isn't a viewing booked."

From the Juliet balcony he caught the thin wedge of
dishwater-grey sea between buildings a quarter of a mile in
the distance. He and Eve had laughed about the "sea glimpse"
description in the spec — even the most pretentious of estate
agents couldn't have called it a "sea view" with a straight face.
He couldn't see the fronds of white today as the waves lashed
the shore, but he could hear them.

"So, what now?" Graham said.

"We're hiding out. Rest, eat and prepare. We may have
to defend ourselves."

Graham's eyes widened, and Barnes made himself remember that Graham's frontline exposure, despite his almost-complete service, had been curtailed early.

"Try to stay calm. We'll be sitting around a lot, so we can get to know each other, and devise some kind of 'what next' strategy."

* * *

"So, remind me, what was it that led to your medical retirement?" Barnes said, rifling through the cheap first aid kit he had bought to deal with both his and now Graham's injuries.

Graham looked sharply at Barnes — it wasn't meant to sound like a challenge, but it did. It was a slightly indelicate question anyway, but Barnes was pretty much past caring.

"Back injury," Graham said. His voice was a mumble. "I was chasing a suspect who was garden-hopping. Slipped climbing a fence, fell awkwardly, that was that."

"Did you catch him?" Barnes passed him a packet of biscuits.

"I did, actually. Well, slowed him up. My oppo actually got the cuffs on him, then had to call an ambulance for me."

They were sitting on the bare laminate flooring, a sad-looking candle between them, coats bunched up against the wall, cheap supermarket blankets draped around them.

"Quite apart from the discomfort, I can't see this being a long-term solution," Graham said, shifting uncomfortably. "We're squatters."

"Shame you haven't yet bought your smallholding," Barnes said. "Did you speak to Miriam?"

"Yes. She's not happy."

"No surprise there."

Graham eyeballed him again.

"It's funny," he said. "All the arguments and silly bickering Tamsin and I engaged in, and I didn't realise until I met Miriam how much I learned from it."

Barnes looked at him. *Don't go there.*

244

"I just matured so much in my outlook," Graham continued. "I can count on one hand the amount of times Miriam and I have had a cross word."

"I must be responsible for at least two of those occasions," Barnes said. "Sorry. So, what *did* she say?"

"I won't lie — she did blame you. She blamed Tamsin more, though. Those cross words I mentioned — they were all in the early days, when things were still quite raw and Tamsin and I were still arguing quite regularly after separating, usually about the girls.

"She wasn't happy about having to move out. She's gone to her sister's, but she took some persuading. She didn't mince her words. She said something about my ex being more important to me than she is."

Graham looked at the floor.

"She's never spoken to me like that before," he murmured. "Worst argument we've ever had."

"Sorry about that."

"I nearly backed down."

"For her sake, it's good you didn't."

They debated whether or not to order pizza, but in the end decided any kind of footprint would be a bad idea — they were squatters, after all — and instead piled their way through packets of nuts and supermarket biscuits.

"Anything from Jersey? Or Gabby?" Barnes asked.

"Gabby?"

"ACC Glover."

"Nothing. Jersey are still searching." He shivered and pulled his blanket around his shoulders. "It's colder in here than outside. I could murder a cup of tea."

"How's your . . . you know." Barnes wiggled a finger at Graham to indicate his various injuries.

"Could be worse. I think it's just cuts and grazes." Graham picked at a plaster and grimaced. "Showboating, as I said."

"You were still lucky."

"With round two imminent, apparently. Are we just waiting, Barnes? Should we not keep moving?"

"We can, but not indefinitely. Conditions are treacherous and we have no identified safe house — this is as close as we can get. As I said, we need to rest, regroup and come up with some kind of strategy that doesn't involve us just waiting by the phone."

"I just don't understand how we can stay perched here like sitting ducks waiting for them to turn up."

"Going out in the elements is not wise. You might feel better for being on the move, but it's a false advantage. And look, you don't have to stay with me. If you'd feel safer calling time and heading to the police station, or A&E, or somewhere else big and public, then I'm not stopping you. I just figured we might do better if we've got each other's backs. Besides, the minute the weather breaks I'm on the next flight to Jersey."

Graham was silent.

"Let's doss down here tonight, sleep and then see where we are in the morning. You've worked kidnaps. You know it's all waiting."

"It's only waiting if someone else is actually doing something," Graham said.

Don't I know it, thought Barnes.

"You want the empty bedroom, the empty study or the empty lounge?"

Graham managed a sour smile. He was nervous and scared — it was obvious. Being cold, displaced and uncomfortable undoubtedly didn't help.

Barnes moved to the window again and carefully scanned the street at both the front and the rear. It was a townhouse on three floors, and the vantage point was pretty good.

Nothing of note. Cars on driveways. Dark pavements. Flickers of television screens through net curtains. Lamp posts shuddering alarmingly in the wind. Sleet heaving haphazardly across the glass in vomited sheets. A single dog-walker in head-to-foot hi-vis orange, battling through driving wind and slanted precipitation, looking like they were being attacked by the vegetation being blown this way and that in front gardens up and down the street.

CHAPTER FORTY

Barnes was already awake when he heard the noise.

It was shortly after midnight, and, unlike the previous night, he was unable to sleep, a combination of physical discomfort and nervous apprehension. And so he lay there in the dark, his girlfriend's ex-husband snoring lightly in the other room.

He knew they were coming.

Barnes coughed in the darkness. Normally the sound would have been absorbed by curtains and furniture and the like, but as the house was totally untroubled by such things, the cough reverberated around the bare room.

Then he heard it. A low squeal of brakes. An idling car engine, so close it had to be right outside the house.

The engine died. All was silent again, but only for a moment, and as Barnes lay there, staring at the ceiling, hands gripping the blankets as if pushed into the floor from above, he made an observation. The sound of one car door slamming would be okay. Two, likewise — maybe a taxi dropping off some late night revellers.

But four? Four car doors could only ever be bad news.

For just a moment, Barnes lay on his makeshift bed, hands flat on the floor, unable to move, pinned by an unseen but irresistible force called Fear.

The immediate sound of activity at the front door — clicking as the lock was interfered with, the *clunk* of someone trying the door handle — brought him to attention. He rolled onto his front and moved on his elbows and knees into the next bedroom, where Graham was snoring.

He had reached out to Graham with an outstretched hand, the finger of his other hand to his lips, when their visitors gave up on stealth and instead went loud.

There were three heavy *thuds*, and then the front door crashed open and slammed into the plasterboard behind it.

Loud, deep, baying voices. Like being on the receiving end of a search warrant, only with less rules. Smashing glass. The metallic *thunk* of weapons.

Graham awoke in a panic and pushed himself into the corner, tucking himself into a ball. Barnes shut his eyes and tried to count the voices as they spiralled up through the stairwell.

At least four. Front and back.

Barnes picked up the heavy Maglite from his meagre collection of hastily procured supermarket supplies and brandished it over his head like an angry Saxon about to charge. He knew, in descending order, that preventing capture presented the greatest opportunity for survival, followed by escaping while in transit, with escaping from a static secure location being the least likely.

Heavy bootsteps thundering up the stairs. Barnes's heart began to hammer in his chest. *It's all a front*, he thought. *We know that. We're the police. We're loud and dominant and intimidating to inspire compliance and submissiveness to gain control and achieve operational objectives. It's all psychology.*

He kicked the carrier bag at his feet and the contents spilled out onto the bare floor. There was a kitchen knife in there, still strapped to the cardboard packaging. He used his heel to kick it backwards towards Graham. It skittered across the hard floor and hit Graham's foot.

He looked behind him. Graham's eyes were wide, blank, staring at nothing.

Man down, Barnes thought, and faced the upper landing just as the first of the men appeared on the stairwell, glinting weapons in gloved hands.

He swung once, twice, forehand-backhand, collecting the first man two good solid blows on his balaclava'd head. The man grunted and stumbled backwards onto the top step — Barnes kicked out with a boot and the man tumbled down the staircase.

It was a far better result than Barnes was expecting, and he felt a surge of energy. Could he actually pull this off? The man would have fallen all the way to the bottom had he not collided with three others rushing up behind him with crowbars and sledgehammers.

They stepped over their stricken comrade and charged Barnes. Barnes swung, missed, leaving himself open. Something hard was rammed into his gut, and he doubled over. He felt the skin on his head break open and blood spill out as something hard and blunt was jabbed into his scalp.

Two of the men rushed past him and into the bedroom. Graham mewed and pleaded in his semi-catatonic state. Barnes heard strikes and whimpering.

The blow sent him to his knees, the world spinning, the streetlights outside somersaulting in his vision. A gloved fist swept past, connecting with his jaw, and he went sprawling forwards onto the landing carpet. He was still conscious; he felt plastic cable ties being zipped tight around his wrists, and the curious sensation of blood pumping from a wound like an oil spill.

They didn't strike him again, but hauled him to his feet and pulled him roughly down the stairs — his legs buckled under him on more than one occasion, and he was half shoved, half dragged the rest of the way, then pulled out onto the driveway, where a panel van waited, rocking in the freezing wind, its yawning side door leading into a sightless interior.

Barnes tried to yell, but his jaws felt gummed together. His brain felt like soup; even so, he wondered why the

249

neighbours were not calling the police at the almighty disturbance from the supposedly empty house next door. Even the howling gusts couldn't mask it.

He couldn't see or hear Graham. Where the hell was he? God, Miriam really *would* love Barnes after this.

He spluttered laughter, and then vomited.

"Got some spunk, this one," one of the men said. "What's so funny?"

It was probably no more than the concussion, but there was also something of a perverse relief — all the days he'd spent watching, worrying, waiting, looking over his shoulder, then when the monsters finally appear, you realise the anticipation was the worst bit all along.

He was pushed into the van, and he fell face first onto the floor, his cheek scraping sawdust and grit on the plyboards. A second body was shoved in after him, whom Barnes presumed was Graham. He lay still, making very faint whimpering noises. Rain drummed on the van's roof.

"Graham," Barnes said, his mouth as thick as treacle. He gave the still form a nudge with his foot. "Graham."

"Shut up," somebody said.

He tried to sit up, but the van moved off, pushing him back down. He shook his head, but it felt too heavy for his body and it caused another pulsing wave of nausea anyway, and so he tried to *blink* himself awake.

"Graham."

"I said *shut up*."

The world exploded in a white flash of dazzling light, illuminating the inside of the van like the fifth of November. Scorching, molten pain radiated out from the centre of his skull, and he felt thick blood begin to stream down his face. He hung his head and groaned, now more unconscious than not.

"Fucking teach you."

The man sat back down opposite Barnes, still holding the nine-mil that he'd used to strike Barnes in the nose.

They drove. Barnes had no idea how long or how far. He drifted in and out of consciousness, the feeling of wanting to sleep completely irresistible, his nose an aching mess of frozen numbness.

When he regained some small degree of consciousness, he tried to get his bearings. All he could ascertain was that they hadn't done much cornering and were travelling at a reasonably steady speed; there were no sounds of cars passing them with any regularity, which likely ruled out motorways, so Barnes went for an A-road. The A27 west just up from the coast, or any of the tarmac fingers stretching north to London — A21, A22, A23.

He looked to the front to see if he could get his bearings from the view out of the windscreen, but the rear of the van was completely enclosed and bereft of windows.

So he eyeballed the man opposite instead. Bright, tiny little eyes radiating hate, recessed in a black balaclava.

"Short straw?" Barnes said thickly. "You don't get to ride up front with Mum and Dad?"

He wasn't quite sure where his fat mouth had come from — it must have been a combination of delirium and the oddly exhilarating feeling of the bogeyman now being out of the shadows. He might get beaten to death, but at least they couldn't make him jump.

"You mouthy little . . ."

The man leaned across the van again, and with fat fingers, jammed an oily, dirty rag deep into Barnes's mouth. It reeked of WD-40 and industrial glue, and a particularly grimy patch smeared itself against Barnes's tongue.

Unfortunately, being pistol-whipped meant his nose was filled with blood; as he could only breathe through his mouth, this shut off his airway completely. His eyes widened and stretched in panic, and little staccato grunts like a kick drum emanated from this throat as he tried to force air into his lungs.

"Take that out of his mouth, ya donkey," a voice from up front said. "He'll choke. Don't want him dead. Not yet, anyway."

The man grunted and did as he was told. Barnes sucked in ragged gulps of air, and another quip formed on his lips.

The man sensed this and held up the pistol with a look that said, *Try me.*

Graham suddenly stirred, and groaned like he was in labour, taking some of the attention off Barnes.

"Graham? Graham, are you okay?" Barnes said.

Graham groaned again — and then sobbed, a single, involuntary honk that was so plaintive it was almost shameful.

"Oh Jesus," Barnes said. The man was terrified, which took the edge off Barnes's bravado a little. "Graham, sit up. Are you hurt? It's going to be okay, Graham."

The man carefully placed the barrel of the nine-mil against Graham's temple; Graham mewed again and pulled his knees up to his chest in a ball.

"If you speak to him again," the man said, "the shot will be point blank, so close to his skull that the undertaker will think he set his own hair on fire."

"I think you mean 'pathologist'," Barnes said.

"How long?" the man said, banging on the flimsy partition separating them from the cab. "I'm likely to kill one of these two soon."

"Did you really just ask, 'Are we there yet?'" Barnes said.

The man hissed in his balaclava and raised the weapon again. Barnes winced and braced himself, and then all three of them tumbled the same way as the van took a sharp turn into what appeared to be a decidedly poorly maintained and extremely bumpy road.

Up front, somebody switched on the radio. There were, apparently, speakers in the rear of the van. It was a news bulletin, the nasal tones of the newsreader strangely comforting to Barnes, like looking at normal life through a telescope:

"Enquiries continue into a chemical incident in Eastbourne, in East Sussex on the south coast. The seaside town, known for genteel afternoon teas, walks on the promenade and wall-to-wall sunshine, had its Victorian legacy shattered earlier this month when six people died following the release of a deadly, and as yet unidentified, toxic nerve agent just half a kilometre from the beach. Despite a coordinated response between emergency services, Defra and government authorities, both the

cause of the incident and the nature of the chemical itself remain a mystery. Police say that a deliberate act cannot be ruled out . . ."

The radio was switched off.

"That . . . now that was a fuck sight easier than I thought it was going to be." The voice from up front was muffled, and laced with steel. "I thought maybe I'd have to give up a few casualties of war — you know, toss the law a few breadcrumbs — but *fuck me*. Their total lack of a clue surprised even me. So much so, I might do it again. If you can kidnap a kid without a second look, you could rob a bank, take down a multinational, siphon product off your competitors. Sky's the limit. Christmas market in Brighton city centre next, I'm thinking."

Even through the fug of pain, Barnes's physiologically inexplicable sense of exhilaration evaporated. He swore he knew the voice, but more than that, in half a minute his suspicions had been confirmed. The chemical attack, the consequent chaos and Maggie's abduction were not coincidences. And he could tell no one — no phone, hands bound, snatched bodily out of his former house to probably go and dig his own grave somewhere.

All of it, just for him.

Only one person hated him that much.

CHAPTER FORTY-ONE

The van rolled to a stop. The front doors opened and slammed. Footsteps. Then the side door growled open and a snatch of cold air ghosted into the van.

Graham was yanked out first, mumbling, and dumped on his backside on the ground; Barnes was next. They were marched across a black field laced with ice, stumbling over the uneven terrain — thick, sucking mud that had frozen in a crazy stage of twisted craters and mounds like an armadillo's back. The snow was falling thickly from a heavy, portentous sky; Barnes idly noted that the wind had dropped, and imagined that, if they hadn't already, flights would be resuming soon. In so doing, he also realised that, although his face and head were throbbing, his mind was comparatively clear.

As if to emphasise the point, the overhead twinkle of a low aircraft and two-step sound of churning engines shifting down caught his attention. When another couple of aircraft followed in quick succession, he realised they must be near an airfield.

Surely not Gatwick bloody Airport again, he thought. But, no, the craft were too small. They sounded like props or similar. One of the smaller rural aerodromes, maybe.

There was nothing else to indicate where they were. No street lights, no distant traffic, no signs of civilisation at all. This stood to reason, given the circumstances, but it didn't make Barnes want to walk any faster.

Something up ahead. Lights. They walked for another few minutes across the open field, and Barnes saw another van, engine idling, headlights on main beam across the darkness, catching the outlines of four men.

Four *more* men. Standing still. Waiting.

Eight in total.

They reached the second van. Barnes realised the four new men were standing around a large open hole in the ground, and a cloak of dread settled upon him as he realised this was it. He was going to die, here, in the middle of fucking nowhere, his body covered in boggy mud in a shallow grave that wasn't all that shallow. Technically, he hadn't been suspended yet, so it would still sort of count as death in the line of duty. His name on a plaque. Some cash for Tamsin. A drink with a colleague or two. Then forgotten.

You win, Stratton.

He was forced to his knees inches from the yawning hole, opposite the blinding headlights of the van. Graham was moved to the other side of the hole so they were facing each other, his back to the headlights.

One of the men from his group walked over and stood beside Graham. He faced Barnes and carefully, almost ceremoniously, pulled his hood down with both hands, the headlights from behind him enveloping his form in a halo. Barnes couldn't see the features of this apparition, but he recognised the naked skull and the sinewy frame. This was the man up front. The one that played the radio clip. The one that spoke to him.

"Thanks for not making me dig it myself," Barnes said, nodding at the hole.

The mouth again. Two of the men looked at each other. One tittered.

"Hello, Stratton," Barnes said. "I thought you were in a cell."

The skull spoke. Barnes just about caught the blue serpent tattoo on the side of his scalp. The men from his group fanned out around the hole as if at a funeral. Barnes forced himself to look away from the headlights. They were dazzling, and rendered him unable to get a proper sense of his surroundings.

"You're gonna die here tonight, DI Barnes. You're gonna die not knowing what's happened to your family. You're gonna lose. I'm going to win. Then we're square. An eye for an eye."

At his feet, Graham seemed to wake up, insofar as he began to sob and moan uncontrollably, sinking down into a hog-tied ball.

"Please . . . please don't kill me," he said. "Please don't. I'll do anything you want. Anything."

He began to babble. The headlights of the van caught a sudden wisp of rising steam as Graham lost control of his faculties. One of the men shifted uncomfortably. Another laughed.

Barnes's eyes began to slowly adjust. He looked over his shoulder. There was a whole lot of darkness in all directions; the van's headlights cut a narrow path ahead, but besides that, there was open field. He couldn't even see the van they'd just left. To his right was the black hulk of some kind of copse at the edge of the field. Maybe thirty, forty metres away. Everything else was just black oblivion.

Graham whimpered. Barnes's mind raced, the pain focusing his thoughts, adrenaline shifting gears as his fight-or-flight began to work double-time. *Fear paralyses*, he thought. *But you can't touch it.* He thought of the cases he'd worked where criminals had walked free because of the victim's fear; conversely there were those that had been banged up because their victims had fought tooth and nail, the offender's skin and blood buried deep in their victim's nails, their skin, their teeth. If you fight, if you make them work for it, then you could still play a part, even dead. There was something about

Graham's complete shutdown that was somehow galvanising Barnes. As a minimum, he should try to keep Pearce talking.

He didn't want to be a plaque.

"How did you break out this time, Stratton? EAWs are pretty hard to wriggle out of. I imagined you in some six-by-four concrete box in the bowels of Malaga airport or something."

Pearce stared at him. The silhouette of his chest swelled slightly, like he knew he was being manipulated into talking about himself, but figured he had the time to indulge it.

"Four times I've escaped from custody, DI Barnes. Four. None of you ever learn. I have friends. I have resources. I have skills. And I *cannot* be caged."

Pearce produced a handgun. Its silhouette against the van lights was so sharp and clear as to be offensive. He stood there, the weapon by his sides.

"Bit risky you putting in an appearance, then, no?" Barnes said.

"I wanted to look you in the eye again. Last time we met, *I* was wearing handcuffs. Now it's *you*."

"Releasing a bunch of chemicals in a seaside town was a bit extreme. I'd have given myself up before you had to do that."

"Catch one by killing a load. Nobodies."

"What was it? The chemical? They still can't identify it."

Pearce tapped his nose with the end of the barrel and grinned.

"You said there was going to be another one? In the van. Another attack?"

"I haven't decided. But it doesn't concern you now, either way."

"And the court case? Getting me back here?"

"Mate, that was a fucking doddle. A bunch of phone calls with my best gibbering lawyer act, that was it. No one had to be hurt, no one had to be paid off. The best bit was that fucking Duke Kenley even had to be told that his trial was being moved up. I wish I could have seen his face.

"You lot — police, CPS, prisons — you kill me. Think of the game you're in, the people you have to bang up. And yet I can get your phone number off Google, I can find out when you're next on duty by calling the switchboard, I can even get a meeting room booked in CPS HQ. *And you lot never question it.* You never question who you're talking to on the end of the phone, you never check. You just go along with it."

Barnes had to admit, the man had half a point.

Pearce moved off to the side slightly, and pointed the weapon at the back of Graham's head. Barnes inhaled sharply. Graham didn't seem to notice. He continued to murmur, babble and sob in low tones, chattering some kind of nonsensical last rites to himself, or so it sounded.

"I didn't kill your family, Stratton," Barnes said.

Pearce lowered the weapon. He took a step closer, his toes almost at the edge of the pit.

"You don't talk about them. Ever," he hissed. Graham wailed a little louder.

"You're going to kill my family," Barnes said. "But I didn't kill yours."

"*I* couldn't protect them because *you* locked me up."

"How does that logic work? You'd been in exile for the best part of God-knows-how-long. You wouldn't have been there to protect them even if you *hadn't* been in custody. You chose this life, and they got hurt."

"Fucking end him, Stratton," somebody said.

"The same applies," Pearce said. "You chose your path, and now your family will settle up."

"Did you kill my wife, Pearce?" Barnes said.

"Not yet."

"My first wife. She died in a car crash. A van being pursued by police, occupied by three shitbags driving all over the South East — burgling houses, robbing old ladies, dealing drugs — smashed into her. I can't do anything about it now. But I know it was you. At least be man enough to admit it."

Pearce moved the gun, and pressed it against the side of Graham's head. It took a second for Graham to register what it was, and then he was obviously struck again by another wave of pulsating fear. It didn't manifest, this time, in any kind of coherent pleas for mercy, but took the form of a fresh bout of wailing and sobbing, like a man whose mind had already turned to mush.

Barnes again looked at the copse to his right. It was a little clearer now, and he realised there was a faint slice of moon attempting to appear from behind a canopy of cloud. The spread of leaves had the rounded fullness of oaks rising above a hedgerow that demarcated this field from the other.

The copse was closer than he thought. Maybe twenty metres. The dark spread of ground between here and there looked relatively innocuous, but Barnes knew it wasn't.

There were two ways out of this. Three, if you included succumbing to an anonymous death. Persuade Pearce not to kill him, or create a distraction of some kind and make a run for it. Both had very long odds, but what did he have to lose?

"Did you notice how this little prick hasn't mentioned his family once? He's all *me me me*." Pearce punctuated each *me* with a jab of the barrel against Graham's head. "*Don't kill me, spare me*, blah blah blah. What a fucking worm."

"He's scared, Stratton. You don't have to—"

Barnes didn't fully realise Pearce had fired the weapon until Graham Wall's lifeless body sagged forward in an instant, like he'd been unplugged. His hands were still tied behind his back, and he collapsed forward into a ball, like a hedgehog trying to escape danger, his face taking the brunt of it as it collected the frozen earth beneath him.

CHAPTER FORTY-TWO

Barnes yelped. The suppressed pistol had made a *zzzippp* noise. There had been no muzzle flash. Barnes's eyes and brain frantically tried to work together to process it.

Silence. Just the idling diesel chug of the panel van, and the collective breathing of ten, reduced by one.

"Graham. *Graham*," Barnes whispered.

Pearce stepped forward, and with a size-ten boot rolled Graham's body into the muddy pit. It landed with a squelch, and snowflakes quickly began to cover it.

"Where's your piss and vinegar now, DI Barnes?"

It was a good point.

Barnes looked down at the hole. It suddenly seemed deeper and darker, somehow, and Barnes found his distorted vision could no longer detect the bottom. All he could see were the faint reflections on the surface of frozen puddles, and the dim shadow of Graham's sprawled body.

Suddenly, Barnes didn't feel the same degree of fear. The pit looked warm and inviting, a duvet of snow and mud, his final resting place. He felt the dregs of his energy leave him as he prepared to face the music.

Then — there was something. Not much, nothing you could hang your hat on, but something. Something Pearce had said: *Now it's you in handcuffs.* For the first time since being tonked on the head in the house he'd been squatting in, Barnes thought about his bound wrists. He wasn't sure if it was the cold causing his vessels to constrict, or dehydration, but there was the tiniest amount of give there. Even a gang of armed mercenaries couldn't legislate for all the cause-and-effect variables in a dynamic situation — which way someone was going to fall, a splinter flying into your eye when the door crashes open, how tightly you apply the handcuffs.

He worked his wrists gently, not wanting to catch anyone's eye. His skin had sweated under the cable ties, creating a small amount of *de facto* lubrication. He flexed his shoulders and pulled at them.

They could very well go.

Barnes shut his eyes, and got up onto one knee.

"Oi," somebody said.

"Piss off," Barnes said. "I'm losing feeling in my leg."

"You'll be losing feeling all over in a minute, mate."

"Like your mother."

It wasn't even a crude insult, but it did the trick. Barnes found himself yanked to his feet by an angry goon.

They were right by the edge of the pit.

"*What* the fuck did you just say?"

"Your. Mother. Has. No. Feeling."

The goon yanked his balaclava off, and Barnes saw a shock of dark hair, a square jaw and angry, heavy-lidded eyes.

"What the fuck are you doing, Anton?" somebody said from the other side of the hole.

"Don't say his name, you fucking dullard," someone else said.

"He'll be in the pit too, in thirty seconds. The fuck does it matter he sees my face?"

"Good point, *Anton*," Barnes said. "But every contact leaves a trace."

It was tough, because Barnes's throat was still in agony, caked now with blood from his burst nose, and his palate was as dry as old toast, but he hawked violently, leaned his head back, and spat a gob of blood and mucus into the centre of Anton's face.

"*Gaaarrruuuhh!*" Anton yelled in a guttural squawk, his eyes instinctively screwing themselves shut, his hands flying to his face.

Barnes knew he had a split-second, maybe less. His bound hands proved to be a useful counterbalance; using his hips as a fulcrum, he dropped low and swung his right shoulder into Anton's side.

The contact was solid enough — Anton was only slightly knocked off balance, but it was enough for him to slip and tumble into the muddy grave with a screech.

Barnes was off and running before Anton even landed on top of Graham's body.

Roars, shouts, the scrabbling of feet behind him. He had, he knew, disappeared into the darkness, and was hedging his bets that most of them had been drawn like moths to the headlights of the van and, as such, had lost visual on him almost immediately. He had, he figured, a matter of seconds before someone swung the van around to act as a searchlight and torch beams swiped the air.

He pumped his knees high to his chest, getting up on the balls of his feet, trying to minimise the amount of time his feet had contact with the ground, by turns reducing the likelihood of the mud sucking him down into hell or turning an ankle in a frozen rabbit hole. As he ran he pulled at the cable ties.

Footsteps, slapping on the icy mud. There was someone on his shoulder, but as he felt them reaching for him, the man slipped and went down onto the mud.

"*Gaaaarhh!*" the man yelled.

Then suppressed shots, zipping around his head like angry fireflies. They were firing blind, he knew, and even with a steady aim and lots of light, handgun accuracy was pretty much a lottery beyond about ten metres. He only had to make it to the copse. It wasn't far.

He heard the van's engine gurgle and rev, and the headlight beams swung around in an arc — and then the engine cut as whoever was piloting stalled it. The beams reduced to practically nothing in the darkness, and then, as the engine caught again, he heard the wheels spinning in the increasingly sodden mud.

Barnes pumped his knees harder, thanking whichever branch of Fate, God or Chance that had seen fit to smile upon him at that moment.

He reached the hedgerow and hurled himself over the lowest part of it, landing on his back in the field on the other side. There were another ten metres or so of open surface before the copse. He scrambled over on his back and was enveloped by the density of the trees just as the first dark figure clambered over the hedgerow.

He opened his mouth wide to try to grab the air he needed without making any noise. He hadn't seen or heard a dog among the group, but still figured that hiding would prove fatal, as would running, and so, as quietly as he could, he turned and walked deeper into the impossibly dark copse, turning this way and that to create some semblance of a zig-zag trail.

The group behind him were still shouting and yelling, creating — along with the unrelenting rain — a form of unwitting cover for the sound of his movements. He reckoned they would have to abandon the van; if not, then it would take at least three of them to try to get it unstuck. In these conditions, the pit was just about deep enough for Anton to be unable to get out unaided, so if they'd left him there, potentially there were only four on his immediate tail — three, if someone had stayed behind to pull Anton out.

There was a torchlight beam swinging behind him, but the foliage was so dense, all it would pick up was the vegetation immediately in front of the user. There were voices either side of him, suggesting the copse was being flanked by the remaining searchers, maybe hoping he would pop out the other side. So maybe two in the copse, two outside it.

Minutes passed — five, ten, fifteen. He kept moving. He worked the cable ties as he went, feeling them become ever looser as he walked. Not enough to get them off, but he was getting there. He could see practically nothing, and trying to maintain a decent pace was challenging when his instinct was to pick and feel his way through the darkness as slowly as he could. He took deliberate steps, lifting his feet high over unseen trip hazards, bringing them down firmly to squash any potential underfoot treachery.

The copse was widening. It was larger than he'd first thought. The voices outside it were, to his exhilarated disbelief, growing fainter. His eyes were acclimatising to the darkness; by contrast, those behind him with torches and headlights were actually being hindered by those things. He daren't allow himself to believe he might actually get away with this, not yet, but the fact that he hadn't already been caught, shot and dismembered spurred him on.

He walked.

And he walked.

And then lights.

Ambient traffic noise, swishing past.

The copse opened out, and Barnes saw a row of overhead arc lights, the metal of an Armco barrier and a line of traffic hurtling past like determined insects.

A spread of wet, dark ground between himself and the barriers.

He chanced a look behind him.

No van. No figures. A faint swivelling of a torchlight beam in the distance.

They thought he was hiding in the copse.

He put his head down and pelted for the barrier, waiting for the shouting and the shots flying around his head.

None came.

He climbed ungracefully over the barrier — despite his progress, his hands were still bound behind him — and wrestled for four-tenths of a second on how to engage his newfound liberation. Try to flag down a car? Run up the hard shoulder?

He did neither, and instead walked straight into the westbound lane, faced down the oncoming traffic, and shouted.

Blaring horns, flashing lights, swerving cars, screeching tyres, spray from surface water pluming up from tyres. An artic juddered to a stop, and looked dangerously for a second like it might jack-knife.

And then, the blue lights of a traffic patrol lit up the urban tunnel, and Barnes sank to his knees on the tarmac, while the rain continued to pummel the earth.

CHAPTER FORTY-THREE

Tamsin was afraid to move. Afraid to stretch her limbs. Afraid to wake up, even.

She didn't know where she was. She could see absolutely nothing. The colours dancing behind her eyelids were brighter than the room she was in. The black air was damp, and cold. There was no sound besides the *drip-drip-drip* of an unseen leak slowly echoing in the darkness.

She was sitting on some kind of rubber mat, her back against a solid wall. Eventually, the paralysis eased and she felt around the mat. It was about five feet by four; beyond that was damp stone. She stretched her hands out as far as she dared, then recoiled in the black, terrified of what might lie beyond it. She felt behind her. The ridges and dips in the wall behind her felt like breeze block.

She felt around the mat again, in case her children were here too.

But she was alone.

She moved all her limbs, trying to swallow down the panic at what might have happened to Maggie and Ellie.

Maggie.

The kid had been traumatised once — now, here she was again.

She tried to think back to Jersey, but her mind still felt soupy. Why would that be? Cold? Lack of food? Had she been drugged?

She remembered speaking to Barnes on the video call — the rest had happened so fast.

They'd been waiting. Positioned at all the exits. They took the girls first — to fast-track Tamsin's compliance. *Don't hurt my children.*

They'd taken all the traceable devices, shoved them into a bag, doused the bag with bleach. Led them out to a van. One of them had driven Tamsin's car. Guns. Guns pointed in their faces.

Ordinarily, Tamsin would have yelled *fuck off* and screamed the place down. But the holiday home was in the middle of nowhere, and they had her *girls*.

There was a boat, she remembered that. Tamsin had no sea legs whatsoever — the gang didn't know that, but it was a sure-fire way to suck all the fight out of her instantly. It was like turning off a tap.

After that, it was hazy. She remembered the girls whispering to one another, and one of the men shouting. Then another man had told the first man off, and had apologised to the girls. He chatted to them, made jokes, reassured.

Tamsin didn't know what to make of that, but it had allowed her to focus on her nausea for a while. Then it had eased a little, and she must have fallen asleep, because they were travelling by road thereafter, in some kind of truck or van. Driving for hours in a haze of semi-consciousness, until she'd finally persuaded them to stop to allow Maggie a toilet break in a petrol station. She was still kicking herself — *kicking* herself — for not raising the alarm, but she'd felt sluggish, light-headed, dizzy.

Not least because, shortly after that, they'd been separated and the fog had suddenly lifted, big time. She'd fought and bitten and kicked but was eventually overpowered, while the girls had been hauled off into the shadows while she screamed.

The murk returned.

She couldn't believe the darkness. There were no shadows, no shapes; even after several minutes blinking and straining her eyes, it stayed a single opaque wall of black. The echoing drops of water were the only indication of the size of the room — it felt big.

She could feel the panic in her chest rising, threatening to consume her, and she fought to zero in on her own personal brand of steel — potty-mouthed, fearless, unquestioning protector and saviour of the afflicted.

She had to channel that now. She didn't know how long she was going to be here, so she needed to use that time to think — rationalise, use logic, work out a way to *escape*.

Whoever her captors were, they'd made the mistake of thinking that prisoners sit idle, worrying, panicking, pleading, their brains passive, empty and unthinking.

But when you work your mind, minute after minute, hour after hour, with nothing else to do, it becomes sharper, leaner, a taut muscle.

Tamsin needed that now if she was going to get out of here. She needed to think, fight and *graft*.

To devise a plan.

To get her kids back.

To *escape*.

The alternative was lying here in a puddle of her own weakness, passive, waiting, pleading. Unquestionably submissive in the hope of a milligram of her captors' mercy, even if it was spat back in her face.

They wanted a *victim*.

Fuck that.

CHAPTER FORTY-FOUR

Barnes sat on a metal box bench in a dimly lit holding room in Newhaven police station, leaning forwards, his hands still bound. He was flanked by the officers who'd found him on the Firle straight. His saviours. They were quiet, tense. They'd initially pegged him as a mental health case, but then had seen the cable ties, heard his story — including his purported occupation — and had summoned the detectives. Barnes had tried to tell them what had happened, but they had just shushed him in soothing tones and tried to find his ID.

The door opened.

Gabby.

He was in uniform, but wore no tie, and didn't look like he'd changed his shirt in a week. His head, usually as smooth as a cricket stump, featured a few days' growth, as did his face, and he looked like someone had attacked a photograph of him with a brown felt-tip pen.

One of the officers stood up immediately. The other stayed sitting.

"Standards slipping," Barnes said, addressing the floor.

"Sir?" the one standing said. "We were expecting the DI."

"On her way," Gabby said.

He leaned against the concrete wall opposite and regarded Barnes. The thick layer of whitewash was pockmarked and grimy with handprints and other dirt.

Gabby frowned, and addressed the officer.

"Sit down, for Christ's sake," Gabby snapped. "Why is he still bound?"

"We . . . were waiting."

Gabby expelled a jet of air from his nostrils, like a snorting bull.

"Cut them off. Use gloves. Drop them into an exhibit bag. Make a note of where and when you did it. Your oppo here will witness it."

"Yes, sir," the officer said.

The relief was incredible. Barnes rolled his shoulders and rubbed his wrists. They were purple and raw from the biting plastic, the cold and his efforts to work himself free.

"My hands," Barnes said, holding out his muddy, raw, bloody fingers to the officer. "I was attacked in my hotel. Before we were abducted. I got away. There's blood and skin under my nails. You need to swab them."

The officer looked at Gabby, unsure.

"For Christ's sake, this OCG is like a bunch of ghosts. This is a direct line to a possible ID." Barnes fought to keep his voice level.

Gabby nodded at the officer.

"We're searching the area you indicated," Gabby said.

"And?"

"We've found a big hole, a bunch of footprints and some tyre tracks."

"That's it?"

"That's it."

"There will be blood on the ground. They executed Graham Wall right in front of me. Point blank, with a suppressed SLP. Kicked his body into the hole."

"Snow's pretty heavy. Rain too, now."

"Heavy enough to wash away a body?"

"We're still looking."

"He says he's job, sir," one of the officers said. "No ID, though. Nothing on him at all."

"Oh, he is," Gabby said. "Though for how much longer, I cannot say."

"Sir . . ." Barnes said. "Maggie's abduction and the chemical attack. They're linked. It's confirmed."

"Confirmed?"

"Stratton Pearce. He was there. He *told* me."

"Barnes, he's in a bunker in Bratislava or somewhere, awaiting extradition."

"Sir, with respect, he bloody isn't."

"You can identify him, can you?"

Barnes thought, suddenly putting himself in a future witness box. All he'd actually seen was a spectre lit up by a van's headlights. A shred of tattoo. That almost skinless physique. It was him. He knew it. But a good defence advocate would have a field day.

"I recognised his voice. He's got the motive. Sir, he has my *family*. Why will *no one* listen to me?"

Gabby pushed himself off the wall.

"Samson Kane."

Barnes shut his eyes.

"Sir?"

"He's missing. His house is a forensic bonanza. What do you know about it?"

"I don't—"

"Yes, yes, I've seen the intelligence report. Tina Guestling tried to pass it off as an unknown source, anonymous call directly into FIB. But I don't buy that for a second. You went to his house, didn't you? You went to his house, realised he'd been snatched, and called it in via poor Tina because you were worried about getting yourself in more trouble. Am I right?"

Barnes didn't answer. He suddenly felt like not talking, that continuing to do so with his present audience could subtly result in a large dose of largely groundless self-incrimination.

"Much as I despise the man, I don't particularly like it when my superintendents are whisked off the street. Have you spoken to him?"

"No comment."

Gabby's eyes widened, and then he gave a sour smirk.

"From collegiate to adversarial in the blink of an eye. Is that really the line you want to take?"

Barnes folded his arms. "Once you start giving me some reassurances that there is an active operation ongoing to find my family and that you're going to develop the intelligence about a possible secondary chemical attack, then I'll cooperate. Until then, I'm saying nothing more. And I want a lawyer."

"Well, have it your way. Until you're arrested or served papers for misconduct you'll have to fund the lawyer out of your own pocket, of course, but I'm still happy to make some calls."

Barnes shook his head, suddenly exhausted. "Why are you being such a prick? You know that if my family is hurt because of you, I'll never let it rest."

"That sounds like a threat."

"What if it were your family?"

Gabby inched closer, and bent down so his eyes were level with Barnes's. "It wouldn't happen to my family," he hissed. "I wouldn't let it. I would *protect* them."

Barnes lurched forward, swinging, but was pinned back on the bench by his two highway rescuers.

"They're going to kill them, don't you get that?" Barnes yelled. "They're going to drop more of this shit in a town centre somewhere and while you're running around with your thumb up your backside, they're going to kill them!"

Gabby straightened up while Barnes struggled. "You'll know that there's no cell space here at the station. Doesn't have a functioning custody facility any longer. Nearest block is Brighton. But we could find room at Brook House for you. Just up the A23. You could watch the planes land."

He eyeballed Barnes for a moment, then made to leave.

"Miriam," Barnes said.

Gabby turned.

"What? Who?"

"Graham's wife. Partner. She needs to be told he's dead. I don't know anything about her or where she is. Graham sent her off to her sister's to keep her out of harm's way. Somewhere in Lancing. You'll need to sort it."

Gabby stared at him for a moment, then left the room.

* * *

The lawyer was in his fifties, with smooth, bright pink skin, a deep chin cleft and collar-length white hair swept back over his head. He wore thick Harry Palmer spectacles and a leather jacket, and carried a battered briefcase that looked older than he was.

Gabby had given Barnes the option to sleep in the holding room and await the arrival of PSD detectives in the morning; technically he would still be at liberty, but if he made to leave he would be immediately arrested for being complicit in Kane's disappearance, as well a host of other peripheral ingredients that amounted, in Gabby's view, to misconduct in a public office.

Barnes, exhausted, hadn't protested the point or argued his right to *habeas corpus*, and he'd sprawled on the metal bench, one of the cops from his earlier rescue stationed on the door.

He sat up and eyed the man warily. He didn't have a great deal of time for defence solicitors generally; the fact that he now probably needed one had not particularly diluted this outlook.

"Are you the legal rep?" Barnes said, knowing it would likely wind him up.

The man twitched.

"Robert Peverell. I'm not a rep, I'm a solicitor," he said. There was an antipodean curl to his vowels.

"Am I getting billed for this? I'm not under arrest."

"That could yet change, by all accounts. May I sit?"

Barnes slid up to the other end of the bench to make room. He turned to face the lawyer, leaned against the wall

273

and propped his knees up. Peverell sat down and spread the contents of his briefcase across the surface of the bench. Barnes caught a waft of some kind of citrus-tinged aftershave.

"Have you had disclosure?" he said.

"If you can call it that," Peverell said, looking at the papers. "I told your boss — Mr Glover, is it? — that if I did not receive sufficient disclosure to be able to advise you, then you would most likely answer 'no comment' when questioned."

"Let me guess: he shrugged and said, 'I don't care what he has to say.'"

"More or less, actually," Peverell said, glancing at Barnes over his glasses. "No love lost between the two of you, I'm guessing?"

"You could say that. What, specifically, is he laying at my door? I've got fourteen years' worth of shit he'd like to stitch me up with, but I can't imagine he's got the time to show you his scrapbook."

"He seems to think you might be complicit in the disappearance of your superintendent, a Mr Samson Kane." He peered at the papers. "He says Mr Kane has been missing for several days, and all indications at his home address are that there's third-party involvement — in other words, that he's been kidnapped. He says you were at the crime scene, made a back-door phone call to Intelligence, coercing some analyst to pretend it was anonymous information, and then fled."

"Most of that is correct, actually, but I didn't kidnap him."

"Well, the evidence is largely circumstantial, and there's no clear motive, but, really, there are gaps that can be plugged after charge."

Barnes went cold. He sat up straight. "Charge? *Charge?* You can't be serious."

"Well—"

"What about my family? What about the intelligence of a secondary chemical attack in an urban centre? What about Stratton *Pearce?*"

"Inspector Barnes, I must tell you, they're not believing much of it. To his credit, Mr Glover has dispatched resources to the area you described and says he's found a load of fields, a two-hundred-foot man and not a great deal else."

"Two-hundred-foot . . . what?"

"My apologies, I think he was being flippant. He was describing the Long Man of Wilmington, I believe."

"Oh."

"By all accounts, he's allowed for a ten-mile radius as a margin of error, and so far, his conclusion is that you must have made it up."

"Jesus, this bloke," Barnes said, rubbing his eyes.

"Is there anything else you've got? Anything else you can put up to verify what you're saying?"

"DNA. Under my nails. They've already swabbed them. Just need to make sure they've actually sent them off to the lab and haven't just put them in the bin."

"Leave that to me. We'll get you out of here."

CHAPTER FORTY-FIVE

Gradually, ever so gradually, Tamsin thought she began to hear sounds. She'd taken it upon herself to establish more about her surroundings. Her cage seemed to be purpose built — a concrete box a little smaller than a single-car garage, with a low ceiling, with smooth, cold walls and not a lot else. She'd found what she thought was the door, but there was no handle, no latch, no hinges even. No light whatsoever. Not a shred. Was this place underground?

While performing this cursory inspection she'd kicked over an empty plastic bucket, one of three standing in a row besides the mat. Next to this had been a pile of fabric that turned out to be a tracksuit in a polythene wrapper, and she'd realised she was still in the clothes she'd been wearing when they'd been taken. This, too, had made her think. It was the middle of winter, and she'd found no radiators or anything, but although she was cold, it wasn't unbearable. This meant there was an — admittedly meagre — heat source somewhere in whatever building she was in.

The buckets suggested a degree of care. A degree of routine. She had no idea of time, but reckoned it was coming up for twenty hours, best guess. That meant soon she was going to need to use the toilet, and food, and — crucially — water.

This would have to be supplied. If it wasn't, her health would deteriorate fast. Eventually, she thought, forcing herself to think the words in the interests of survival, she would die. If that was the intention of her captors, why leave the buckets and tracksuit?

And the sounds, so faint she thought she'd been imagining them. Footsteps too, maybe voices, she couldn't be sure — but a door had definitely slammed. A metal door. It hadn't sounded particularly close, either — certainly not next door. Maybe another floor. No way to tell.

In any case, on hearing this confirmation of the presence of at least one other, she'd pressed herself against what she took to be the door, and screamed herself hoarse for five minutes straight.

Maggie! Ellie! Mummy's here! I will find you! Be strong, girls.

Then, after a brief pause:

Let me out of here, you bunch of bastards! I'll find you too!

She screamed and screamed, eventually working herself into a paroxysm of tears. She sank to the floor, her palms sliding down the naked door, crying for her children.

* * *

The weather was starting to finally lift. Strips of cloud were spread across the ice-pink sky as Tina pulled into the overgrown driveway of her bungalow, having pulled another all-nighter.

Red sky in the morning, sailor take warning, Tina thought to herself.

She crept into the house, then realised Nicky was up and about — dishwasher on, kettle boiling, percolator percolating. The radio was playing a Keane track.

She kissed her daughter on the forehead. "What you doing up, baby girl?"

"Busy day ahead. Coffee? You're swaying."

"I shouldn't, but I can't sleep anyway. I've been wired for days."

"You're certainly pulling the hours."

"It's mental at work, but that isn't why."

Nicky passed her a mug. "Tell baby girl."

Tina perched on a bar stool and set the mug down. It *chinked* on the countertop.

"There's this guy. A DI."

"Own teeth, solvent, loves opera?"

"No, no, nothing like that. He's in trouble. And he just seems to lurch from crisis to crisis."

"He's *in* trouble, or he *is* trouble?"

"Bit of both, maybe."

"Steer well clear, then. Sounds like baggage."

"Nicky, I'm not dating him. He's seriously loved up, anyway."

"So what's the story?"

"From what I can gather, he put away some pretty nasty criminals."

"His job."

"Are you going to let me tell the story or what?"

"Sorry, Mum, I'm playing. Please, continue."

"And these criminals have taken it upon themselves to make his life a living hell. Remember that weird chemical cloud in the town centre?"

"How could I forget?"

"He thinks that was a cover. A diversion, put in place so they could snatch his daughter."

"Shit, really?"

"It gets better. The boss of the chemical investigation — big boss — didn't want to hear it, so Barnes — shit, I said his name — found her by himself."

"You helped him, didn't you?"

Tina nodded.

"Are you in trouble?"

"Maybe. I don't think so. Who knows? I'm not doing anything illegal, just some additional tasks on the side. Like a pet project. It helped find the main suspect for the chemical incident."

"Well, that's okay, then. You don't need them. You've got—"

"The casino?"

Nicky popped some toast and started to slap butter onto a slice.

"I was going to say your studies. You'll be a doctor soon, then you'll be earning twice what the big boss is on."

"I think that's probably unlikely, but anyway. My point is, he's still in trouble. He got his daughter back, and so they all went on holiday to recover. This gang *followed* them there, pulled Barnes back home and while he was here, they *took* them."

"His family?"

Tina nodded, and took another slurp of coffee. Nicky frowned.

"You know, he sounds like my friend Bonnie. The amount of drama in her life, it's like she craves it. Like she *creates* it."

"That's pretty harsh, Nic. Some people just have bad luck. In Barnes's case, he locked up the wrong people, and now they want their pound of flesh."

Nicky looked at the ceiling, thought about it, then shrugged.

"And while he's definitely not making it up, I've had a bunch of seriously weird phone calls from him," Tina continued.

"Weird how?"

"Just . . . I get half the story, then something happens in the background and he has to go. Like he offloads on me but doesn't really hear what I'm saying in return. Last time he had to leave a crime scene in case he was being watched."

"He *is* trouble. As well as paranoid, by the sounds of it. Why won't the boss make it official? Doesn't he believe him?"

"It's not that so much, it's more that he sees him as, I don't know, a problem child or something. Or, like you said, he thinks he's brought it all upon himself."

"How did you come to be helping him in the first place? You specifically, I mean. Wrong place, right time?"

"Kind of. He knew I had a daughter. Appealed to my maternal instincts."

"Oh God. What, the big boss doesn't have children?"

"Who knows? I can't imagine anyone wanting to, you know . . . with him. I don't know, maybe he was a catch in his younger days."

Nicky giggled. "Mum!"

"The point is, what do I do? Do I keep helping Barnes, or close the door and tell him it's got to be official or bust?"

Nicky thought about it. "If you *don't* help him, will you be able to look at yourself in the mirror? Will you be able look him in the eye? Will you be able to sleep again?"

Tina smiled at her daughter's insight.

"And I mean, God forbid, you don't help him and something bad happens to his family . . ."

". . . That's on me."

Tina thought about this for a moment, then finished her coffee.

"There's your answer, then," Nicky said. "You go be a hero, I'll finish my toast and browse the jobs pages."

"Find me a good lawyer too."

"Consider it done."

"Thanks, babe. Great coffee." She kissed Nicky on the forehead for a second time and disappeared off towards her bedroom. She would send Barnes a text. Maybe an email too. Sleep on it — a few hours only — then motor ahead with her personal mission to rescue the unfortunate DI.

"Mum?" Nicky called.

"Yeah?"

"Find them, okay? Find them safe and well. Doesn't sound like anyone else is going to. No pressure, by the way."

Tina smiled. She was such a good kid.

CHAPTER FORTY-SIX

Tamsin's stomach was practically eating itself with hunger. She felt weak, her skin parched and her mind cloudy from lack of water. She lay on the mat, in a ball, growing colder. How long had it been now? She had no idea. The sounds had stopped. The slamming door had been an anomaly, a one-off. She imagined some minimum-wage knuckle-dragger getting a telling off for failing to observe protocol.

Maybe it was their intention to let her die after all. Maybe the buckets and clothing were simply to torture her with false hope.

Jesus, where were her girls? It was the only thing keeping her going. That, and the desperate hope that Barnes was out there trying desperately to find her, marshalling the cavalry for a dawn raid. How he was going to find them, she had no idea, but that was his job, wasn't it?

She forced herself up, dragged herself the eight feet or so over to where she thought the door was, and banged it feebly with what remained of her strength.

You bastards. My girls . . .

A square of white light like a solar flare suddenly shot into the cell. Tamsin recoiled — she hadn't seen any kind of light for, she thought, well over a day, and her eyes were not expecting such an ocular assault.

There was the sound of plastic scraping on concrete, and then the light disappeared and the room was plunged, again, into darkness.

Tamsin blinked, suddenly energised. Any event, a change in routine, a break from the nothingness, gave hope.

In the five or so seconds that the room had been illuminated, she'd deduced, rather than seen, that it had come from the bottom of the door. She had seen that the walls of the box were smooth, grey and, apparently, newly painted.

She crawled over to the door, feeling her way for whatever waited there, wild colours dancing where flash images of the room had been burned onto her retinas.

Her fingers bumped against an object she quickly established was a plastic tray. She found a plastic bottle of water, an apple, a sandwich, a bag of crisps. And, in a discovery that made her laugh out loud, a paper napkin.

You want me to shit in a bucket, but bring me a serviette for my lunch.

She shovelled down the food and washed it down, feeling guilty in case Maggie and Ellie had not been afforded the same courtesy.

She felt better almost immediately.

Energy.

Strength.

Hope.

You'll regret feeding me, you bastards. Oh, yes you will.

* * *

Barnes still wasn't answering.

Tina's taskings for the day were a fraction more pedestrian than they had been for a while. She was still in the Op Console incident room, alone. The dark golf course stretched away outside, making Tina feel exposed — a square of light beamed out across a black spread of land. She was still working through a list of actions for Op Element, but the shooting of the suspect at the airport had caused the urgency to dissipate somewhat. It was still running next door, but the tabloids had moved on and were now concerned primarily with the death of Ronnie Biggs and a ceiling collapse in a West End theatre that had injured almost a hundred people. They still hadn't been able to identify the stuff, and in terms of motive, as Maggie's abduction had never made the news, it didn't have the same newsworthiness as, say, terrorism or Russian gangsters.

She sighed. Christmas in a week or so. She thought about inviting Barnes for Christmas dinner — if his family was still missing, of course. It would be a bit awkward, but she felt sure Nicky wouldn't mind. He'd put his life on hold — eating, sleeping, washing — he was just hunting, hunting, hunting, unable to break away or do anything else until he found them. She could maybe browbeat him into eating some turkey.

Unless there was news between now and then.

Tina was methodical, diligent and meticulous. She saw patterns and links where others wouldn't. Crucially, she looked *beyond* systems. She didn't wait for databases and algorithms to make links for her and drop them in her inbox. She had once identified a serial house burglar that had been so prolific as to be a reverse Father Christmas, and he had baffled investigators, analysts and senior officers for months, causing misery to households that numbered in the hundreds. The only potential lead was a neighbour sighting someone suspicious in the middle of the day wearing a red jumper.

Theorising that burglars didn't just burgle, and that the arrest rate for burglary was the inverse of shoplifting — another pernicious acquisitive crime — Tina trawled several months' worth of custody photographs and property records of suspects arrested for shoplifting, until she had a shortlist of twenty-seven that had been arrested wearing a red jumper in the last twelve months. By process of elimination, she removed static variables — the dead, the imprisoned, the medically detained — until the shortlist was in single figures. From this she found three with prior convictions for burglary, all of whom had been released from prison in the previous six months to a designated address in the local area.

Their perp was caught in the act less than a week later.

Tina had an ability to place herself at a scene. She could visualise the surrounding variables — passing traffic, nearby doctors' surgeries, public transport timetables — and she could extrapolate links from otherwise inconsequential details. She believed that no matter the meticulousness of the planning, or the professionalism of the unit, there was no way every possible eventuality could be anticipated. And the more audacious the crime, the more likely the unexpected variable. Have-a-go heroes. Passing trucks ploughing through kerbside puddles, drenching attackers. People putting out the bins at just the wrong time. Conversations picked up by baby monitors. Traffic cameras. Millions of individual decisions and choices criss-crossing each other in a series of ripple effects.

The world was shrinking. Digital footprints had fewer and fewer gaps. Even the most hardcore criminals needed to buy food, fill the tank, use the toilet, and so Tina would place herself in the street, refusing to believe that the crime could have passed undetected, and she would sift through great chunks of bland data until a pattern emerged.

She got to work. She sifted through intelligence reports, crime reports, ANPR data, prison releases, passenger manifests, traffic camera catches, CCTV placement. Things like financial data didn't lend themselves particularly to speculative searches — they required you to know who the individual was first — but some friendly calls and helpful data-sharing protocols meant her colleagues up town would alert her to large or suspicious transactions occurring around her hot times. Things like ransom payments — although that side of the enquiry was the SIO's remit — and motive did seem to be eluding them at present.

The one thing she did spend some time focusing on were suspicious activity reports. These were a veritable treasure trove. Curtain twitchers, overzealous neighbourhood watch coordinators, chairs of residents' associations — not to mention, Tina noticed, retired police officers. In many cases, they were the worst of the bunch.

Collectively, they reported huge swathes of inconsequential matters. Cars without tax, hawkers, collecting conkers without a permit, misuse of parent-and-child supermarket parking bays — in many cases they reported things that had simply irked them personally, or threatened to interfere with their own civil equilibrium, the carefully cultivated steadiness of their lives. Matters that were reported with such zeal that the call taker had to fight not to roll their eyes.

But this didn't dissuade them. They remained undeterred. And they continued to furnish the local constabulary with a join-the-dots pen picture of suspected bad behaviour in their area.

And, every so often, they hit the jackpot. They found the missing piece of the jigsaw.

And they got the last laugh.

Trawling a month's worth of her own suspicious activity reports was easy enough, but Barnes and his family had opted to travel by ferry to the island, and had departed from Portsmouth. If you assume they had been brought back to the mainland by their captors — if for no other reason than they would have found it hard to stay hidden on an island the size of Jersey — then it stood to reason they would have returned to some isolated cove on the south coast in the dead of night.

So Tina put in her request for all forces along the south coast to batch-dump their SUS_ACT reports in her inbox.

They obliged, with varying degrees of cooperation — and thus speed — and it took her email account some time to recover from the onslaught.

States of Jersey had, after some gentle encouragement, pinged Tamsin's phone. The cell radius was not especially helpful — half of it was in the sea — but by all accounts her phone had not left the island and its last activity was on one of the Jersey mobile networks.

It stood to reason. An organised gang of kidnappers was not going to allow their hostage to retain their personal effects, much less a traceable device. They knew what was low-hanging fruit to the authorities, and it was all going to go either in an industrial incinerator or on a cargo airliner destined to fly in the opposite direction.

Tina's car had been driven or taken from the holiday home to the ferry terminal. That was a matter of record. Barnes said the car at the terminal might have been a false trail, or that it played into the conceit that Tamsin had left him. He'd also said if they'd gone via commercial means, with some kind of extended family subterfuge, then Tamsin would have raised hell if there was any hope of mucking up their plans.

But would she? What if they had her kids? What if they'd threatened to hurt them if she didn't comply? Barnes's better half certainly sounded like a feisty one, but as Tina knew all too well, a gun to your kid's head would take the wind out of anyone's sails.

And she was fragile. She'd already lost and been reunited with one of her daughters in the space of a few days, and then the nightmare had begun again. She might have been hysterical. And what if the weather had put the stoppers on the crew leaving under their own steam? What if they'd had to go by ferry as a Plan B? They might have had to rush it.

They might have made mistakes.

When she had collated all the SUS_ACT reports from the start of December from Kent, Hampshire and Dorset, she stared at the pile. This didn't help with the theory that they had travelled back here on a small craft and had landed on a deserted beach anywhere along the UK coastline, but it was a start.

Still, the pile of reports from these counties alone was as thick as her wrist, and she suddenly felt despondent. She would work all day and all night if she had to — coffee and pizza would be her rocket fuel — but that was still going to be several days' work, days they might not have. Jersey was the priority — there might have been some otherwise innocuous report around the time of Tamsin's car being left at the ferry terminal.

A presence behind her. Gabby wandered in — no tie, hands in pockets, sleeves rolled up, half a shirt flap untucked. He needed a shave — all over, by the looks of it — and Tina recoiled slightly. When the leader is putting in the hours and is the one turning the lights off at the end of the day, it's a great motivator; but there was a fine line between being in the trenches with the troops and being so exhausted it caused glances to be exchanged and muttered conversations about whether the boss needed replacing. ACC Glover was usually so well turned out that his current state was verging on alarming.

"You look like you need some sleep, sir," Tina said.

He grunted.

"How's it going?" she continued, nodding towards the Op Element incident room. "Any progress?"

"Substance identification is a dead end," he said. "Can you believe it? I've got all the chin-strokers in there — Defra, STAC, PHE, MCA — and they can't work out what it is."

"Takes time, I guess."

"Apparently it's *our* fault for not getting a sample of the stuff. I said we were a bit busy catching bodies to get out our sodding test tubes."

"No idea at all?"

He sighed, sat on the edge of a desk, and helped himself to a custard cream from an open packet.

"They know there was a distinct cloud of the stuff floating through the town. Elevated ozone levels, but the speed and severity of symptoms means there was at least one other chemical as well. Some survivors said it smelled like chlorine, others said ammonia, others said it was odourless."

He rolled his eyes.

"Where do they think it came from?"

"The best they can tell me is that it probably originated in the Channel. Maybe a disturbed shipwreck, maybe a barrel of something fell or was pushed off a container ship. That's only a guess, though. There were no maritime incidents reported that day, so it's not supported by anything real. They *now* can't even tell me it was a deliberate act. Newspapers have walked away."

"You don't look too sorry, sir."

"Nor would you, looking like this."

"Have you been home at all?"

The shake of the head was so slight she wondered if he'd even had a say in the matter. She decided that he didn't just look tired, he looked *beat*.

"Does that mean DI Barnes's theory has any more weight?"

"Theory?"

"About the chemical incident being a distraction by someone. To abduct his daughter."

He shrugged. "It's as good a theory as any."

She didn't say anything.

"I know what you're doing, you know." He nodded towards the stack of reports.

A cold feeling pulsed through her system.

"I know you're helping him."

She took a deep breath. "Sir, look . . ."

"You want some help?"

CHAPTER FORTY-SEVEN

The care routine was perfunctory and infrequent, but regular — food was brought once a day, water twice, and Tamsin had established that if she put the buckets and the tray by the invisible hatch then they were collected, cleaned and returned.

Tamsin had seen nothing — just the square of blinding light and the sound of plastic scraping into her cell. Beyond the earlier door slamming episode, she'd heard nothing. No voices, no comings and goings, nothing. At one stage she wondered if it was just one captor in the place, but then she remembered the group at the holiday home and realised that this was a larger enterprise.

Then, after what her body clock told her was knocking on for forty-eight hours, the door opened.

It slid to the side on grinding metal runners into a recess in the wall, flooding the concrete box with brilliant, blinding light like a gateway to infinity.

She couldn't suppress a pained squeal, and covered her eyes with her hands.

"Get up," a voice said.

She stood, both exhilarated at the prospect of developments but also terrified at what they might entail.

289

"Where are we going?"

"Come on. Come here. Wash."

She tried to place the accent. Not sure. Not local.

"I'm not going anywhere until I know where my girls are."

"Suit yourself," the voice said, and the door slid shut again.

She wanted to scream in protest, to plead and beg for a second chance, like an errant child who finally links poor behaviour to revocation of privileges, but she clamped the symptoms of submissiveness deep inside her and forced herself to listen to the girl who stood up to bullies, the teenager whose rebellious streak lasted into adulthood, the woman who healed the sick.

"Fuck off, then!" she shouted, then collapsed in a heap and began to sob as quietly as she could.

It was four, maybe five hours later — or maybe only two; she remembered how slowly time went during maths class — when the door slid open again.

"Come. Wash."

She silently obeyed, holding her forearm up to the light as she walked over to the doorway.

"I want my girls," she muttered. "Where are they?"

The man — head to foot in black combat gear, face concealed by a ski mask, SLP on a lanyard in a tactical thigh holster — didn't say anything.

"Come on, you prick," she said. It was out of her mouth before she could stop it. "Two words: 'They're fine,' and I'll do anything you want."

Silence. He led her down the corridor and she opted instead to take in her surroundings.

The dark grey colour scheme continued out into a network of corridors, with tunnel lamps bolted to the ceiling in steel mesh guards. The main corridor was easily a hundred metres long, and the box she was being stored in was one of several in a symmetrical pattern, each with an industrial padlock on the door, and she realised it was some kind of enormous storage unit. There wasn't a window anywhere, and although it was only assumption on her part that they were underground, it certainly felt like a reasonable one.

There was no sound, and Tamsin's footsteps slowed in growing dread as she imagined that all of these makeshift cells contained people. Old, young, dead, alive, her daughters.

That frantic feeling surged in her throat again, and she fought to stay calm.

At the end of the corridor was a small vestibule, with half-width breeze block walls jutting out from the main corridor walls to create a staggered chicane, affording the user a degree of privacy.

That's a bloody joke, she thought.

Her escort waited at the first of the breeze block walls, and indicated that she should proceed. Adrenaline surged again, and she went ahead alone, eyes scanning for anything she could use as a weapon, an escape, a distraction.

Nothing.

The chicane opened into a square area with a simple shower and toilet cubicle. Anything that wasn't bolted down looked likely to crumble in her hands. Even the towel was some kind of degradable paper that would disintegrate if she tried to strangle anybody with it.

She tentatively stripped and stepped into the shower. It was hot and powerful, and incongruous to her situation as a consequence. There was soap in a dispenser on the wall, and after she had tossed her clothes into a plastic bin and finally relented with the tracksuit in the packet, she stepped back into the shower stall and pumped handfuls of soap into her open palms.

The escort led her back down the corridor.

"What, that's it? No snooker table? You don't want a quick frame or two?"

She saw the open door of her own cell at the end of the corridor, the blackness beyond the threshold like a yawning gate into hell, and she knew there was no way on this earth she was going back in there.

She took a deep breath and slowed her pace.

The guard turned. "Come on. What are you—"

Tamsin swung her hand in an arc, slapping her palmful of soap across the eyes of the guard. She pressed down hard, her fingertips meeting the surface of his eyeballs, a feeling like skinned grapes, and he growled with pain as the substance met his eyes.

With a venomous shriek she swung a foot as hard as she could into his crotch, and swung the other arm into his throat. All told, it wasn't a bad attempt at incapacitation — her aim was bang on, certainly — and she made a scrabbling grab for the SLP, unclipping the holster in a surprisingly deft movement and yanking it from the lanyard. His attempt to prevent it was half-hearted at best, distracted as he apparently was by three separate clean strikes to the most vulnerable areas of his body.

And she ran, weapon in hand, through the network of grey, metal, endless corridors.

"Maggie! Ellie! Where are you? It's Mummy! Oh, babies, where are you?"

She banged on cell doors as she ran, turning this way and that, lost in a maze of subterranean grey.

What the hell was this place?

There were shouts somewhere behind her. Or ahead of her, she wasn't sure. In any case, her soapy-eyed escort was clearly not alone.

After half a minute or so, she rounded a corner — and came face to face with the open door of the cell she had not long vacated.

"No!" she screamed. "For fuck's sake!"

She turned on her heel, rounded another corner — and saw that her balaclava'd escort had multiplied by four or five. They were helping their temporarily stricken colleague to his feet.

"There!" one yelled. "Get her!"

She turned again, pointed the pistol behind her, and let off a round. The report was deafening, and she prayed someone might have heard it.

She didn't stop to see where it went; it ricocheted around the metal enclosure and she heard a yelp as it apparently made contact with one of her pursuers.

She kept running, ears still ringing, trying to keep going in a vaguely straight line, despite being forced around countless corners.

She *must* be able to get out. She had a gun, for Christ's sake. Could she take them all out? It didn't seem likely — they had all sorts of body armour on and she wasn't confident of her aim. She wasn't sure how many rounds the gun held, but she didn't think it would give her much margin for error. In any case, she resolved to empty the clip anyway, to create as much ruckus as possible.

She reached what looked like another main corridor, and saw the vestibule where she had showered at the other end. They were all chasing each other in circles — all that was missing was the theme tune from Benny bloody Hill. By the vestibule there was a narrow grey door that she hadn't noticed before. She'd assumed it was a broom cupboard or something . . . but maybe not.

She pinned her ears back and went for it . . . and then her pursuers appeared at the end of the corridor, blocking the maybe-exit.

She skidded to a halt like something out of a cartoon, and they charged her. She stepped backwards, the gun gripped in both hands, and screamed at them to hold, to stay where they were, or she would start shooting.

They were maybe a hundred metres away — less, perhaps — and they kept coming, ignoring her commands. She didn't hesitate, didn't even really give a great deal of thought to it, but, with the weapon clutched in shaky hands, she screamed, and emptied the clip in the direction of her custodians.

The noise in the confined space with the low ceiling was unbelievable. Somebody must have heard that. God, *please* let someone have heard it.

There were more rounds in the magazine than she was expecting. Fourteen or fifteen, maybe. Several flew over their heads, but at least three of them hit their targets. To her horror, they kept coming. She wasn't sure, but one of them looked to have taken two rounds, maybe in the thigh or lower torso, while she appeared to have only winged the other one. The remainder of the group didn't return fire, but, apparently safe in the knowledge that there was no longer a ballistic threat, put their heads down and charged.

Three of them took her out like it was a Six Nations ruck, and she howled as the gun clattered across the floor. She thrashed and screamed and struggled, but one of them socked her in the jaw, taking most of the fight from her, and she was removed bodily from the corridor and placed indelicately back in her cell.

The door slid shut, and the cell returned to darkness.

Tamsin screamed.

CHAPTER FORTY-EIGHT

Tina couldn't quite believe it. Within twenty minutes of Gabby's offer of help, she had found herself supported by another analyst and two researchers, all of whom had been told to report to her and do as she instructed.

She wasn't quite sure what — besides ruinous exhaustion — had led to Gabby becoming a slightly more human shade of crimson, but she decided not to question it.

She put the phone down. Her opposite number in Jersey had proved to be an unconditionally helpful colleague — something to do with the intelligence sorority, maybe — even if the update wasn't especially helpful. Barnes's observation, that Tamsin's car has been tactically placed to make it look as though the crew had escaped the island by passenger ferry, was looking like the most likely theory.

What the opposite number *had* provided, however, was the list of SUS_ACT reports for the forty-eight hours preceding the ANPR hit on the car. It was thick, but not that thick — and Tina now had help. She figured she had to start somewhere, and theorised that any launch of a small vessel, irrespective of its motive, was likely to head directly for the nearest piece of coastline. That meant Weymouth or Poole — or somewhere less prominent in between. Size, range, fuel type were all considerations too. In simple terms, the further the distance needed to travel, the larger the requisite craft. A ten-person RIB was not, for instance, going to make it to Felixstowe from St Helier.

She added Dorset to her pile of reports, and divvied them up between her new team of researchers. She told them to index the reports by beat codes, prioritising those on the coast, then working inland. Once they'd cleared Dorset, they would move east systematically through Hampshire, Sussex and Kent.

She herself would take Jersey.

She sat down. She had only her knowledge, experience and a strong hunch that this line of activity was a worthwhile one. It was an approach that had served her well before — but then again, there was a first time for everything. If it proved fruitless, then she had wasted time she knew they didn't have.

She covered her face with her hands and tried to think. It made sense that they wouldn't stay put — the island was too small — but why would they come back here particularly? Why, for instance, wouldn't they go straight to the continent? St Malo was three hours due south, but far less if they headed east to the nearest unlit beach on the Cherbourg Peninsula, and they put an international jurisdiction and a large body of water between themselves and the nearest interested law enforcement authority in so doing.

Or, maybe, there was an in-between option. A port, but a small one. Some kind of backwater outpost that technically counted as an international border crossing point, but which was staffed by one man and his dog in a hi-vis and was closed on Sundays. There were a handful of these along the south coast. You avoided the scrutiny and security infrastructure of larger ports, but you also avoided the rather unsubtle spectacle of crunching a launch into the shingle at Pevensey in the middle of the night.

She worked her brain harder than she did the squat rack. What were they trying to achieve? They were not sexually motivated. They were an organised crew, but no ransom demand was involved. As far as she could establish, Stratton Pearce was a garden-variety psycho who was enjoying the sport of dangling Barnes like a puppet before serving up the ultimate revenge. That meant keeping well below the radar — difficult to achieve with three feisty females who didn't want to be there, and doubly difficult in France, unless there were significant connections, resources and equipment available, and that kind of thing left a trace. So, for now, returning to mainland UK seemed the most likely eventuality.

Not that she was discounting anything out of hand — Tina worked with probability, logic and reasoning — so it was more a case of what to focus on first. If the first avenue didn't strike oil then you moved onto the next one systematically.

The trouble with this approach was that it didn't lend itself particularly well to a rapidly shrinking time frame.

She kicked out and cursed, her foot striking the plastic waste bin under the desk, as a sharp needle of frustration fired through her. Where was the SIO and the team of investigators? They should be the ones setting the policy direction on this, working up hypotheses, confirming priority actions. *It's great you've given me a team, Mr Glover, but come on!*

She tried Barnes again. He wasn't answering, and she was starting to worry about him in a way that she could hear Nicky teasing her for.

What was it he had said about the ex? Barnes was going to try to form some kind of alliance with him. Maybe she should try him.

She flicked back through her daybook — kept partly through meticulous habit, partly in case she needed it for the public inquiry when the shitshow finally landed in her lap — and found it. Graham Wall. Some quick-time open-source research and internal data pulling got her an address and phone number.

She dialled.

It took a while to connect, with crackling on the line, but then it began to ring.

She couldn't quite work out why, but when it did, a bolt of nervous electricity shot through her, and she ended the call before it was picked up.

The ringing in her ear was a long, flat continuous tone, instead of the Hyacinth Bucket trill of the UK networks.

Graham Wall was abroad.

Why would he be abroad?

With everything going on?

This was not reason, logic or probability — it was a good old-fashioned sixth sense, a twisting in her gut.

And it was telling her something was badly wrong with this picture.

* * *

Over the next few hours there was darkness, and silence, and not a lot else.

Tamsin lay there on the mat, huddled in a ball, when she became aware of faint sounds.

Voices.

Crying.

Maggie? Ellie?

She stood in the darkness and strained to listen. The sounds were faint, but definitely there.

"*Mummy . . .*"

"Ellie!" she screamed. "Where are you?"

Sniffles.

Tamsin moved around the cell, feeling the walls, trying to trace the source of the sound.

"Maggie? Ellie?" she said. "Where are you? Answer me, babies, please."

The crying continued.

Her tears became sobs, which in turn became incoherent muttering as distress and despair began to take hold.

And then a little voice in her head spoke to her.

They're toying with you.

As if to prove the point, her fingers closed on the fine mesh of some kind of grille, about the size of a slice of bread, in one of the upper corners of the cell.

A speaker.

She was right.

The grille vibrated with the sounds of the voices. They were trying to drive her mad.

The door slid open, and that terrible light flooded the cell.

A silhouette appeared in the doorway.

It stood there, hands by its sides.

"What do you want?" she said, puffing out her chest. "I don't need another shower already."

"Hello, Tamsin."

She recoiled.

She knew that voice.

CHAPTER FORTY-NINE

Barnes swung his legs around and sat up. He felt hungover. He felt his pockets — they were all empty and he couldn't remember if he'd surrendered his belongings or if they were out there in a Sussex field somewhere.

He felt numb. Worrying had wiped him out, and now he just wanted to forget. He was giving up, he knew, was on the cusp of starting to think they were never coming back to him, and what do you do then? Get up, make the tea, fill the car, buy the bread, all the while knowing they are *still out there* — for one, five, ten years. Never going back, never moving on, a constant presence, an infected wound that refuses to heal.

And then, he realised, the narrow strip of window near the ceiling was revealing pale blue strips of winter daylight.

The storm had passed.

It was time to catch a bloody plane.

He stood up and peered through the laminate glass in the door. There was a cop in plain clothes stationed on a chair outside the holding room. At least, Barnes assumed he was a cop; they *were* inside a police station, but the baseball cap and hoody suggested otherwise. Barnes could only see the back of his head. He had his legs crossed and was reading something.

Barnes banged on the glass.

"It's not locked," the cop said, not turning round.

Barnes turned the handle — and recognised the vivid pink scars on the man's neck.

"Holy shit," Barnes said. "Samson."

Kane stood up. "In the lasered flesh."

"What happened to you? You look . . . bloody awful."

And he did. His eyes were bloodshot, and his body was decorated with dressings like a Christmas tree. There was a large graze down the side of his face, like he'd come off a motorcycle and scraped his head along the road surface.

Barnes waited for an answer.

"They came to your house . . ." Barnes started him off.

"Four of them. Masks. Threw me about a bit, then dragged me off through the back garden to a van. Kept me in a garage for a couple of days, then just threw me in the back of a van and dropped me on the tarmac outside the RSCH. I mean, literally dropped me. The van didn't even stop."

"When was this?"

"Day or so ago."

"No one knew?"

"Gabby knew."

Barnes's mouth tightened. "What did they say?"

"Nothing that surprised me particularly. 'Stop investigating. Stop trying to find them. Back off.' Blah blah blah."

"And then they just let you go?"

"Think about it. They nobble enough people, enough cops, then they keep building the sense that we are being infiltrated. That we're *losing*."

"Just like that?"

There was suspicion in Barnes's voice — not intentional on his part, but it came out anyway.

"Barnes, I can guess at what you're probably thinking, but there isn't enough money on this planet to make me willingly stroke my own chest with a soldering iron for the sake of a ruse."

Barnes swallowed. "You were tortured. Jesus." He placed a hand on Kane's shoulder. "I'm sorry. This is my fault."

"No, it's not."

"Yes, it is. Too many people are collecting scars because of me."

"Come on. We've got work to do."

CHAPTER FIFTY

"You haven't changed," the voice said. "You've proved quite the tempestuous challenge for my men. Three of them out of commission — two with gunshot wounds, the third remains unable to see."

Tamsin curled up on the mat, staring at nothing, forcing herself to breathe normally. It surely couldn't be.

"Tamsin."

The voice was closer. It had moved from the doorway over to where she lay.

"Tamsin."

Closer still. His breath near her hair.

"If you come any closer, I'll rip your head off," she said.

The voice gave a low, sallow chuckle. "That spirit. Undimmed, despite your incarceration. I am impressed. And speaking of undimmed . . ."

He clapped his hands, and electric lights in the cell powered on with a *thunk*.

Tamsin covered her eyes with her forearm.

"I take it you didn't think to clap your hands?"

"Very fucking funny, Graham."

She lowered her arm, squinting in the glare.
Yes, it was definitely him.
Her pissant ex-husband.
Graham Wall.

CHAPTER FIFTY-ONE

There was nothing in the Jersey reports. Nothing immediately relevant to their cause, anyway. Double-parked vans, people loitering, houses with front doors wide open. Oh, sure, Tina could go back and follow up on all of these suspicious citizens — calling them back, clarifying details and vantage points and the like — but there was no time for that. She'd been looking for something that jumped out at her, and none of these did. She — Tamsin — didn't have time for a fishing trip.

In any case, she'd been side-tracked slightly by her discovery that Graham Wall was abroad when she called him. It just didn't sit right with her.

And nor did the fact that she was now researching intelligence that might put some meat on her suspicious bones. She felt like she was snooping around Barnes's underwear drawer.

But there was plenty.

And it was right there in front of her.

Graham and Tamsin Wall had history with the police. A stream of reports of controlling, possessive, jealous behaviour, none of which in and of themselves amounted to a crime. Tiny, individual episodes of subtle manipulations and gaslighting that were as difficult to prove in a court as they were destructive to their victim in the home. A historic rape allegation, made in an almost throwaway manner when the police responded to one of her 999 calls, and shut down again just as quickly by the alleger.

Tamsin got scared. She got scared when Graham shouted, or hid her money, or interrogated her on her movements, or threw crockery. And when she was scared, she called 999. Then, when the fear dissipated, she backpedalled. The cops would turn up — Graham, part of their alumni, would be jovial and agreeable, and would cheerfully agree to stay somewhere else for the night. More often than not, one of the responding officers would chuckle or wink as Graham got into the back of the patrol car. He remained calm and amiable, while Tamsin, in her heightened state, was just made to look neurotic. On one occasion, she'd shown an officer a diary she kept — times and dates going back seven years when Graham was at his worst. The officer had rather diligently transcribed most of it verbatim onto the investigation enquiry log, but nothing had come of it.

So she'd pick up the phone, but that was it. She might agree to a caseworker making contact, but if you wanted to try to get her statement of complaint or get her to go to court and support charges against him — no way.

Tina read, open-mouthed. It was sobering stuff — stuff she had seen all too frequently — and it had been going on for years. A long catalogue of domestic abuse going back to well before the girls were born, alleged with just enough scarcity as to render fruitless any attempts to investigate. No arrests, no prosecutions, no convictions, and certainly no substantial impact on Graham's then-occupation. Graham recorded as a disputant, or a person of interest, or an involved party — never as a suspect or an offender. It may as well have never happened.

Tina clicked her tongue. She knew how *that* felt.

She didn't want to, but she had to get this to Barnes.

She set the Jersey reports aside and, with her diligent, uncomplaining researchers working through Hampshire and Dorset, turned her attention to the Sussex stack.

She worked through them. Suspicious vehicles, groups of loitering men, delivery vans with their hazards on for longer than it took to make a delivery, unattended shopping bags, baby strollers with no babies in them, lights on in vacant shopfronts, house callers purporting to be police officers — the list was practically endless. Tina noted that the vast majority of the reports had been closed without further action by the control room, and she wondered how many actually held the key to unsolved puzzles.

Over a three-day period, she circled twenty-seven different incident reports that were worth a second look. Most of them involved vehicles; a handful concerned reports of people in residential areas hanging around looking shifty, like they were casing houses or something, usually in the middle of the day.

None of them featured reports of a mother and two kids kicking and screaming in the middle of a shopping centre, or clawing the insides of a van.

They were all long shots.

She got to work, prioritising, indexing and eliminating. If she were lucky, there would be some kind of slip-up by the group — they'd drink-drive, or run with a headlight bulb out, or flip the bird at the traffic while crossing the road.

Eventually, after she had got the list down to ten, she took a break. She called Nicky, and thought about the gym. Drive there, work out, shower, drive back . . . she didn't think she could spare that much time. She'd be itching to get back the whole time, and so she opted for a brisk walk around the new, purpose-built paths criss-crossing the Bridgemere estate and then got back to it.

When she returned, she noted she'd circled one more than once, in heavy red marker pen.

She frowned. Why had she picked that one in particular?

She opened the incident log and took another look. The report was of a panel van parked on double-yellows just outside the entrance to Newhaven port. It was half on, half off the kerb, hazards blinking feebly as the battery slowly ran down. By all accounts, it was closer to the check-in lanes than the main road itself, and yet it seemed to have been reported by a civilian rather than anyone from the port authorities.

Tina checked the date. It had been reported the day after Barnes and his family had gone to Jersey. When Tina cross-checked it against the ANPR records database, she saw that it had arrived in Newhaven the day before that; not only that, but the same set of records indicated that the van was moving eastbound the day after Barnes landed back on the mainland. According to the ANPR trail, it had gone north on the A26 out of Newhaven, turned east onto the A27 at Beddingham, and had then disappeared.

So far, so good. It told her nothing concrete other than it corresponded with the time frames of Barnes leaving for and then returning from Jersey — but, in her view, was worth a closer look as a result.

The woman that reported it was a local resident, and had given her name as Sheila Snow. Tina called her back, and learned that the van had been there for almost two days when she reported it. The van was old and a bit battered, she said, and looked to have been sign-written once upon a time; a dirty stencil had been left behind by the removed decals. She said that on at least two occasions there were clusters of men hanging around by the van, smoking, talking and looking around. Sheila generally regarded it all as very suspicious, and she'd wondered if they were people smugglers or something — that said, Tina got the distinct sense that Sheila was more bothered about the blatant parking infringement, and then started talking about her blue badge exemptions and how she tried not to overstep her bounds.

Tina thanked Sheila and ended the call. She put the phone down, leaving her hand on the receiver while she thought. She'd not learned much more, but it was still more information than had been taken when Sheila made her original call.

She looked again at the list of incidents. How many more of these would yield more information on a second callback?

She had a decision to make. Keep digging into this one, or spread herself across a few more? More ground, or more depth?

She could also, of course, lobby ACC Glover for more support. She glanced up at her researchers, who were still working through their own lists. She could voice her concerns about being unable to contact Barnes — who had of late, it seemed, resorted to making snatched, cryptic phone calls from various corners of the country.

Maybe she shouldn't push her luck.

She opted to go with her gut and return to the van. There was a reason she had circled this particular report so heavily with red pen.

She ran the van through both PNC and local systems. DVLA listed the official colour as red, but Sheila had said it was so old it was closer to brown. The DVLA records showed no current keeper, but it carried a valid MOT, was taxed, and was insured to a named policyholder living in Great Yarmouth.

That piqued her interest. Someone had taken the time to ensure the van was roadworthy. So many criminals didn't bother, and being pulled over for driving while uninsured had been the key that unlocked far more nefarious schemes. Given that it seemed to be a complete shitheap, this could mean that someone didn't want more attention on it than necessary.

Locally, there was no trace. Never been stopped, never been used in a crime, never been implicated or complained of by its fellow road users.

She sent a tasking request to Norfolk Constabulary for a patrol to go and knock on the door of the insured party, not expecting it to bear fruit or even be a real person, and then turned her attention to the period of time between the van's last ANPR footprint and now.

She threw the pen down. She couldn't work like this. She brought a map of the area onscreen and then got one of her researchers to go and obtain an A0 printout from

Intelligence's industrial printer, the one they reserved for major enquiries.

When the task had been completed, she pinned up the lush green map and plotted in a circle, creating a radius of possible routes from the last ANPR hit, and worked her way out, cross-referencing it with the list of SUS_ACT reports.

And then she saw it.

To assist risk assessment and prioritisation within the command-and-control environment, and in recognition that many calls to the emergency services can be long and complex, the open incidents screen contained a list of pedigree information — incident number, date, time, location, caller details, location and a short title that gave the briefest sense of what that particular CAD was about. The user could then click into any CAD and delve into the whole sorry story. Generally, short titles were linear and uncontentious, like ASSAULTED or THREATS BY PHONE or SILENT 999 or COMPLAINT. Sometimes, when the call was a bit more complicated and didn't lend itself to a three- or four-word summary particularly well, the call taker would have to get a little creative.

The short title for this particular CAD was CHILD PLAYING?

Tina brought the job up on the screen. It was a call from the duty manager at the Selmeston service station, a tiny rural facility on the A27 between Lewes and Polegate, and the only stop along thirteen miles of busy trunk road that sliced through the sprawling green fields of the South Downs.

The manager had reported that a mother and child had come in to use the facilities. They'd only been in the shop for a matter of minutes, and although they hadn't bought anything, they'd browsed unconvincingly, the mother hanging around while her little girl took interest in some colouring books and the revolving stand they were mounted on. The manager wasn't sure what sort of vehicle they'd arrived in nor if anyone else had been with them.

When they'd left, the manager went over to where they'd been standing and had checked the area because, she admitted, it was a CCTV blind spot and she thought the mother had seemed a bit spaced out, and the manager thought she might have been stealing.

She reported that she'd found nothing untoward, but then had noticed, on the floor, a pink felt-tip pen. It was missing its lid, and when she bent down to pick it up she saw the lid had rolled under the display.

As she stood up, she saw that one of the colouring books on the revolving stand bore a free gift — a wipe-clean white-board and a packet of felt-tip pens. The packet was damaged, and one of the pens was missing.

The manager had taken the book off the display.

She was sure it was nothing — the kid messing about or something — but she reported it anyway. You know, just in case.

Something had been written on the board, in pink felt-tip pen.

Not *hi there* or *my name is* or *i love zebras*.

Just one word.

help

CHAPTER FIFTY-TWO

Tina put on her best silky voice and called the duty patrol sergeant for Seahaven and Lewes. He was gruff, and sounded harassed — today he was unexpectedly covering the whole of Wealden as well — but he softened a little as Tina spoke to him, even though he probably knew she was after something. Nobody called the duty patrol sergeant unless they were after something.

The CAD had been assessed by the call taker, who, in fairness, had escalated it to a supervisor to review. The supervisor had researched potential links to reports of missing people and domestic abuse in the area around that time and, finding nothing obvious, had written a long screed on the incident log arguing why no further action was appropriate and proportionate in the circumstances, and that, on balance, the little girl was probably messing about.

Tina asked the sergeant for a unit to get to Selmeston, interview the manager, and try to get hold of the CCTV. As a minimum, she said, she wanted to try to identify the vehicle the mother and child arrived in, and, for preference, secure the colouring book and pens.

The sergeant's interest appeared to be mildly piqued — so often, what were colloquially referred to as "good intent" calls amounted to absolutely nothing; on the rare occasions that they actually did, most people wanted a piece — and he agreed to queue it for his next available unit.

* * *

"I hope you've eaten something besides pizza over the last week," said a voice from behind her.

Tina turned — Barnes, and Superintendent Kane.

Before she knew what she was doing, she had run across the room and thrown her arms around Barnes's neck.

"What happened to *you*?" she said, as she released him and then imagined Nicky rolling her eyes and shaking her head.

Barnes sat down, and nodded towards the giant map. "You've been busy. And . . ." He indicated the researchers.

"They're mine," she said. "Mr Glover gave me a team."

Barnes and Kane exchanged glances.

"A team? For what?"

"To help find your family."

Barnes rubbed his eyes. "I must be dreaming."

Kane assimilated the information fast. Barnes listened as he spoke to Gabby on the phone and rattled off his theories, policies and resource requests. It was an impressive argument from Barnes's point of view; more than that, from what Barnes could ascertain, it didn't seem like Gabby was mounting much of an argument.

About bloody time.

Two DCs joined them a short while later, and there was an armed tactical team made available under the direction of a wide-eyed commander who looked like he lived in his car.

"Seriously, what happened?" Tina said. "I've been trying to call you, and update you, and . . . you look like you were dragged through a hedge backwards."

"Not far from the truth, actually."

"You haven't told me yet, either," Kane said.

So, Barnes told them. He told them about how, after discovering Kane's place had been ransacked, he sought out

313

Graham. He told them about their short period of exile, their surreal bonding in an empty house and their abduction. Tina's hand went to her mouth when he told them about how Graham had been shot dead at point-blank range and kicked into a not-terribly-shallow grave, and Barnes's thousand-to-one escape attempt that resulted in him being scraped off the A27 by a traffic unit.

He stood up and indicated the approximate location on the map, and then described being debriefed by Gabby, who claimed to have found nothing besides a big empty hole and some tyre tracks when they'd searched the area.

When he'd finished, Tina was raging.

"He *knew*? Glover? He was holding you at Newhaven and didn't tell me? I've been banging on about being worried about you and he just shrugged."

"I'm sorry to say, nothing much surprises me about him anymore," Barnes said.

"I guess that would explain why Graham's phone was ringing out with an international tone," she said. "They probably put it on an air freight flight to Cairo after they killed him."

Kane frowned. "Why would they take you there?"

"What do you mean?"

"I mean, why there? They could have taken you to any remote field in the country. The UK is full of them. They can't just have randomly chosen it. There must have been some reason they took you there. Even unconsciously. Convenience, symbolism, local connections, no matter how small — there has to be a reason."

"You should be an analyst," Tina said.

"What's this?" Kane said.

He pointed at the map, where Tina had inserted two pink pins — one at Selmeston service station, one at Newhaven port. Barnes seemed to go a little grey when she told him about the colouring book and the felt-tip pen.

"You said there was an airfield nearby, yes?" Kane said to Barnes. "A small one?"

Barnes nodded.

"There's two here — what, five miles from the service station? If that? You're not telling me that's a coincidence."

"Maybe it isn't," Barnes said. "We don't yet know that the van at the port and the petrol station thing are anything other than totally innocent."

"We don't. Not yet," Kane said. "What did you say you'd done about the petrol station?"

Tina flushed. His tone was verging on accusatory.

"There should be a patrol enroute," she said.

"Good."

"Any minute now."

CHAPTER FIFTY-THREE

Dave Sloan was tired. He was only on his first early shift after four rest days, but his days off had been interrupted by a spontaneous summons to court for a case that had unexpectedly been bumped up the list. The overtime at such short notice would be reasonable, but he wouldn't even see it until his January pay packet. Ah well, maybe it would help with the post-Christmas credit card bill.

He was tall and lean, verging on gangly, with a dark sweep of hair and an Adam's apple like a golf ball. He was only just twenty-five, and, despite three years' service, still had a bit of keenness about him, a bit of interest in doing the job for the right reasons and not just because he knew he'd get in trouble if he didn't.

Sloan was single-crewed, which meant he was buzzing around like a mad thing shovelling up after nights — taking statements, revisiting witnesses, collecting CCTV, a bulk harvest of stuff that would probably never see the inside of a courtroom. Selmeston service station was just another one of those enquiries — albeit, he had to admit, when he'd been briefed, it didn't sound like your usual run of the mill enquiry.

Maybe he was getting jaded, he thought. Maybe it was time to apply for firearms or traffic or something, while he was still relatively fresh.

The duty manager was called Carol, and once she realised the police were following up on her call about the mysterious message and the broken packet of felt-tip pens, she became consumed with helpfulness. She made Sloan a cup of tea and busied herself with retrieving the CCTV. When asked if she'd happened to put aside the colouring book and damaged packet of pens, she became slightly crestfallen, and admitted that she'd put it back on the rack with a sellotaped repair job and a discounted price. Sloan explained that *not* preserving items just created avenues of ready-made defence further down the line — yes I might've touched it, but I was just walking past — but that he would take it anyway.

He felt her eyes on him as he dropped the colouring book with gloved hands into an exhibit bag, and then he returned to the counter to view the CCTV.

It wasn't brilliant quality, but it was as Carol had described. Mother and child enter the store, quickly use the loo in the back, hover around inside for a moment and then leave. Nobody else with them. No purchases. Knowing how downloading CCTV from smaller retail outlets was hit and miss at best, Sloan made a note of their descriptions and then used his phone to video-record the footage on screen.

"What about external?" he asked. "I need to try to work out what vehicle they arrived in."

"Do you think this little girl is in trouble, then?" Carol asked, fiddling with the machine. There was a slightly gleeful edge to her voice, Sloan thought. Maybe she was totting up the reward money in her head.

The forecourt, if it could be called that, was no more than a poorly kept concrete spread with four pumps up the middle, with just about enough room for one car beside each. There was a hardstanding out back that doubled up as a car park for people just using the shop — behind that, a whole load of greenery stretching back to the Arlington Reservoir and beyond.

Carol rewound the tape and changed the view to the outside of the shop. The mother and the child walked into the shot from the bottom, heading across the forecourt to the entrance of the tiny building. There was something not quite right with the mother's gait — like she was summoning considerable effort to walk in a straight line.

"No vehicle," Sloan said. "Did they come on foot?"

"Forecourt gets busy," Carol said. "There's a bus stop just before the turnoff. They might have parked in that. Cameras don't cover that far."

"Why wouldn't they have used the car park? Was that busy too?"

Carol found the right camera. The car park was busy, but there were spaces.

"It's not the easiest thing to get into," Carol said. "Just as easy to leave it in the bus stop if all you need is a wee."

"Can you show me the widest shot of the road?"

Carol obliged. It didn't improve much, just a hint of the kerb and the verge markings. You could see wheels and maybe the bottom sill of passing traffic, but that was it.

"Play it from when they walk off the forecourt and out of shot."

She did so. The mother and child left the frame, and Carol flicked the view back to the camera out the front of the building.

It was impossible to identify which vehicle might belong to them — they zipped past at such a speed — but then Sloan noticed the trundling wheels and dirty red-brown bodywork of something moving much slower than the ambient traffic speed.

Like it had just moved off.

"Thanks for your help," Sloan said, and stood up. "Can you burn that for me?"

"If they come back, I'll call you," Carol said, inserting a disc into the machine.

"Yes, please. 999."

"I tried that last time. There was a rude woman who told me it wasn't an emergency and I should try the other number."

She passed him the disc.

"It happens. Thanks," Sloan said.

He took the exhibit bag with the colouring book in it and headed out to his car, reaching for the radio on his chest as he did so.

"Comms, from Echo-Sierra One-Oh-One, come in," Sloan called up.

"One-Zero-One," said a tinny voice.

"Show me all done with my assigned," Sloan said. "Exhibits collected. Who wants it, again?"

"Someone in intel, One-Zero-One."

"Roger that. Should I run it down to them?"

"Negative, One-Zero-One. I've got a ton more jobs queued for you. Have to be the pony run. Or do it later."

Sloan sighed. Internal post it was.

"Roger. Send me the next one, then, I guess."

"On its way. One-Zero-One, am I resulting this job as sus?"

"Maybe," replied Sloan, looking back at the service station's tiny, chalet-style shop. "Maybe not."

CHAPTER FIFTY-FOUR

"You did a pretty good number on my men," Graham said. "I expected you to put up a fight, but not quite to this extent. If it wasn't the last place they'd want to be seen, three of them would need to go to hospital rather urgently."

"Your men? *Your* men?" Tamsin said, still unable to believe her eyes. "How do you get a bunch of rent-a-thugs to do this kind of thing for you? You wouldn't even confront the neighbour when he kept parking over the driveway. In fact, the only person you've ever squared up to is *me*."

"Common goals make for convenient alliances," he said.

"What the hell are you on about, you lunatic?"

"Or, put another way, more hands make light work." He reached out a hand and closed it gently around her throat. "Please don't call me a lunatic."

Tamsin froze, a combination of bad memories and the sheer unreality of her present situation being her ex-husband's design.

"*Alliances*," he said again.

A second figure appeared in the doorway of the now brightly lit cell. He moved slowly inside, hands dug deep into a grey hoody, a blue serpent tattoo crawling up the side of his pale, hairless head.

"Hello, Tamsin," he said. His voice buzzed like a chainsaw. "You're a feisty one, no doubt about it."

Tamsin had never met him, but she recognised him immediately.

Stratton Pearce.

Barnes had, through necessity, shown her Pearce's picture relatively early on in their relationship. He had wanted her to go in with her eyes wide open, but also to know what he looked like for her own safety.

Graham removed his hand. Tamsin swallowed. Barnes hadn't told her everything, but she knew this was the man responsible for killing his first wife.

"Quite the bromance you two have going on," Tamsin said, unable to keep the tremor from her voice. "Where you going on honeymoon? Niagara Falls? Or just a staycation in the House of Hell?"

She drew a rainbow in the air with an upturned palm.

Pearce walked over and squatted next to Graham. He smiled. It looked like a metal zip on a pair of jeans.

"I would love to knock that bloody mouth of yours into next week. Or maybe do something else with it."

Her heart began to drum in her chest. The effort required to summon her usual front began to increase exponentially.

"You can try what you like," Tamsin said. "But I guarantee you, as a minimum you will lose an eye. And I bite," she added.

Pearce shook his head and grinned.

"I love it. You turn that on for that husband of yours? I bet he loves it too."

"Please, please, can we dispense with the jousting," Graham said, looking, Tamsin thought, a trifle uncomfortable. She wondered if he was in over his head.

"You've got a sodding nerve," she said. "Are you telling me that you've cooked this up together? You? You're responsible for kidnapping me and the girls, dragging us off in a bloody van for hours on end and dumping us in this underground Hannibal Lecter pit? You're more of a psycho than I thought. And that's saying something."

Graham stood up, frowning. "Are you hurt?"

"Yes, I bloody am."

"You've been fed. You've washed. The only injuries you've sustained were simply to subdue you. If you hadn't tried to escape, you would be unhurt. You shot three of my men, but did they return fire? No. These are mercenaries, Tamsin, and the reason they did not shoot you is because they were under strict instructions not to."

"I can't believe you'd do this. To me, maybe, but our girls?"

"I resent that. I'm offended that you think I'd let any harm befall them."

"Then what are you *doing* this for?"

"Come with me."

He led her out of the cell, Pearce bringing up the rear. She didn't give it much thought — being out in the corridor with these two was better than being cornered, and she was not going to turn down another opportunity to get out of there.

They headed along the metal corridor again, Tamsin noting patches of brown on the floor from her earlier handiwork.

They headed for the shower, and she noted, with some irritation, that the narrow door she had subconsciously overlooked as a broom cupboard was, in fact, an exit. It led into a narrow stairwell, dimly lit by yellow wall lamps. Their feet clanged on the industrial steel steps as they headed further down into the facility, Tamsin feeling like she was on board some kind of space-age craft.

They stopped on the next floor down. The corridor and padlocked container cells were more or less identical, but when they stopped outside a container halfway down, Graham unlocked the door to reveal a brightly lit vestibule.

The wall opposite featured an enormous plate glass window — the light was coming from the other side of it. Tamsin rushed up to it. On the other side were Maggie and Ellie.

Alive.

Unhurt.

They were in a colourful nursery of sorts, decorated with rainbows and unicorns. Ellie was in the Lego box; Maggie was laying wooden train track pieces across a green carpet decorated with painted trees and bushes.

"Girls! Maggie! Ellie!" Tamsin yelled, banging on the glass. She looked around frantically for a door, or something she could use to break the glass, but there was nothing. She hammered on the glass until her energy reserves began to dwindle, and she sank to her knees, sobbing. The girls didn't register her presence.

"One-way glass," Graham said. "They can't hear you."

"Why are you *doing* this?" Tamsin moaned.

"I wanted to show you that I would not allow any harm to come to them."

"They're prisoners."

"They're being extremely well looked after. And, of course, they have their father."

"They need their mother. They need their home. They need to be *out* of this madness, Graham."

"And they will. In the fullness of time, they will."

"Maggie was abducted, Graham. By your hand."

"She was never harmed. The operator was under strict instructions."

"Are you kidding me? She's not the same person. She'll be traumatised for life. And now you've done it to her again! You released deadly chemicals in the town centre? You killed all those people, just to create a distraction?"

"She was nowhere near it."

"She was two miles down the road!"

Her hand dropped from the glass, and her shoulders sagged.

"There's no point. You're completely off the charts, Graham. A headcase. And it's just me you want to punish."

Graham squatted down beside her. Pearce lurked in the doorway.

"I want to hurt you, Tamsin. You're right about that. I want you to suffer, as I suffered. I want to punish you for ripping the family apart, for taking my girls from me."

She shook her head. "You don't change. Always some-one else's fault. All those things you did to me over the years, all those things I couldn't prove but you and I both knew happened, trying to drive me out of my mind, and you still want the last laugh. Why can't you just let us go?"

"The girls, I will. You, I'm afraid . . . well, I can't say what will happen."

"And you think that will be good for them?"

"In time, they'll get used to it. They will *forget* you."

He held out a hand.

"Come along, sweet girl. It won't be long now."

Tamsin, suddenly clear on her fate, and mind racing as a consequence, allowed herself to be led back to her cell.

The two of them hovered in the doorway while she walked obediently back over to her mat.

"You might think you have common goals," she said, turning to face them and sinking heavily to the cold rubber, "but you know he won't let you do it, right?"

She nodded towards Pearce, who was leaning his bald head on the doorframe, watching the exchange with what appeared to be malign amusement.

Pearce stepped forward into the light, hands thrust in his pockets, and breathed steadily while regarding Tamsin. "He's had a hard-on for me for seven years. I was in a van. Me and two others. I was driving. We'd just done a burglary. Had blue lights on our tail. We collided with his car. The impact killed his wife."

He squatted down and gently lifted Tamsin's chin with a finger, forcing her to look him in the eye. He smelled of menthol gum.

"It . . . was . . . an . . . accident. Could have happened to anyone."

He stood again.

"But no, he had to take it personally. Locked me up for all manner of invented shit. Locked me up, so I couldn't protect *my* loved ones. And they died. That's on *him*."

His lips curled into an amused sneer.

"You realise I'm telling you all this because I can afford to. Got nothing to lose. You won't get a chance to *tell* anyone. Know what I mean?"

Oh yes, Tamsin knew what he meant. That didn't mean she was going to be cowed like something out of Mansfield bloody Park.

"The way I hear it, he locked you up for some pretty hefty crimes. Conspiracy, people trafficking, murder. What, he was just supposed to let you go in case something bad happened to other people while you were inside? It's his *job*. How about, *you* put your family at risk by deciding to be a criminal. You and you alone. You ever think about that?"

Pearce's sneer vanished. Anger blazed in his eyes. He took a step forward; Graham gently stretched a forearm across his chest, and he stopped.

"All he wants is to ruin Barnes's life," Tamsin said to Graham. "That's it. The more destructive, the more brutal, the better. You think you'll be able to keep a bit for yourself, you're in la-la land."

"Well, there's a statute of limitations on that. Barnes is, about now, probably just about finishing digging his own grave in a field in the Weald Basin."

Tamsin felt the bottom fall out of her world, and, with it, a curious sense of resolve. Know where you're headed, and you can plot a course.

"Why would you build something like this?" she murmured. "What's wrong with you?"

Graham rolled his eyes. "Stop *saying* those things. It's beginning to piss me off."

"Come on, Gray," Pearce said. "She's trying to get a rise out of you."

"You're in over your head, Graham," Tamsin called as the cell door slid shut. "There's no way out."

CHAPTER FIFTY-FIVE

Sloan's next assigned job was to follow up on a pub assault from the night before. There was a suspect in custody, sleeping it off, but the complainant needed to be seen when he wasn't three sheets to the wind.

After shouting through the letterbox for ten minutes, annoying the neighbours and repeatedly phoning the guy, Sloan gave up. If he tried too hard he'd end up having to report him missing. He returned to the car, and found his mind drifting back to the enquiry at the Selmeston service station.

He brought the job up on the car's MDT. He'd only been briefed over the air by the control room as to what was required, and hadn't actually read the CAD.

He frowned. There was more on it than the controller had let on. Some kind of live kidnap operation running, with a possible, if tenuous, suggestion that the service station job was linked, that both the child and the mother had been under duress at the time and that the kid had attempted to discreetly raise the alarm.

Brave, Sloan thought. And smart.

The requestor was an FIB analyst, Tina Guestling. She answered on the second ring.

"Hello? I'm looking to speak to Tina Guestling?"

"Speaking." She sounded breathless.

"PC Dave Sloan, Echo-Sierra Response. Been to that CAD you raised out at Selmeston."

"Oh, that's fantastic. And?"

"I've got the CCTV."

"Fantastic," she said again. "Anything on a vehicle?"

"No. They walked in off the street, by the looks of it. If they were in a vehicle, I think it stopped short. Bus stop, possibly."

"Shit. Okay. How good's the inside footage?"

"Not bad. Shows most of what the duty manager reported."

"Is it them?"

"Well, I've no idea. I don't know who 'them' might be."

"Of course you don't. Sorry. Can you get me the footage? Like, yesterday?"

"No problem. Where are you based? HQ?"

"No, the incident room is in Eastbourne. Major Incident Suite."

"Okay. I'm in Lewes, just finishing up on a job. I'll come straight there."

"Brilliant. See you shortly."

Sloan put the phone away. There was a tap on his window. A stocky guy stood there in his boxers, with last night's flat top and a black eye that was practically vibrating.

Sloan wound down the window. The booze stink was like a warm blanket.

"You woke me up," the man said. "What do you want?"

"Later," Sloan said, and started the engine.

* * *

Sloan crawled through Lewes town centre, debating whether or not he should use his blue lights, then finally he broke free of the one-way slog and cut through the Cuilfail Tunnel and out onto the A27.

He cruised down the Beddingham flyover, the Ouse a steady constant below him, fields stretching away to his right, a carpet of green leading to the sea, edged as it was with filaments of white from the recent snow. Above him, the brightly coloured aerofoils of paragliders drifted lazily off Mount Caburn, dotted around a pale — and no doubt freezing, Sloan thought — blue sky.

He traversed the Beddingham roundabout and headed onto the Firle straight, a steady drumbeat of oncoming traffic *whomping* past him, trying to decide whether he should stick to main roads or cut through the Cuckmere Valley and then bomb along the coast and drop into Eastbourne from the Seven Sisters. Both routes could be shit — it just depended on the traffic.

As he passed over the River Cuckmere and continued on the straight to begin the climb the hill up towards Milton Street, one of the oncoming vehicles caught his eye. He almost missed it, but something about it made him follow it in his rear-view.

A van.

Red-brown — it couldn't make up its mind.

In any case, it was a shitheap.

He hadn't been able to pinpoint the driver, or see the number plate, but something about it . . .

He hit the light bar and two-tones and spun a U-turn as neatly as he could. There were five or six cars between them, but the road was dead straight and he made good ground.

The van pulled over in a long lay-by just before the Drusillas roundabout. In season, there would be a white wagon selling fresh strawberries there, but today it was just Sloan and his quarry.

No movement from the van. No one trying to get out or make themselves known. Sloan clocked the number plate, made a note, and then called up the control room to inform them what he was up to, and where.

He walked slowly up to the back of the van. There were no windows. The side of the van had once been sign-written, but the decals had long since been pulled off, leaving a dirty stencil behind. If Sloan had been armed, his hand would almost certainly be resting on the grip of his pistol.

He reached the cab. Just the driver. No one else up front. She was smiling and looked eager to cooperate. She certainly wasn't forgettable — she had short pink hair and a tattoo on her neck, and she seemed to be wearing a white jumpsuit.

"Good morning, officer," she said brightly, in heavily accented English.

"Good morning," he said, suddenly acutely aware that his reason for the stop was pretty skinny — sixth sense at best, and he had little in his pocket should she refuse to cooperate. "Mind telling me where you are off to?"

"I driving to Brighton. Seaside."

"What's with the jumpsuit?"

She shrugged. "Work."

"Just you?"

"Just me."

"No one in the back?"

"Please, take a look," she said, unclipping the seat belt.

"That's okay," he said. "I'll look. You stay there. Please."

"No problem, officer. I do as you say."

"Find me some ID while you're waiting, maybe?"

He moved back the way he came, an Armco barrier between himself and the green countryside sprawl and a whole load of sky, A27 traffic whipping past him on the other side as he did so. He reached the double doors at the rear and racked his baton in a single movement.

Nothing. The rear was empty. Dusty plywood floor. A balled-up tarp. That was it. That wasn't to say it wasn't of forensic interest.

The gods of hindsight would have said he should have trusted his instincts and arrested the driver on suspicion of kidnap before poking around the van. At least that way, she'd have been in cuffs, and if he turned out to be wrong, he'd get a civil claim at worst.

But he'd be alive.

He shut the offside door, then moved to the nearside door as his radio chirped into life.

"Echo-Sierra One-Zero-One from Sierra Oscar."

"Go ahead, Oscar," Sloan said, closing the nearside door.

"Your traffic stop. Subject vehicle is of interest to Operation Console, repeat, of interest to—"

The driver was standing right there. She was very short, but there was a certain power about her build.

And she wasn't smiling any longer.

"Hey, I thought I said to—"

The blade flashed up like a silver marine predator clearing the water to claim its prey, and buried itself in the underside of his chin. It cut up through the soft flesh under his jaw, and then continued through his palate and into the centre of his head. It was theoretically survivable, but the length of the blade meant that it finished up with at least two inches of steel embedded in his brain, causing a series of essential functions to be switched off in an instant.

Not that PC Dave Sloan was aware of any of this. There was the strange sensation of having a really bad itch under his chin, followed by the cold metal ramming through the roof of his mouth, and then his vision, hearing and some other critical operations ceased. He was just about aware of his legs giving way and his body collapsing onto the cold tarmac, and the driver's footsteps as she walked away from him and back to the cab, but that was it.

Beyond that, there was nothing but darkness.

CHAPTER FIFTY-SIX

Tina paced the office. Where was PC Sloan? He should have been here ages ago. She'd tried his mobile, but he wasn't answering.

There was a sudden flurry of activity in the corridor. People were rushing into the Op Element incident room. Tina stuck her head out into the corridor.

"What's going on?" she said.

"Officer down," someone said. "Traffic stop gone wrong. Stabbed."

Then they were gone.

Tina retreated back into the office and sat down heavily on her chair. It was Dave Sloan. She knew it. She just knew it. It couldn't be unconnected. It couldn't.

Barnes and Kane were elsewhere in the building. She called them both — they arrived shortly afterwards, wide-eyed. They'd already heard. Kane was on his mobile.

"No way Gabby can pretend *this* isn't happening," Barnes said.

"It's a live job," Kane said, ending the call. "Traffic stop. Driver stabbed the officer once and made off, heading towards Brighton. Units out looking now."

"Who's the officer?" Tina said.

"No name yet. A response officer. Single-crewed."

"And the vehicle?" Tina said, closing her eyes.

"A van. There was already a marker on it. One of yours?"

Tina filled them in on her progress — the van, the petrol station, the single breadcrumb trail left by the little girl.

Barnes's chest swelled and contracted as he processed this.

"The CCTV?" he croaked. "Was it them?"

"I don't know," she said. "Descriptions were similar."

"Only two of them, though. Where was the other one?"

"Held back in the van, maybe," Kane said. "You let them out of your sight, you need some collateral. A guarantee they'll behave. The CCTV will confirm, obviously."

"He . . . PC Sloan . . . was on his way back here to show me when he . . . when this happened."

"I'll get hold of the SIO," Kane said, pulling his phone out again. "We need that footage, even if it does muck up his crime scene."

"They've shown their hand now," Barnes murmured. "They're not worried about covering their tracks. They're going loud."

Kane moved towards the giant map. There were four pins now — Newhaven port, Selmeston service station and the scene of Barnes's rescue, together with the location of the hole and tyre tracks described by Barnes and found as part of Gabby's purportedly fruitless search, near to the Sparrowhawk Aerodrome.

"Where was the stop?"

"A27. In a lay-by between Drusillas and the Cuckmere," Barnes said, reading the incident log off the screen.

Kane nodded, and inserted a fifth pin into the map.

"They're round here somewhere," he said, indicating the sprawl of green between Lewes and Eastbourne, the coast and the inland towns. "They must be. Tina's van never popped up beyond Polegate after the last ANPR hit, meaning it stopped somewhere in this radius, or, if it continued, it took some seriously remote routes to get there."

"It's still a needle in a haystack," Barnes said.

"But we are narrowing it down, are we not?" Kane said. "And if you're worried that our fallen colleague is going to soak up all the resources, then I can promise you that your family won't be forgotten."

"It's still live," Barnes said. "The van is still out there."

He grabbed his jacket.

"Come on. Let's go and find where they're keeping my kids."

* * *

Barnes drove, Kane in the passenger seat, Tina in the back. It was a seven-seat carrier they'd borrowed from the Child Protection Team, and just looked like a family vehicle out for a picnic on the Seven Sisters.

"The traffic is carnage," Kane said, listening to his radio. "They've closed the A27. CSM wants the whole road until they know what they're dealing with. All the traffic is being diverted at Polegate."

"Take the coast," Tina said. "We can cut up through Friston."

"This thing doesn't have blue lights, I've just realised," Barnes said, as they passed Eastbourne Pier, dots of snow covering the pebbles like little white Santa hats.

"Too late now," Kane said.

Kane's phone rang. Tina's phone rang at the same time. There was a burst of chatter on the radio.

"They've got the van," Kane said. "Falmer, by the university. Foxtrot have it boxed."

Barnes gripped the steering wheel as they climbed towards Beachy Head.

"Just the driver, by all accounts," Kane said, breaking off from his phone conversation. "No one else in it. They've got the driver contained. Female. Negotiating now."

He turned his attention back to his phone.

"How's it looking? Fine, listen, you need to tell the HCN coordinator that this is part of a live kidnap. They need to build the hostages into their strategy . . . yes, I do mean ask the subject where they are. No, it needs to be now. Well, if they shoot her, it won't matter, will it?"

He ended the call.

Barnes dropped them down into East Dean and then along the long, snaking road that overlooked Cuckmere Haven and dropped them down into Exceat.

"They need to compare the van tyres with the lifts from the field," Barnes said.

"They will. Can't get near it right now, of course."

"It's the same one. I'd bet my house."

Barnes turned off at Friston Forest and headed inland towards Litlington. There was nothing around here but undulating ranges of stubbled rape and corn, tiny grey lanes weaving through the middle of it, the South Downs rising up behind it all.

Barnes suddenly stopped the car in the middle of the road and got out.

"What is it?" Kane said.

Barnes was standing in front of the car, hands on hips, rotating on the spot as he scanned the field. "Something the lawyer said."

"Lawyer?"

"Australian guy. Weirdo. He said Gabby reported nothing after I told him where to search, besides the hole in the field, some tyre tracks and the Long Man of Wilmington."

"And?"

"He was taking the piss, most likely, but in any event, I popped up somewhere around Middle Farm, south of the aerodrome, right?"

"Okay."

"That's five miles away. From the Long Man, I mean."

"Right."

"It's nowhere near."

"He was taking the piss, as you say. Adding a whacking great landmark to his search parameters."

"But what if he wasn't?"

The mobile phones of Kane and Tina rang again, simultaneously.

"Yes?" Kane said. "I'm listening. Yes, I am cleared. Just tell me what the log says."

In the back of the car, Tina was having a similar conversation.

"That's it? Nothing else? No, that's fine, I can work with that."

Kane ended the call, and Barnes suddenly realised that he didn't think he'd ever seen the man smile.

"What is it?"

"We have them. A fucking bullseye. Raise the cavalry."

CHAPTER FIFTY-SEVEN

They turned off the South Downs Way onto a lane leading north. Barnes rolled forward in the people-carrier, an amphitheatre of green and yellow rising up on both sides of the road, streaked with white from the melting snow. The Long Man, a two-hundred-foot chalk figure incised into the side of Windover Hill, marked their progress.

"There's nothing out here," he said. "What's your information, exactly?"

"Tell you later."

"Some coordinates would be handy."

"There," Kane said, pointing to Barnes's right. "Try and get out of sight. Off the road, if you can. Preferably an elevated position. We need to try to talk in the tactical teams."

"Where? There's nothing except the lane and the hedges. It's like being in Postman sodding Pat. What am I looking at, anyway?"

"*There.*"

Barnes looked. There was an unmade track about fifty metres long, leading to an open stretch of churned mud that looked like it belonged to an abandoned farm nestled in the valley between two titanic opposing hills. There were a couple of hay bales shrink-wrapped in black plastic and a corrugated archway containing the rusted iron of long-abandoned machinery. Behind that was what looked like a strawberry patch — rows and rows of tended plants at least a hundred metres across under a spread of white tarp that formed a series of tunnels suspended four feet above the ground.

"There."

"What is it? Pick your own?"

Then he saw the incongruity. Ancient, rusting, abandoned farmware on one side, new white tarp and freshly churned soil on the other. The site was shielded from the road by a series of angled metal sheets that, Barnes realised, were rows and rows of solar panels.

"I see it."

"That's where they are. No one would give it a second look."

"We need to get in."

"Wait. Wait just a while longer. We can't go in as we are. It'd be suicide."

"Can you see anyone? Anything?"

"Nothing. No movement."

Tina leaned forward from the back, and put her hand on Barnes's shoulder.

"The van driver. She's down. She's been shot. They found chemicals in the van. Sounds like she was enroute somewhere to release them."

Barnes carried on past the stronghold, trying to make their presence look as innocuous as possible in case they were being watched. Once they were out of sight, Barnes turned the car around and began climbing a chalk-and-flint track barely wide enough for a tricycle. The car bumped and jolted, and Barnes could hear the foliage underneath scraping the car's floor pan.

Eventually, at an elevation of about twenty metres, they pulled up into a cluster of gorse bushes and tucked the car out of sight.

Kane got out and produced a pair of binoculars; Barnes paced around the car, jittery, tense, wanting to steam in. On the opposite hillside, the Long Man kept silent watch.

"This isn't the best vantage point," Kane said, lying flat against the frozen earth.

"What can you see? Sentries?"

"Nothing at all. But you can bet your bottom dollar there's some state-of-the-art CCTV down there."

"What the hell is it? A bunker?"

"Something like that. Safe to assume it's at least part subterranean. The strawberry grow looks like a topper."

Barnes shook his head.

"We should research it. Get some more background. There'll be deeds, plans, archives. You can't build something like this as a bootleg."

"No time," Kane said, shifting his position. "I've only got a partial view. We're too far away."

"Christ's sake," Barnes said.

"Don't sweat it. It'll do for now." He pulled out his phone and began to talk earnestly — Barnes realised that he was talking to the team leader of the armed tactical support.

"Well?" Barnes said. "What did he say?"

"He said he likes a challenge. ETA thirty-five minutes."

"Jesus, are they stopping for breakfast?"

"They're coming from Gatwick. All the coastal teams have been soaked up by the van stop. Don't worry, they're not dawdling. Hey, where's Tina?"

Barnes spun round. "She's not in the car."

"Well, she can't have . . . oh shit," Kane said, and put the binoculars to his eyes again. "Oh my God. She's heading down the hill."

"She's what? She'll be a sitting duck! Call her, Samson. Get her back here. She's got nothing but a radio."

"India-Delta-Two from Echo-Golf-Nine-One, come in," Kane hissed into his radio, the binoculars still glued to his face. "India-Delta-Two. Dammit, Tina, answer me. You are to back off and get back to us. That's an order. You'll blow the whole op."

In the binoculars, Kane watched Tina sidestepping down the hill so fast she looked like she was surfing. Without stopping or turning round, she held up her middle digit.

"Shit," Kane said. He fiddled with the radio until he was on a different talk group. "Yankee team leader from Echo-Golf-Nine-One, come in."

"Yankee-One, go ahead."

"Be advised, we have a civilian member of staff attempting a close-quarter recce of the stronghold."

"Nine-One, that is not a particularly good idea. Do they have protection?"

"Negative. We are keeping obvs from an elevated position. She is single-crewed and on plot; she's got comms but nothing else."

"Get her out of there, Nine-One."

"We're working on it, Yankee-One. No promises. Just put your foot down."

Kane ended the transmission before the team leader could protest further.

"She's going to get herself killed," Barnes said. "What is she *doing*?"

CHAPTER FIFTY-EIGHT

Tina stepped down the hill like she was snowboarding, just about keeping her footing as she started to travel faster than her body was entirely comfortable with.

When she reached the road, she pressed herself low to the tarmac and waited, keeping herself below the gnarled, skeletal hedge line separating the lane from the set-up at the end of the track.

Nothing. No sound. Nothing to see. Just the bite of winter wind and the steep hillside behind the botanical grow, the enormous chalk figure blocking out any hint of sun. In the summer, the fields of wheat and maize would be whispering with the breeze weaving through the crops; right now, however, the long-harvested surroundings had been cut back to frozen stubble.

She edged forward, aware of the muffled chatter emanating from the radio on her belt. She turned the volume right down and moved along the hedge line, keeping low.

The gate separating the lane from the mud track was another incongruity that they'd missed on their first drive-past — it was new, and looked to be some kind of galvanised steel construction. It was shackled shut with an industrial padlock. Only a bulldozer was coming through this.

She scanned 360 degrees, then hopped over the fence, put her head down and sprinted for the corrugated barn, pressing herself to the freezing metal. She stuck her head around the corner of the barn, and brought the radio to her lips.

"India-Delta-Two, I am on plot. No contact, nil trace for subjects. Nothing seen at all. Stand by . . ."

"Tina . . ." burst the reply.

She turned the volume down again.

Figuring the rear of the barn was a blind spot and therefore relatively safe, she moved along it until she reached the far side. It was about a hundred metres long. By the time she got there she was practically flush with the foot of the hillside, and had a view back towards the lane that included the rear of the botanic tunnel.

She tilted her head and frowned. From this angle, concealed from the road, she could see what appeared to be inclined steel trapdoors underneath the tarp that formed the tunnel. There were pop-rivets around the outside of the doors and they generally looked pretty sturdy, not to mention invisible from the road. The whole tunnel was about seventy metres long.

She swallowed as she wondered what might be beyond them.

She also noticed a series of arc lights running along the outside of the tunnel, and some heavy-duty cameras positioned at intervals along the tarp.

She looked up. There was another camera above her head, mounted on the barn wall with a red blinking light underneath it. It was pointing at the trapdoors, and it didn't look like one you would have picked up in Comet for thirty quid.

"India-Delta-Two, possible entry point located. East side of tunnel. CCTV in operation. Looks like some heavy-duty doors. Possibly leading underground. Holding here. Superintendent Kane, I'm going to try to send you some pictures from my phone. No sign of life as yet."

"Get yourself back . . ."

She killed the radio, suddenly feeling vulnerable. She couldn't make it back to the road without being seen — in fact, it was entirely possible she'd already been picked up by one of the cameras — but she couldn't go forward either. The doors had no obvious method of opening unless you had some C4 explosive, and even then they looked like they could withstand a solid blast.

Then there was a whirring sound, and the doors opened.

Tina flattened herself against the barn wall, suddenly too scared to poke her head around the side to look. She knew she needed to; if she couldn't give a decent update on numbers, descriptions, weapons — not to mention the presence of hostages — then her little rogue mission was as pointless as it was foolish.

But she felt pinned, frozen, her mind suddenly dulled — with cold or fear, she wasn't sure.

She edged back along the barn wall the way she had come, back to the gate, trying to take slow steps, but fighting the urge to panic and run. Her footsteps seemed to crunch on the frozen ground.

She was about halfway along the barn wall when she saw a figure appear at the end near the gate, about fifty metres away. He was dressed in full combat gear, a long-barrelled weapon slung across his chest. He hadn't seen her — he was smoking, and playing with a phone. He looked like he was providing some kind of flank, for either outbound or incoming traffic, albeit not a particularly industrious one.

She froze. She had nowhere to go, no cover. He still hadn't seen her. Her only option was to make a break away from the barn wall into the field opposite, but he would see her immediately and either shoot or catch her. Or both.

She began to edge back to the corner she had just left, stepping backwards, keeping her eyes on the predator, unable to believe he still hadn't seen her.

A sound in her ear. Loud in the rural stillness. Someone there. The ratcheting of a bolt-action rifle.

"Don't fucking move. Who the fuck are you?"

Tina shut her eyes.

* * *

"What's happening?" Barnes was one sneeze away from running down the hill himself to attempt a snatch rescue.

Kane had the binoculars pressed to his face.

"Nothing. I can't see the cameras she's talking about. She reckons she's found the entrance, but we're on the wrong side of the valley for that. No visual from here."

"Where's the bloody back-up?"

As if answering his prayer, the still winter air over the South Downs began to vibrate. The vibrations quickly escalated to an audible hum, which in turn became a rousing thudding noise as the police helicopter appeared over the brow of the Long Man.

Kane pointed down the hill. Barnes squinted. At either end of the lane were two brand-new, black long-wheelbase vans. Rifle officers in camo gear sprinted up the hill either side of Barnes and Kane, flanking them both as they followed the treeline some fifty metres away.

"Golf-Nine-One, from Team Leader."

"Go ahead," Kane replied.

"We're in position. I have a wide containment on the plot, breach teams either end of the lane, elevated rifle overwatch, an ambulance on standby at the RVP and I've pushed up four armed CROPs to the gate."

"I can't see them."

"That's kind of the point. Your civilian says the only threshold is reinforced steel, so we have three options, as I see it. Wait and see if anyone comes out and breach while the door's open, keep obs and try to negotiate with one of the subjects by phone, or attempt dynamic entry."

"Dynamic?"

"Blow the door. But without getting up close to inspect it, we don't know how hard that will be."

"Okay. Come back to you."

"We've got good visual. Suggest you pull your civilian out of there before she becomes a hostage."

"Oh, shit," Kane said, squinting through the binoculars.

"What?"

"She already is."

CHAPTER FIFTY-NINE

Tina stumbled, fighting to keep upright as she was dragged backwards, her heels catching on the frozen, uneven mud. Her custodian had hooked an arm tightly around her neck, his other hand firmly gripping his rifle.

He pointed the weapon up and swept it from side to side as he moved, scanning for unseen enemies. He reached the steel trapdoors and banged on them with the rifle's stock.

"Hey," he called. "Get up here. We're blown."

He patted Tina down, finding the radio, then released her and gave her an angry shove, putting her at a distance of about six feet. He brought the weapon up and pointed it at her chest. Instinctively, she put her hands up, fear coursing through her.

"Don't shoot me," she said, fighting to keep her voice level.

"Shut up," he said, examining the radio. "You old bill? What you doing out here alone? Who else is with you?"

She didn't say anything. He threw the radio down and brought the butt of the rifle down upon it, hard. It didn't shatter exactly, but the chattering voices were silenced. She tilted her head, listening. A sound in the distance.

He returned his attention to her, the weapon levelled.

"I said who else is with you? Does anyone know you're here?"

He took a step forward.

"I'm afraid so," she said, lowering her hands. "The cat's out of the bag. The place is crawling with armed police."

She pointed a finger straight up as the low thudding of the helicopter grew louder.

Her captor spun around on the spot, weapon pointed at the sky. He couldn't see the aircraft.

There was a clunk, and the metal doors opened. Three more men appeared, all brandishing carbines. Tina noted that they climbed out, boots scraping on a metal staircase. The thing — building, whatever it was — was mainly underground.

The men fanned out to corners of the tarp and pointed their weapons at the unseen foe.

A fourth man appeared from the bunker, carrying a handgun rather than a carbine. He moved with less urgency, but seemed no less intense. He wore a grey hoody and jeans, and there was a blue serpent tattoo on the side of his shaved head. He made Tina think of a cobra about to strike, and she realised that this was Stratton Pearce in the flesh.

* * *

"You need to see this," Kane said, passing Barnes the binoculars.

Barnes flattened himself next to Kane and held them up.

"Holy shit. You were right," he said. "That's Stratton Pearce."

Kane's radio chattered. "Nine-One from Team Leader, come in."

"Go ahead," Kane said.

"Contact black side. At least four subjects plus your civilian. She's under threat. They're pointing a carbine at her. From what we can see, the doors are wide open. They're solid steel, but appear to be manual opening. Can't see where they go. Good opportunity to go forward."

"Stand by," Kane said. "Just stand by."

* * *

"What is it?" Pearce asked.

"Found this one sneaking around. She's a cop. I smashed her radio."

"That was fucking stupid, wasn't it?" Pearce said.

The man's eyes widened, and for a moment Tina thought he might leap forward and tear out Pearce's throat with his teeth, but then he blinked and looked away in grudging deference to the obvious alpha.

"Well, what are we doing?" the man said. "We're sitting ducks out here. Fucking chopper's overhead."

"And if you go back down there, they'll smoke you out," Tina said. "It'll be like shooting fish in a barrel."

"You shut up," the man said. "No one asked you."

"She ain't lying, though, is she?" Pearce said. "Real Hobson's choice. Here's what we're going to do, we're going to surrender."

"You what? Are you fucking mental?"

"What you wanna do? Fight them? You think you'll win? I hate the cops as much as the next man, but I'm sorry to say that their gang is always bigger."

"Stratton . . ."

"We've got a delivery today. It needs to go ahead. That is a lot of product coming our way. We can't risk losing it."

"Divert the delivery!"

"Why, because the old bill are all over us? We'll be fucking pariahs. We won't be able to buy aspirin again, let alone anything else."

"And once we've surrendered and there's nobody here except a bunch of detectives, you think they're just going to drop it off and say, 'Sign here.'"

"You let me worry about that," Pearce said. "That delivery is not stopping for anyone."

"Stratton, we've got semi-automatic weapons and three hostages below decks. Surrendering will take about seventeen seconds off some very long sentences."

"Few hoops to jump through before that happens, though. We can generate some brownie points too. Like, suddenly seeing the light and coming to the defence of another."

He pointed his pistol at Tina, then spun by forty-five degrees, pointed it at his colleague and pulled the trigger.

Tina screamed. Her erstwhile captor jerked backwards and then fell heavily, hands clawing at a wound in his neck.

Pearce tucked the weapon into his waistband, grabbed Tina and pulled her towards him.

"Like that, do you? I can say to the judge that I had a change of heart and saved you. How many more can I kill with that line, I wonder? Come on."

He yanked her by the wrist and pulled her towards the yawning doors of the bunker. They opened out into a metal gantry that led onto a staircase that descended into . . . God knew where. Tina knew she wasn't going down there.

She dug her heels in and wrenched her wrist away. Pearce spun back around to face her, eyes blazing.

"I'm not going down there," she said, firmly. "You'll have to kill me."

"Gladly," he said, and levelled the weapon.

He was only a couple of feet away from her; the barrel was less than a foot from her chest.

She made a grab for the gun with both hands, knocking it off aim as she did so. Pearce was surprised by her strength, she could tell, and if all those hours spent in the gym and at kickboxing classes and spin and everything else didn't count for something now, then they never would.

Pearce recovered himself, and tried to wrestle the gun away from her. Cords and sinews stood out on his neck, bringing his serpent tattoo to life, it seemed.

His strength was incredible, and she could feel herself losing the world's highest-stakes arm wrestle. It wasn't a fair fight, either — she needed to gain complete control of the whole weapon, while he just needed to slip his finger against the trigger.

With a final effort, she pulled the gun away just long enough to remove a hand, which she balled into a fist and swung at the side of Pearce's head.

It connected well enough to send him stumbling backwards — he dropped the gun, tripped on the metal lip of the bunker doors and fell into the doorway, grabbing for both the weapon and the doorframe as he went.

"Bitch!" he yelled.

Tina didn't hang around to wait for what happened next, but put her head down and ran for the barn, grimacing as three or four shots roared in the air behind her.

She was nearly at the barn. Ten metres. Less. She was going to make it.

She tripped suddenly, and collapsed onto the frozen earth. She tried to get up, and wondered why her leg wouldn't move. It was like she had been sleeping on it all night and had been woken up by serious pins and needles.

She scrambled backwards on her backside, frantically making for cover, looking at the ground and wondering what she had tripped on.

Then she saw the line of red in the dirt as she dragged her body backwards, and she realised she'd been shot about the same time the pain of a thousand sledgehammers hit her.

She reached the barn wall and pulled herself behind it. She touched a palm to her hip, and it came away bright red. She pressed it again, and blood pulsed out between her fingers.

Oh God. That wasn't good.

CHAPTER SIXTY

Tamsin pressed her ear to the cell door and strained to listen. There was activity. Running footsteps, shouts, barked orders. The unmistakable — even to an untrained ear — sound of weapons being made ready.

She dared not hope. As far as she knew, Graham was going to kill her — slowly or quickly, she couldn't know, but she was beginning to prepare herself for a long period of wasting away, giving up hope to make the wait bearable, allowing herself to gradually forget everything she had ever known.

This did not feel like part of that. If she didn't know better, she'd have said it was the sound of Plan A being knocked to the side and Plan B having to be hastily enacted.

There was a thump on the other side of the door, and Tamsin stepped back, startled.

The lock ratcheted, and then the door slid open.

Tamsin came face to face with the barrel of a big, ugly looking firearm.

"Come on," said Pearce.

"What's happening?" she asked.

"Fuckin' D-Day," he answered, and grabbed her arm.

He dragged her off down the corridor, armed men running past them in the opposite direction. From one of the other floors came the sound of several extremely loud explosions.

"Oh my God," Tamsin cried. "The girls."

"Relax," Pearce said. "That's just the old bill's light show. Stun grenades. Lots of noise, lots of light. They can't hurt you, though."

"Police? The police are here?"

"Don't get excited, darling. This is where the fun starts."

"Where's Graham?"

"Gone to try a bit of shuttle diplomacy."

* * *

"Shots fired, shots fired!" bellowed Team Leader. "Breach team, push up, push up! Hostage made a break to the south but is down. Get the ambulance here, now!"

Barnes had seen it. Pearce had executed one of his own men in front of Tina, and had then headed back towards the bunker, dragging her behind him. She'd broken free and had made a run for it, only to be flung forward as one of the wayward rounds smacked into her body.

The two black vans rolled down the lane, converging on the gate from either side, lines of CTSFOs in dark grey combat gear filing along beside them, using the vehicles as ballistic cover in a way a skeletal hedgerow couldn't possibly help with. The helicopter swooped low and the fierce barking of angry CMDs filled the air.

There was a distance of less than twenty metres between the officers and the sentry guarding the tarp at the nearest corner. He looked distinctly like the turkey that forgot to go to the back of the queue when the farmer came collecting the Christmas stock. When a series of stun and CS grenades were lobbed over the hedgerow, he threw down his weapon and thrust his hands in the air. His colleague on the opposing corner did the same.

A further line of grey-clad CTSFOs descended the hill behind the tarp site and moved straight onto the site, throwing more grenades as they went. They had no hard cover, and so there was no holding off — the assault steamed straight onto the site.

The two sentries at the rear of the plot didn't surrender quite as willingly as their front-facing colleagues, and they dropped to the ground shortly afterwards — whether they'd been Tasered or shot, Barnes couldn't tell.

Something caught his eye. Over by the barn. A figure. No, two figures. Running from where all the activity was. They disappeared from view along the side of the barn, and then popped up at the rear, past Tina's unmoving body, heading north-east up the hill, partially concealed by head-high shrubbery.

"That's Pearce!" Barnes yelled. "He's slipped the containment. There's someone with him. Oh my God. It's Tamsin. Tam!"

Barnes dropped the binoculars and half-ran, half-fell down the hill.

"Barnes!" Kane yelled from behind him. "Team Leader, be advised there is an unarmed detective . . ."

Barnes didn't heed, didn't wait around to listen. He veered off at forty-five degrees as he ran, both to keep step with Pearce's trajectory and also because the line of CTSFOs would prevent him from going anywhere near the action for his own safety.

Knowing there were rifle officers and CROPs that were invisible to him, he dropped down to the lane and ran south — to all intents and purposes, away from the plot — and then when he was far enough back along the lane, he climbed over the hedge and began the climb up the hillside towards the Long Man, eyes furiously scanning for Stratton Pearce's bald head.

He picked his way through dense gorse and brambles, the crumbling, uneven chalk terrain like a coral reef invisible below metre-long coarse grass blowing like the wild hair of the land beneath.

He turned and began to climb in a more linear direction. He felt like he was stalking through the savannah, but wasn't quite clear on whether he was the predator or the prey.

Pearce was the only one with a firearm, which probably gave him his answer.

He pumped his knees and tried to gain some quick ground. The helicopter was still hovering overhead; Barnes wasn't sure if he had any kind of back-up or if all the attention was still down at the bunker.

The wind was bitter up here. Streaks of snow were still threaded throughout the hillside, and he forced himself to keep moving, to stay warm if nothing else. The sun had long given up, and the sky had turned the colour of chalk as the daylight began to fade.

He scanned, scanned, scanned, and then, when he thought he'd lost her on the hillside in some bizarre gun-toting parody of *Wuthering Heights*, he saw, to his surprise, that he'd managed to get above Pearce by about ten metres.

Pearce had levelled out on the hillside and was now traversing in a flat line; Barnes's ascent had taken him higher. Pearce was stumbling, running, dragging Tamsin along behind him, checking ahead, to the side, behind him — but not above.

Barnes moved ahead, trying to work out where he could head them off; he had the element of surprise, just about.

Pearce picked up speed. He'd found a path of sorts, a narrow stone track gouged into the hillside that was enabling him to walk in a less circumspect fashion.

Barnes tried to match him, but his own terrain was still treacherous, and if he tried to run he would fall, or turn an ankle, or worse.

They were getting closer. Their paths were converging; Barnes could hear Tamsin protesting and calling Pearce every name under the sun.

The track they were on began to rise, and Barnes realised that it was going to intersect ahead of him, much sooner than he was able to effectively judge.

It was too late to change course, or recalibrate, or anything. He dropped a couple of feet from his portion of grassy hillside, and landed on the track a couple of metres behind them.

Pearce turned and raised his weapon, pulling Tamsin towards him.

"Barnes! Oh my God," Tamsin said.

"You okay, Tam?" Barnes said.

"Ask me again in half an hour or so, okay?"

"Where's the girls?"

"They're in the bunker. They're okay, but—"

"Shut the fuck up, the pair of you," Pearce snarled. "For a minute there I was worried you were a real cop."

He pointed the gun at Barnes, then brought it back and slowly rested the end of the barrel against Tamsin's temple.

"We're done, now, DI Barnes. I've strung you along for long enough. Had some fun with it. And actually, this is a pretty good way to make sure you never forget me. That you will never forget this . . ."

Barnes tensed, cold clear adrenaline suddenly coursing through him. Pearce was six feet away. He couldn't get there before he pulled the trigger, let alone disarm him. Pepper spray — useless in this wind. Baton — not quick enough, and suddenly he realised that by rushing up here, ill-equipped, he could very well have hastened Tamsin's demise.

"Don't do it, Stratton. Don't do it."

"Shut up!" Pearce pointed the gun at Barnes again; Barnes decided he would take that. "I suffered. I still suffer. Why shouldn't you?"

"I don't disagree, but why should the girls suffer? They've done nothing. You'll take their mother."

"And you can be the one to tell them whose fault it was. Tell them every birthday. Tell them every Christmas. Say it was Daddy Barnes's fault you've got no mum . . ."

The gun reappeared at Tamsin's temple. Her eyes widened in fear. A reptilian smirk crossed Pearce's face.

* * *

"Stand-off on the hillside, Nine-One," Team Leader said on Kane's radio.

"I see it," Kane said, the binoculars jammed to his face. "Subject holding hostage at gunpoint. Looks like my DI is trying to negotiate."

"How's he getting on?"

"I'm no body language expert, but I'd say he's pissing in the wind."

"Clear threat to life, Nine-One?"

"I'd say so. He's got the gun to her head. He's killed one of his own already. He's going away for a long time. And he looks very, very pissed off."

"Understood, Nine-One." Team Leader turned his attention to his rifle officers. "Romeo-One, do you have a clear shot?"

"That's confirmed, Team Leader. Range is good. Drop is good. Solid backstop."

"Roger that, Romeo-One. Centre mass will not achieve strategy. Instant incapacitation required. Critical shot authorised."

* * *

Barnes didn't immediately realise what had happened. Pearce just suddenly seemed to pass out. He fell backwards, awkwardly landing on his back on the stone track, pulling Tamsin over with him. For an instant Barnes thought he'd shot her, and that the round had over-penetrated and entered Pearce's own head too.

Then, a second or so later, the flat crack of the rifle booming across the valley reached Barnes's ears.

He stumbled over, prised the weapon from Pearce's still-tight grip and threw it behind him. He pulled Tamsin to him, checking her body for injuries and gunshot wounds while she rained kisses on his head and sobbed with relief.

Against his better judgement, he jabbed two fingers into Pearce's neck, under his bony jaw. Nothing. His lights were out. A seven-six-two in the skull would do that to you, he thought.

He stood and looked down at the rigid body, Tamsin's face buried in his chest. Pearce's leg was bent up behind him, his head craned back as if trying to cram oxygen into his airway, his face frozen in a pained scowl, his eyes no more than dead silver slits.

Barnes stared across the valley, Tamsin held tight in his grasp. The wild grass of the South Downs stirred in the wind, the chalk figure of the Long Man looking down on them.

"Let's go and get your girls," he whispered.

EPILOGUE

"Another?"

Barnes shook his head, and covered the top of the glass. Kane shrugged, and signalled the barman for a top-up.

"I can't work out if I'm meant to be celebrating or commiserating," Barnes said.

"Maybe both," Kane said.

They were in the Ship, Kane's new favourite watering hole, tucked away in a corner overlooking Meads Street in green leather Chesterfields with a crackling fire. There was an untouched game of backgammon on the table in front of them. Barnes didn't even know how to play; Kane just felt it added to the ambience.

"This," Barnes said. "I genuinely didn't think I'd be able to enjoy something like this again. You know, the last time I was up this way I was running for my life from a mob that wanted my police car."

"Yes, that did occur to me," Kane said. "Sorry. This is my new favourite part of town, though. Five minutes' walk to the sea, Beachy Head round the corner, and all this *architecture*."

"Architecture?"

"How are the girls?"

Barnes thought about it.

"They're okay, still in a combination of shock and relief. Overall, it's a good feeling. But they will need time to heal. And there will be some scars."

"I'm glad they're okay."

"Thank you. If not for you, they might very well not be. You know, I gave Tamsin the choice. After she was discharged from hospital, and we were all back home, and the girls were in bed, I said to her: you can't live your whole life looking over your shoulder because of me. If I'm not around, that all stops."

"She punch you?"

Barnes thought about it.

"More or less," he said, and they both laughed. "She actually said, 'You're the only one Maggie feels safe around. You can't go anywhere. It will be a good many years before she can trust a grown-up again. You're the exception.'

"I tried to say it was because of me that Maggie was in that position in the first place. Then she did punch me."

Barnes stared out the window. A light dusting of snow was beginning to swirl around the dark street.

"He admitted it," Barnes said. "Pearce. Admitted responsibility for Eve's death. Not to me, to Tamsin. Didn't think she would live long enough to tell anyone. Claimed it was an accident."

"How do you feel about that?"

"I'm not entirely sure. But, you know, I'm glad he's dead," Barnes murmured. "I can't believe I'm saying that, but injured, in custody, even sectioned — he'd still be able to get to us. And even if he couldn't, he'd damn well try. If he'd survived . . . well. If he'd survived, I wouldn't even have given her the choice."

"Most of his crew are coming back nil trace so far, but we got an ID on the sentry that Pearce shot. Matched the DNA found under your nails from the attack in the hotel."

"That figures."

"Sure you don't want another drink?"

Barnes smiled.

"How did you get a fix on the location? We had it narrowed down to a pretty decent radius, but you led us to the front door."

Kane sipped his drink, and stared at Barnes over the rim of his glass.

"I think you already know," he said, wiping the foam from his top lip.

"Duquesne Kenley. What did you do? Bug his cell or something?"

Kane just shrugged.

"You little beauty," Barnes said, "You weren't missing at all."

"It took some doing, but his little show of hubris when we went to visit him unlocked the door. I gave him just enough of what I knew to get him worried, and he folded like a deck of cards."

"Sorry I missed that."

"He'd been supporting Pearce as penance, and Pearce was dangling him like a fish on a hook. It was slowly dawning on Kenley that he was never going to be able to pay off his debt.

"For all his front, the prospect of another seven years in prison, minimum, was killing him slowly. He no more wanted to fester at Her Majesty's Pleasure than you or I. Plus, Pearce still wanted blood, and he was, marginally, an easier target inside than out."

"And Graham?"

"They found him in the bunker in some kind of purpose-built nursery. He didn't resist, exactly, but seemed to be leaning towards using his daughters as human shields."

"Jesus."

"It didn't last. The armed guys shouted at him a lot, then a baton round to the kidneys, then he got Tasered. He was as meek as a lamb after that."

"He's no fool. He'll claim duress or something. That he was being manipulated as a way to get to me. He's not a hothead like Pearce."

"He's a very strange fish. I'm no criminologist, but there's some kind of obsessive-compulsive narcissist thing going on there. The partner, girlfriend, whatever she was—"

"Miriam?"

"She reported him missing when he didn't make contact after all the subterfuge of packing her off to her sister's. The travelling consultant's lifestyle seemed to fit with a double life of underground bunker construction. She was clueless about the whole thing."

Barnes shook his head.

"Him and Pearce, working together. Didn't see that coming."

"It happens."

"Can't believe I fell for that. Faked his death right in front of me. Oldest trick in the book. That, and the links to shipping. Pharmaceuticals. Wanting to buy a smallholding on the South Downs. He dropped the chemical plot like bread-crumbs in front of me and I didn't pick up on any of it."

"Well, you had other things on your mind. And he's not coming out for a long time. Something many ex-wives would be thankful for, I'm sure."

"What about the bunker?" Barnes said.

"It's an old World War Two GPO repeater station, built after D-Day to reset essential undersea cabling to mainland Europe. There's hundreds of them up and down the coast, mostly owned by either local authorities or the National Trust. Most have been sealed, but a couple were sold to private investors on a long-term lease. Graham did a pretty good job of modernising it."

"And Tina?"

"She was very lucky. The round missed anything vital. She's going to make it. I went to see her in hospital — she woke up just long enough to say, 'How come all the good ones are taken?' And she wasn't talking about me."

Barnes grinned. He couldn't help himself. "Thanks, boss." He stood up.

"When are you coming back to work?"

"I don't know."

"If it assists your decision, Gabby's put his papers in. He's going to retire."

"Somehow I think he'll be more of a menace in retirement."

"So, what *are* you going to do?" Kane said.

"Christmas in a few days. I'm woefully underprepared. But I've got one more thing to atone for first."

* * *

Eileen Howlett lived in a terraced cottage near the Redoubt. It was tiny, and cluttered with trinkets and keepsakes — including pictures of her only son. The sea roared in the distance, and a steady stream of seafront traffic flowed past her window.

She insisted on the formalities — a pot of tea on a tray with jam shortcakes and paper napkins.

"It was his first day in CID," she said. "He was so proud to become a detective. He wanted to make me proud. That was the last thing he said to me. He sent me a message: *Going to make you proud*, he said."

"We couldn't find any other family — wife, children?"

"He had all that to come," she said, her voice breaking.

"Will was a hero, Mrs Howlett," Barnes said, putting down his cup. "He ran towards danger to help others. As an officer fallen in the line of duty, we — that is, his police family — would like your permission to support his funeral. Full guard of honour."

Her eyes brimmed with tears, and tea spilled onto the saucer from her shaking hand.

Barnes closed his hand over her trembling fist.

"He died so others could live. Myself included."

He stood, and buttoned his jacket.

"He won't ever be forgotten for that."

POSTSCRIPT

The defence lawyer with the chalk-white surfer's hairdo, Robert Peverell, collected his leather jacket and battered briefcase from the X-ray machine and stood patiently while the prison guard waved a search wand around his body. He made small talk and bad jokes with the Belmarsh guard staff, none of which were funny, but his easy-going manner and Australian accent seemed to thaw them out a bit.

They showed him through to a private interview room, and pulled the steel door shut behind them.

Peverell pulled some papers out of his briefcase and pretended to examine them closely while he waited for his client to arrive.

A few minutes later, the door opened again and a handcuffed Duquesne Kenley shuffled in. Peverell had never met the man, but tales of his charisma and ability to influence sociopaths and murderers verged on legendary.

He wasn't getting that vibe today. In fact, Peverell thought, Mr Kenley looked positively hangdog.

"Good morning, Mr Kenley," Peverell said. Kenley returned a limp handshake.

Peverell made a show of shuffling through the papers. "My, my, you have been busy, haven't you? Positively

362

chameleonic, in fact. And despite your — admittedly unwitting — cooperation, your remaining tariff still extends into double figures."

Kenley looked grim-faced.

"Well, try not to worry," Peverell grinned, shoving the papers back into his case. "There might be a way to get you out of this."

THE END

THE JOFFE BOOKS STORY

We began in 2014 when Jasper agreed to publish his mum's much-rejected romance novel and it became a bestseller.

Since then we've grown into the largest independent publisher in the UK. We're extremely proud to publish some of the very best writers in the world, including Joy Ellis, Faith Martin, Caro Ramsay, Helen Forrester, Simon Brett and Robert Goddard. Everyone at Joffe Books loves reading and we never forget that it all begins with the magic of an author telling a story.

We are proud to publish talented first-time authors, as well as established writers whose books we love introducing to a new generation of readers.

We won Trade Publisher of the Year at the Independent Publishing Awards in 2023. We have been shortlisted for Independent Publisher of the Year at the British Book Awards for the last four years, and were shortlisted for the Diversity and Inclusivity Award at the 2022 Independent Publishing Awards. In 2023 we were shortlisted for Publisher of the Year at the RNA Industry Awards.

We built this company with your help, and we love to hear from you, so please email us about absolutely anything bookish at feedback@joffebooks.com

If you want to receive free books every Friday and hear about all our new releases, join our mailing list: www.joffebooks.com/contact

And when you tell your friends about us, just remember: it's pronounced Joffe as in coffee or toffee!

ALSO BY ADAM LYNDON

**DETECTIVE RUTHERFORD
BARNES MYSTERIES**
Book 1: DEVIL'S CHIMNEY
Book 2: BEACHY HEAD
Book 3: BURNT OUT SECRETS
Book 4: THE CHALK MAN

Milton Keynes UK
Ingram Content Group UK Ltd.
UKHW010822220424
441551UK00005B/434

9 781835 265246